CW01509924

TOFINO

A Novel

Tom Stewart

PB 978-1-7772211-9-5
EB 978-1-0695510-0-9
HC 978-1-0695510-3-0

Lucky Dollar Media
British Columbia, Canada
LuckyDollarMedia@gmail.com

Praise for Tom Stewart

Winning Author of 2023 Whistler Independent Book Awards *Best Fiction Novel*, Immortal North

"Reading Immortal North for a fourth time, and chapter 26 is f_____g art, particularly pages 216-218. Just wow."
★★★★★
-Keren Jackson, Goodreads, 820 books reviewed

"Immortal North is as quiet as snow falling in a forest. Until it is not and then it is a cacophony of violence and sorrow. Less than 10% of my ratings are Five Stars, this one deserves it."
★★★★★
-Lyn Graves, Goodreads, 1900 books reviewed

"Heartbreakingly beautiful, raw, thought provoking, enchanting. This book broke my heart, built it back together only to shatter it again and again, and I would keep going back for more." ★★★★★
-Heather Hays Reed, BookSirens

"Part of Immortal North ripped my heart out and part of it held me close. The novel was atmospheric and stunning in its descriptions. Near the end I couldn't stop. I highly recommend this powerfully moving story. It's something you don't want to miss." ★★★★★
-Jennifer Pritchard, Kindles All The Way Down

"Stewart's mastery of beautiful sentences matches William Gay and William Faulkner. His acrobatic sentences contain some of the best words and most heartfelt, perfectly spoken sentiments I've read." ★★★★★

-Darrell Ingrum, Netgalley

"Immortal North is one of those classic works best savored slowly. I was so immersed in the wonders of the natural world and the mysteries of human love and existence that I wanted the story never to end. One of the finest examples of true literary fiction I have ever read." ★★★★★
-Marcus Lynn Dean, Author, *The Scream of an Eagle*

"I just finished Immortal North and if I could rate it Ten Stars or higher, I would. The writing is spectacular. I will never forget this tale as long as I live. It resonates with me that much."
★★★★★
-R.Z. Halleson, Author, Netgalley

"Immortal North is a once in a lifetime book. Stewart gives us a master class in intensity and anticipation: we know what's coming, we hope it doesn't. The novel ends with a climax so drenched in beauty it made my hands shake." ★★★★★
-Amanja Lambert, Independent Reviewer, "Amanda Reads too Much"

"This land is so well described that it becomes a character in and of itself. Immortal North requires an emotional investment from a reader, but if you are willing to give Stewart your time, he will give you a piece of the trapper's and the boy's hearts. And you will find by the midway point that you have given them all of yours. Very highly recommended." ★★★★★
-Jamie Michele, Readers' Favorite Reviews

Dedication

Dedication to follow.

I

SUNDAY – VANCOUVER

A calm ocean surface hides surging tidal currents.

Valerie lay in bed in the middle of the night thinking of the Pacific but listening to the rain. Her phone on the night table beside her. Its dark screen a portal to chaos. She didn't reach for it. She was trying to do less of that. All the emails can wait. They can't wait but they will. Who gets a panic attack while running? Just who is attacking whom? Does the enemy within look just like you? How does one achieve the proper perspective to see an autonomous assault?

The tighter you grip the reins the worse the burn when the world rips them from your grip.

Valerie with a fist balled in bed.

Heavy patter.

Heavy dark.

Nameless weight.

Rain dripped to her puddled balcony with such regularity she believed she could measure her own decay. She wondered if it was raining in Tofino. She turned in bed. Part of her wanted to unwind this thing. Maybe she herself was contributing to building the mother of all complexes, maybe my very efforts are only making things worse for so many. Valerie Roy and her sprawling empire of inferiority, they'll say. They might have already said that, she had stopped reading her socials. The queen who cues the trumpeters of self-help and self-development and self self self. Is that me? Am I that? She realized she had forgotten to text her dad to ask how he was feeling. Lying in the dark she made a mental note. She actually visualized a fountain pen scrolling the notepad of her mind. Saw the note there among so many, ink dripping from the letters' loops. She listened. She heard the ink drip.

She recently made a joke to herself that her two closest friends were her earbuds. When she did see her friends, connections were thinning. Even the thread to Stacy, her rock, was starting to fray. Listen for it to land like a pebble in a pool. She listened. Ploop. The rain outside. Two months ago Stacy said she looked thin. They met for dinner every month but Valerie cancelled on their last. As lifestyles diverge, so too diverges concerns, goals, outlooks. Language changes when definitions morph: *meaning*, *purpose*. Driftwood hardly distanced yet somehow taken by distinct currents. Gaps expanding. Is that such an uncommon story?

Outside her condo a drop falling for every concern, who could count them all. Pooling to amorphous puddles, puddles connecting. Taking on some shape of the past? Some fear of the future? The wind blew and rain peppered the big pane of glass. But this will pass. A storm of such intensity never lasts very long. It's like love, in that regard. Not that theirs was love.

Last night, looking down from her condo, she thought it might again have been his truck on the street outside her building. That would have made it three nights in a row. She didn't want to call the police but she figured she probably should. She had had a scare once before. She told herself on the second night that if she saw his truck on the third she would call the police. This was the fourth. She hadn't seen it earlier this evening and before she lay down she looked but it was hard to see in the dusk and light rain. Slowly there was nothing to see in the dark and heavy rain. But this wasn't about a man. He was only one drop among many.

She should have broken it off sooner when she knew early it wasn't a forever thing. She figured he knew that too. They would go for dinner and he wore a suit—*he wore a suit*. His naturally big frame filled out from manual labour. They went for dinner and he ordered a bottle of wine without consulting her on its selection. She wasn't used to that. Sometimes he didn't ask her, he just did things. Just took things. At times what she saw as his shortcomings were on other occasions his virtues. One time in the kitchen he didn't ask. She knocked over the pepper and salt shakers. He lifted her up onto the counter and they knocked over her wine glass, a crack but not a shatter. See the thimble of spilled Shiraz, its deep red curved head snaking over the marble countertop. As if with a life of its own. To the counter edge. Couldn't see the drips hit the floor. Couldn't hear them like she could hear them now. Wine drips skinnying its length. She watched the glass rolling radially, that its arc would roll it off the counter. She kept her hands around his neck and he didn't stop. She watched it disappear. They heard it break. He didn't even look.

Once while walking home after dinner. An alley. She said her dress. My dress. Even in the alley he held her wrists above her head. A hand on her throat.

Outside, black as the heartbreak night, rain cast by wind gusts and though the peppered pane withstood, the rain's perfume infused the room and inhaling deeply she did smell rain on wet pavement. Who gets a panic attack while running? She didn't perform all that poorly on a six-hour-sleep but for too long it had been closer to five.

That first night she didn't notice them, his scars. Details masked by the dark and the drink and the overwhelm of sensation—carnival of flesh, it had been a little while. The second night she did notice them. His belly. She saw them, all of them. She didn't ask. That wasn't her style. You can't force a flower to bloom by prying at its petals.

On their first dates she would do most of the talking. Years ago before work became life she had travelled enough to know she wanted to travel a lot more. She said to Trent that seeing the pyramids was on her bucket list. Fly to Tonga to swim with a whale. He was mostly quiet. That's fine she wasn't trying to change him. Been down that road before. And anyway with time will come the exchanging of small passive pressures. He was quiet but not simple. She didn't run out of things to say just things worth saying. She was the first to bring her phone out at the dinner table and then felt badly and apologized. She told herself they both knew it had an expiry date. Maybe fewer dinners out until things run their course and one of them ends it. Their bodies had a language and a part of her wanted to keep that conversation going. Can't sometimes one love language just speak loudly enough for them all?

Tell yourself that.

They were lying in bed, the sheet loose over their waists. She had mostly made up her mind about it. They were lying there and her fingers so light on his stomach delicately touching his past and he hadn't told her about it and she never asked. That was the night he told her. Now it was she who was quiet. She listened but he didn't say anything more and she wiped her eyes and they just lay in the dark. As if his burning words stole the oxygen. Any words she might speak made sparse by his so dense.

Sometimes silence says more than words. So let her bare presence be a hopeful ointment to his pain. Maybe that's not nothing. Maybe in the deep waters of our psychology there is a knowing truer than words, a Mariana Trench of understanding articulated other ways than through speech. As if sometimes nothing else will do more than ablest silence. Those times that it doesn't become its own empty goodbye. After a minute she started to say something, then tried again. She didn't know he hadn't told anyone else. That he told them other things.

That night a stronger connection than any other night, than all those nights added up together. She wished that was enough. But if compassion is a type of love it's not the romantic kind, and pity is only farther from it. She finally found some words but he had closed back up. That's what wounds are supposed to do, right? All in the fullness of time. And other such lies.

The next day she was leaving Vancouver for business in Toronto. The forced idleness of transit so conducive to deep reflection. Get a ten-thousand-foot view from a ten-thousand-foot view. Thoughts once ignored if not suppressed from work's relentless routine now with a chance to float on up. Endless thoughts like endless clouds above a broad, prairie blue sky—Oh Canada, one day I will know the expanse between your shores. Clouds churning with concerns, clouds dense like sopping sponges soon to be squeezed by some spiteful god's clenched fists.

When facing important work decisions she would step back, identify the hurdles, the opportunities, the options, put it on paper, dissect, then execute with surgical conviction and not look back. Why with my personal life do I hesitate, vacillate? Monthly, weekly, my God daily. Does one maintain their sanity by constantly questioning everything? Everything. Is that normal? Do I want normal? Why lately are islands of achievement surrounded by oceanic doubt? Outside the plane's window, shrinking cloud gaps, the sky becoming a grey stratus sea.

Since day one her job was more than a passion. Still is, isn't it? Nothing's changed. So what's changed? When passion becomes obsession, even what you love can shackle. Decisions becoming harder to make. That certitude, that intuitive knowing of the right decision, slower to arrive. This brain fog. This plane in cloud.

She arrived back with more uncertainty than she had at her departure. But shortly thereafter, at least in one domain, she found resolution. His disrespect of boundaries. Please put down my phone. After a quiet dinner she ended what she knew in all honesty was a mistake from date two. She figured he knew it too.

He didn't.

Back on her own again. Solo. Every broken connection came at a loss even if she had done the severing. This loss like other losses still cut. The cut drained, dripped, thinned the body from which it leaked. Starting over, again. Like last again. In the three weeks since their breakup she had gone on one date and would have gone on a second but he never called. Thirty-eight. Thirty-eight is not twenty-eight. Your math checks out. This wasn't about a man. She wasn't even sure if she wanted one of those. She had met Trent at a point that might be called spiritual depletion. Maybe that brought a false positive. His looks, his quiet confidence, his build, their sex. Starvation transforms a slice of bread into exquisite fare. Emotional isolation transforms a smile into a work of art. Not that he smiled so much. Rain pooling. Her heart rate. She listened to the bleeding sky.

Valerie's employer was uncompromising, relentless, stubborn—more than once she told her that to her face—a perfectionist, rarely a word of praise. I'm already working dark-to-dark seven days a week. There was friction.

Four years ago at thirty-four Valerie had made Canada's *Top Forty Under Forty*. Valerie founded the company. She was its CEO. She answered to no one but herself.

At times her virtues were also her shortcomings.

For how large her company was rapidly becoming, most of her work was online. She herself was doing the backend, coding and software engineering—not technically trained but YouTube is Disneyland for an autodidact. Her team growing but she herself filled many roles. Maybe eight years wearing so many hats has fractured my being, diluted my story. The stories we tell ourselves. Eight years. *Eight years?* On her shortlist of distrust, time ranked high.

Valerie had built a solid team, women she respected and felt lucky to work with. But the hierarchical dynamic prevented deep bonds. She offloaded tasks but that itself comes with its own preoccupations for the control addict whose uncompromising pursuit of perfection was the very reason her business had grown—is growing—faster than bull kelp rising off the seafloor. Few things in the natural world exhibit such ascendancy as bull kelp, bamboo, and *B2P*—her business. Humans are natural, thus natural are their creations.

Invasive uncertainty.

Drip.

Anonymous weight.

Drip.

Is it one thing or all the things? Lack of identifying the thing becomes one more thing.

Drip.

Was this gradual or sudden?

Drip.

I wonder if it's raining in Tofino.

Vancouver's coastal winter weather must have saturated her mind and Valerie fell asleep into a wet forest. Normally the feeling of falling wakes you up but this descended her deeper. Her landing softened by a damp woods that though dark, the leaves so green they might be electric. She poked a small patch of moss which squished like a sea anemone, its closing mouth retracting soft tentacles. Surrounding her, big leaves dripping fat drops and the rain coloured by what it wet as if the paint of this dream still fresh, green and dusky woods smeared and glistening. A strange call. Not a bird, this too wet even for robins. Aquatic acoustics, notes in bubbles, some melody piping through a wet medium. She couldn't see the source and got up from where she kneeled on the forest floor. Walking on fawn legs, her eyes saucered as a doe, the night woods began lightening with a false sunrise.

She woke in unnatural light. Reached to the night table to check the time and saw her iPhone already lit with an incoming email. She forgot to airplane mode it. A sign of slipping. She was not surprised to hear her first thought on this new day at 3:03 a.m. was self-critical. Her phone's harsh white light violating the night, doe pupils aghast and rapidly shrinking. Above her dresser a watercolour whale swimming on the outskirts of her phone's diffuse prism of light, more grainy in its heights. She swiped her screen. Work emails, texts. One was from Trent. Maybe a good sign. That was fewer than normal. He stopped calling because she stopped answering but a text still sends a message. She didn't respond to his texts and eventually he would understand and move on. So why haven't you blocked his number? she asked herself. She didn't answer that. She had already told him too many times that it was over, but every time had said it kindly and now silence was the best way. Right? Talented silence wears many hats. So let the acid bath of silence dissolve the bones of this brief, now dead relationship. She was sorry for him but eventually he would understand. Time will heal. So they say. But if you distrust time perhaps you're doubtful of its curative power. She silenced her phone but not the rain now far too heavy to call them drops. The room faded to black and the surfaced whale returned to its depths.

A two-hour ferry ride to the island plus a three-hour drive to Tofino is nearly a foreign getaway in your own country. She had read so much about it. Valerie reached into the dark now shocked blacker after the brief and luminous violation of her phone's screen. She lifted the moon-snail shell from her night table. It was big, even for a moon snail. Sometimes she imagined herself as a mother, soothing whatever in the night was bothering her little girl. She would tell her: *Here's what you do. With other shells you only listen, but with this one you can talk. You get to whisper. Before bed you whisper into the shell.* Her little girl would ask, already whispering, just what she should say. *Anything you want, you decide.* Secrets? *Yes, if you want.* She would turn the shell over and show her the whorls that spiralled up to the apex. *Put your finger there.* She'd take her little girl's finger and touch it to that point, it softly indenting her skin. *That's how it sends them through the night to where they need to be.* Where does a secret need to be? The child's simple question with a wisdom defying her youth, as if Socrates was right and knowledge is only recollection. She'd have to think about that. *And in the morning when you wake up, the first thing you do before you get out of bed is put the shell to your ear like this.* She'd hold it not to her own head but up against her little girl's, the round shell nearly half the size of her head, her mouth open, listening carefully. *Do you hear it?* Her little girl nodding, turning to her. *What do you hear?*

Valerie put the shell down. She reached for her phone and the wall-whale resurfaced and she didn't open the deluge of work emails and in the rainy and heavy dark she read what she read last night.

Are you ready to awaken a deeper sense of wonder? Here, the full power of the Pacific comes to rest on vast sandy beaches. Ancient forests calm the spirit with mist and mystery. Quiet inlets ripple with life. Situated within the traditional territory of the Tla-o-qui-aht First Nation, we're surrounded by the breathtaking expanse of the UNESCO Clayoquot Sound Biosphere Region—cherished for its profound biodiversity. We savour our acclaimed food scene and delight in the creativity of the coastal arts

9

community, while treading softly and sharing respect for all who call Tofino home. Because here, everything is connected.

She read that last sentence again. She hadn't taken a vacation since B2P shot over the moon. Not even one full day free of work? She mentally replayed as many Christmases as she could recall, and even if placed on pajamas she saw her work laptop.

Earlier in the week Valerie scheduled a silent retreat held at an off-grid location boat-accessible from that small town with a storied past fronting the Pacific. A floating retreat anchored at the end of a quiet inlet, quaint accommodation like an archipelago of tiny homes. Disconnect. Reconnect. Take a break from the concrete—concrete city, concrete work, concrete patterns. A much needed rest and reset because sometimes even what you love can shackle and passions can bind. So go to nature. Breathe rainforest deep down into your belly. She scrolled through images of cedar boughs and sandy beaches, taco trucks and breaking waves. Her room otherwise dark but this blue sea flooding her walls so keep your eye on the whale. She actually smelled the ocean. How strange, she thought. What's the name of that phenomenon? She was scheduled to attend the retreat in four days but at 3:13 a.m. she just booked an Airbnb in Tofino for today.

II

Sunday – Tofino

"Tofino? No, he had never set foot here. Captain Vicente Tofino de San Miguel. A rear admiral in the Spanish Navy. An astronomer, mathematician and the king's hydrographer."

White boats on a calm sea. Seen from above they'd look like ivory play pieces scattered over an exotic blue gameboard. Crestless swell under a blue-grey sky. A marine world fresh in the morning air just cool enough to make you appreciate it, occasionally blowing into your balled hands like they held a pair of dice you wish to bestow some luck. A few seagulls bobbing, some calling. Boston Whalers, Pursuits, and Grady Whites. The fleet of guided fishing boats trolled off Portland Point southwest from town. Steve and Russell, American clients, sitting the two stern-facing chairs. Alex their guide standing in the aisle between them watching the rods. In one of the fish boxes inlaid to the deck under Alex's green Dunlop rubber boots, one bled Chinook salmon.

"What's a hydrographer?" Steve asked.

"Russell?" The guide passed off the question.

Russell exhaled cigar smoke. "Water-mapper."

"Succinct," Alex said.

"So the Spanish were first?"

"Yeah, Pérez sailing up from a naval base in Mexico. Then the Brits, Americans, French. Some say the Chinese may have sailed over before all that, the fifth or sixth century even. But very first would have been whoever crossed Beringia. The last ice age had glaciers extending well out to sea. So this here was ice." Alex pointed outwards, then up. "Ice two-kay thick. Hard to imagine that."

All three looked up.

"Though there are other accounts. Some say people were trapped in a clam shell and that guy there freed them." Alex nodded high to a cruising raven. "I like that version. After the big melt, sea levels were much higher than now." He turned looking down the coastline and pointed northwest. "That mountain there that you guys climbed, Lone Cone, would only have had its top visible."

"What's a kay?" Steve asked.

"I believe we went over this yesterday."

"I know but I just can't quite seem to keep your fucked Canuck lingo straight."

"Base-ten number system. Just give it a chance."

"How many key-low-me-turds in a mile, again? The same as the number of toonies in a greenback? Right? Three point one four five?"

"Yeah, see, you got it. Easy peasy." Alex stepped to the port-side downrigger and tightened the reel's drag a quarter turn then reeled until he regained the rod's deep bend. "You guys just need to join the rest of the world already. Water freezes at zero. A hundred centimetres in a metre, a thousand metres in a kilometre. Isn't that just easier? It's fun, I think you'll like it. Just try it just for a minute just to see how it feels. Take it home and try it on and don't decide right away. You have to break these things in. Then we can all speak the same language. What can we offer in trade? I'll do you a favour. Canada will drop the u in favour if you adopt the litre. That's fair."

"Litre of cola." Steve looked at Russell. Back to Alex. "Well we talked about it. Not going to happen."

"I'm willing to negotiate the pronunciation of the last letter of the alphabet. Zee for zed. Though that trade will ruffle a few of my countrymen's feathers." Two unflapping seagulls cruised off the stern.

"The hell is a zed?"

"Or what if we drop the *c* in defence?"

"Do what? The Canadian Navy? You must be joking. Alex, we wouldn't run fair-weather whale-watching tours with the Canadian Navy."

"Not that sea. D-e-f-e-n-c-e," he spelled it. "We could swap in an American *s*. Would you just look at us here." Alex broadly gestured. "Consulates for continental improvement. This is a big step. Posterity will speak praisingly about the historic compromises that took place today at 7:41 in the Outcast, a humble Tofitian fishing boat."

"Ambassadors," said Russell. A churning puff of exhaled stogie.

"Right. Ambassadors, not consulates. I mean, the Imperial System has roots to the monarchy, right? The name says it all. Isn't the basis of the right to bear arms an assertion of your independence from the colonial fatherland—which amendment is that?"

"The freedom-loving second."

"So flip the bird to the crown and like an American bald eagle shaking its feathers free of rain, imperial reign, make the switch to metric. Unite the continent." Alex held out his fist for Russell to bump and Russell gave a cough or short laugh while not bumping it and Alex moved his fist over to Steve while saying the twenty-first century kindly holds out a hand to you. Steve sort of grabbed and shook it, rather ambiguous like.

"The thing is," Steve said, "your bacon is inferior to our bacon. This morning my hotel served me my breakfast meat as a circle. I just looked at her. I mean, if you guys can't get pork right—" He paused as if to weight the gravity of his coming words. "If you can't get pork right we're not deferring to you on weights and measures."

Faint honking like an aerial traffic jam. Alex looked up to a northwardly vectored gaggle. Nearly atmospheric, high flight makes tiny geese. This feathered meteor breaking up overhead, a leading bird peeled off to trail the V.

"You know what the girl said to me at the hotel yesterday," Steve said. "I said Tuesday we need an early checkout so I'll pay now. She goes, *yeah, no, for sure.*" Steve looked from the open sea to his guide. "What in the very hell. I just looked at her. Is that some kind of misdirection? Is that a triple negative or just some kind of fucked-up double? She told me it was 1250$ and I laid down a few Benjamins and waited for my change."

"If you're implying ours is Monopoly money I was going to say you kinda remind me of that game's spokesman. The moustache, mostly."

Steve twisted one short white handlebar. "Maybe I should have tried speaking her language. I got my toque on so which way to the gong show, eh?"

"That's actually not bad. Your Canadian English is coming along nicely. Seems all our time together is paying off."

"But not in salmon."

Alex laughed. "It's a little slow."

The Outcast was powered by a pair of 150 horsepower, four-stroke engines. The twins, he called them. One was turned off and the other trolled them forward at about three knots, purring quietly like a happy cat. Scotty downriggers holding island-built Islander reels, their machined aluminum the same colour as this morning sun presently glinting in their gold as if it took credit for their polish. Ten-foot-long black graphite Shimano rods bent devoutly to the sea. Ninety-nine feet below, as if death hadn't cleared up life's confusion, a dead anchovy corkscrewed through the dark water. "Any moment we're going to get into them. One down, three to go." Alex lightly stomped the floorboards. "In the meantime, we'll practise. We'll start slow. Try saying centimetre."

"Slow as the fishing?" Steve said.

"Keep it up. Here we go: cent."

"Ce. Ceh. Seeee. Inch. Can't do it. Inch's shorter. You guys are wasting so much breath. In the U - S of A we value efficiency. It's how we get shit done."

"Then I guess we're at an impasse. I can't suggest to my parliament—"

"Your what?"

"I can't suggest to my parliament that we adopt the Imperial System. We'd be setting humanity back. It'd be like trading in astronomy for astrology. So I guess our both nations are hooped."

"Primed Minster. I'm saying that right?" Steve asked.

"Yes."

Russell smiled around his cigar, smoke merging with engine exhaust. Off the stern in another boat someone was on the rod playing a salmon. Steve and Russell watched. Alex watched. Steve nodded towards it, then turned to Alex. "Hey Alex, what are they doing over there? Are they in some kind of trouble? Think they need help?"

Counterintuitively, sometimes getting one's balls busted brings a smile. Alex turned to the plotter, confirmed their current tack was over yesterday's waypoint marking their double-header.

"I mean it's gotta be easier to clean your boat if it's not all fishy. Right? That's just smart, Alex."

Alex smiling shook his head. Guiding these two felt like fishing with friends.

"So it was whoever crossed the ice became the Indians here?"

"Maybe." Alex moved to the stern and engaged the starboard-side downrigger, the cannonball rising. He reeled up with tandem pace and stopped the Scotty at seventy-nine feet. "Not sure at what point you call people by a different name than the place they left. One night in the new lands? One year? First born? My friend Elizabeth would know. I mean, at that point they would have just left Russia, though not sure what they called Siberia in 15,000 BC."

"Probably just cold," Russell said.

"But the word these days here is Indigenous, or First Nations, I think. I believe Native or Aboriginal is accepted, or maybe as capitalized adjectives. Truthfully it's a little confusing, and changes. And depends who you ask. My buddy wear's a ball cap with Native Pride written across it. I asked him once what word to use. He said Douglas. Comedian. Names here can be a little confusing and these are sensitive times. Let's not even get into gender pronouns. I consider this fishing boat a safe place from gender pronouns."

"Call me anything but late for dinner."

"Does that pass for a joke in America? Tell me, are your roads really paved in gold?"

"They are, yes. But you'll have to take my word for it. We generally don't allow fishing guides to cross the border."

"Catch all your bass is why."

"Indians. We just say Indians. I think they're okay with it."

Alex shrugged. "So, whoever it was and whatever you call them arrived about ten, maybe twenty thousand years ago. Archaeological evidence has this area, Clayoquot Sound, inhabited for over four thousand years."

When the inconstant morning breeze did blow it was light. Alex steered the boat along yesterday's tack. Half the screen was a map and half sonar. "I'm seeing bait at sixty feet. Herring or needle fish."

Steve said, "I assume you're messing with me."

Alex a poor multitasker couldn't solve that riddle in real time. "*Feet*, hypocrite."

"Ha, actually yeah no that wasn't intentional." The variable breeze swirled cigar smoke. Alex smelled it. He liked it. Reminded him of being a fishing guide twenty years ago in northern Canada where he also guided Americans. He liked Americans.

"Break that name down for me, Cap'n. Clacckit Sound."

"Sound is the term for water between the mainland and islands. An old Norse word, *sund*. I didn't know either when I came out here from the prairies. Ask a seaman to kindly forgive the ignorance of an easily confused prairie boy who finds himself far from his native wheat fields. And then C-l-a-y-o-q-u-o-t." He spelled it. "It's the anglicized term for a group of various peoples, various tribes or nations. Tla-o-qui-aht. The suffix aht means people."

"Nations? I thought there was just one Canada, *eh? Eh,* Alex?"

"To emphasize certain peoples' sovereignty, or desire for it, I believe."

Steve dramatically gestured an arm to the sea. "Amateur historian, salmon enthusiast: book your charter today with Alex from Outcast Adventures, an odd duck in his strange Tofino pond. I don't recall getting regaled with history last year. Traded in your winter ticket to Mexico to go back to school?"

"Well. I figured a guide ought to be able to entertain his beloved guests during the slow patches. So, my choices: comedian or historian."

"Entertain or distract," offered Russell.

"Exactly, Russ. Actually I did go to Mexico again last winter. I was surfing at La Ticla, which I wish translates as The Tickle, but sadly it does not. A very small and rural town in Michoacán. A few years back cartel and bandito violence escalated. I have a friend who was surfing there years ago and one night the banditos woke everyone from their cabanas to rob them at gunpoint. His buddy ran away. Right then just fuckin' up and runs for it. The balls, hey? They actually fired shots after him. The Natives down there who own the stores and restaurants got tired of all that. Bad for business. So they armed themselves and took back control of the town. Now when you arrive you have to drive through a roadblock of pick-up trucks with clandestine folk-soldiers. Rather intense. Blue jeans and collared shirts and sombreros and assault rifles. They do not smile, though this surf tourist does. But the waves are high quality. The tacos too. The businesses are friendly to surfers. Surfers eat a lot of tacos."

The starboard rod faintly twitching and Russell sat up but Alex said it was just the line bouncing off that baitball. "Just wait," he said, "it's coming. So what has two thumbs and a decent cutback and a good hookset and eats a lot of tacos?" Neither of the stern-facing occupants turned to see a gesture of self-pointing thumbs. "This guy." Only one of the Outcast's crew here laughed.

"I'll have to take your word for it." Steve deadpan turned to Alex. "About the hooksets." Then he blinked slowly, still looking at Alex. As if a blink is the subtlest slapstick. Then he turned back to the untwitching, unspringing, fishless rods still devoutly bent like twinned worshippers long prostrate asking for a little bounty from the goddess Sea. Today, after all, was Sunday.

Alex laughed. "You know, I really love you guys. So where was I going with this story?"

"Distraction or entertainment, irregardless, Alex," Steve said, "I truly have no friggin' idea."

"Oh yeah. So after a month there I was heading home but wanted to see the capital. The country's capital."

"They speak Mexican down there, correct?"

Russell looked at Steve like oh stop.

"So I booked a food tour."

"A what?"

"A food tour. The Tripadvisor said ten to fifteen people plus the guide. I show up at the meeting place, the first restaurant, and it was just Raúl and me."

"Rah-ool."

"I got a three hour, one-on-one private tour, the guide taking me to ten different restaurants. From dive hole-in-the-walls where for certain you know you will not get the shits in the middle of the night because they're not going to wait that long, all the way up to finer dining. Not *fine*, but finer. Walking from one spot to the other in the warm Mexican evening, while the guide—eloquent, perfect English, charming Raúl—"

"Rah—oowell."

"While my man educated me on the city and the food and the history. Man I loved that."

"Prediction?"

"Yes, go ahead, Steve."

"This story ends with a churro."

Alex and Russell both laughed. "So you've heard this one before. I'm always going to book a food tour on vacation. Finally, *finally* boys we arrive to the long-winded point of this story."

"Thank god damn."

A guide in another boat took up his net and lowered it to the surface, his client on the bent rod. He dipped and scooped then stood the net's long handle vertical so the weight would not bend the aluminum, then boated the fish. Alex's crew listened to that boat cheer.

"Must be nice," Steve said.

"When I got home I thought it would be interesting to know more of the history here. Interesting in its own right, but you know, also good for business. If it ever happens, if it just so happens to get a bit slow."

"Alex. It's a bit slow."

"Yeah." Alex descended the port downrigger back to ninety-nine feet. He called it his Jay-Z depth. Fifteen years ago his friend who taught him salmon fishing told him to only run lines at odd numbers. He did not question it. Some traditions are worth blindly respecting. There is more to them than the literal. There is more to life than the literal. "I started reading some history books on the area. Talking—well, mainly listening—to my friend Elizabeth. Something of an anti-historian."

"Okay Alex." Steve put up his hands. "Okayyy I'll bite. Because the flippin' fish aren't. What the heck is an anti-historian?"

"It's a hundred-year-old lady without many friends who gives me nightmares. Often can be found at Shelter Restaurant. She's like the Johnny Cash of history."

"Thanks for clearing that up."

"So I had a day off and I was heading fishing."

"You had a day off from fishing and went fishing."

"Never knew the flat sea could echo, Steve. Keep interrupting and you'll have to tack on an extra charter day to get to the end of this pointless story. So I left Tofino Harbour. Passed Grice Point and Duffin cove and Felice Island, entered Van Nevel Channel. What is that? You know what that is? That's me driving through history it sounds like, right? I was like, okay—I'll start there. Just started reading about some of the coastal names. A coast logs history uniquely. The names of channels, islands, beaches, like the dog-eared pages of history." Alex turned to the contoured coast as if he was looking at a historical picture book. "Makes it easier to remember. And interestingly, it's not all named after history's noblest actors. Good, makes it harder to forget. Geographical names ought to have a mixture of the reputable and the disreputable. Among your Tranquil Bays and Pretty Girl Coves of the world, you outta throw in some Mao Mountains and Hitler Hills and Pol Pot, Pol Pot… Pol Pot… Someone help me out here."

"I got you," said Steve. "Pol Pot Puddles."

"Not many significant puddles is the problem, Steve."

"Pol Pot Pole?" He swung again.

"Eh. Kinda better, but there's simply too few poles. You got your North and your South. I believe that covers them."

Quiet Russell was potentially an adherent to the valid fishing philosophy which states that waves lapping boat hulls speak truer than words from flapping lips. But if such was his allegiance he did break faith to throw a tyrant's-lifebuoy to his drowning shipmates: "Stalin Shores."

"Stalin Shores. That's very nice." Steve reached across the gap between the two seats and touched Russell's arm. "We get back let's call our travel agent. We'll order matching Cossack hats."

"The history of this area is straight Hollywood, almost too wild to be believed. Spain capturing British ships in Friendly Cove then shipping the imprisoned captains south for trial. Ships cannon bombing coastal villages. The crew of a trade ship is slaughtered but one survivor hides below deck, then the next day when the looters return he blows himself and the ship sky high, killing scores of his enemies."

"Jesus. Okay tell us that one."

"I'll do you one better, Steve. I'll take you to the site where she sank, on our way back after I limit you out." He winked and stomped the floorboards covering the fish-hold. "We're gonna git into 'em. Stay with me. Then I'll take you there and with that sun poking through we might be the first to spot one of her sunken brass cannons.

"Okay, history continued. This area becomes an international trade hub starting in the late 1700s. Basically from then on it was one crazy boom-bust cycle after the next. The curse of areas richly blessed in natural resources: devastate one, move on to the next. But Clayoquot Sound shouldn't feel so special, just fitting in with a timeless pattern the world over. Exploit the natural resources then send in the missionaries. It all started with the sea otters. Soft gold, they called it. Actually back then their pelts were worth more than their weight in gold."

"Why sea otters? Beavers I get. Everybody loves beaver."

"True. Sea otters have the most hair per square inch of any critter, land critter or sea critter. They have no blubber so it's that hair density which keeps them warm. Though not so warm as to insulate them from the cold touch of humankind." Alex squinted and spoke wistfully.

"Nii-iice. How's the side-gig writing coming, Alex?"

"Sales are slower than I'd prefer. I'm working on it."

"I suppose they're cuter than the beaver. I've seen them hold hands."

"Yeah. Just too cute, hey. The hand holding. To keep them from drifting apart in the wild currents of life. Evolution, no doubt, was a romantic." Alex was debating whether to disclose the sex life of sea otters. He looked at Russell, at Steve. These large and rich and innocent Americans. Whether he should mention how at times the male otter will bite the female's face to the extent flesh tears from her nose, hold her underwater, and ultimately kill a significant number of his mates—either

22

through drowning or resulting infection. Not romantic at all, evolution likes it rough. Alex recalled the sight he had seen six years ago. A sea otter capturing a baby seal from Cleland Island. He hadn't told anyone that story and had no plans to. Things of nightmares. How the baby seal squealed as the otter dragged it from its sun perch on the rocky shore, the pup squirming, the otter flipping it over on its back, then taking a mating posture, it held the little seal underwater until the pup drowned. But it was only getting started. It then became repeatedly and vigorously amorous with its limp and lifeless body. He had watched it with curious horror for an hour. That night he read that their necrophilia could last days. *Days*. Jesus Christ. No, he would not disclose such lurid details so sharply visible they would only pop the bubble protecting his innocent guests.

Steve said, "Heard their sex life is fucked-up beyond belief."

"Otters—killed them all by the early 1800s. They're only back now, frolicking, playing, raping because they were reintroduced. Found a few hiding out in an Alaskan cove like shipwrecked refugees. I'd assume shell shocked and entirely PTSD'd. Probably their species has some deep-rooted complexes. Well they caught some, darted 'em, released 'em here."

"Happily ever after."

"Then you've heard this one too."

The starboard rod twitched and so did Russell but Alex said that was just a weed. Stare at rod tips for two decades and you can read a subtle language invisible to most. "Okay back to Tofino boom-bust cycles. Next it was dogfish, then seals. Huge international business, British Columbia found its economic footing in sealing. Rough numbers, the seal population along the coast dropped from five million to one hundred thousand. In one spectacular year, *one year*, six hundred thousand seals were killed. What a fantastic bloodletting, eh? Some of these animals weigh up to six hundred pounds. Picture big ships cruising right where we are now, their decks whitewashed from milk leaking from dead pregnant seals. Well we just about killed 'em all."

Steve looking out at the cobalt sea, which perhaps for his wide eyes was curdled and creamy. He said somberly, "The Tripadvisor review of Outcast Adventures is going to be most unique, buddy."

"Next boom and bust we have whaling. In one year in the early 1900s, four whaling stations processed over fifteen hundred whales. For the oil but also the *sea beef*. I actually don't think that branding is so bad. *Sea beef*. I'd try it."

"Yeah I'd try it."

Russell opened their cooler and picked out a juice box and spiked a straw. So, cigar and juice box. Alex thought that was funny. Russell didn't ask he just passed one to Steve who said obliged. Passed one over his shoulder to Alex who also said obliged. Flavour: tropical storm, blue typhoon.

"Moving on. There was a short-lived gold rush. Forestry continues today. Commercial fishing—salmon, of course. Most of the salmon we're catching aren't wild they're hatchery, so that story tells itself. Then we have my personal boom-bust favourite, that of the herring roe. Apparently it's a delicacy in Japan. Or, at least in the 1970s it was. Back then Russian and Japanese herring stocks dwindled while this west coast surged. Hundreds of boats showed up to capitalize. Japanese businessmen walked around town with briefcases of a million dollars and I am not making this up. They'd hand out sizable cash gifts to captains, simply requesting that they remember them when they dock their load. It was said that from the huge influx of cash to the coast, no hundred dollar bills could be found west of Winnipeg." Alex didn't wait for Steve to ask. "The geographical centre of Canada. Birthplace of yours truly. It was said ladies of the evening—potentially my favourite euphemism of all time—I mean just try to top it."

"I always thought *coup de grâce* sounded nice."

"It is nice, you're right. Coup de grâce. It's quite tasteful. I like, *sleeping with the fishes*. That sounds very peaceful. But then again I've always had a soft spot for the mafia."

"*Ethnic cleansing*—oh hell, I almost missed it. The best: *Manifest Destiny*."

"You're right. That might be the best. Sounds so valiant yet so dreamy. Maybe never a prettier mask worn by something so ugly. But, *ladies of the evening* will always have a special place in my heart. If your daughter says that when she grows up she wants to be a *lady of the evening*, you'd be like, I get it, that just sounds dignified and enchanting." A nearby boat throttled up and set off in the direction of town. "So these ladies—let's stop beating around the bush and call a spade a spade: these soul masseuses who plied their trade with delicate touch through the flesh of the weary roe-fisherman arrived by yacht—I said yacht—from Vancouver and were said to accept payments for their services in roe. And get this, prices rose from sixty dollars per ton to *five thousand per ton*. The bars would have been wild. The town stunk with cash."

"And fish eggs."

"Now Tofino's present-day boom tops it all. The god of West Coast booms: tourism. And I don't see this boom ever busting. Wouldn't take DaVinci to predict that sea-otter-pelt hats might one day fall out of fashion. But beaches have been popular since man first wiggled his toes in the sand. No shelf life to the sea life. Am I right, fellas?"

"Captain, who needs salmon." Steve crossed his legs on the gunwale and maybe that comment only half in jest as he did look rather pleased, as if blue water and morning sun and a boat with good company might just make superfluous any riches yet outstanding. He sucked and squeezed his wheezing juice box.

It was this type of good-natured, low-pressure, genuine people that Alex always wanted to work the hardest for. He checked his speed and course. He went to the stern and started rigging up a fresh anchovy, sliding its head into the purple-haze glow-in-the-dark teaser head, securing it with a piece of broken toothpick, slightly curving its slick silver body in his palm while being careful not to impair its tiny scales, then bedding one hook of the barbless treble along its lateral line, shaping the bait to roll in slow spiral, the motion a wounded anchovy swims after being slashed by a salmon tail.

"Believe it or not, surfing actually tops it all, tops fishing even." He stepped to the starboard to bring up its lure and swap in this fresh one when the port rod-tip started jerking spastically towards the surface. "Fish!" Alex lunged to the rod and gripped the cork with two hands and slid it out of its rocket launcher then reeled down to take up the slack and gave the rod a short jerk upwards to free the line from the quick-release clip. He reeled down again to find the fish then swept the rod up into a deep hookset. He held the ten foot pole steady, gauging the fish's size by the pull, the bend. The pole throughout its whole length liberally bent. The fish taking line and that precise metallic whir composed by countless tiny ticks is a beautiful sound if you know it. Like vizzzzzzz. He loosened the drag a touch. Russell had the last one so he passed the rod off smoothly to Steve already standing. "Here you go."

Alex had to restrain himself from over-coaching because these two here knew what they were doing. He didn't want to take anything away from it. His voice, his instruction, if not needed would just break the spell, adulterate and infringe on a type of union, the connection of fisherman to fish. He watched

Steve and watched for other boats and kept his eye on the other line.

Alex liked netting and gaffing a fish as much as he liked playing one on the line. It had its own skill. Controlling the boat and keeping the line out of the motors and downriggers and watching for other vessels and if the fisherman was novice, then coaching. That all took more skill than playing the fish. Above all he really liked seeing another person catching one. It made him feel good, seeing another's joy. A momentary break from the consuming world of self. Liked it the first day he guided a guest to a fish, which he could remember because he had somehow lost his purple hat on that big Northern Pike. Liked it this day, seeing Steve fully absorbed in it. Someone with a good fish on the line. The eagerness to see what was hooked—a salmon, yeah, but you wanted to see its individuality, its particular colour and size and shine. Alex thought maybe it was like how as you age, giving a gift becomes more enjoyable than receiving one. How giving nourishes the giver who does not ask for recompense.

Steve was standing and had his rod tip up and wasn't forcing the action and wasn't muscling the fish, just letting the bend of the rod do the work and feeling for what the fish allowed, reeling when it tired. There is so much feel to this and you earn that feel by doing it a lot and listening. You screw it up sometimes but you learn from those and get better. By listening and feeling. Not a dance not an art but it's something, deeper than craft, more substantive than mere technique. Maybe better unnamed. There's no rush when it's all about smoothly keeping that barbless hook engaged with steady pressure. It's something you feel, something you learn to feel. You can become excellent at anything, no gifts of nature required. Believe it, he did. Earn it, is all.

Alex leaned in under the bent pole and reached to the Scotty and turned its knob to auto-retrieve. There was camaraderie when a good fish was on the line. Nothing as strong as the bond of soldiers or firefighters or even the machined synchrony of a pit crew during a tire swap—box box box—but still an unspoken union from each well-executing their own role in a shared pursuit. How old is this. It's old. It might be timeless.

The salmon was off a stern corner when the flasher broke the surface disrupting the line's tension and a lesser angler, fooled by the momentary slackness, would think the fish had gotten off. Steve said something to the fish or to the water or to himself or more likely a word to each at once and he reeled to find the fish and smoothly reapply tension.

The salmon was closer now with less line to stretch and absorb the strong head jerks. Twenty pounds of muscle in the water, in its element, trying to stay in its element. Steve feathering the drag lighter. He had his fingers just beyond the knuckle-buster knobs. The downrigger stopped with the cannon ball a foot under the surface and Alex turned the small boom sternwards.

The fish close but swimming under a patch of sun-stained surface and they couldn't see it but then they could see it. The fish being pulled out from under that sparkling water like Steve was reeling in something from a dream. Now he stopped reeling and angled his pole forward, sweeping the salmon in closer. Its body a couple inches below the surface. Its body at once shimmering and dark, as if of two worlds. Purple-black-dark green-silver fish. This salmon's vibrancy matched its species' most colourful story. Few species like this in the world and maybe none. Speed, power, beauty, fight, sustenance, history. A fish hatched inland in fresh rivers, frys falling down rapids, sliding over boulders, swimming narrow channels, over winding shallows to awaiting predators at the brackish shore. Their sea run—a year, up to eight—out to open ocean waters, to Japan, to Russia. King Salmon I've heard you run ten thousand miles. Returning deep inland seeking out natal waters, even to the very same calm pools that hatched you. Nature with a performative wisdom beyond intelligence, beauty beyond design. Your bodies feed the bears, the birds, the nitrogen of your decay nourishes a forest, hardens trunks, towers growth. Legendary fish. Hard to fabricate a myth about a species that defies one's imagination. Purple-black-dark green-silver fish just below the surface like it rose straight up from lore and not a small part of Alex wished to allow its return.

When Alex took a salmon he would use the whole fish, whether frozen as fillets or chopped into rounds to pressure can in mason jars: skin, spine bones, and all. Eat the roe raw. Bury the carcass in the garden. By law you could take ten Chinook. He didn't take that many. That's not virtue signalling, it's not even exactly about conservation because if the sustainable limits were set by informed biologists then a fisherman could take ten in good conscience. So what is it? He just happened to not like killing them, preferred beautiful things alive in this world. He had killed enough beautiful things. It wasn't fear of them haunting him of which some things did. He had accepted living with ghosts. He just preferred not to kill beautiful things. A preference that collided with his valuing their extreme nutrition, and to live a life where food is lifestyle. It wasn't some traditional background, he wasn't raised a fisherman. This had nothing to do with heritage or history. It had something to do with fish, values, maybe beauty.

The Chinook tried for one more run and angled its head away from the boat, this time weaker. It tried to run but couldn't run. You're the fish. Alex leaned over the gunwale. You're the fish one day. The boat straightened out the salmon's course, as if a force stronger than a trolling motor was at work here. Alex reached below the gunwale for his three-foot wooden gaff. Wrapped his fingers around the contoured handle, hardly a gesture more primal, pick any land including this one and this could be a war club of olden days.

The wooden gaff was fitted with a curved metal shank. He reached out to hook the fishing line. The line refracted at the water's surface, accenting the schism between these two worlds. He gently drew the line in while watching the single barbless hook in its snout. He didn't breathe lighter because he wasn't breathing. Smooth motions to not spook the salmon out of its tired truce and into a desperate run and shake the hook or snap the line. He transferred the line from the gaff's hook to his hand. He pulled the line in while raising the fish to just below the surface, his reflection merging with the fish in the water. He raised the barbaric gaff. When the fish was about to break the ocean's thin liquid skin he swung the gaff blunt-side down onto its head, now not even covered with enough water to splash, then loosened his grip and spun the gaff a half-turn and with a half-swing drove a stainless shank through something beautiful. In the same motion that he gaffed the fish he swept it from its liquid home and into its new dry world to die. He laid the stunned fish down on the white floorboards. Not yet dead but too concussed to even quiver. A skinny line of bright blood leaking from its torpedo-shaped cranium did not seem entirely out of place with its pageantry. This red flair, crimson accent. But to Alex, something distasteful there. Over the white floorboard the red blood ran towards a scupper ported to the ocean, like it knew what it was doing.

Infinities move among us. Eternities go here. Leaking life reddening the floor. Alex gripped the fish's tail and in holding it he felt within himself something at once light and heavy. As if emotions exist on a continuum, at times twisted by the weight of heavy circumstance, connecting the otherwise discordant.

Places where reverence bridges to fear, wonder to doubt, feelings of absurdity intertwined with profundity, as if he held a god by its tail and knew beauty entangled with dread. Something he had keenly felt no more than a handful of times. Once in the North, a wolf its yellow eyes, head held low over red speckled snow. Once in a canoe at night at the edge of a forest fire burning like the night itself roared. He had known it another place too.

Death drains colour, the black and silver fish like it left some paint in the water. Him gripping its muscular caudal, where its streamlined body narrowed between torso and tailfin, before it fanned out into an irregularly black-spotted tail, like some kind of exotic fan gifted on its journey. He raised the gaff.

III

At 6:00 a.m. Valerie's music-alarm started playing a light piano riff. She had four playlists. This one was called *Day Break*. She had an app that randomly chose one of the many songs and started it imperceptibly, crescendo over song length.

The rain had lightened. She didn't see Trent's truck. She went through her morning routine: journal, meditation, a run with music along the Stanley Park Seawall, shower. Valerie's condo was immaculate, colour balanced and modern. She had a cleaner once a week when really once a month, or never, would have sufficed given her tidy nature and that she herself swept and washed. It was a flat that could appear in a magazine. It had, in fact. A CBC interview. She and Peter Mansbridge each sat a chair on the hardwood floor in front of her tall living room window, its many framed panes of small square light. Over the course of the interview two broad monstera leaves level to the floor turning from green to golden, like platters of sun, or beggar's hands a charitable sun engoldened. On one side of the wall next to the window hung a large modernist painting, thick oils looking wet, three colours, no definable shape.

Val found that the fit and colour of her clothes influenced her mindset. She chose her attire with intention. It was style but not just style, not just fashion. As a girl she hadn't cared much about style. Then later, as a young woman, something changed.

Her reasoning trailed her actions because one day she noticed she was looking forward to choosing her attire. Personal style as a way to praise the day, a type of playing with her world, celebrate beauty—those flowers, that song, human kindness—in a type of humble accompaniment. Her aesthetics were for herself, nevertheless, she believed that the ultimate drivers of the mind are often hidden, consciousness often the last to know. She was agnostic as it concerned underlying motivations. But she was certain that this red dress she just packed looked pretty and wearing it was fun. There's some truth there. She finished packing for Tofino. Texted Stacy: *Val leaves Van. Besos y besos!*

On the ferry from Vancouver to Nanaimo she parked on deck four, designated with a cartoon crab. She strolled the main deck and noticed that the window-facing bow seats had three times as many people as the window-facing stern seats. She wondered to what extent one can psychoanalyze seat selection. What awaits, versus, what's left behind.

The big motors' low rumble churning up the sea in a tumbled white froth. The heavy ship pulling away from harbour and the coastline receding. She took out her iPad from her duffle bag and responded to three emails. Two more arrived. One from a large healthcare-technology company. A letter of intent. That makes it the second one she had received. There were no dollar values in this acquisition proposal. She recognized the company's name. She Googled it and found it to be a subsidiary of a multinational consumer goods company, a household brand. The last proposal came four years ago. Her rejection of that offer had found its way to the business section of the Toronto Star. This company would certainly have known that a thirty-four-year-old female CEO—female, because for all of Canada's progressiveness, every article still mentioned her gender—had declined selling her four-year-old company for twenty-five million dollars, a seat on the board and stock options. That was four years ago. Four years for B2P was not most companies' four years. Invite the kids to play on the chart of her gross sales because it looked like a skateboard quarter-pipe: hypergrowth, to make any sense of it, graph it in log scale.

Funny timing. This is funny timing, she reflected. As if the doctor prescribed for my panic attacks a business sale. Off behind her travellers lined up for food. She considered the poutine. She read the email again for any hints alluding to just how much they wanted her business. She would sit down with them like she had the last offer. She liked meeting new people, networking came naturally. She joked with her dad, the civil engineer, your work rubbed off on me because I like building bridges. Her dad who when she brought home A-papers wouldn't say so much, wouldn't praise it because he already knew her to be a top student and expected nothing less, so why should her meeting his expectations impress him. He had her rewrite those papers even when the teacher was not accepting resubmissions. "Because you're not doing it for the teacher." She still had some of the papers. She still had all of them. She considered the poutine.

For that last acquisition meeting she reminded herself to not set the pace, as in, no need to play dumb, but at certain times she found it more productive to downplay her cognitive abilities. Those times being around particular men. She found the interactions went smoother if the counterparty didn't feel intimidated. Her mind did not intimidate all men, just something she sensed from those who perhaps were the insecure ones. Some modern-day version of threatening the patriarchy? Something that historically got some women in trouble. Men perhaps confusing the source of their insecurities. It's not me it's you. She'd never say that. She'd smile. She was just being practical. And partly, it's fun to underplay your hand. Praise their flush—genuinely because it really is a great hand, they feel good about that, she liked that for them—not duplicity not manipulation. It just happened to be the case that in certain dynamics, proposals, negotiations, she held a full house, held quads, a straight flush. So she reminded herself that time not to set the pace, follow it. It's just better for everyone that way.

That first acquisition meeting was 2018 downtown Vancouver at the corner of Seymour and Robson, where she was supposed to meet Evan Miller, chief operation officer. They had exchanged emails. While she was waiting, a lady approached and said hello, maybe mid-fifties. That seemed a little strange, but maybe someone recognizing Valerie from one of her interviews. Val politely returning a hello while keeping an eye open for Evan. The woman introduced herself, "I'm Evan Miller." Val laughed at her own prejudice. Then she laughed at the café choice: Incognito Coffee. That's fun.

Ms. Miller sat not across but beside her. Valerie wondered if that was some negotiating strategy, starting off on the same side of the table. Putting unconscious nudges to work. The server asked their orders and Valerie ordered an oat-milk matcha latte and Evan Miller said the same and Valerie smiled. Then she listened to words of praise leading a pitch. Evan Miller halfway through her coffee slid the tablet over the table then touched a finger with a clear gloss nail to the screen. Scrolled the contract down to the offer highlighted in yellow, eighteen million dollars. It wasn't spelled out: $18,000,000. Valerie figured the zeroes had a stronger psychological effect and wondered if the numerical representation was intentional. She wondered that because those zeroes were doing their job. As if they were trick hoops and she a SeaWorld dolphin.

"What do you think, Ms. Roy?"

She took a moment. She snapped the small biscotti and dunked half. What do you see in those hollow 0's? What will you fill them with when you sell your four-year-old—their malapropism—not business: baby. Then you'll have all the time to figure out how to spend your time. Lots of time to look for some meaningful way to spend your money. Spend it trying to buy your way back to where you are now. To the *pursuit*. Pursuit of what? You know what. Then you'll be wishing you didn't act like some poor harried woman in a strange bazaar selling her baby.

Back then there was hardly anything to think about but she delivered her rejection more deftly. Then bit the softened cookie.

Ms. Miller's smile showed neither traces of surprise nor resentment. She touched and swiped the screen and a different contract waiting in the wings was loaded. Finger scrolling the pdf. A new number, this one bolded, highlighted yellow. $25,000,000.

Valerie did take a moment because there can be delight from flattery even if one has no intention to dance. She was taken aback by the praise but not blushing. Blushing is coloured embarrassment, and she was not that. She said oh my. She sipped her latte. Then with enough sweetness to make an Italian cookie tart she rejected her first commercial suitor. She said she was truly flattered and that perhaps one day they could revisit the proposal, while in the meantime she saw to greater growth. Val turned it down not because the price was wrong, but because, in her words: "It's hard for the price to be right when you really love what you do."

Ms. Miller said, "Keep raising the peak, hey?" A play on the name of Valerie's company. "Well, I respect that. More. I admire it." She smiled. "But I'm still going to see if we can't make that decision harder for you. This isn't our last conversation, Ms. Roy." She smiled and powered down the tablet and leaned back and pulled her mug in. "In the meantime, while I see about fattening the cheque, you keep doing your thing. Just one small request. When the next proposal comes, Valerie—and it will come—please tell them Evan Miller said to go fuck themselves."

Valerie said she certainly will.

Four years ago? She on the ferry trying to account for the impossible compression of time. How is yesterday not yesterday? She reread this letter with enough absorption that if her churning mind were to become audible it might match the ferry's low rumble. It wasn't about the money, but you can't help being curious of the coming number.

Valerie had a nice place, nice car, nice clothes. Having that she didn't want any more. She had read the happiness studies, knew of the hedonic treadmill: the trap of constantly trading up. When a person has enough to cover basic needs and no longer stresses finances, the spiritual-emotional returns from greater wealth diminish rapidly. Statistically, poor people were less happy. The stresses from food and housing insecurity loom large. But wealth's contribution to deep fulfillment seemed capped. She didn't need more things and disliked accumulation's clutter. She lived below her means and donated to an environmental organization to offset her carbon footprint. She liked to travel, or she told herself such a story about her former self who once made time for it.

Her iPad on her knee over crossed legs, white sneakers unsmudged. A sailboat off in the distance. A troller. At the horizon, blue water met grey sky and she squinted but could not see a definable line of separation. The timing is rather funny. Fate holding a feather gives an uninvited tickle. How strange is it that you can't tickle yourself but you can pleasure yourself? she wondered. You'd think if evolution can prevent self-tickle, it would also keep you from self-pleasure, from venting the urge to mate. Is that what you call it? She rolled her eyes at herself on the ferry. Venting the urge to mate? Hot. Too sexy, Valerie.

Sweep one hundred emails to the recycle bin, perhaps start sleeping like a normal person, or even living like one with a social life? Take thirty million dollars—or what, thirty-five? forty? and start striking-through my bucket list. She watched shrinking Vancouver shores. Somewhere in there was her shrinking condo. She could imagine her shrinking self still there behind a screen. Why was it a recycle bin? Who wants their messages recycled? Garbage bin. What will you do if right now you see a whale—fin, fluke, or spout—then what? Breaching up out of your bucket list right here. She wasn't superstitious, and tried as best she could to not centre herself within her worldview. But who isn't a little sensitive to synchronicity, that the simultaneity of two events has meaning beyond mere coincidence? If I see a whale in the next ten seconds I'll sell. She counted down from ten. By seven that gamble actually made her nervous because the words of her pledge could be chiseled into stone. At five seconds she had mixed emotions. With two left she heard the ferry's intercom click on. Even before the captain spoke she held her breath.

"If anyone wants to see a little marine life in the Strait of Georgia, there's a basking sea lion off port." Clicked off. Clicked on. "For all you landlubbers, that's the left side." Likely some passengers waiting for him to come back on and clarify what "lubbers" is or are.

The moment the captain said basking was time enough for her to be biochemically injected with a mixed barrel of nerves, her mind anticipating the next word to be whale. They do bask.

Enough people moved to the port-side windows Valerie wondered if a ferry could list. Only one person went to the starboard window. You'd think that person was confused. Valerie over the years had seen several sea lions. She had this thing where she wanted to cultivate uncommon perspectives, try to see what goes overlooked. Not an antisocial snub to norms, and not like right now she actually expected to see anything out the starboard window, more like trying to entrench neural pathways of an orthogonal thinker, someone open to contrarian views who simply adores creative thought. Even silly small things like sometimes brushing her teeth with her left hand in hopes of sending a few luminous neurons to light her mind's dimmer corridors. You lose what you don't use. Just small ways she found to play with her world. She stood at the starboard window alone. But if you are the contrarian constantly giving your world a second look, it might reinforce a distrust for that world. Or did the distrust come first?

She standing alone at the starboard window looking out at the spoutless Strait of Georgia with little to show but a moderate breeze. Calm and sparkling sea, as if at arts 'n crafts the kids had run beads of Elmer's glue along wave crests they dusted with glitter. You bet it's pretty.

A man dashingly dressed approached and touched her elbow. Charming smile and squinting eyes. Approximately two hundred years old. A cane. Val was 5'4" and she outstood him in his wool newsboy cap. "It's the other side, dear. Come on, we'll go together." Voice as youthful as his fashion. He turned holding her elbow like he hadn't even considered she'd disagree and Valerie thanked him. They began walking to the other side. Shuffling across the ship's midpoint she felt more bond in half a silent minute with him than with most people she had passed several days. What was that? He with his hand on her elbow but anyone watching would know just who was steadying whom. He paused his stroll, immobile, as if a delayed heartbeat stilled him to intermittent fossil. Then he refound his stride and they returned to shuffle. When they arrived to the windows, most people had left or were leaving, some pocketing their phones. They approached open glass and he gestured invitingly for her to have a look. "This is port side." Her saviour. She said right and he said no left and she put her hand over his on her elbow. "I used to be in the navy, you know."

A lady looking like the other half of the collector's set—charmingly small, red beret—walked up and took his arm. "There you are you little flirt. I leave you for one minute." She looked up at Val. "We have to watch them, don't we." She looked at him. "Was she impressed that you were in the navy?" He released his frail grasp and sunk his head between his padded and now-raised shoulders, gaping mouth not unlike a guilty turtle, or one whose tail was in the clutches of an inconvenient yet harmless kitten. Kitten said, "Now you're buying me a Mars bar." He smiled at her and winked at Val and they turned at about the speed of a pivoting ferry.

Valerie looking out the window but not really looking, wondering, is there a number large enough where you must say yes? Sell at your expense for the greater good the proceeds could do in the world? A thought she'd keep to herself so as not to give people diabetes from her saccharine words. How large is the offer that you can't decline? Come to that number before their proposal. Her dad had taught her to always arrive to negotiations with your values predetermined. She texted her dad, his health on her mind. She walked for the stairs to the outer deck.

This rippled ocean a shattered mirror of ten thousand suns. Like, my God, splendour. Take a moment to bask like the missing sea lion in the sun of this flattery, because tomorrow brings a trough. As her company grew her profile broadened. Comments both positive and negative arriving to her socials. It's a curious physics when two substances made from the same matter can have drastically different weights. The weights not originating with the matter but with she who does the weighing. Of course she researched that peculiar psychological concept. Losses loom larger than gains. Apparently, negative comments hinder disproportionately more than positive ones bolster. Such is the human mind, hers for certain.

One person on Twitter said that "B2P raking it in does not fit with a health and wellness company. The pyramid logo fits their scheme, Roy sits at the top." Her stomach dropped. Another comment another day. "Signed up for the highest-tier membership. Nutritionist never showed. Same thing with the breath workshop. Skipped the yoga class because I'm too bent out of shape. Three weeks now without a refund." She had tried to track that person down and offer a year of free membership.

She had started B2P from her basement apartment, financed it with 18% APR credit-card debt. Her own struggles spawned the business and its scaffolding was her bones and comments like that were a kick in the shins. She believed differences could be resolved through good communication, truly try to see the other's perspective. She had replied that the company's valuation didn't tell of its profitability. Many companies vastly larger—even behemoths like Spotify and Amazon—were for years, or still are, unprofitable. Companies valued not on actual but potential profit. There were levers of monetization she could pull that she hadn't pulled and didn't want to pull. That if she sold, went public, for certain they'd all get pulled. She responded saying she was making a comfortable living but that in comparison to other CEOs of similar-sized businesses, she would absolutely be at the bottom of the salary totem pole. The next two comments called her racist. The third was an emoji of a purple eggplant. Fourth said I love you Valerie Roy. We push and we pull.

The outer deck fresh in sea fragrance but the breeze quite cool. She buttoned up her long coat over her knit top. Sharp waters, sun glinting sea chop like polished serrated blades. That social-media fallout was five years ago. Stace helped. From elementary school onwards, Stacy had been Val's closest friend.

Surface connections are never so hard to come by but depth is exceedingly rare. Stacy was a big girl—big mouth, big boned. Made Val laugh. Some things hadn't changed. She didn't much worry about Val. Most didn't see past her outer layer, took that as innocence all the way down. Stacy knew her sweetness misdirected most from seeing her grit, stubbornness, fierce independence. Surfaces are often secretive of the core. Valerie looking at the sea here.

During that negative Tweet storm, Stacy came over to Val's condo with a gift wrapped in white packing paper. No ribbon but a pretty red bow. Val unwrapped it. White shirt, small black centred lettering. You couldn't read it very far away. She held it up by its shoulders, laughed, turned it, draped it over her chest.

You don't like me, bet against me. -Ma$e

Hilarious. That shit's hilarious. Still hilarious to Valerie three years later. Stace said she considered *Fuck bitches get money* but the message wasn't as clear.

Val said I get that, the ambiguity of whether one ought to forsake the pursuit of the fairer sex in order to strive for financial reward, or if one ought to endeavour on both fronts. Val still had the shirt. She found it fit a bit big, and the egotism about XXXL, but her best friend's sweet gesture made her laugh and perfectly fit her love of '90s rap. Sometimes she wore it to bed like an oversized cotton hug.

Even through texts Stacy detected this most recent dejection. She would dig into her at dinner. The first Thursday of the month the two of them always went for dinner at Italian Kitchen on Burrard Street. Val had declined last month. That was a first. Thirty days later Val cancelled again. Stacy said okay no problem. An hour later she was banging on her door like Val owed her money. She said a normally infatuated foodie declining the best meatball in town is like an athlete spitting blood.

"I'm concerned you're dying and not telling me. So I'm here for your Tesla." Stacy with her hand out, perhaps for the key fob.

Val smiled and said she's just working through some work and things. She hadn't invited her in.

Stacy said cool, I get it, life, right? Then she put her hand on Val's chest and walked her backwards and took from her purse a thermometer she had brought purely as a prop and said bend over and held it up and pursed her lips like she was going to spit-lube it and Valerie laughed and covered Stacy's mouth to keep her from spitting because she probably actually would spit and then they had tea by candlelight like medicine.

They sat on the couch. Stacy had found a candle, a new one, looking artisanal, tall, white with grey swirls and a red string threading a small label hand-written about beeswax and coconut and coffee and rum and other such fancy things of which Stacy didn't further read. Elegant concoction like an upper-class waxen cocktail. She asked for a lighter and saw Val's look and teased the control freak saying I'm lighting it deal with it it's a candle and she did and they sat on the couch.

Getting Val to talk about herself was about as easy as getting her own husband to not talk about himself, or getting her four kids past the one minute mark of the Silent Game. She made the game up. Like probably every other mother has. Is necessity the mother of invention, or are mothers the inventors of necessity? Who can go the longest without making a sound. Prize: Mom's sanity. And a cookie. Or just all the cookies, forever. Stacy on the couch inquired, "What's going on?"

"Ah just the norm, really. How are the kids?"

It wasn't even intentional. Stacy discreetly broached Val's deflection. "Start fucking talking."

"I had a panic attack. While running."

"Weird. Where?"

"By the Stanley Park Seawall. In the morning, the other morning."

Stacy waited and it says something about the company you keep when someone answers a question that wasn't voiced.

"I don't know. I guess I just feel stretched thin. To the point I wonder if others can see through my chest, my crinkling lungs like two paper sacks sucking in and out." She put her hand on her chest. "I'm lacking my normal clarity."

"The work?"

"No. I dunno. Maybe. I don't even know what it is. Not for certain. It's either all the things or one thing or a combination of them. That I'm certain about."

Stacy didn't laugh.

"There's no shortage of potential candidates. But none of them are new. None of them feel like the culprit, you know? I like my life. I've chosen it. I often love it. Like daily, I mostly love it, I think. I can point to things, big obvious things that look like the guilty party. But it's not direct. We don't always know. We have ideas, stories. We give them names. Overworked. Stressed. Insecurity. I don't know. Loneliness? Routine? Self-criticality? Self-doubt? Sometimes it's hard to trust my feelings when for no apparent reason I just find myself crying. What is that? Hormonal? I feel the effect but the source is subsurface."

"Well start with the big obvious then."

She shrugged. "Maybe a cognitive dissonance at play. Holding the reins of a self-development company while feeling like the person who should be enrolled in all its workshops. I mean, I started it for my own benefit. So is it an imposter syndrome? Maybe not, because a lot of the time I do feel confident. Nothing quite fits. Who knows how these things work. Maybe some kind of subliminal jive. A perfectionist syndrome has been suggested."

"Or control freak." She stroked the cylindrical wall of the prettiest artisanal candle she'd ever seen and probably the most expensive. A taunt that came with a smile. Then she topped up Val's tea.

"That too. But I just don't know. You point to one thing when really it could be something else, or things interplaying, or just some temporary hormonal imbalance, deficient in some macro or micro nutrient. Who knows, maybe it's as simple as a lack of vitamin D."

Stacy nodded like a sage. "Dick."

Val smiled, "The other vitamin D."

"Sunlight, yes, equally important. Studies show sunlight is nearly as important as vitamin Dick. I take your point." Sometimes Stacy tried to speak in Val's language, communication morphing into Stacerie, similar to Spanglish.

Val said "I know you're messing with me but you're actually not wrong. Social connection, dick or otherwise, has biochemical effects. Even right here, this is below the surface too. I mean, maybe this is what I needed."

"Oh, I'm deep dicking you alright, baby."

"Maybe just some temporary imbalance manifesting as heart arrhythmia on a jog, yet the psychoanalyst says you're repressing that afternoon at the pool with your uncle, or whatever. The mind is so complicated and we don't even have access to the iceberg's tip. Never mind how different issues over your life are interplaying and flywheeling off one another, everything amplified by low sleep. Or that I don't even know for certain what's causing it is itself a type of lack of control. You know? Meta-uncontrol? Or." Her eyes low to the candle on the coffee table. "Certain past things. You work on things and feel like you've addressed them. But I mean, we just plainly don't know what's ever fully resolved. I once fell and gouged my knee when I was twelve. There's still a scar." She pulled up a pant leg. "It tightened the skin around it." She pulled at the old scar. "It makes you wonder if our deeper wounds were properly sutured, you know? What does the mind's scar tissue look like? The heart's?" She didn't go into those other things and Stacy knew what she meant anyway.

"How long have you been feeling a bit low?"

Sitting on one end of the couch Val held her mug with two hands. "A little while."

Common rules of engagement don't apply to closest friends. Stacy fired point blank. "When was that panic attack?"

"The first one was three months ago."

Stacy leaned back. Quiet. Maybe hurt. Between them, small cracklings from the candle's wooden wick mimicking campfire. Few ambiances are abler to receive divulgences than firelight. "And the most recent?"

"Friday."

She prodded more and they talked. The breakup with Trent didn't feel like the culprit and the first panic attack came earlier. She didn't tell her about his truck only because he had not been physical and she had resolved to call the police if things escalated and sister bear here would only overbear. Val talked of work. She said towering walls while raising a hand gripping a phone.

Stacy while still looking in her eyes reached out and peeled her phone from her hand and set it behind herself where Val couldn't see it and said go on. There were not many people Val would allow that. Actually, there was no one. Not specifically taking the phone, rather that patronising authority. She smiled quite sweetly and Stacy said I know that smile.

"I hate complaining. Like, I sincerely hate what we're doing here."

"Keep talking."

"Gah. I know I've got discipline in spades, that sometimes it's harder to do less, to relax and let go. I tell myself to break

47

patterns but that becomes its own type of pattern. All this is laughable and petty. Like next I'll be crying over how all my devices require different charging cords." She shook her head. "Meanwhile in other places in the world some people are just trying not to go hungry. Let's move on. What about your work?"

"Keep going."

She inhaled heavily because for some voicing afflictions is harder than bearing them. "Maybe just all the little things. By themselves they're nothing. Just silk threads." She drew a hand across her chest. Again. "Imperceptible on their own. One day you find yourself bound. Like there are parts of me becoming restrained. Things I can no longer see because it's like I can't even turn my head and it's my own fault for making my world small. Like those horses with blinders. And I value the opposite, vision. Okay let's stop now. Do I sound like I think I sound?" Eyes back on the candlelight. She uncrossed a leg and pushed her toes against Stacy's knee.

"You should hear you. Would you be as unsympathetic to me as you are to yourself? People with good jobs that have things can also feel low. I mean, obviously they can. That's the most fucked-up type of elitism I've ever heard." She laughed and teased her friend.

"I sound like a privileged little whiny girl."

She shook her head. "You don't."

"You'd tell me if I sounded like a little bitch, right?"

"Probably not."

Valerie sighed. "That's what I thought. It's like we can tell ourselves, but not resolve ourselves. Like your words fall on your mind's own deaf ears. We know the right things to say, but whether in the murky depths of our own psychology we're actually listening is another thing altogether."

A few years back Stacy suggested Val take herself on a backpacking trip across Europe. Val said, "Uhh. Nah. Kinda yeck. That's just not me. I like the pursuit of..." She was going to say excellence but it sounded so grandiose and self-important she did not say that. She just said, "I like building."

In this evening's coconut-rum-coffee air she reminded Val of just how many people were benefiting from her work. "Tens of thousands of women. Valerie. Take a minute. You should hold that close. That's just actually incredible."

At that point B2P had closer to five hundred thousand members. "Thanks Stace." Stacy arrived at 5:00 p.m. and at 7:30 she handed Val back her phone saying, "Babe, I just got off the phone with your therapist. She prescribed: lasagna. Put on somethin' pretty for me. I'm taking you to the hospital that smells like garlic."

Since high school, planet Valerie and planet Stacy had been spinning farther apart. Measured by preoccupations, lifestyles, goals, a galaxy expands between them. But laughter proved interstellar. Valerie actually did order the lasagna and Stacy got the pappardelle saying it was from her unconscious daddy issues. Val thought that was hilarious and accused Stacy of ordering it simply for that punchline, she wouldn't put it past her. She loved this woman tremendously. They talked of life, work, dumb dates and husbands and their occasionally redeeming qualities, love and its lacking, music and Italian food—really, the only things that matter. For dessert they shared a cheese plate paired with Tawny Port in glasses narrow-rimmed and tall-bowled.

Stacy said that from her changing palette she can tell she's matured. "I used to hate blue cheese and responsibility. Now I don't mind blue cheese."

Val got the bill. Stacy dropped Val off. Val stayed up. She got her notepad and turned down the lights and relit that candle and put on her baggy purple sweatpants and her Ma$e shirt and hit play on a down-tempo playlist. The music atmospheric, like a prelude to a dream.

Diffuse focus brings psychological sickness? Drain the swamp. Cull the mediocre. There's beauty in excellence and I love the pursuit. She sat with that. *Disrupt patterns and break routine? (Plan spa date where I pamper Stace-the-babe!) Prep for Ted Talk—do it even if you don't love doing it—there are things larger than your self-concern. Open up to new connections in uncommon forms. Whatever that might mean, whatever that might look like. Getting away is not running away. Catch your breath and come back stronger. Tofino?*

She could feel some kind of outstanding concerns refusing to surface. Things morose and broody. Felt uncertainties at the tip of the tongue shy of exposure to a naked page. She wanted her belly, her heart, the little girl and the old lady inside her to run the margins. Purge this lurking unnamed. Why is the unconscious so obscure? Why only hints and allusions? Why not just reveal the issue so it can be addressed and resolved? Aren't we on the same team? Inhabitants of the same mental globe yet isolated linguistically, trying to communicate across the gulf? The subconscious orchestrating panic attacks and strange dreams, or you find yourself singing song lyrics with an uncanny description of current preoccupations. Yet if someone told you to sit down and come up with a song that captures your present concerns, it would not come easily.

She knew she had not pinned it all down but negative awareness is not nothing. She made that term up. Knowing exactly where you don't want to go still helps with direction. Knowing something remains hidden fuels the search. It was that night she came up with the idea of Tofino. It had been too long since she'd last travelled and she heard so much about it. She called it an escape, then didn't like that word. Called it a retreat, no better.

Getaway—funny the defeatism in vacation words. Restorative sojourn, she settled on that.

This morning's cameoed sun slipped behind silver curtains. The ferry's outer deck cold even with her long coat, hair tucked under its double-breasted collar. She had heard that pods of porpoise sometimes swim beside the ferry. Dark green shores of Vancouver Island closing in. She went back inside. She strolled the ship's oval walkway and passed, seated quietly, hand in hand, newsboy cap and red beret and she smiled cornered eyes without turning their way. At the little store near the bow she didn't browse the clothing but she did the magazines. Forbes, Newsweek, Macleans. B2P had received coverage in all of them but none this month. Softly from her purse played a piano. She had set her mom's ringtone to a calming song *No One Knows Me Like the Piano* by Sampha. It mellowed her for the call. She loved her with a love not easily defined nor had it taken its final shape. Probably nothing takes a final shape when both parties are continually changing, she thought. She and her mother were different people and every advancing year wasn't shrinking that gulf, but the waters were calming. And every year they curiously seemed one less year apart. So distrust time. Still mother and daughter, but categories broached and lines crossed. Sometimes they were two women that talked. Her mother never used to share her insecurities. Her mom had been caring and supportive and controlling and impassively hard on her dad, and her mother had been loving and complicated and irreducible. Sometimes she'd let that song play for a couple bars.

"Hello Mom."

She took her for a lap around the ferry. Told her of the little charmer who had taken her by the elbow. "No, sadly he's spoken for. I know." Her parents separated and to Val that made her mom's current concern for her ex-husband's health rather touching. Apparently in some form, love from *I do* can carry through after *I don't*. I guess that's not nothing. Mom had a student arriving. She had tried to teach Valerie piano when she was young, and though the keys didn't come so easily, in one way perhaps she had gotten through because music for Val was elemental. A passion fully core that reached its limit just short of her fingers. Val sensed that that was something of a disappointment to her.

The cafeteria line had dwindled and she ordered the poutine because: vacation. She sent Stacy a pic of that hot Quebec mess, captioned it, *Gravy and curds with a side of fries*. She didn't check her email again and told herself a break from work means a break from work and promised herself less phone more Tofino.

"Please return to your vehicles."

She seeks the cartoon crab.

IV

Late morning. Black Tesla like a seed spat from the ferry's belly. She leaves Nanaimo Harbour, Valerie driving cross-island towards that raw western shore. Playing through fifteen speakers a playlist she titled *Thump My Ticker*. Some of them older songs she didn't much play anymore but would have felt bad deleting them. Skipped one. Skipped the next. Almost didn't skip the next because the song was heard as much by her heart as her ears, but it was too slow for present purposes. She set her thumb to the steering wheel's skip button but then allowed Wallen to make his case for a heart on the run and she did wonder in light of the fact that Tofino is literally the end of the road, if her unconscious had her running away. In the silence until the next song's arrival she was thinking about the pretty line about the magnolia tree. She was not sure what she was looking for, listening for. Sometimes you don't know until you find it. When she found it she sang and didn't care that the story wasn't hers because the story doesn't have to be your story to be moved by it. She wasn't singing another's song she was moved beyond restraint of silence by the beauty of their composition, by their humanity. Music doesn't require permission. Tame it like you'd tame a sunray, imprison the wind, bind the water. At times the song pitched high beyond the range of her vocals.

She reached with a cracked voice. None shall be excluded from pursuit of high registers.

Nearing Coombs she considered stopping to see the big farmer's market with the goats on the grassy roofs. She'd seen Instagram pictures, a billy above you as you wait in line for a mini donut. That's hilarious. Cuckoo's Trattoria with their beautiful covered courtyard patio and its fountain and all the plants and a pasta lunch wasn't something she ruled out until she was two full kilometres past the turnoff. She drove past Cameron Lake then slowed down for Cathedral Grove but did not consider stopping to appreciate the little sliver of old-growth trees the timber baron MacMillan had, after sustained public pressure, graciously agreed to leave standing, exclaiming, "All right! You can have the goddamned grove!" Instead she just turned her head towards that impressive facade of behemoth Douglas Fir towering beside the road. Eight-hundred-year-old sentient pillars feeling the rumbling over their roots. A drive-through museum of sparse relics who evaded the saw. Do they tell more of extant beauty, or beauty lost? she wondered.

Three years ago at the Fairmont Pacific Rim she attended a fundraiser building awareness of old-growth deforestation. The presenter narrating the slides, clicking through forests, before and after. From majestic groves to clear cuts. He said over eighty percent of the Island's old growth has been logged, old trees still being cut today at a rate they'll be gone in but a few more tomorrows. Truthfully she hadn't given it much thought since then. Now driving through this breathing cathedral, its huge arching canopy cast a shade darker from guilt. She recalled those slides of fallen old trees like war atrocities, severed torsos of slain giants leaving ghastly stumps. With the final slides he said that in certain old forests live rare trees a car-width across—click—sustained by the tiniest fungal threads of truffles—click—which smell like pineapple and dark chocolate, whose spores are spread by feasting flying squirrels—laughter, click—themselves evading predation by the endangered spotted owl. You could hear in the crowd a riffle of hushed wonder, a sound not so dissimilar to a breeze blowing through leaves of old trees. Valerie slowly driving, momentarily spellbound by the ancient bark's deep channels, her driver's-side mirror hit a rubber stanchion divider and her heart jumped and her grip tightened and she centred car and mind. Watch the road.

On the outskirts of Port Alberni she saw a hotel's sign advertising its sushi restaurant, her mind logging it as a future option for the return home, the same way one skilled in bushcraft might register a bubbling spring, curl of birchbark. But she wanted to arrive to Tofino hungry. Tofino doesn't have beaches and surf and sea life—it *is* that. She had read that. Not things on offer, things defining. She liked that. So who are you? What are you? Tofino knows what it is. Or does it?

Sproat Lake on her left, she drove on, ascending into Sutton Pass. On her right appeared heavy rapids. She cracked her window and the frothy flow of Wally Creek in full spring glory powered by funneling mountain snow-melt thundered down the rocks. She looked for the Love Lock Fence she had seen on Instagram. Those countless colourful padlocks on the little chain-link fence. Was it taken down or did it fall from the weight of bearing a thousand promises?

Black Tesla cruises skinny Highway Four, winding and elevated, expansive view of Kennedy Lake, twisting road beside tall rock walls, hair-pin turns bordering sheer drop-offs, beauty entangled with danger, this road nearly population control. A construction flagger waved her into the alternating single-lane and if wide-spread unemployment from automation is coming you'd think it not begun if we're still paying people to hold up signs. Valerie waved to the coal mine's orange-breasted canary.

55

Her route descended towards Kennedy lake then levelled off while the temperature of this temperate rainforest continued to fall.

In the early afternoon she pulled up to the Tofino-Ucluelet junction. She was headed right but left did pull. For every single mention of the aquarium that catches live in the spring all its creatures, circulating their tanks with fresh sea water, to release them healthy in the fall, and for every mention of the Wild Pacific Trail and the Ucluelet Brewery, came two mentions of a pizza joint. She would travel for pizza and it's not the Leaning Tower that calls her to Italy—twice booked twice cancelled. At the junction she turned right, but from the edges of her rear-view mirror grew green basil leaves curling with char.

Long Beach. She slowed. She sent her father a picture of the sign. Her father the World War Two enthusiast told her how Tofino Airfield, based just inland from here, housed Kittyhawk fighter planes and bombers that flew sorties eight hundred kilometres out over the Pacific to hunt Japanese. That on this beach, fighter pilots in training strafed machine guns on the shores and only a few years back an old bomb was found lying under the sand.

She turned for the beach's first parking lot and parked among only two other cars. Sea fragrance funnelled down a sand path through the headland's grassy dunes. Her sneakered steps in the loose sand made for awkward walking. Black stretch jeans with bare ankles, a long-sleeve knit top. Her long jacket in the car.

She walked out between high dunes latticed with driftwood bordered by Sitka spruce plated with bark like miniature shields for assaulting rain and ocean spray. Some trees missing their tops appeared not to have given them up so easily. And there is the sea. And now you feel small. The long beach and big sky and endless sea. Where she stood she felt in appropriate company: she one speck among countless grains of sand. The big water today is not very blue but dear sky you're luminously grey. A dozen grey shades on an arching canvas vastly textured. Grey like it had something special in mind for the colour and anyone saying grey is dismal might just be seeing a colour she was not seeing. Like someone had told the sky grey can't be pretty, that's for blues, sunset pinks, and it said we'll just see about that. She looking to the big water, to the far reaches of beach scarce of people on even this mild spring Sunday. Two people strolling in the distance, a couple kids playing by the shore. For a pleasantly lost minute she watched them, pails and shovels building castles in the sand. As if believing the world would respect their walls. Where Val stood the sand was dry.

A big raven scavenging a small, washed-up upturned Dungeness crab. Tangled clumps of sodden eel grass still vibrantly green so evenly spaced all down the beach as far as could be seen, as if a sea creature by every step had shed a weeden dress until she walked off naked. A seagull on the beach opened its wings into the wind like it was preparing for flight, but it didn't take flight. It just resettled its wings.

Self-development. Sometimes that word sounds to my ears... not how it once did. But I still just love the idea of personal growth. Sell the biz? Scale the biz? Hate the biz? Love the biz? Clenched fist in a pant pocket. To that preoccupied inner voice she said bitch, don't kill my vibe. A soothing here that doesn't ask permission. Waves lapping like music, like this rhythm archetypal for all melodies to come. There are easier places to sustain a problem than a beach. She exhaled, her fist relaxed. Waves lapping the shore making sounds a mother might to soothe her daughter. She took her shoes off, her socks. Cool sand on bare feet. She walked towards the water. A rookery, the barren islet of Incinerator Rock, many small birds flittering its top. Two surfers to its right. As if an official greeter, the Northwest wind seemed happy to meet her, playful in her shoulder length hair.

A chill where the wind grazed her nape. Small architects at work in the wet sand. The flooding tide in search of walls.

She drove past the old Tofino cemetery where a man is laying a blue flower at the headstone of his beloved. She drove past Cox Bay and the turn-off to Chesterman Beach, and at the Outside Break parking lot she did not keep driving and turned right and slowly drove to the end of a gravel lot and parked by a little taco truck.

V

"The Giant Pacific Octopus that inhabits the coastal waters off British Columbia is the largest octopus in the world. One has been caught weighing two hundred and seventy kilograms with an arm span of almost ten metres."

"What did you memorize its Wikipe... oh." Steve turned and saw Alex was actually reading that off his phone. He turned back to his jigging rod.

"I mean holy shit. Thirty-foot tentacle span! My god. They eat anything, sharks, crabs, fishes, seagulls, other octopuses—pi? pussies? Russell?"

"Pussies, yes."

"I'm starting to think lingcod don't like jigs or sarcasm." Steve bounced his lure off the reef.

Alex scrolled. "Lays a mere four hundred thousand eggs. Ends up starving to death while caring for her young." He looked up. "And I thought my mother was quite nurturing."

"And you free dive in these kraken-infested waters eh? Eh?"

Alex had guided his guests to their daily Chinook limit, two each. They had put the salmon rods away to the canopy-mounted rocket launchers. Midmorning and closer to shore here they jigged short stiff rods in ninety feet of water. One lingcod already in the inlaid fish box.

Russell nodded sideways to the uninhabited coast. "What's this area called?"

"This is Gowlland Rocks. If you hiked in from shore here you'd end up where that World War Two bomber went down. You did that hike last year, hey?"

"We did."

"Thoughts?"

"Meh." Steve waffled a hand.

"Yeah. Same. Underwhelming. It wouldn't make my Top Ten Tofino Attractions."

Steve opened the cooler and took out two Tupperware. One with carrots and celery and one with dip, white with flecks of green, likely dill. He held that out to Russell.

Alex had his eyes on Russell's rod tip most subtly twitching and Russell said between a bitten cigar, "Just nibblin'. Come on. Come on now."

"An incredible array of people came through this area in a short amount of time. Spanish, American, and British trading ships. Danish, Swiss, and Belgian clergy. Scots, Chinese traders and labourers. Norwegian and Japanese fishermen. When the town was incorporated in 1932, a third of the two hundred and fifty residents were Japanese. Rather astounding that so many people came to give it a go without knowing much about it. Not sure if it speaks to their sense of adventure or the quality of life they were leaving.

"In many regards this was an unwelcoming area. In some regards it still is. Tuff City, no road until 1959. Travel was all boat, and that routinely limited by weather. Raging winter storms and huge seas. Countless ships sunk. More than ten feet of annual rainfall. *Ten feet*." Alex, like most Canadians, capriciously moves between measurement systems Metric and Imperial. "An ungodly amount of rain but the cedars drink it like fishing guides drink Lucky Lagers. Forget about seasonal sadness, here you just try not to drown. Back then would have been some long dark wet winters. Nowadays all Tofitians in the winter go to Mexico. Not a single person left in town. You could rob the place blind in January. In January, one third of all Mexicans are Tofitians."

"Fact," Steve said. "I'll be updating Wikipedia when we get back to the hotel."

"So you got your utter biblical quantities of rain, you got your occasional tsunami every few hundred years, your impenetrably thick bush. But apparently the Pacific Northwest was one of the most densely populated geographies in all of North America prior to contact."

"Contact with explorers," Russell said.

"Yeah."

"Intensely wet winters but unlike much of the northern hemisphere in the winter months, you aren't going to freeze or starve to death. A temperate coastal rainforest has its soggy perks. The average square kilometre here has more living mass than any other ecosystem in the world, including the Amazon jungle. Did you know that?"

Steve just looked at him. "Of course I didn't know that."

Alex laughed. "Heaviest biomass there is. I'm considering branding it. At minimum, we should make bumper stickers. My biomass is bigger than yours. I like big biomass and I cannot lie. Etcetera. This place was bountiful. I mean, it's not what it once was and it still is bountiful."

"I'll have to take your word for that." Steve twitched his rod. Alex stomped a heel to the floorboards twice and Steve smiled.

"And not just salmon and halibut. Herring and lingcod and all kinds of rockfish, seals, sea otters. Dozens of shellfish. I mean every rock on the coast you look at has mussels growing on it and aren't they superfoods? Clams on every beach. Geese in the fall.

The Natives ate whales, orcas even, eagles, porpoise, you name it it was probably eaten."

"Eagles?"

"Yeah I read that a hunter would put out bits of salmon onto the beach then hide under clumps of seaweed. When the eagle landed he'd simply reach out and grab its legs."

"Huh. I didn't see that coming."

"Yeah you and the eagle."

Two fast ducks flew by on whistling wings just above the water. Alex speaking over the back of his clients' heads. Three heads watching two rods. "And sizable humans from all that quality food. People got big and strong here. Not like in parts of Asia, small people eating rice." His clients couldn't see his squint. "I don't think that's racist. But fuck me it could be. Everything's offensive today. Point is, people thrived here. This area had something like seventeen distinct tribes, nations, bands, peoples, whatever word."

"And now?"

"And now there are less."

"Russell missed his ling there and nothing seems even faintly interested in my grub, as enticing as I do have it dancing." Steve right then wondered if this style of fishing was named jig after the dance. He twitched his rod. "So, what happened?"

"My friend Elizabeth says when history is summarized it's false. But what happened. The largest part of the story is the same story as the rest of the Americas. On the bow of the tall ships the nautical figurehead wasn't a scantily clad woman or a swan or a lion. Death in a black cloak. And before here it had already mowed down swathes of Europeans, Chinese, Africans starting who knows when. They've found mummies with tell-tale skin rashes. Might go back as far as ten thousand before Christ. Might have killed the philosopher king Marcus Aurelius. It was killing nearly half a million Europeans a year in the 1700s—royalty, peasants, it didn't play favourites—buried something like half a billion people in its last hundred years before we eradicated it. Jesus Christ those numbers. Infected Lincoln, Mozart."

"Smallpox," said Russell.

"You always hear of it in the Americas but it was laying down scores of people the world over, long before here. But it came here. Boy did it ever. History's vilest stowaway. When it got to Caribbean shores, that scythe unsheathed. People fell like wheat stalks. Captain George Vancouver sailing the coast saw so many deserted villages. This province's biggest death toll in a single year was 1862. Maybe *fifty, sixty percent* of *Indigenous died*. Just catastrophic, just heinous shit. Stories of the sick taken out into the woods and left with a blanket and a couple salmon. The trauma that would have followed, a type of societal collapse. Then came other diseases, TB was a scourge. Reports of one family from this area losing nineteen of twenty children. It's just..." Alex was looking over the long shoreline. Solemn trees. Jagged rocks as hard as history. "It's just horrendous."

A line of flapping ducks skimming the surface, torpedo shaped, quick-beating wings, one trailing.

They jigged and drank juice boxes.

Russell whipped up a stout rod. "There we go."

"Fuckin' A," said Steve.

"I assume you spelled that suffix in your head with e-h."

Russell reeling in the ling said that actually fuckin' A is an emphatic affirmative. "Comes from the military."

"Fuckin' A is American? Ah hell you gotta be shittin' me. I wanted that one."

Steve smiling looked at Alex. "You bet your sweet maple-sugar ass it's 'Merican. But you can use it. Just cost you a pipeline or two, is all."

The rod-tip tapping but this stout pole, capable of landing hundred-pound halibut, barely bends on a ten-pound cod. The high-gear-ratio Shimano reel quickly surfaced the ling. No subtlety to this. Slimy body mottled grey and brown, big pectoral fins and an outsized head as if a troll had been hooked from its cave. The barbed treble hook piercing both its lips silencing its protest.

Alex took up his gaff from below the gunwale. He had etched in burnt cursive: *Lucille*. Most fishing clients that knew music thought he had named it after a famous guitar. He had but not directly. He named it after a pool cue that was named after a famous guitar: *Jeffrey, break out Lucille*. Fresh Prince, it's the little things. Lucille was marked off in centimetres. He laid it alongside the ling for contactless measure. Human hands contaminate the mucus barrier, introducing pathogens while drying the slime that slickens their swim. He never touched a fish unless it was the last thing it felt. "Seventy-two centimeters. Fair game. Sorry my ugly friend." He gripped, swung, bonked, spun, gaffed, boated, dispatched. Swift and ethical.

The fish in repose on fibreglass floorboard, he held the line in his left hand and used the gaff's metal shank to remove the hook from its dead lips, upper, then lower. He slipped the gaff tip under a gill and raised it before them. Gaping mouth, rising wisp of soul? He pointed. "One of nature's toothiest. Over five hundred teeth. And they lose them as fast as they grow them. Twenty a day if you can believe that."

"No shit?"

"I know."

"A face only a mother could love."

"Yeah. If she didn't try to eat you."

Geometric patterns in various browns, slimy body in reef camouflage. A thin long goo too viscous to free-fall drooped from its tail. He poked its fat belly. He had sliced enough to bet it was stuffed with small crab. He opened the floorboard's hinged lid and laid the limp ling beside their catch. A catch mirrored in the other fish box. From the transom he grabbed a short fillet knife and slit its gills, draining its blood and preserving its meat. "Nice fish there. Nice work on the reel, Russell. That's a ling and two salmon a piece." Legally they could take more. "How you guys feel about that?"

Steve didn't look at Russell. "That's plenty."

He liked these guys. Alex had just worked thirty days straight. Before a much needed break he was sending his final satisfied group home with their fish. That felt good. Doing a good job. It feels good. Elevates coming pleasures to the status of sweet reward. Russell and Steve each unclipped their lure and handed the rods to Alex who stepped down into the cuddy and laid them on his free-dive wetsuit, itself reef camo like ling skin. He came back up and fired up the second motor. "You guys set back there?"

"Take us home, cap'n."

He pushed the twin throttle levers and the girls pitched the Pursuit then levelled her out into plane, frothy wake trailing. Alex was looking starboard trying to judge the surf at Cox Bay. The spring temperatures still a bit cool and the beach for a couple more months not so busy. A few surfers sitting their boards. From the top of one wave came a little bursting spray as the white underside of half a shortboard was put through an aggressively vertical turn. He praised it with an unspoken fuck yeah and planned to get in the water on his coming staycation.

Off the port, three boats were fishing Lennard Island, too far to make out their decals or boat names. One with its lower hull painted red, another blue. He waved to guides he knew well. He half-turned his head and spoke louder than the motors and pointed to an island off their port. "You'll have heard that name. Wickaninnish. Translates to nobody sits before him in a canoe.

A chief so powerful that all the Indigenous within several hundred kilometers of here, even distinct tribes, conducted their trade exclusively through him. Said to be both loved and feared by other chiefs."

Ahead and off starboard near Tonquin Beach idled four boats single-file like a funeral procession. Their crews facing shore. Alex throttled down and puttered in closer. Over the VHF some fishing guide was chattering away as if he thought himself the host of a talk show. Alex turned off the marine radio. Some four hundred yards away rose a sleek black fin, call it five feet tall. Glossy black, its tip swept back, the matriarch blowing a warm breath into the cool and calm air, and that puff did not so rapidly disperse. Mist hanging above the surface as if she were responsible for making the clouds. Legendize her if she's not already. Behind her the surface slit by two rising black fins and smaller puffs.

Steve said, "That is so impressive. That's three. I wonder how many there are. This is incredible." In back another glossy fin rising out of the sea and its back not yet crested. Tall fin getting taller and no curved tip, the bull's fin standing like an ebony obelisk. Two others emerged and six whales swam stitching through the water.

"I see them a few times over the summer, every summer. I never get used to it. It's as impressive to me as the first time I saw it. Me, I eat about three thousand calories a day. Sitting down for a Schooner rib and ravioli night, maybe I get up to four. One of these big boys here, I read about three hundred thousand calories a day."

"Insane."

A fleet of salmon hunters watching a pod of salmon hunters. "At this time of year in Tofino it's the start of a lot of migration, feasting, mating. And sometimes the wildlife also engage in that behaviour." First Russell laughed then Steve laughed. "So here we are at Tonquin at the end of the Esowista Peninsula."

Russell asked, "And it means?"

"I'm actually not sure."

"I feel good about that," Steve said. "Makes it less likely you were making the rest of the stuff up." The whales submerged.

"So this is the site of that epic tale I mentioned, The Tonquin, a two-hundred-and-ninety-ton, hundred-foot-long American merchant ship. The Holy Grail of British Columbia ship-wrecks. To this day its brass cannons lie somewhere underneath us. I'd love to find one of those, mount it on my deck. Fire off a gratitude blast every Thanksgiving. The Tonquin story would salivate a Hollywood producer."

"Well we got our fish. Not only is there nowhere else I need to be, there's nowhere else I want to be." Steve popped the cooler and distributed a round of tropical storms and sat back in his chair under the midday now-greying sky and put his feet on the gunwale and scanned calm waters for the next whale. "You in a rush Russ?"

"The ship was built in New York, 1807. Three-masted. Its crew of twenty-four rounded Cape Horn on a trade charter to the Qing Empire in China. They survive a typhoon, made it back to New York with a ship full of goods, then it charters out to Australia, Fiji. At one point the ship got so low on water the crew was rationed to just three gills of water a day. Only three gills."

"How much is a gill?"

"I have no idea."

Steve shook his head.

"Makes a stop here and there so crew members can stretch their legs and tend to their black gums. Eventually the ship is bought by John Jacob Astor, your country's first multi-million-aire. At his death, the richest. Maybe you know this? Real-estate mogul, fur-trade monopolist, opium smuggler. The ship sets sail again from New York heading south to round the Cape for the Pacific Northwest and the fur trade. Big international business at that time. The Tonquin was captained by Thorn. By some accounts, a prick of a skipper. Wouldn't even let his crew sing sea shanties."

"What's even the point of becoming a sailor?" said Steve.

"They stop in Hawaii and a few crew members run off but the Natives there return them to the ship like delinquent school boys."

"That's kinda funny. We don't want these. You can keep these."

"Captain flogs one, shackles another. They leave Hawaii in the spring heading towards the Oregon coast. There's a big bar in that area."

"I believe I had my heart broken there," said Steve.

"The other kind of bar."

"The others are chin-up, which I avoid at all costs, chocolate, which I advocate, and crow. I believe that's the extent of my bars, Alex. So what in the flippin' orca whale are you talking about?" He pointed at a surfacing black back and Russell held up his phone to take a pic.

"Where a big river meets the ocean it can stand up large waves. Bar."

"I'm logging all this for your Tripadvisor. We left Tofino with frozen fish and a seaman's vocabulary. Ask Alex about the bar."

Alex laughed. "The one at Oregon is notoriously dangerous. The Columbia Bar. Thorn sent out a small boat with five crew to find safe passage. They die. Sends out a second boat. Most of them die."

Two orcas humping through the water and Russell said this is incredible and Alex said thank you I've been working on my delivery and Steve made a sound like a two-tone fog horn.

"Eventually the Tonquin gets around that bar and they arrive to Clayoquot waters. They anchor up somewhere right around here."

Steve looked around at the water, the shore, as if history was surfacing.

"Okay, so at that point in history, the American—Tla-o-qui-aht trade relations were on rocky footing. Turns out things like lying, stealing, murders, arson, strain relationships. And Wickaninnish by all accounts was not someone to fuck with, to put it mildly. From here there are several versions of what happened but they all originate from the only survivor, a Native who was hired in Washington to act as interpreter. The Tla-o-qui-aht paddle up and are permitted on board. Thorn and the chief-trader haggle, not Wickaninnish, a relation. Thorn says the sea-otter pelts are priced too high, his counterparty says they're not. They get nowhere. Thorn's exasperated and starts pacing the deck. The lead trader follows him. Some say he taunts him with insolent words, holding out the pelt at every turn. Thorn loses his patience and grabs the fur and rubs it in the other man's face. The Natives of this area did not take disrespect lightly. The following morning at daybreak, Thorn still asleep, the Tla-o-qui-aht return, friendly, eager to trade. A watchman allows them aboard. More canoes paddle up and the ship is crowded and the agitated crew wakes Thorn. They trade but with these numbers Thorn is feeling uneasy and suspicious and orders his men aloft to make sail, the anchor to be hauled, the deck to be cleared. And that command was as if he himself had signalled the attack."

Both Steve and Russell turned from the orca-less surface to Alex.

"The crew's firearms are below deck. The Tla-o-qui-aht armed with concealed knives and war clubs draw and start butchering. One man, Lewis, bent over some blankets in trade is stabbed in the back and he falls down into the cabin. Thorn fights off several attackers, kills one, cripples others. Then he's overpowered and slain. Women in canoes finish off the men who fall to the water. The unarmed and outnumbered crew is mercilessly slaughtered." Alex looked up like he was posing the sky a question. "What about those men still up high in the rigging?"

"Shit," Steve breathed. He looked around the calm Tonquin waters here as if that ghost ship might just sail on by, as if he might look up into its tall masts, see those few doomed men up in the rigging, feet in the ropes, swaying above a bloody deck where below a hundred warriors massacre his mates, hear the war whoops mixed with the cries of the dying, a deck littered with bodies, awash in blood.

"So one of the men Weekes is up in the rigging. He and others inevitably descend and he gets mortally wounded but five of them retreat below deck. Find stabbed Lewis there ailing but alive. They barricade the door and get the guns then bust a few holes in the door and start blasting. The attackers flee to their canoes with that interpreter, taken as captive. The crew eventually leave the cabin and survey the carnage, see their whole crew hacked-up lying on deck or dead in the water. The attackers haven't fully retreated they're in their canoes safely out of musket range. The men man the cannons and let them buck and drive them back farther. The day passes and a night. The next morning the Tonquin still lies at anchor. Loose sails idle in the morning air and the deck unmanned. The ship full of valuable goods. The Tla-o-qui-aht cautiously approach. Just one crew member appears on deck. Lewis. Lewis waves. Maybe truce?" Alex tilted his head towards a shoulder. "Maybe not." Tilted it the other way. "Lewis disappears. Of course the Tla-o-qui-aht must consider that it could be a trap. But they've got them vastly outnumbered and they can see the cannons unmanned. Eager for the spoils the warriors do approach. Canoes debarked and ship boarded. It's said that nearly the whole tribe is either on the ship or alongside in canoes. Lewis must have gone down in the ship's hold. What else did they keep down there?" A theatrical question Alex posed only to his rhetorical self. "Powder kegs. About four tonnes worth of explosives."

Russell raised his eyebrows and Alex nodded.

"Fucking lights it. Huge, huge blast. Tears the rear of the ship apart. Bodies ripped apart. Fire, heat, thick smoke, splintered canoes, wood shrapnel. Nearly everyone injured or killed. Wounded people trying to swim in cold water for their lives. For days afterwards limbs and bodies wash up on the beach. One account says up to two hundred people died.

"Later an escaped boat is found in a cove with the four men. Apparently Lewis refused to join them. Knew he'd die of his wounds and so set his mind to vengeance. The winds kept that small boat from making it out of here. They're questioned by that interpreter. Tortured to death. He eventually escapes and brings the stories to America."

The fishing fleet idled south pacing the whales. A whale watching boat coming around Wickaninnish Island slowed and joined the flotilla. "That's a hell of a story," said Steve.

"Yeah. Just brutal. Trade relations were uncordial before that and the sea otters nearly extinct. This sealed the deal. Trade ships avoided Clayoquot Sound for decades after that." The orcas' straight route had turned circular. Alex said they were likely feeding. The boats stayed the legally required four-hundred-metre distance. From the direction of town a boat cruised around the corner, smaller, fibreglass. Everyone from every boat watched as it drove towards the whales and one person in the flotilla had their hands raised. One with their phone raised. "That captain is going to face some social media scorn." The boat cruised over the orcas now submerged, who probably heard it coming long before any of these fishermen did. The only thing the boat killed was the moment.

"Alex, tomorrow's our final day in Tofino. What do you think we should do?"

If they were surfers he'd have told them that the south swell just starting to show up on La Perouse buoy meant some beaches that don't normally get waves will be worth a look. He would have told them to check Long Beach and Florencia Bay. There were a couple other spots, the best spots that go off on a good south swell, but he wouldn't have told them about those ones. After fishing yesterday, Steve and Russell had rented kayaks and took a tour of the Big Tree Trail, said they saw the Hanging Garden, a tree nearly sixty feet wide nearly two millennia old. So he didn't mention it. Finally he said, "Don't seize the day, eat it." Conviction of a foodie. "The beauty of this town not found anywhere else in Canada attracts a certain amount of affluence and those dollars put talent in the kitchens. This town knows food. You could rent e-bikes. Guide yourselves through your own food and history tour. Radar hike, Sunset Point, all the rest, stop at all the beaches, take in the sights, sample the tacos. That's actually what I would do. What do you think about that?" He looked to see if they were as excited about this as he seemed to be. "You could start early and hit the bakeries and coffee roasters. Eventually you earn the Brewery and the patios. Draw straws for designated e-bike driver. Maybe there's an e-bicycle seat built for two and you guys can double like Jim Carrey and Jeff Daniels."

Steve whapped Russell across his jacketed chest and he coughed a puff of smoke. "Tell me you packed our pink and blue suits."

"Blue and orange, aren't they?"

Steve turned to Alex and said, "Well that sounds like a yes."

"Or what about Hot Springs? Did you go there last time?"

Now farther away four puffs vented in succession as surfacing backs arched in marine choreography. "I got that one." Russell with his phone up.

"I think last trip it was closed." Steve looked at Russell and said as if translating his quiet interest, "Actually that would be perfect. A soak on our last day. Do you think we could book a tour last minute? It's a Monday tomorrow."

"Hard to say. Depends how many spring charters are running. But I think those tours book out at least a few days in advance."

"How would you feel about running us up there? Rather take a private boat anyways. We'd make it worth your while."

"Normally, yeah sure. But I actually scheduled myself a few days off. It's been a long stretch, boys. I never used to, used to just work the whole season straight through. Go hard for the summer and take it easier in the winter. But reliably, by about mid-season, I tended to become an asshole." He smiled to soften that word. "This is just better for boat morale and likelihood of return clientele. And tomorrow, fellas, tomorrow is date three." He held up three fingers. "I promised her a boat picnic. If I blow it with her, boys I dunno. The dating pool of this town is hardly deep enough to drown a worm."

One boat pulled away from the flotilla.

"Some people's biggest issue with this area is the winter rain, or that jobs are limited and mostly tourist-facing. But Jesus the dating scene is piss poor. About two thousand permanent residents and I wish I was bi-sexual. If you don't wish you were bi-sexual we just look at the world differently. Because math is real. I could double my dates if not my wardrobe. But I just happen to find—other than my own—the penis repulsive. An appendage utterly grotesque."

Steve spat in the water.

"The lingcod of anatomy, really. Mine, however, being quite the opposite. More salmon-esque beauty."

"Go on."

Alex figured Steve probably meant go on as sarcastic incredulity, but it could be interpreted as an encouraging interjection for Alex to continue his line of phallical thought. Of course he elected the latter. "Like picture that scene in that old movie Ghost."

"Which scene?"

"There's only one."

Steve kinda shrugged like Alex's reply was ridiculous but also fair.

"But it's not Demi's and Swayze's hands shaping the clay, it's the Lord's hands. The Lord's hands spinning and shaping my member into being. That's about how I see it."

Steve leaned over the port gunwale where it sounded like he was purging deeper this time. Then he stayed there a second. Then he dry heaved. Probably joking. He leaned back in his seat and wiped his mouth. "Do not go on," he said.

Alex laughed. The whales had found some distance. Dark fins heading southwards like black shipless sails.

"Okay back to the math. And I should say that though I take history seriously my math skills are highly suspect. Town of about two thousand permanent residents. So right off the bat, given my most inconvenient heterosexuality, you cut that number in half. Say one thousand potential dates. I'm forty. One nice thing about being forty is that the age range you can date expands. I mean most sixteen-year-olds date sixteen-year-olds, right? But when you're forty, you can date all the way down to what, twenty-five?" He waited to see if they would give him a judgmental look. "Twenty-two?" He waited. "Let's say twenty with a clean conscience? And all the way up to what? Thirty-nine?"

Steve was smiling. "Oh I bet that joke kills with the ladies."

"I've actually used it twice with an all-female crowd. Never has there been night dark enough to hear such crickets. Okay, so from a thousand to what? About three hundred in one's age range? How many of those are in a relationship? Most. Let's say two-thirds. We're down to one hundred ladies. Keep what follows off the Tripadvisor, Steve. Now we account for body-shape compatibility. Then trim the women with very short hair. Cut all the ultra-hippies who don't shave those parts which ought to be shaved. Cut those that define themselves by they—that's not bigotry, I simply cannot handle more than one woman, it's just me knowing my limits. Cut those occult abbreviations on the dating apps, ENMFPQ, pan-, pam- pamb-sexuals. Whatever it even means. And the cold math arrives us home to a lot of quiet evenings. Tending the fire, fellas."

"Watching Ghost by yourself. Shaping your clay, huh?"

Alex laughed. "Basically it comes down to if you're willing to date the lady who brings you your mail. And when things inevitably don't work out, you're always going to be wondering if she's messing with your deliveries."

"No longer caring for your package, just fucking with your deliveries."

"Well said, Steve." Two boats pulled away and Alex figured it was time to cruise on back to the docks.

"At least summers must be nice. Hey? All the ladies coming through?" Russell asked.

"Russell, Steve, if you look to the top of this vessel's VHF antenna you'll see I fly the flag of romance. I'm done messing around. Short-term rentals might be the economic backbone of this town—short-term romance, I've had my fill."

Steve actually leaned over and looked up to the antenna. There was no flag. "Oh I see it there. Rainbow, huh?"

"I'm just a classical romantic." He squinted and looked at the sky whose sun behind cloud could no longer be seen. "Tofino winters may know rain but my love is without season."

"Oh boy. Hey Alex, turns out we should be heading back. I'm a little concerned for your motor there." His words seemed to reference one of the Yamahas but he was staring at his guide. "It sounds a little overwrought. Might want to get that looked at."

Alex was trying to think of a flower that bloomed all year, if such a one existed, and employ it as an analogy.

Steve discarding his juice box turned and looked at Alex's silence and said he thought he heard a whimpering orca but I guess it's just the gears squeaking in Alex's head.

"Just looking for that true love, that ride or die, you know? You feel me?" He once again held out his fist for a pound. Steve did bump it this time. Russell too. Two of his favourite guests of the year were limited out and happy and he was happy and heading to harbour. So wrap this up.

Four fins faintly visible, made hazier from their own breath, shrinking back down below a liquid skin. The cloud makers swimming on south, stitching through the water as if tying two worlds together—myth to real, past to present, surface to what lies beneath—these workers in a dream factory. Russell lowered his phone. "That made my trip."

Steve turned to him. "Surely you're not referring to the fishless ravings on history and love from our mad guide? Oh." He gestured to the phone still in camera mode. "The whales. Of course."

Alex said I love you guys. "We're outta here." He throttled-up and cruised for town.

Coastal houses along the waterfront bluff. He was thinking of their request, Hot Springs. He did want to make it happen. Humour even stupid humour is more than humour. Indicative of similar lenses and similar minds. Alex didn't offer out of good entrepreneurial business skills and he didn't offer from his own financial obligations because he had no kids and the boat and mortgage were paid, he just happened to like these two. He said it would have to be the same rate as a full day of fishing because they'll be motoring a lot further and gas is priced like the throaty twins here guzzle truffle oil. Greedy pigs. But he said it would all depend if he could sell Alina on it. "Boys, there's just no telling with her. I mean, there's no telling with any of them, but certainly not with her. But I'll see what I can do."

VI

A lex hated chin-ups and cold ocean swims and dying. He hoped the first two might help some with the last one. Still in his Carhartts and Dunlop rubber boots he pulled himself above the bar for the eighteenth rep at the end of the set at the end of a long stretch of work. He believed that whatever is your goal, cardio paired with strength training is that goal's long game: desk work, the trades, the arts, no difference. He went to the chicken coop and fed and watered las tres mujeres rubias, his three golden hens, and shoveled their soiled pine shavings into the wooden compost which looked like a cedar beehive and spread fresh pine shavings down. He changed into his bathing suit on the back deck and walked down to his property's foreshore and dipped into the ocean cove. Scrabbling back all pale like an albino mink over the rocks he considered drinking a celebratory beer in the shower but figured he'd delay his indulgence. The hot shower on his tight chicken skin felt absolutely glorious and so this staycation begins.

Alex lived at the end of town and town centre was only a five minute walk away. He called Alina to sell her on the extra crew for their boat-picnic date but no answer. He figured she was probably with a client. Outside the CIBC someone had left groceries in their bicycle's basket. Three crows ate through a bag of Wonder Bread while a fourth cawed. He would have flushed them and stood by but the widely scattered crumbs suggested the whole loaf was compromised. Across the street in the post-office he unlocked his box and peeked in.

"Hey Alex."

He turned. "Hi Michelle."

She was holding a package.

"What'd you get?"

She shook it. "Actually, decorations. I was thinking I'd come by your place Wednesday if that's still alright and set things up."

"Yup no problem. Let me know if you need anything, extra chairs or cutlery, champagne flutes or whatever."

"Okay sweet. And hey thanks so much for letting us use your place. It'll just be nicer having this little bachelorette at a friend's rather than booking a resort."

"Completely my pleasure. I like sharing the place. And I'll be outta your guys' hair at Jeremy's working on the dancefloor build, so it's all yours and free of boys."

"I'm looking forward to the ceremony but I *cannot wait* for the dance party!"

"Me too." His back against the glass door, she at the farther one.

"Okay, I'll see you Wednesday, or if not, then at the wedding."

"Nice. Sounds great." Alex passed an acquaintance he had met at a beach clean-up. They traded brief and unoriginal reflections about the weather. What he used to see as a pitiably banal topic he no longer did. Now he enjoyed such empty musings. It wasn't about the weather.

He walked back down First Street and turned left towards the Community Centre and took the forested path towards Industrial Way. A full kilometre away he could smell fermenting yeast, pungent sourness as if it rose from the very bogs beside him. It fondly reminded him of a Crown Royal Whisky tour he'd taken in Gimli, Manitoba with his family as a kid. He wondered to what degree the same particular smell common to distinct experiences linked them in one's mind. For certain it linked them to a degree. He texted Alina. *Hey darlin. Thinkin bout ya. Two extra crew for our boat date tomorrow, two clients as a favour. You're going to like them. Russ is quiet but smart and Steve is a riot. We'll head up for a soak and after I'd love to take you for dinner at Wolf if you're still free.* *wolf emoji* *cheersing wine-glasses emoji* He thought about a heart emoji. Send.

The Distillery later could be busy but on this spring midafternoon only one other table was occupied. Two women sharing a flight of mini-cocktails served on a rectangular wooden platter. Alex thought they looked good, the cocktails. He sat and Daniel one of the owners joined him. The table a big wooden spool bare of thread. Alex with a whiskey soda. The whiskey was only being released in small batches and you had to ask for it. He wasn't a big drinker and would sometimes go weeks without one. Sometimes he'd impose random goals for the satisfaction of disciplined living, and then the pleasure of earned indulgence from meeting them. He sipped the whiskey-soda-lime with his back to a wall of stacked casks of Portuguese oak aging West Coast spirits made from organic British Columbian grains. Big polished steel tanks shining from high-window lighting. His tumbler hued golden as if coloured by a memory of a Manitoba wheat field and it tasted sweet as that fine past day. Two customers walked in and Daniel got up and went behind the bar. Jeremy came over from the distilling side.

"Hey." Alex smiled.

"Hey." He nodded at the afternoon drink. He sat.

"A little reward after working thirty days straight. Now a few days off."

"Attaboy. What are you going to get up to?"

"I'm taking Alina and two guests for a hot springs soak in the morning."

"Very nice. I haven't been up there in a couple years. So how's that going?"

Alex when he had picked up his drink from the bar took a toothpick and skewered an olive. The olive eaten he now poked an ice cube. "Well. To kindle love's faded coals nearly dead inside me takes a stronger breath than the average date can blow."

"First sexual Shakespearean innuendo I've heard today."

"Up until recently I was beginning to wonder if my cock had become ornamental. So, at least one of life's mysteries solved, though others remain. But I'd say, overall, we're still testing the waters."

"I'm happy for you and your ornament."

"Thank you Jeremy, that means a lot to me. Yeah I'd say we haven't yet hit it out of the conversational park together. But." He made a sideways finger motion. "We're working on our swing. She's got a great swing."

"Is her little guy coming with you?"

"Nah her ex has him this week."

The two short customers at the bar had selected a bottle of vodka and said to Daniel they had read that for brunch they should check out Long Beach Lodge or The Wickaninnish Inn. "But we go to Long Beach and no restaurant there and so we go Wickaninnish Beach and *no restaurant there!*" He put his flustered hands up.

Daniel said don't feel bad, I'm sure it happens all the time. "Long Beach doesn't have a lodge and Long Beach Lodge is at Cox Bay. Wickaninnish Inn isn't on Wick Road or Wick Island or Wickaninnish Beach, it's at Chesterman Beach. While we're at it, I may as well save you a few headaches. Schooner Restaurant is not found in Schooner Cove. Beaches Grocery is not on the beach. The town's main street is not Main street—it's Campbell Street, Main Street being one street over. That should get you started."

The man looked over at who was probably his wife because they had matching rain jackets. He looked like he was hoping that she understood a single word of that. He pushed up his glasses and pointed to a bottle and said I pay.

"Wednesday can you still help whack together that dance-floor?" Jeremy asked.

"Definitely. I just saw Michelle at the post office. I'll head your way when she and your bride-to-be and her entourage are coming my way. I'm looking forward to this West Coast wedding. We should space out the stringers and engineer a little spring to that red-neck plywood dancefloor. Expect to see me in my finest dancin' boots."

Jeremy looked below the big spool top. "Which are those same Blundstones that you're wearing now? Correct?"

"Those would be them, yes. But spit polished. Expect to be able to see yourself in them on your big day, my man." Alex on that point would have cheersed him but Jeremy was working. "Alright I'm gonna run." The last sip of whiskey-soda-lime is always the sweetest and Alex savoured it a second under his tongue then brought his tumbler to the bar and bumped a fist with Daniel and said hi to Kate who had just walked in. At the open door he looked up at a bright grey and textured sky. In front of the row of industrial garage doors a car was driving down the narrow parking lot. Muffled rumple of rubber over loose gravel and a soundless engine from a car with bass as if it ran on rap. Black Tesla. The car turned for a slot. The door opened and a sneaker was placed on gravel and he saw bare ankle and his phone vibrated.

Sender: Alina. *i thought u said day off!?* The first letter wasn't capitalized. How does that even happen? he wondered. Alex smiled. He could have seen this coming. He hadn't put his phone away when it vibrated twice more in his hand.

wtf!?

just take them then

Not even an emoji. He smiled and almost laughed. He knew that wasn't the end of it. Drama just seemed part of her language if not her very nature. But it's the wild ones that keep you on your toes. And maybe she was right. Maybe my bad for crowding our date. So what? Apologize and bring her flowers? He was holding the door open for Tesla without much looking at her, texting with one hand his fuming love interest.

Valerie walked in and Alex walked on and in that same moment ten thousand love stories went unwritten.

VII

Valerie bought a bottle of Old Growth Cedar Gin for Stacy and left Industrial Way for Tofino town proper. Arriving, it barely looked real. The blue harbour, the boats, the background mountains' snowy peaks. She almost drove into a concrete barrier protecting the bicyclists. At the B&B she didn't set down her bag. She turned to the accommodation owner, the old man. Her voice was sweet and her genuine smile hid her mild disgust "What's up with the carpet?" On the stained carpet she could see vacuum lines so it wasn't exactly unsanitary, but the white carpet, a clear sign its owner was short on the ability to project their self into the future, looked like it could tell more than a few stories. Though a history nobody wants to hear.

"My wife," he said. His wrinkled face like a Shar Pei with a similarly heavy brow. "Twenty years ago, I told her. But she says white." He shrugged. "What you gonna do? Boss says white we go white." He said that before they changed their policies the room had been host to various partiers and dogs. Now they don't allow the drinking.

Valerie had seen a dog's water bowl in the common room outside her door. She asked about breakfast and he said his wife serves fruit and muffins outside the door at 8:00. He pointed behind her at the small coffee-maker and mini-fridge. "There's cream in the fridge. But there's no fridge in your suite." He winked and she didn't know what that meant, his playful admission to an infraction of a local bylaw. He turned down the hallway. She looked around and didn't see a cat but her eyes starting to itch soon to water seemed certain they had.

Cheap pressboard furniture. The old lamps not old enough to be called antique, so just old. A painting of a girl with a horse, in this town with no horses. The girl centred in the painting, half of her perceptibly sun-faded seemed to impart the portrait with greater interpretive depth. Concerning the folded throw-blanket at the foot of the bed she had two theories. One, given that the policy of many reputable hotels does not mandate washing duvets as frequently as the sheets, this amateur accommodation's sanitation schedule for the throw-blanket here was likely even more relaxed. And two, that it covered a stain. She flipped up one side. Then the other side. One hypothesis was confirmed by a faded red blotch she told herself was wine. She didn't smell the blanket to confirm her other conjecture. So this is 275$ a night in Tofino?

Valerie took out her phone from a jacket pocket. She'd heard camping beach-side was glorious and she liked that idea and did own an old two-man tent her dad had given her, but hadn't brought it. She scrolled. She tapped. A couple Airbnb's looked good but this one had looked good, so who knows. She stopped scrolling. In four days she was off to an isolated silent retreat, and though a privileged getaway, it was still ascetic privation. Lengthy meditation sessions beginning at 5:00 a.m., Ashtanga Yoga, fasting the day through until a small vegan dinner then early bed. Why would I pick that for vacation? Is that actually restorative because it sounds depletive. Bah. She scrolled. *Rustic Elegance on Nature's Edge*. After three pictures she had seen enough. She called and the concierge said there was indeed availability.

The B&B owners lived above the three suites. She went outside and up the small stairs and knocked and the old man said above the volume of the television, "Yeah just come in it's open." She pulled the squeaking screen door. He didn't immediately look away from the television. The cat on his lap matched the carpet, or, likely it once did, the cat appearing better preserved. Valerie pointed to her reddened eyes now tearing, as if cued by the fluffy proof. "I'm really sorry, but my allergies are acting up. I feel bad cancelling last minute, but I would just be sneezing through the night and keeping you guys up."

He looked but briefly and waved his hand. "My wife snores like a two-stroke Merc and I sleep with earplugs." Turned back to U.S. political news.

Valerie sniffed. "Well next time I'm going to bring my allergy meds. Would you please tell your wife I'll be missing out on her muffins."

He sighed, whether from details of a foreign federal election or the duty of customer service. He picked the cat up off his lap, limp torso and drooping legs as if a feline egotism expected the world to rise up to its paws. Set it down on the carpet. "If you really want to try them they're from the Co-op. I think they get them from Vancouver." The cat followed then overtook him and at the island desk near the door it jumped up effortlessly. While looking at Valerie it sashayed over the desk and papers. Its eyes saying it knew something. Whatever that was, you could tell it knew. Dogs can detect odor signatures of cancer, but cats in other sensibilities seem heightened. Who knows what they know. The pussy conveying a superiority if not an inter-species taunt, unblinking eyes and daintily placed padded steps with little concern for where it set them. Valerie sniffed. The cat set a paw on the POS machine the man was trying to work and he had to redo it saying I'm trying to credit you back half while Ms. Kitty here wants to double it. The cat reached the end of the desk and still hadn't looked from Valerie and turned around without breaking eyes and then sat the counter edge closest to her. Its tail slowly wagged once, then again. Black vertical slits in emerald orbs tinged yellow at their outer circle. Coldly sapient peeps, oracular eyes like it would see into her soul. Now waiting for her to confess what it already knew.

A short forested drive between old cedars and hemlocks and Sitka spruces. Her lowered window, she didn't need her car's digital map to tell her the ocean was just on the other side of the big trees. She slowed for the small security booth positioned well before sight of the Inn and lowered her passenger-side window. Ahead at the main building the valet welcomed her and took her bag to the luggage carousel and they spoke briefly but warmly. Under the grand entryway she wished it was raining so she could watch the long links of little inverted copper pyramids funnel rainwater. The big awning supported by huge hand-hewn cedar pillars. The big posts appeared rippled, like the adze hewer on every swing had been inspired by the scalloped sea. She glided two fingers over shallow grooves so defined she could see thin wooden curls at her feet.

The problem with making a room so beautiful is that it's only going to be hard to leave. A soft jazz singer welcomed her from a bedside speaker. Come away with me. Seems we're already here, Norah. Pretty fireplace unlit. Parted white curtains bordering a sliding glass door to the ocean-front balcony. Oh my. This is too much. On the desk among complimentary chocolates and other local goodies, a ten-year-old Port in a single-pour vial. She pulled the cork and smelled its syrupy scent rivalling in richness the seaside perfume. Oh my. She sprawled like a queen on the king bed, like a starfish that floated up at high tide. Her sleek white phone looked right at home on the luxury bed. Blank screen concealing chaos. Just like me. May as well dress you in a suit. I'll tie your tie for you, honey. She poked her bedside partner and the screen coloured to life and she responded to a few emails. One from her lawyer. "Liabilities increase alongside business growth; we need to think of risk in terms of vulnerability and attack vectors." She scheduled a meeting for her return. She reread the acquisition offer.

She once had a dream and in that dream she in the rain rode a horse blacker than the night, couldn't see it, her fist full of mane. Felt both thrill and fear. Even with a white-knuckled grip she couldn't hold on and was tossed to the sand. Listened for the runaway horse she never saw, but maybe hooves are quieted by sand or the rain, or maybe dreams or dream horses don't have sound, she wasn't in this reflective moment actually sure. That night she woke up with her own hair in her hand.

She used to be dismissive of dreams until someone pointed out how many breakthroughs have come from them. Kekulé's benzene molecule, Mendeleev's periodic table. Or just Paul McCartney's, *Yesterday*. She didn't think dreams were necessarily the insight from an inner oracle, but undeniably there was still the potential for insight. Even if the images sparking in the night were only loose associations from neuronic firing scarcely more coordinated than clams in the night spurting up out of the mind's sand, randomness can reveal if awareness brings reflection. Take the letters on the Scrabble stand and rearrange them. Or perhaps at times the content of dreams was more ordered. The subliminal brain trying to decipher the day's murky residue of stimuli and ideas, occasionally percolating an insightful bubble up to the cognitive surface.

Outside her door North Chesterman beach under an overcast sky. Rosy sun in a dignified grey-suit sky. Her view to the beach framed by cedar trees, not even wind enough to sway the ivy vines.

The first panic attack came while she was using the Tabata timer on her phone. Your life is a Tabata timer. Jog for three minutes, sprint for thirty seconds, repeat. *H-I-I-T.* She had completed over half a dozen intervals and after the last sprint she depaced to a jog but her heart rate and breath kept on sprinting without her. Her body fleeing in all ways but her legs. She stopped jogging and put her hand on the seawall but the seawall towered up beside her while she shrank. She dropped to a knee. The mind is funny. Her head dizzy and vision tunneling to a single pebble on the pavement, yet triggered by her pose she recalled an article on the Russian mafia, the Bratva that tattoo stars on their knees. *You kneel to nobody.* Her on one knee and her vision tunneling. The fuzzy outer-ring blackening inwards. Who gets a panic attack while running? She was more inconvenienced than scared, more curious than alarmed. Such is her nature. You gotta be kidding me. She'd find out later that a panic attack while running isn't so uncommon. The physical exertion elevating one's heart rate and blood pressure, sweating and shortening of breath. She figured her mental anxiety now paired with this physical stimulation had her psyche recognizing the physiology of evasion. *Time to fight or flee.* The whole system except that tiny detail of consciousness certain of imminent threat. Concern from the depths surfacing rather indelicately, her world turned inside out. Afterwards, she tried to recall which thought, which triggering concern, had sprung the attack.

She smoothed the bedsheet beside her. She let the acquisition offer float in her head. Float like a raft on the sea outside her window. Just to imagine. Floating away. She hadn't seriously entertained that first offer years ago. Am I now? Multi-million-dollar indecent proposal? Oh my. I'm flattered. Even a little curious. But, sigh, I'm married to my work.

She pushed her phone away and Norah said something really nice and Valerie rolled onto her stomach and looked out at the beach. Lying on her belly she watched waves breaking on the sand. Hours from sunset but the sky's lapel-pinned rose of a sun looked to have pricked a heart now bleeding through the silver sky. Two surfers sitting on their boards. She couldn't see their faces. Their longboards' noses pointed towards one another like spy-hopping whales. The swell rose and dipped them. Rose and dipped them. The next wave building, more shadow to its face. One surfer pointed their board to the beach then lay and paddled with the wave mounding up behind. The rider bending her legs up behind her to shift weight forward and she stroked deeply one last time and the board was caught by the wave. Valerie on the bed had unconsciously bent her own legs up. The surfer popped up to her feet and angled down the curving water and rode with a relaxed and easy style the peeling waist-high wave, cross-stepping from the tail to the nose, movements smooth and fluid and lanky, arms for balance but balance with style. Her hair and Valerie's hair looked about the same length. Valerie imagined those movements to the point she could, for a turn or two, almost be her. They took a turn together. But she didn't want to transpose herself onto that girl's wave. Beauty appreciated, not possessed. She wanted to admire her, celebrate her on that wave. Some girl Val would never know who would never know that right now someone was admiring her. Seeing her as beautiful. Who knows who loves ya. She watched her flow, cross-stepping back to weight the tail and pivot the board and turn with easy grace like a bird in the air—a lark, an eagle—and her hair swept out on the turn as she carved the wave then rode down the line, a watery V trailing the board, a smaller one from a finger channeling a liquid groove in the smooth wave face. Valerie silently celebrating her. Some beautiful woman unnamed. Who knows who loves ya.

Someone should bottle this beach smell. Maybe a diffuser or a scented beach candle? Or maybe just move here? She flipped through a brochure of the Inn's services. Not even desiring anything in particular, just enjoying the peruse. She flipped a page then flipped one back. A picture of a grotto, The Steam Cave. She called down to the Ancient Cedar Spa and asked if there was availability and if also they could accommodate a request. "With extra olives, please."

VIII

Wrapped in a towel wearing a robe she needed her second hand to draw back the grotto's heavy door. Steamy cave, grainy light, low ceiling, empty, hot and humid. Two-tier benches looked and felt like natural stone and for all she knew they might have been. Her feet on the warm and damp stone floor. Who knew rock could feel so welcoming. To her left a clouded glass door opaquely light leading to a seaside patio. She hung her white robe on a hook and pressed the big button for the steam cycle and in her towel stepped up to the higher bench. Dully glowing glass sea stars embossed on the low ceiling. The small grotto spaciously luxurious for one. She lay down. Eyes closed and hands over her towelled chest. Repose of the momentary death of concerns. Tofi-no? Tofi-yes.

Gurgling up from a hidden vent the humid room churned with cloud. The patio door cracked and Val didn't mind company but it was only the spa attendant saying her gin Caesar awaited her. And so now I'm dreaming. This is too much. She half-opened her eyes. "Thank you very much." The sound of her words having taken on the atmosphere. The door closed and little steam was lost and though the drink's cool umami pleasure awaited her she remained reclined. She imagined the blood-red drink, tower of ice, flecks of horseradish and dark curl of Worcestershire, a rim granulated with Montreal Steak Spice if the world in this moment would be most kind. Toothpick of skewered olives. She wondered if phenomena other than time were elastic because she seemed to stretch some of the drink's pleasure from patio to cave.

I am an imposter in a story of false achievement. The vent gurgled and steam rose. One coming morning I'll wake up and read of my ruin. B2P's walls all crumbled down in the night. A red sea star glowed. And faded. A yellow one softly pulsed. Attack vectors and vulnerabilities, the lawyer said. Even work you love can shackle, even meaningful pursuits can stretch you thin. And this. This here indulgence is the very opposite of your coming Ted Talk, no?

Sometimes she had to defend herself from herself. She realized long ago that she didn't need to be an asshole to herself to be a decent person and remain highly motivated. Condensed steam dripped from the ceiling sounding sporadic percussion notes. She told herself she will do more and do it better if rejuvenated. First getaway in nine years is probably allowed. No? Not a getaway, a restoration. She knew her mind that guilted was the same mind that motivated and she lay listening compassionately to gurgling thoughts and percussion doubt until her glistening skin was soft and pink. The sea stars dully glowed and faded.

Alone in the sensuous cave made more private by the thickening mist she loosened her towel. Her hand massaging her tense shoulders, her upper chest. Her fingers tracing down to her belly. A wandering hand. She lying on her back like that night she was lying on her back. Right now she listened to ceiling drips, but that night the rain. That night no towel, no top. Trent neither. On the couch his weight over her and she sliding lower to accept more of it. He was just about to put himself inside her. His eyes on her eyes but her eyes on his belly. He probably saw that. She hadn't asked. She exhaled smoke. She smoked one or two, maybe three cigarettes a year, not enough to be a bad habit so she wasn't trying to quit. She went to touch his belly, being careful with the cigarette. He took it from between her forked fingers and dropped it in a wine glass which hissed and thinly smoked and seemed more than one type of wrong and with one hand on her knee he closed her legs and in that split second she felt rejection but he only used that motion to roll her to her side then he grabbed her hips flipping her to her belly and he put her arm behind her back—not painful but almost painful—then paired it with her other, using only one of his hands to hold both of her forearms bound behind her back, she bearing his weight, him bending her lower back, pushing her down into the couch with her face half-buried in the cushion and the other half covered by her hair and then less hair because he had wrapped it in his fist and pulled her hair while putting himself inside her not forcefully, but her gasp then her moans saying the line between pleasure and pain was very thin. Hard to imagine it thinner. Breathlessly thin. His weight over her lower back bending her, like he was taking from her what he wanted. Or trying to.

Sometimes his virtues.

Her heavy exhales in the hot grotto as if she now the source of the billowing steam. She went for the bloody Caesar.

IX

S hed's evening patio was quiet and the hostess seated Alex at
the bar. Small restaurant with a little wood stove. He pulled
back a bar seat, draped his jacket, hung his hat below the bar
without looking for the hook. Alex for years now had a crush
on the topless mermaid suntanning on the chalkboard under
the beer taps. In his head now he said something really sweet to
her.

The screen behind the bar was streaming a World Surf League
competition. Right-hand point break with set waves so evenly
spaced and perfectly peeling the surf looked engineered. He was
pretty sure it was Jeffreys Bay. He had been watching the live
stream that day in 2015 when Mick Fanning was waiting for
a wave and a grey fin rose beside him. A Great White Shark
and it wasn't just having a look. Fanning scrambled wildly and
punched the shark and paddled possessed and the shark actually
bit through his leash and the jetski swung in at full speed and
picked him up. South Africa you can keep your perfect waves,
I'll stick to sloppy beach-break Tofitian waters.

He looked from the screen to the plate beside him. Flat-iron
steak, grill-scored and charred, white plate with red juices being
soaked up by the leading edge of parmesan truffle fries. The guy
slicing into the meat wore a ball cap. Big dude. Green Dunlop
rubber boots set on the low rail. Alex looked at him. "Did you

just pull your arrow out of that? I assume you're wearing a loin-cloth gitch that you made from its hide."

The guy didn't turn. He didn't stop slicing. He didn't look impressed, though he didn't look unimpressed. Maybe the steak so well-seasoned that this impropriety couldn't leave a bad taste in his mouth because he was chewing and didn't seem to want to rush that. He set down his fork not his knife and looked to the source of the indecency, looked Alex up and down and didn't smile. Turned back forward and reached for his pint glass nearly drained. "Imagining me in my underwear, hey? Is this you coming on to me? Fuckin' steal anyone's land today buddy is the better question. Is that why you look so tired?" He looked then looked away. "At least for another ignorant white man you seem to understand my traditional ways." He lifted the corner of his shirt like he actually was about to display loin-cloth underwear.

Alex laughed. "No I haven't stolen anyone's land today. What are you drinking?"

"Tuff Sess."

Alex turned to the bartender. "Jeff, two Tuff Sess's, please."

The bartender set down two cloudy copper pints. Alex raised his glass just off the bar top and a couple inches to his side, a dull clink sounded. He liked that sound. He sipped. Toasted malt and mild hop, from bottom to top the cloudy pints slowly clarifying. "How'd it go today Doug?"

"Slow. But we got 'em. You?"

"We got 'em. But it was slow."

X

In the evening air over Main Street cruises a crow. The tips of its wings are upturned, small ruffle in its spread primaries, the bird flying flat with no flapping and it flares and near weightlessly lands on a powerline while its beak grazes a transformer and its body completes a circuit. The bird quietly smokes then falls stone dead to the parking lot outside the Credit Union and triggers a fault that trips a breaker and town loses power.

Valerie had eaten dinner at On The Rocks, the Wickaninnish's bar. The bartender brought her the bill and then they both looked around in the novel quiet softened with natural twilight. He told her power outages are pretty routine in this town. They couldn't hear it but the generator kicked in and the lighting returned and part of maybe most people's inner child there was a little disappointed in that.

She changed into her bedtime shirt which said in small lettering: *Invert, always invert*. Investment wisdom, a reminder to try and look at outcomes and incentives. But also, the sexual innuendo on a nightie did amuse her. She turned off her bedside lamp. She had her arms above her head on the pillow. Scent of her own light body odour, very light, but it was there. She rolled her head. It didn't so much smell uniquely her or even distinctly female, rather, just human. She smelled it. She liked it. She wondered if that was a lonely thing or a very lonely thing.

If feminism was a belief in the equal rights, opportunities, and treatment of women, then she was one. Years ago before she parsed out the nuance of that definition to satisfy herself and nobody else, she wondered if a particular guilt was a signal of betrayal to the movement. She recognized that a part of her at times desired the security and comfort she felt in certain masculine presence. She wondered if that urge wasn't rooted in endless millennia of primitive living in a threatening world, coded into the base biology and built into the very bone structure of humankind. At times she wanted to feel protected if not taken care of. No longer did that bring a tinge of guilt. Now she believed anyone telling a woman what a woman is, however well-intentioned, and including any feminist, was part of the problem.

But this wasn't about a man. She wasn't entirely sure if she wanted one of those. People will tell you to follow your heart. Sure. But it's hard to know what the heart really wants. A girlfriend once said to her, "That's why I trust pleasure." She called it her argument for and defence of hedonism. "Truth is hard. But you can't doubt an orgasm."

She had met men with whom spending time felt comfortable, more comfortable than being on her own. It was nice and comfortable. *Comfort*. Do I want the highest expression of my short time to be comfort? Men she thought could be an island of respite in this sea of loneliness, while deep down knowing none of them were the one.

Everything has trade-offs. Single life is wide open and today felt so nice. Would I be leaving a state of occasional and mild emotional deficiency for a state of constant mundanity? Every new day brings the potential for uncommon connections. Pursuit of pleasure and meaning unconstrained by traditional norms and domesticated roles. Do I want traditional? Or a life unfettered. Sex heightened by lovers more impassioned when intimacy isn't a certainty. Better to go months without it than having it scheduled like clockwork every Sunday, predictable, stale, set your watch by it—not just the day but the duration. Most couples I see are not basking all day in fulfillment. So often I see stale dynamics of transactional relationships communicating in a loveless language. Life has deep meaning in my work and my passions, cuisine, music—travel, this lost love refound. Scent of light body odour.

Her mind like that dream horse that likes to run in the dark. She needed to rein it in promptly after lying down or she'd never corral it. She had come up with a sleep mantra. She'd never heard of that concept before, a sleep mantra. Just made it up, then made up the mantra.

My bed is a sanctuary. My body calm. My mind at ease.

She'd slow the words, elongate her breaths to draw out the spaces between them. Open her mind to open space. Lazily scan her body, feel each limb relax. Release her face of lingering tension, cheeks, jaw. Start her mantra again, so very calmly, if she found herself heavily thinking. It helped cue her mind to drift away. Falling and rousing but then finally falling. She called it her ketamine lullaby, tranq that wild horse mind. She'd let the words float around however they pleased.

My body at ease. My bed is calm. My mind is a sanctuary.

***

Down the coast from the Inn, Alex is dreaming and in his dream he's on the beach. It's sunny. The girl ahead on the sand. He runs, then she runs. He slows and she slows. Her hair in the wind. The smile, the playfully devious smile that she also smiles

101

with her eyes. He tries again. This game. He runs and then she runs. That silly game that did make him laugh. Then she tells him to stop chasing. She doesn't say it. In the dream her eyes say it and there's no mistaking their message. Small figure getting smaller down the coast. Until the only evidence she existed are her steps. His nervous eyes on the foamy edge of the tide. The flooding tide pooling into her depressions. Him standing there alone in sinking sand in a dream of a sunburnt memory.

XI

When Valerie found out she had a sexually transmitted infection she didn't feel like something had been given to her, she felt like something had been taken away. She lost her virginity when she was seventeen. That never felt like the right verb. He was seventeen. They had trust because they said they did. With words. l love you. I trust you. Words. She wanted him to be her first. She told him that. He gave her herpes. He said he didn't know. He may not have. The nurse also had some words for her. "You have it for life. It lives in your spine."

She'd always remember him. The calendar says that that was a long time ago. But time is a farce. She was seventeen but still cried to her mother and her mother held her and couldn't remember the last time she held her. Her mother deeply saddened by her daughter's anguish felt a tinge of guilt from getting to be a mother who again holds her daughter. She told Valerie that the infection actually increased intimacy because it was a type of secret and a little personal idiosyncrasy and a type of privileged knowledge she would only share with the man she thought was worthy enough of knowing it. Some mothers in addition to being mothers attempt locksmithing, bomb defusing. Well-meaning but not without implication. "So it's a secret?"

Later her mother said she looked into it, not naming *it*, and said *it* wasn't a very big deal if you knew anything about *it*. Stepping around its proper name like you skirt shit on a sidewalk. Her mother continued, if someone isn't going to be understanding, that's a good way to weed out the close-minded. Valerie found all those words, words which she didn't entirely believe, both patronizing, or matronizing, and also a bit comforting.

The day before they had sex, the boy who had given it to her was a kid with no outbreak, and the day of their intimacy he was a kid with a mild outbreak. His willful blindness—a great human talent to believe what suits us, and reject what doesn't—perhaps reducing his scrutiny. His brain in his young and stupid and horny skull that afternoon was short on its normal volume of blood. If a boy at fault then a boy with a story, and a boy who had gotten it somewhere else too. A story without end.

There are few villains in history and there may be none.

She had told two friends about it. One friend who she had since lost—lost never felt like the right verb—said this does not make you unclean, and Val said I know that and she hadn't used that word herself and her friend felt like an idiot. It was just truly a verbal mistake. Some small wrongs aren't easily righted, some never get righted. Some small things are big things. The smallest effort of one's pinky finger can dog-ear a book page. Stack a building on it the crease remains. You'd think something that your pinky can bend, your whole body could straighten. Nope. The infection found a home at the base of her spine but that comment's residence was more cerebral.

She read on a health website that the emotional impact of being diagnosed with genital herpes is often worse than the condition and it doesn't deserve the upset it causes. But since when has logic cured complexes? Back then Valerie felt her

STI was something like a modern-day equivalent of losing her virginity before marriage, as it would concern those cultures where premarital sex was a great dishonour—not to the woman who chose it, or to whom it was forced upon—but to some bullshit, besmirched honour imposed by a patriarchal culture. All the countless young women who lived in that imposed and fabricated shame, the ruined reputations, the disowning, the acid washes. *Acid washes*. She read that acid washes were on the rise in India. No thank you, India. She felt like it was a cousin of that. Surely not for everyone, but it was for her. She had lived with her infection for twenty-one years and she didn't much think about it anymore and in any given year she only had a few mild breakouts. It was fine. The infection didn't define who she was and it was just something from her past. She was stronger than it. Whatever that means. She considered herself stronger than it.

She sometimes thought about it.

Something closed up back then. Not her legs—how dare it think it could take sex from her. Something else. Something unnamed. A constraint that kept her from opening fully. Opening ugly, words she'd written in her journal.

Valerie journals every morning. Before running and meditation she writes in unpunctuated free-form-flow ideas in the predawn dark before a self-imposed disciplined regime. She writes in cursive. One small artistic act, the flowing and elegant loops, an engagement with a part of her mind if not the world she wants to keep close, words curling like wild vines, her own tiny defiance to the ordered day where with executive efficiency she retakes the helm of running a multi-million-dollar, continent-wide company. It also just looks nice, the writing. Isn't there some kind of truth in beauty? So seek small salvations from the optimal.

After that she reads through self-development goals. Goals that started as a few lines. A practice she had been keeping for years. It was now four pages. She just didn't feel like she could delete any. So she'd read over a few lines each day, then next day move down the list. Eventually after a couple weeks she'd start over. She'd read a couple favourite inspirational quotes. *Don't let perfect be the enemy of the good. When I let go of who I am I become what I might be.* She considered getting a dog so she could name him Lao Shih Tzu. Adages easy to say but hard to internalize.

Valerie runs every morning. It isn't a chore it's a pleasure, a ritualistic one, and so vacation isn't a reason to stop running. This morning now 6:00 a.m. she laces her second bow and her tights fit well and her running top does too and she puts her hair in a ponytail and the hood of her hoodie up like a boxer. She runs better and feels better when her clothes fit well and she likes them and she looks good in them and feels good in them. She buried her buds, picked her playlist—her third of four. She titled her workout playlist *Pick It Up*. Mix of old and new songs that she was constantly curating. She hit play and listened to the opening vibe, double-tapping her right bud until one spoke to her. In support of her distrust of time, some music doesn't seem to care how many years have passed, some old songs retain their power. Some songs going on a couple hundred repeats and yet their freshness perennial.

She left through the front door and turned for the beach and the dawn waters behind the Inn. Already the fragrance. Cedar trees more pungent from the dew, scent of sand and seaweed, salt brackish, rot sweet. The short wood-chip trail soft underfoot. She stepped out onto North Chesterman all fresh and brisk and clean in the cool, sea-scented morning like where have you been all my life, like you didn't even know something was missing until it arrived. A small wave measuredly breaking on the beach, its white crest falling in a long line appearing as an invitation if not a challenge. Let's go. She set out after it. Music low enough it didn't dilute the beach sounds, it complimented them.

Beach houses to her left by the headlands surrounded by tall trees hoarding sun glow. She made it a policy of disclosing it to every romantic interest before they arrived to the bedroom. She was well practised in the conversation. She found power in ownership. It's all outlook, everything's framing. She with a *why* can bear any pitiable nineteenth-century misogynistic philosopher. She thought from total ownership of her issues, self-honesty and a fortitude earned from discipline and effort, she could arrive at as much resolve as ever would be possible. Absolutely there were mountainous gains there.

After she had contracted it from a man another man called her a word. First she told him about her situation. She said "confess." She didn't use that word anymore, but that was the word she had used when she was still figuring things out. She is still figuring things out. That young man had then used a descriptive word. She held onto his word. Maybe it was true. Its specificity imbued it with a type of precision. Precision seems like truth. So she held onto that word. Even today. Kept it close. And he held onto her. Not physically, with a tighter grip than mere hands can hold. He let her know he was doing her a favour by staying with her, given her situation. He never said that explicitly. He said it every other way, so he didn't need to.

Sometimes she nicknamed her men. Right before she left that one she nicknamed him Newton. He constantly trying to pull her down like gravity, reinforcing in her mind that her primary direction is up. Goodbye.

She paced on morning sands while the glorious sun spread wide over the water, as if claiming its empire of dawn. Of course the fear of a panic attack happening again fed the anxiety—vicious cycle. The inability to control it only inducing more fear—negative loop. She came up with a way to address it: Fuck you. Come at me. I'm right here. Her gapped tracks in the sand large enough that self-doubt could alternate in a step, if it could keep up. She still in the cedar shade but the ocean now two waters. A sun-lightened blue advancing to shore as if the colour was carried by waves.

A couple men became guiding stars. Some stars are best aligned behind you. Orientation no less true from a repelling navigation.

The first mental-health worker she saw was a psychodynamic therapist, one year after contracting the STI. Some of the literature suggested psychology's legitimacy was in question given the *replication crisis*, that the majority of research conclusions could not be reproduced. Arriving at your first session doubting the merits of talk therapy might preclude any potential benefits from even a placebo effect. She voiced her concerns. The therapist responded rather bluntly, "Do you believe everything worth knowing about yourself you can learn from yourself? Why would that be the case? Tell me about the back of your head. Couldn't there be useful personal insight from a perspective not fixed in your footing? Whether we like it or not, keys other than one's own voice may be required to unlock certain doors of the mind." She went to six more sessions and there was benefit there but she stopped going. A man had not fixed her. The second professional was a cognitive behavioral therapist and together they addressed self-image inconsistencies and negative language and Valerie saw her monthly for a year and then cancelled, mostly from work-related time constraints. A woman had not fixed her.

Here's how she fixed herself: she didn't. You don't fix a work in progress, her words. A revelation that inspired the founding of her business, *B2P*. Comfort and struggle. Self-belief alongside self-doubt. Confidence as well as uncertainty. Her chaos harnessable because one must have chaos inside to give birth to a dancing star. Why must that misogynist write such pretty prose? she wondered. You don't fix the elegantly imperfect—her words. There is no truer rejoice than a broken hallelujah—a combination of her and Cohen's words. The spectacularly unwhole—her words. She was considering a tattoo of the spectacular unwhole but trying to figure out what that might look like and where to put it.

She sweating seaside. The easternmost branches of the trees were now sun saturated and leaking rays of westward gold, the top of her hood bathed in sunwash like some astral baptism. She ran. She looked to the water now uniformly a lighter blue. Whoever called depression the blues must have seen a different colour. She and the sun both reflecting on the water as if in some kind of joint ritual or shared prayer or communal praise of the sea.

Ownership, strength from honesty. She was not saying it was alright. It fucking wasn't alright. She did not want the infection. She detested it. Some men she had known she wished she hadn't. Her people were those who in defeat remained unbroken only to be propelled by loss, wounded, limping if need be, stepping always forward. She hadn't met most of them and never would and she liked that a lot.

Base to Peak. That's what she named it. *B2P.* A sprawling business sprouted from humble roots. Two decades ago a therapist recommended she attend a women's group for those currently dealing with or living through the aftershocks of an abusive relationship, whether physical or emotional. A sharing circle really wasn't her thing but keeping an open mind was. She went. She talked a little, listened more.

Valerie once read a longitudinal study on social connection. In 1985 participants were asked how many friends they could turn to in a crisis. Five was the most common answer. In 2010 the most common answer was zero. The study's conclusion suggesting that technology was responsible for social disconnection and loneliness. Texting versus phone calls, video versus live, cycles of dopamine hits and drops from social media. Some called it the loneliest era. She researched the research and it actually didn't seem that today was a more lonely time than other times. These things are hard to accurately measure and the data set is shallow. But, undeniably, a lot of people were lonely. It doesn't have to be *most* for it to be *lots*, for it to be significant and problematic.

She read that in maximum security, prisoners misbehaving will be put in solitary confinement as punishment. They take you away from the company of murderers and rapists and give you a timeout with your thoughts. She thought that was hilarious. She looked further into the so-called epidemic of isolation. One researcher: "Not humans with broken parts, but rather, unmet needs." At the time when she started B2P there was a leverageable confluence. The widespread crisis of loneliness was exacerbated by trends of individualism, while at the same time legitimacy *of* and eagerness *for* distance learning was accelerating. She didn't buy into the narrative that digital interaction was inherently negative, rather that most of the current options were not being maximally utilized in ways that strengthened well-being. *It's not the tech, it's the application.* So she built a better application. Events to come like a global pandemic's mandated isolation only stoked the B2P ground fire.

A dog walker. A jogger. Both returning smiles. She wondered, looking at the water, if Tofino offered scuba-dive excursions because she had never used her pool-trained PADI. She ran.

That loneliness is epidemic is not entirely a lonely thing—isn't it heartening to know you are not alone in your loneliness? If many feel a sense of disconnection then many want connection. Logic is sexy, tell Stacy to make the t-shirt. She had an idea, an idea that turned into an obsession resulting in fast-tracked diplomas in counselling and business management, then not a degree in programming or software engineering because she just taught herself to code—YouTube, baby. The foundation of her business was three-fold: theoretical, practical, personal. What professionals she didn't meet in the women's group, a friend had a friend. Making the website was easy. Making the app was hard. Credit cards financed with credit cards. It all came together so quickly that she would describe it as some collective drive to connect, heal, grow through genuine care, support, and play, had itself built the business.

Businesses like hers do not build themselves. Of course she would describe it like that and not all the years of lost sleep, the risky debt, her very real and ironic social isolation from dedicating herself to bootstrapping a business to counteract widespread social isolation. In the interviews, she mostly just said, the thing basically built itself. Not duplicity, distortion: her lenses of the world.

Four years after founding B2P her dad forwarded a link to an excessively lengthy headline from the online edition of the Vancouver Sun. *Social Media Accelerates the Winds of Loneliness Churning a Perfect Storm of Disconnection: In the eye of that storm, Valerie Roy, CEO, unfurls her sail.* Verbose and indulgent, but recognition for serious efforts feels all right. Her dad printed and framed that article for his office.

The podcast host, Guy Raz, of *How I Built This,* in an interview said to her you're the perfect figurehead for the company. "Oh. No. Not at all. I mean, I'm an eager student of this collective project. I'm working hard for it, but I also just attend a lot of its workshops. It was something we started for ourselves." "Why does one so accomplished still doubt her capabilities?" "Just gifted I guess." She lost sleep on how that came out, unprofessional she could live with, but not ditzy. She knew people would see her for what she was. In the following days a flood of new users crashed the app. She considered firing the developer, but then she'd be out of work. For several days B2P ranked number one downloaded app in the App Store Canada, and number three in the U.S. Another headline: *The Real Woman Behind this Company's Unreal Growth.* B2P vibrated a groundswell that rolled east towards Toronto, southwards into the States.

The CBC's Peter Mansbridge interviews Valerie Roy at her home in Vancouver, B.C.

Video transcribed for CBC.ca. November 21, 2018

Valerie Lou Roy, born February 2, 1984, Vancouver, Canada

Occupation: Founder and CEO of Base to Peak

Education: "Long story"

PM: Last month you became an honouree of Canada's *Top Forty Under Forty* and at thirty-four you're running that list's largest company. What drives you, Ms. Roy?

VR: I watched you while I was growing up, Peter.

PM: [Smiles]

VR: Peter, if I make you laugh, would you consider regrowing the moustache?

PM: I'll think about it.

VR: Deal. Firstly, thank you for having me. The CBC is special to me. I grew up with it. The Walt Disney Hour. The Raccoons. Olympic coverage. The National, of course. I don't watch hockey but I like that opening theme song. [VR hums a bar.] I hope we didn't lose too many people about the not watching hockey comment, Peter. It's my pleasure to be here. What drives me? So very many things. People. People that come to B2P wanting to be better engaged with their world, that want to be happier and healthier. Then seeing people make those gains. Getting to work with my amazing team—intelligent, creative women all believing in the power of positive tech. Our belief daily strengthened from seeing our work benefiting people. Then there's this aspect of just wanting to make a beautiful thing. Like the beauty of design that comes through in this business, in our app, is something that a pianist and a cabinet maker and a mathematician all must know. A type of truth manifests in different mediums. Does that make any sense? I think beauty shows up in many places and it matters. Also—is this answer too long?

PM: Not at all.

VR: Also, I like the variation. I do like working with people but I also like working with code. The logic side. Surprisingly, they harmonize. Does that make any sense?

PM: I think so. What does the name *Base to Peak* mean to you?

VR: I think life is about connection. And there are many types of connection, with one self, with others, connecting through passions and art, and nature. I absolutely do not have things figured out. Like, I'm kind of a mess, Peter. Really though. But for me, strong foundations benefit all those paths and pursuits. Strong foundations allow for greater reach. So that figures into the name. In a time when many of us feel a type of disconnection, B2P is about developing certain strengths that enable us to find more connection, to hold more love, is really what it is.

PM: I hesitate to ask this next question and when we were brainstorming, the team was evenly split on whether to pose it.

VR: Well now I'm curious. And a little nervous, Peter. I'm guessing I'm not going to be answering lasagna or pink.

PM: *Founder* and *CEO* are positions primarily held by men. If you or anyone in our audience find something limiting by my framing your achievements in relation to gender, then I do apologize. But your perspective could be informative, and empowering for a young woman watching this right now. I think that makes it worth asking. So, how are you where you are? And why aren't there more women in your position?

VR: Well this is funny because I do get to answer pink. As a girl I played with dolls and liked pink. I still do. The colour part, not the dolls, Peter. I wasn't exactly a girly girl, more like, a nerdy, kinda weird, girly girl. Not a tomboy. What I'm trying to say is that I don't think I exhibit relatively more masculine tendencies than other women, characteristics that might point to why I have my position. [VR pauses.] I don't think I have a good answer to this. The interplay of nature versus nurture is not so well understood and the concept routinely oversimplified. It is not nature *or* nurture. It is nature *and* nurture plus genetic variation. It's complex and interrelated. Who we are and what we're capable of might be better described as heritability interacting with experience filtered through the random nature of development. Just last week I was listening to an interview with a professor of complex systems who publishes on the history of intelligence—intelligen*ces*, not a singular concept. His research suggests that given the neuroplasticity of the mind, environment plays a larger role than genetics. Intelligence might be conceptually reducible to good memory and concept linking. There are cognitive tools for increasing mental storage and improving recall. Sorry, what I'm trying to get at: are behavioural traits less malleable than intelligence? I would find that hard to believe. [VR pauses.] I think a person can, to at least a significant extent, and if lucky to be living in a free culture and raised decently, become what they want. Importantly, no one can prove that that isn't the case and it's reasonable to believe it, and so that's the world I choose. I'll tell that young woman the same thing I would tell a young man, just reach out for what you want. Don't ask anyone's permission. Let your work ethic do the talking and hope for a bit of luck on the way. I've had a lot of that.

PM: Who inspires you, Ms. Roy?

VR: Stern but fair Canadian anchorman.

PM: [Laughs] Natural, chevron, or handlebar?

VR: We'll put that poll to the people!

PM: Who inspires you, Ms. Roy?

VR: So many people. And most of them do not know it and never will. All the women who raised the families and cooked the meals and cleaned the floors and never got enough credit for their efforts. So that's about a billion or two there. My father for the work ethic he inspired in me and my mother for being my mother. Too many artists and musicians to start down that conversational road. We'd run your printers dry.

PM: Among personal development companies, Base to Peak is one of Canada's largest. To what do you credit your success?

VR: Luck mixed with curiosity and stubbornness, I suppose. B2P had more than a little *right place at the right time*. I'm simply humbled by how many people see value in our project. We've spent exactly zero dollars on marketing. *Zero*. For the first two years we grew by word of mouth and realistically we grew too fast for our team to keep up with demand. Things were not perfect. The app is our keystone and it was buggy and constantly crashing. That fault inexcusably lay with our developer. [VR lifts her hand from her lap.] And we had overworked instructors not showing up to courses. Group Zoom sessions going dark. That fault lay with the company's software engineer. [VR lifts her other hand off her lap. Lowers them.] Somehow most of the clients and all of the team stayed. Stayed and grew. I... It's hard for me to convey just how that makes me feel. Somehow I'm getting to do what I utterly love. I get to play in my world. My work and my play don't have a defined line of separation. Long hours are my privilege and I'm big-time grateful."

PM: Last question, Ms. Roy.

VR: Is it too late to ask that you call me Valerie?

PM: Valerie, where do you see yourself and Base to Peak in ten years?

VR: The last ten years passed overnight. Time is an enigma. I'd very happily take ten more years of the last ten years.

PM: Thank you for your time, Valerie.

VR: Thank you, Peter.

Ditzy if not rambling, infantile and self-obsessed. She hated that interview. Calls for interviews continually came. She started declining. Even though she thought she didn't convey herself well in interviews she wasn't averse to them. Anything for the business. But the real power of B2P was its distributive nature. Its value was the community. Making herself the figurehead undermined the project. If you see the Buddha, kill the Buddha.

Valerie's pace steady, her heart-rate climbing. On the sands by Frank Island she turned south-east onto South Chesterman. A longboarder walking out to small surf. Base to Peak was founded on multi-disciplinary practices for identifying, coping with, healing from, growing through various psychological afflictions. What started as a small, women's support group had virtually exploded. It blossomed into more general social connection. Integrating diverse ideas from Stoic philosophy to peer-reviewed research on cognitive-behavioural therapy, to positive psychology. Eventually a myriad, holistic approach under one smart-phone app with various routines, workshops, courses both zoom and in-person. From daily timers for optimizing morning sunlight exposure, to basic nutrition—hold up your camera to the fridge and its native AI would output healthy recipes—exercise regimes and sports meetups, meditation techniques and classes, sauna locations. All booking services were integrated into the app, locations for group cold-water plunges, scheduled reminders for improved sleep practices, supportive group talks with various topics. The software used location services like dating apps. Users selected their interests, inputted their availability, and nearby activities were displayed. The instructors and coaches were first vetted by Val's team but eventually became user-rated like Uber. Yoga, breath workshops, running groups, book clubs, gardening classes. The list was constantly growing because it was not top-down it was bottom-up, user-run. Craig's List meets Facebook meets Tinder for well-being.

The positive health effects of various self-development practices, both physical and mental, paired with routine social engagement among genuine well-wishers was practically opiate. The psychology department of University of British Columbia was running observational studies on her clients. Doctors referring patients suffering from anxiety, depression, loneliness, obesity, poor sleep, and on and on, calling it "social prescribing," without medication's typical side-effects: no dizziness, nausea, diarrhea. Many doctors themselves were joining. It was fun.

One afternoon she was at her computer and considering pairing her wide-leg trousers with a cute low-cut blue Kevlar vest for all the flack she was taking. Among many gripes, she took heat for B2P being exclusively female. She thought her critics had a point. There was a reasonable chance she was on the wrong side of this. The company's female orientation wasn't exactly intentional, it had just started that way. She considered putting it to a vote, letting the clients decide. Of course the community aspect would change if it was co-ed, but would it change for the worse or better? She wasn't sure.

Ahead, a fluorescent group belly-paddling on the sand like bright-pink foundered seals. Rather hilarious and she might have laughed if she had breath to spare. Maybe she would take a surf lesson. Maybe I should add surf groups to B2P? Running she recorded an out-of-breath voice note.

Her team integrated incentives into the app to keep people engaged. Some social commentators were critical, but they didn't attack B2P, rather its CEO. Her app was not *invasive* or *predatory*, as they called it. It wasn't the black algorithmic box of other social media where one could hear the echo of lost mouse clicks as users spiralled down dark rabbit holes, while companies logged all their clients' data. B2P's code was open source. Incentives were designed for positive results: social check-ins, buddy systems, team building, certain premium features unlocked when one user assisted another or brought a friend to the app. The company took a percentage of all bookings and generated fees from tiered memberships.

Her position endowed influence. Influence is power. A powerful individual becomes a target. But power in virtuous hands can do good. She lowered her hood. It takes power to counter negative forces. The good witch. One recent vlogger called her a white knight in a black Tesla. She saw all the levers that could be pulled to bring large monetization—advertisements of products that wouldn't necessarily best serve her clients, or selling user data. She put tiny black bars across those levers: lines of fine print protecting privacy. B2P was one hundred percent hers. In its first years she took on debt rather than give up equity. But heavy lies the crown. Criticisms often ending with a *y*. *Cult-y. Pyramid-y. Monopol-y.* It weighed on her. In dealing with the vocal backlash she and Stacy one night recalled the wisdom of a sage: *If they hate, then let them hate, and watch the money pile up.* –50 Cent. Not that this was about the money. She paid less attention to the haters on her socials because she was too busy building her own.

At the end of South Chesterman she stepped a running shoe up to the big bedrock outcropping, spat and turned. What she wanted was to execute at her ablest level. Surround herself with competent people and come to terms with trusting their abilities. Hard for one whose success came from controlling every single little detail. Hard to trust when certain partnerships burned you in the past. She wanted to give herself up to the pursuit of this thing that felt so special and not screw it up or let someone else screw it up. Get to work. Just get to work. Time away is time wasted. The sun warm on her sweating face. Her pace quickening like she'd just turn this run into a biathlon and swim on back to Vancouver. Her heart rate. Panic and passion can appear awfully similar. Nearly sprinting now. She loved people feeling good. That sounded cloying in her head. One of those things that she'd keep to herself but other people's joy was a big part of her heart. Somehow she had the privilege to put herself in the service of others. She wrote a piece of code which every day at 9:00 p.m., when she normally stopped working, would send to her phone the total number of people—not users—people that had joined B2P that day. The largest single day was 3,425. That night she didn't sleep. Not because she couldn't—she didn't even try, didn't lie down. Coffee and a standing desk. Computer keys tapping away like rainfall, her hoodie up. Just get to work. Some people conjecture theories on space travel. Some hate on the person building the rocket ship. A few others set foot on the moon.

This morning's golden yoke fully broke, a Pacific coastal world now oozing with mellow sun, brightening waters so vibrantly blue they almost match her Slavic eyes. Finishing her run near the Inn she looked out at that big body telling little of what lies underneath. Off behind her by a walking path at the forest edge, standing among tree shadow, is Trent. Trent is here.

He knew her patterns. In Vancouver she was up early to jog. This morning he had returned to the Chesterman Beach parking lot. There he could watch both the road and the beach. Even if it would have meant driving all the residential roads and hotel parking lots, Trent would have found her car. But he didn't need to go to those efforts. Before she broke up with him, well before that, he had enabled her phone's location sharing. He arrived late last night and drove down the long entrance of the Wickaninnish Inn. Pulling up so late to the security booth he couldn't think of something to say. The attendant kindly asked that if he didn't have a booking nor a reservation for dinner to please turn around. He parked at the lot by the beach and pulled up Google Maps and then walked the sand right up to her hotel. Confirmed her car then left and slept in his until a by-law officer rapped his windshield. Drove back and parked on the logging roads. The town's accommodations were not at capacity.

XII

A lex with an early-morning coffee in a travel mug kicked out two portside boat bumpers. He tied up at Method Marine fuel docks. As he was wiping the dew off the seats Steve and Russell walked up.

"Tofino Coffee?"

"Two days in a row." Steve held up his cup.

"It's good coffee. You guys got your trunks?"

"I thought you said Hot Springs Nude Cove."

"Oh boy."

Behind them a floatplane screaming down the length of the harbour sounded like some kind of apocalyptical air-raid siren. "I guess the town's up now." At about ten after seven Alina showed up. Alex logged a data point on one of his many theories on women. He didn't have a theory concerning mothers stopping at their ex's to drop off a Cheese Whiz and pickle sandwich for her boy. But he had one on female punctuality. He smiled passing her a coffee in a travel mug saying it's probably still warm and she asked if he'd added Baileys yet. He pinched her side and she weakly smiled or grimaced. The sun was peeking over Meares Island and though some fishing boats had left before them, Alex hadn't seen any tour boats cruise by.

He untied the lines and Steve shipped the bumpers and Alina sat beside Alex while the two guests faced stern. They idled away some distance before engaging the twins so as not to rock the docked boats. They cruised over placid morning waters. They cruised through the narrow gap beside Deadman Island where every other year a boat runs aground. He was quite sure there was truth in its name as he himself had almost driven up on it. The fog thickened nearing Elbow Bank as if the priests hadn't left at all and the boat was navigating through the clergy's heavy fabric. Van Nevel Channel on their left joined Heynen Channel, Father Charles Channel feeding into Maurus Channel ahead—the Outcast in the fog here surrounded by four spectral priests like some kind of clerical ambush. At least he could spread his life's confessions out among them. Murky Christian confluence as if the smoke of the burned-down churches and residential schools still hung over the water. *Forgive you Father for you have sinned.* They cruised on to other reverend waters, Calmus and Millar up ahead. Alex watching his radar. He was going to point out Ahousaht Village but it was shrouded away.

The marine murk began to clear behind Flores. Alex spoke over the motors. "The largest island in the area." He throttled down. Their trailing wake continued on its way and bobbed the boat and Alina sipping her coffee got a mouthful. She looked like she was going to say something. He cut the puttering motors and the silence was stark and immense. Like they had arrived to something significant that preceded them. Not even a bird, not even their wake yet to shore. He was going to tell a story but for a moment he didn't want to interrupt the silence.

"This happened on this island here in 2013." His voice enhanced by the water's acoustics, at once theatrical and intimate. "A couple lived on the other side. The sixty-year-old lady was working in their garden. A cougar comes out of the bush prowling towards her. She fends it off with a rake. Another day it happens again and she wards it off, now better armed with a machete. They called the conservation officers who came out with a tracker and hounds but heavy rains masked the scent. One day her partner hears screams. He had bought an eight foot, cold-steel boar spear that he kept by the house. He grabs it and runs for her. Sees the mountain lion has got her from behind. He runs up and just starts stabbing." Alex with a two-handed motion. "The cougar runs off. Her skull partially crushed, her skin degloving. He calls the coast guard and she's air-lifted to Victoria hospital. The police search for the cat and find it dead not far away."

"Well that's terrifying," said Steve.

"He saved her life with a boar spear."

"Incredible," said Russell.

"There's actually only been half a dozen fatalities in the past century in this province. Bees kill way more people but it's hard to be a villain wearing a rather adorable black-and-yellow-striped outfit."

Five sharp cracks behind them. Like claps but harder surfaces than hands. Strangely out of place but more so because the claps were coming from the water. They all turned. No one had heard it surface. Thirty feet away a sea otter was balancing a rock on its belly and in its very cute and innocent and loving paws it gripped a clam. It started smashing the shell on the rock, generating an impressive amount of force for its little arms.

"Aw what a cutie," said Alina.

"Well that's clever," said Russell. "Never seen that before."

"Indeed. A cute rapist."

"What?" Alina turned.

"I'm looking for an acute therapist."

"Well that doesn't answer me at all. But now I don't want it answered."

"Probably best."

They cruised on through Shelter Inlet and he switched off the radar and by Starling Point the only fog remaining was wisps like snared cotton in the trees. God's breath, some call it, or remnants of her whisper. Twin eagles were perched on a tall tree, its drooping top distinguishing it hemlock. On the opposite shore a big coal-black bear scavenged at low tide for mollusks or crustaceans. It upturned sizable rocks with little effort. It rolled a two-foot-wide boulder as if a foam-filled stage-prop. No doubt the bear could hear the boat but it cared not. Alex said we can stop but getting the hot springs to ourselves is far less common than a bear sighting. He looked to Steve. "Your call." Steve flagged them onwards.

A small bay on their left with a fenced ring like an aquatic corral for miniature water ponies. Two green shacks and a floathouse connected with narrow walkways. Alex noticed Russell looking, and said to him, "Sea horses."

Russell said, "I believe you."

"Open-net fish farms with their visiting Atlantic salmon."

"Why Atlantic?"

"Great question, Russell. I've heard for their faster growth rates. It's all very contentious. Escaped Atlantic salmon interbreeding with wild Pacific salmon. Alaska doesn't want anything to do with them, there's none up there."

"'Merica." Steve said.

Alex liked when they leave the *A* off. "You guys actually have a lot of great wildlife programs."

"The hell do you mean *actually*?"

The water between Flores Island and Openit Peninsula blue and broadening to big open water, next landfall Japan. Alex said to Alina, "If we don't stop we can make Japan for breakfast. About five days from now, but still breakfast. What do you think?"

"I'd eat ramen for breakfast," she said.

Alex steered the Pursuit northerly along the coastal fringe. Just north of here were all kinds of histories this boat ride too short to tell so he didn't mention Good Friday's tsunami that destroyed eighteen Hesquiaht homes one cold March night over a half century ago. The power out. People swimming with their babies under the full moon as rising water swept their homes away. He didn't tell them about Cougar Annie, the homesteader arriving at twenty-seven years old in 1915 and who over the next seventy years went through five husbands, birthed eleven children, survived two cougar attacks, shot sixty-two cougars and eighty black bears. This wild coast, these wild histories in Alex's mind.

The boat jostled through Sharp Point's choppy waters, a surface confused from a strong tide sucking over submerged pinnacles. They cruised on into the mouth of the long cove with its calming waters. On this windless morning they seemed to be entering the very archetype of tranquility. Ultra placid, this. Alex reduced power. Had he oar locks he'd spell off the twins and row the remaining distance. A glass surface so still, individual insects appeared to be walking on a mirror stretched bank to bank. A resting water-spider twinned to its inverse as if all this wet expanse was their shared web. He could see individual leg hairs. It made him shudder. Some kind of death incarnate. A grimmest creature representative of earth's most uncompassionate domains. He saw fangs. He looked away but none of its eight eyes did. Liquid trees so defined they appeared not as reflections but veritable trees opposingly sprouted from a shared seed. One trunk reaching for the sky, the other the water. As if the Outcast had cruised into the home of a forger, this cove a stash of coniferous fakes. You nearly had to give it a minute to tell which version real, which mirage. Or look behind at the eerie wavering replicants.

To starboard a vertical mist and Alina said, "That's them." Steve and Russell were already looking. They couldn't see the hot springs trickling into the ocean water, just the steaming proof, and the mist fit very well here.

"We'll drive up ahead to the start of the boardwalk trail and walk back to them." Beside the boat an angled deadhead, the ebbing water bending around it like molten glass. The long L-shaped dock vacant of other boats. He puttered to the inside of the long dock and Steve kicked out the bumpers and Alex turned the boat to point their departing direction and sidled up and turned off the motors and lashed two port lines. He got out first and offered Alina his hand. He offered it to Steve and Steve slapped it. The steep ramp at low tide creaking metallically under their steps. Mounted to a tall pole at the end of the pier a small and idle wind-turbine, just looking at it cued in Alex's head its threshing sound. At the unmanned toll box Alex had a twenty-dollar bill out but Steve said put that away my good man and he slid USD cash into the honour system's envelope that he dropped into the yellow lockbox and Alina thanked him.

Single file the crew stepped to a boardwalk trail leading them into dense and lush greenery. Russell stopped to take a picture of a mossy tree. Alex said, "That's Old Man's Beard. Also known as Methuselah's Beard. Oldest man in the Bible, living to be 969 years old, and this is the longest lichen in the world. Only grows in old forests."

Steve turned and said I'm lichen your flora facts and Alex said that's not bad for a morning pun. "The bar obviously lower than for an afternoon or evening pun." They walked on in an old woods under bearded trees that for all their wisdom might not totally understand the concept of dry, broad canopies casting an everlasting shade over eternally damp moss. Underfoot, some of the planks bore letters, mostly boat and family names. He'd seen them all before but he still liked watching them pass. "What would you router into a plank?" He put that to his crew.

Alina said reflectively, "I dunno."

Alex said, "*I dunno. Sincerely, Alina*. I get that. It's philosophically honest."

She called him an ass.

"Maybe something about your star sign?" Purely teasing but she didn't laugh. For Alex, astrological conversations were a surer contraceptive than condoms. He had a theory which held that the superficial beauty of a woman correlated with an interest in astrology.

Steve said, "*Yeah no for sure.* And then about six or eight boards later, *Sorry for making you trip.*"

Russell asked Alex what he'd carve. "A plus A in a heart." Alina turned and made a face and Steve said, "Aww."

Just before a set of stairs they came to the only plank bearing a question. *Clara, will you marry me?* Alex said, "I hate to break this to you all. On a plank just up ahead she goes on to decline that offer." Alina said he's lying and Alex said true. Etched into another plank, a single word, *UNFORGIVEN*. All caps. Alex was always curious what offence inspired it. Or if carving that heavy word helped to unload a burden. He was going to ask his party their thoughts on the mysterious injustice, but on a morning like this he didn't want to populate their heads with such misery. He wished he could drag with the sole of his Blundstone all of its letters across every other plank. Spread it out over the trail and everyone could help bear its load.

The rainforest's thick canopy moderated the sun into select shafts of slant, penetrative light. He wondered how often a cougar or bear used this same walkway. Probably very often. Maybe nightly. He occasionally looked behind them, touched his pants to confirm his pocket knife.

Sulphurous air, sounds of rushing water, sights of rising steam. Steve and Russell up ahead paused on the short boardwalk bridge to watch the smoking creek fall to the first pool, patient water melting over the lip. Steam lingering above the small waterfall that had carved out a narrow channel between tall rock faces. Cascading pools eventually draining into the ocean. Dark green trees and grey rock. Alex said, "Probably just somebody painted this." Alex had once visited Japan, a country where hot springs, *onsens*, ran deep in their culture. He liked knowing that people living on opposite sides of the world, speaking different languages, valued the same things. People not speaking the same language, speaking the same language. Psychic cleansing and spiritual renewal through rocks and water. Just rocks and water.

Alex hadn't smelled this sulphury odour for some time. His crew walked on ahead the short remaining distance. Memories are not always stored in the mind. You encounter them in movement, in sound, in fragrance. The scalding past itself occasionally bubbles up to the surface like natural hot springs. You keep busy and burn through days only to find the past keeps in muscle, that it's stored in fat. The last time he was here was with a woman he loved tremendously. The smell recalled her smile recalled her goodness recalled his loss. If even fragrance will cue the past there may be no phenomena too slight, no object so inert, that the past will not make of it a place for it to dwell. You move through a world armed with hidden triggers. Sometimes it seemed like his heart was sovereign, that it didn't respect time and wouldn't listen to reason. Sometimes part of himself respected it for that.

They changed into bathing suits in the wooden shelter and walked barefoot down the short path. Alina said, "I love this place." They all soaked in the first pool, the hottest, closest to the falls. Heavy water pounding just beside them. Then like a piece of loosened moss Steve slipped down to the next lower pool, and the group followed. Each pool successively milder. At the lowest pool they left to scrabble over the rocks for a cold dip in the salty lagoon. Then chilled bodies leisurely retraced their descent to warm back up. Alex looked straight up the sheer rock face and saw a face looking down at him. Then a second face, white and black fur, palest blue eyes. A couple res dogs eyeing the bathers. Maybe husky-wolf crosses. He watched one jauntily cross the little bridge and its back and shoulders looked very strong.

The waterfall was so hot that most people didn't stand under it. For those that could, you get the heavy water hot and pounding on your upper back like water mallets tenderizing your meat. The hot water falling on Alina. Her hair was wet and she was doing something with it. Her raised arms lifting her chest. The water falling on her. Alex was thinking that a woman looking like her, wearing what she was wearing, that if she just stood a while, had there not been a waterfall, eventually you might just see the rocks start to fissure, see a trickle in the bedrock. A woman pretty enough to make stone cry.

When it came to the potential for romance, Alex evaluated women by their face and body. He figured it was one of his many character flaws. It was something he tried to get past but so far couldn't get past, nor did he have any idea how to. Maybe you can ask yourself to see something different. The image of the rabbit-duck, two faces or a vase, an old woman with the big nose or a young woman with the jaw line. These perspectival shifts. Then again, see how far you get trying to convince yourself blue cheese or cilantro is tasty because someone told you so. Maybe you like what you like and it's not open to rationalization or Gestaltic shifts. Or maybe it won't be long until one can neurologically engineer their preferences. Checkmark the empty square of the desired attribute box and hand the iPad back to the brain attendant and stick your head in the machine and come out purified. He wondered if supposing he flipped that switch how it would affect the rest of his world. Marvel at a lingcod and all things become beautiful? Or would it take beauty off its pedestal and henceforth one would be unmoved by a sunset, a song, a work of art? Would these hot springs then evoke as much feeling as a traffic intersection? Is one allowed their subjective tastes without being called shallow? Maybe I'm genetically pre-disposed to fit female forms and symmetrical faces. There must be an adaptive advantage as to why beauty attracts. As a sign of health? He genuinely was not sure. For Alex, intelligence and humour and kindness are the long-term relationship's perfect tits. So he wasn't sure why initially he got hung up on a pretty face. Probably just shallow, he thought. My prejudice is my poverty.

This specimen under the waterfall. He liked looking at her. Look at her. Even still, if they stayed together long enough no doubt his sex drive would drop off a cliff. Go from wanting it twice daily to once weekly. He wouldn't become blind to her attractiveness though, he'd still appreciate looking at her.

Alina's eyes were closed or mostly closed and she turned and faced away from him. Long dark hair wet down her back. Slim waist. Peach being rinsed in the water. He could see the line where the back of her thigh met her ass. Get the most talented origamists together in a room they couldn't make a better crease. Just, goddamn, is the thing. It's not even fair. Alina under the water again doing something with her long hair wet down her back. She turned. Up on Industrial Way was Tofino Fitness and he knew she was a regular. Her body like a weapon, and not exactly concealed carry. She took pride in it, a little flaunt to it. Why shouldn't she? he thought. What was her body if not a display of discipline and effort and care and health. Aren't those things their own type of beauty? Water down her chest and he wasn't sure who sized her for that bikini. Or does hot water shrink? Though no Savannah cats in Hot Springs Cove her leopard print bikini didn't look so out of place and she could have passed for some spotted variety of the native puma. That analogy in his head almost made him laugh.

Alex wondered if Steve and Russell were sneaking peaks but he didn't want to look at them or it would look like he was monitoring. And if they were, and they saw him catch them, that would be awkward.

Alex had a theory that women who got their breasts done were trying to fill an inadequacy they felt imposed on them by society. He didn't have a theory that a girl who was bullied for her weight and ethnicity, tormented and ostracized by schoolmates for years, exacerbated by trouble at home, had developed a depression and decade-long eating disorder, who years later through hard work and effortful therapy finally arrived at an enduring state of compassion *for* and acceptance *of* herself, who through disciplined exercise and nutrition arrived at new levels of mental health and physical energy, yet who every time she looked in the mirror saw misshapen breasts her former cycles of anorexia and binge eating continuously tightened and relaxed like yoyos, leaving them permanently lop-sided and sagging from the weight of childhood trauma. Who even with all her efforts still continued to see, naked in the mirror, those hurtful schooldays. Alina who didn't ask anyone's approval to gift herself breast augmentation. But he had no theory on all that. His poverty.

She facing him, her eyes closed. He could hear the heavy water landing flatly to her shoulders and so she could hear nothing else. The waters aren't steaming they're fuming from this smoke show, he thought. In the safety of his forty-year-old skull he laughed at the enduring immaturity of his adolescent humour and was smiling when she opened her eyes slowly and they opened in a squint landing directly on Alex, like she knew he was there, like she knew what she was doing. Them bathing in hot water and ancient stones but she like her nature knew an older ritual. She smiled small and wet. She raised him a middle finger.

Alex shook his head, cleared his throat and grinned and shook his head and looked away as if that was easy.

He asked if they were all ready to start heading back and they all said no and he said yeah me too but we probably should. He turned in survey to see if there were any nymphs on the ledge, if a surfaced mermaid was sunning by the lagoon, herd of unicorn grazing the tufts of grass growing between the rocks. There's a reason this place gets so crowded and he'd avoid it during peak season. He turned for a last look, the waterfall, the rocks, the leopard-print babe, the cascading pools, the two large Americans soaking in a hot puddle where Steve leaned and put his hand on Russell's shoulder and kissed him. He didn't want to stare so he turned his head, but he did angle his eyes because it was a rare and strange sight to see overweight American men pecking by a waterfall. Not like a traffic accident, though neither for him like a rainbow. His eyes did register something a little sweet there. Then he recalled the boat: the celery sticks and dip. Hadn't seen that before between two men on a fishing boat. He tried to recall not if he had said anything stupid but just how much. He was smiling when he turned and looked at Alina climbing up over the rocks and said to her did you see that?

"You seriously didn't know?"

He figured that was about right.

Steve and Russell were leaving the top pool and Alex and Alina up in the open change shelter had their jeans on and she with her bikini top on and Alex pulled her to him and their cool bellies came together, not quick enough to slap but a bit of stick to the skin. He kissed her just small and she said I'm cold.

The rainforest's sunlight shafts now steeper. The crew flushed and buzzing walked the narrow boardwalk. Song sparrows and thrushes and robins, those resonant calls deeper in the forest sounding like echoes. Halfway back they met the first tour group. Exchanges of good mornings, people tuned into the same pleasant frequency of an old forest's beauty. Alex wondered if he detected in just one or two of their faces the most minor bit of disdain in not having been the first to soak. Humans, like all primates, are highly attuned to even the most subtle facial expressions. If maybe their tour guide, knowing he was the first commercial boat to leave the harbour, had told them they would be first ones in. Alex also wondered if sensing that disappointment in a passing glance was not possible and so he was really only seeing an aspect of his own self, his projected version of the world reflecting off those oncoming faces. He wondered if what he thought he saw said more about him than them. And given he had been aloof to a homosexual romance taking place in his immediate vicinity, for two boat trips over two years, the acuity of his social perception might fairly be called into question.

Another oncoming group. Both parties filed into two tight lines. Steve and Russell ahead of Alina, Alex in caboose. One woman at the end of the pack seemed less focused on the oncoming group than the old bearded trees smoking wisely in the sun. The phone in her hand must be for pictures as there is no cell service here. She strayed a half-step too sideways and Alina moved over even closer to the boardwalk's edge but the lady still bumped into her then stepped on Alina's toes.

"Oh I'm so sorry." Inflection of a genuine apology and who wouldn't be distracted by this enchanted forest. She stepped back to her side of the shared boardwalk. So pry up that sad plank ahead and swap it in here for the blank one underfoot, buff its *UN* away and leave only the word *FORGIVEN*.

Alina just looked at her. The lady put her phone away. Then she walked on with her group while Alina watched after her. Alina turned back to the direction of their boat, said under her breath, "Fucking tourists."

After a cleansing soak those words most jarring to Alex's ears. Like it would be hard to know how they even found their way here in the otherwise graceful morning. Whether Alina's words repelled him, or the voice of the apology pulled him, his head did turn. Alex for a moment watching her walk away. Blonde hair trailing a tour group. He could feel her steps vibrating over the boardwalk. He wondered, in this connected world, if such vibrations ever end, or just reverberate. And so a splash, however light, is never wholly contained to its pond. The wave from a tiniest dropped pebble, from even a fallen feather on a still pool, light as a batting eye, light as exhalation, wakes your rippled life. He watched her walk away.

He turned back ahead while taking a step but Alina yet hadn't, she had been watching him watch the toe-stepper. Alex inadvertently put his right Blundstone heavily onto her ankle.

She said Jesus Christ for her own suffering. She looked at him, with the same look she'd given that tourist, given Valerie.

Two groups diverged in a misty woods and in that same moment ten thousand love stories went unwritten.

XIII

A fter the boat ride back from the hot springs Valerie walked up the hill from Fourth Street dock and put her bag in her car and walked down Main Street. She passed the small Anchor Park Lookout. She looked up at the large totem pole. A few people were watching the harbour. She hadn't recognized Trent standing off to the side of the small park, not looking like he was looking her way. He had watched her boat depart and watched it dock. They'd been broken up for longer than it took to grow a beard. She'd never seen him in a hat. He wore different clothes. He hadn't worn sunglasses around her, unsurprising given they connected in a grey Vancouver winter.

Valerie in this early afternoon with the lingering and soothing effects of the springs. She could still smell sulphur. Funny, she thought, if you knew it was rotten eggs you'd be repulsed. But when the fragrance is from a natural hot springs you like it. Does it always come down to the story we tell ourselves?

She was hungry and felt like she'd earned a good meal but strolled leisurely. She stopped at a pretty bench with a view and watched the fishing boats. The docks with fishermen in green rubber overalls and orange rubber gloves carrying totes and stacking crab pots. A sailboat with furrowed sails slowly cruising on motor, pulling a tender. Small islands heavily treed. She wondered if the one she was looking at was Tibbs Island.

She had read about it. Fred Tibbs in 1912 building a three story castle with towers and battlements and a piano and gramophone and cutting down all the trees except for one, a hundred foot spruce on which he built scaffolding and would climb every morning to serenade with his cornet the town, Tofino, just across the water. One day he rowed out to a navigation buoy but while servicing its light his skiff floated away. He tried to swim for it but died from exhaustion, becoming one more ghost in the sound.

The big eagle's nest at Deadman Islets was too far to see and the eagle sitting in the top of the hemlock in the yard of the small church behind her, just above Trent, was close but too high to see. She noticed she hadn't thought about work most of the day. A morning in nature was all it took to dam the stream of preoccupations into a settling pool starting to clarify.

She walked past an idling car without anyone in it. She listened to the motor but louder still she heard her own judgmentalism. But supposing that just one out of one hundred cars were idling because a man had raced off to his pregnant wife. Would that entail my restrained disdain of its pollution? This like the other day at lunch with poor service. It took a while for the server to greet her and bring a menu, no eye contact, no smile or engagement and slow on drinks and the bill. She wondered if there wasn't a chance his dog just died or if that day his lover had been diagnosed. How often would that have to be the case for me not to reduce the gratuity? To in fact be more kind. One in one hundred? Higher, no? It wasn't even about kindness per se, it was about probability and impact. But she did wonder to what extent such charitable interpretations warp one's reality. Nevertheless, when some important things can not be proved true or false, you have to ask yourself: what world will you believe in? Create the world before which you will kneel. So said her favourite misogynist.

She stopped outside the window of an artisanal goods shop. Crafts, coastal paintings, handmade pottery. She always had an eye open for the perfect coffee mug. Her morning coffee required choosing that day's particular mug. She walked on, up then down streets. A boutique shop. She browsed coastal prints, earrings, clothes. Looked at a handbag. She had been keeping her eye open for one and had passed on Fendis on Guccis on Pradas. This one hand-cut from premium top-grain leather with natural brass hardware. She tested the magnetic closure. She flipped it upside down and looked at the seams. Righted it. Looked inside and drew her finger along the cuts, the stitches. Attention to detail. Hung it over a shoulder. Turned to the mirror. Turned in the mirror. Subtle yet elegant. She looked at the tag. A price approaching luxury without fully crossing an indulgent line. She smelled it, the leather. Valerie not one for proverbs but a fragrance cued a quote from her dad. "Price is forgotten long after the quality is remembered." Her dad with his same leather wallet for thirty years, sitting on it for thirty years, and he'd told her that about thirty times. She texted him now. *Tell me again how much you hate leather. You're on your third wallet this year you said?* She put her phone in the handbag and she bought the handbag.

She turned up First Street and walked past the Maquinna Bar and Hotel, an establishment affectionately nicknamed *The Dirty Maq*. Perhaps for its history of romances both short and long but mostly short. She passed Co-op Hardware and Co-op Grocery and came to Campbell Street, the town's busiest intersection. No traffic light. One stopped car, its hybrid motor now restarted. She crossed and passed the post office and walking in sweet fragrance wondered if it was coming from the blue hydrangeas ahead and smelled a flower that though beautiful was neither sugary nor effuse and looking across the street she knew Common Loaf Bakery had cinnamon buns. A Japanese maple with tiny sharp-edged arterial-red leaves grew just in front of its open door from where she heard music, "High tide or low tide, I'll be by your side." Valerie knew but little Shakespeare, some Angelou, stray passages of Yeats, Keats, and Dickenson, but on a line-by-line basis she'd bet Marley could hold his own.

She crossed Neill Street and how many hospitals in the world have such a view, and could looking out at stunning water expedite recovery? She thought it probably could. A man leaning on the railing smoking and they exchanged hellos. The scent of smoke recalling her last. She crossed the street and that memory followed her as if invited to lunch. A few years back she had seen this restaurant on *Dragon's Den*. SoBo Restaurant's tiny patio displaying various-sized flowering planters. Driftwood picnic tables and an unlit fireplace with a tinder teepee, as if it, like much of life, was just waiting for a spark. She opened the glass door where just inside hung a large carving of a ceremonial mask. The host seated her window-side. She ordered a fresh key-lime margarita and when that arrived she ordered a mushroom tofu-pocket, three polenta fries, and one killer fish taco. She wanted the halibut ceviche and the corn bread and smoked salmon chowder and only one dozen other things too. But in holding off she knew one day she would have to come back. Strategic restraint.

Like a prohibited curl of smoke might suspend in this establishment's calm air, a cigarette memory lingered in her mind. They lay together that night and the feelings almost felt enough. There was something to Trent. Something just below the surface. She could sense it but not name it, not quite understand it. And they did have a connection, it's not like there wasn't one. Their bodies got along. That's something. Who really connects on every level? She had felt a bit of something. She wanted to feel more. She thought she almost did. Or maybe in those moments there was a type of love? A wordless love. A hot dark physical love. A glass-breaking wine-spilling kind of love. Categories are made up and things come in different shapes and sizes and maybe singular connections can still be profound ones.

Tell yourself that.

That evening, the bottle empty on the end table, them sitting on her couch, opposite ends. Not saying much. The rain outside. She blew a narrow stream of smoke, not straight at him. But close. To provoke his sex. Not rude, playful. And she could almost tell him she felt something because for a part of her it might have been true. She was about to speak but he took the cigarette and dropped it in the bottle, a wisp of rising smoke, a hiss in the bottle's remnant ring coloured like the dying blood of their shallow relationship. Then he fucked her. Wasn't that what you wanted?

Valerie looking out the window to the liquor store across the street. A sip of sour margarita and a lick of salted rim. The server set down two small plates and one basket lined with a crinkly checkered liner. The taco spilling a kiwi cube. She took a live picture which caught a tumbling blueberry. Sent it to Stacy: *Fruit in a fish taco it's officially vacation.* *taco emoji* *How is Mom? Wish you were here!*

Trent was quiet but not simple. More time wasn't really peeling back his layers because someone wrapped the skin of that onion so tight. But how does one even pull the curtains back on another when it seems a life's work to draw them open on yourself? When one's own thoughts arrive unwilled, born from some mysterious inner womb. She hadn't seen him engage with friends, hadn't met his family. She blamed herself for the misconnection. But that's not why she broke up with him. And it didn't have anything to do with his scars. Seeing his scars humanized her own. Her skin scarce of blemish but her body not without wounds. The reason she broke up with him: she just wasn't that into him. Her own mind was active and craved being engaged. His quiet nature bored her. She felt very bad using that word and would never say that to him. She thought maybe it was one of the absolute worst words you could call someone. She told him honestly that they were different people, that she wanted to feel more with him than she did. She was sorry. She looked sadder than he did, whatever he felt on the inside.

A couple of her friends put a lot of stock in the Five Love Languages. Valerie thought they were arbitrary and nonsensically reductionist and that really they were not discrete categories. "When I think about it, they really don't make sense." She said that while walking False Creek Loop with Stacy. "One of the languages is *Words of Affirmation*. Isn't that a type of gift? And aren't certain physical touches, like giving your partner a massage, a *gift* and an *act of service* and *quality time?* They all blend together. How is *Quality Time* its own language? Isn't quality time the *very basis* of all relationships—just spending quality time together? Isn't that like ground zero and the other languages are definitionally also that one? Stacy, who's buying this stuff?"

But in knowing those categories were meaningful to others, she tried to fit them like lenses before her eyes, see how others saw the world. She wondered if Trent's language was touch because she hadn't seen anyone react to it the same way. Is it genetics or upbringing that causes one language to be more communicative? *Nurture* didn't feel like the appropriate word to best describe who or what raised him. She asked him his thoughts. That went nowhere.

Not the night of the cigarette smoke, another night. Not the couch, the bed. The sheet loose over their naked waists. She was looking at the marks on his belly. She hadn't asked and wouldn't ask but then why were her silent eyes so softly inquisitive that she turned up to him. His bare belly. She reached her hand very slowly towards them. Her hand not halfway there and underneath its travel his pectoral muscles flexed and his abs got defined and his whole body tightened like his muscles might rip his skin apart. Like armour. But a battle being fought subsurface. His face looked strained and she couldn't see that his lower back hollowed enough a mouse could run that arch. Her fingers moved lower and she almost stopped, concerned each pregnant little packet of abdominal muscle might pop. His rapid breaths shallowing. Normally he wasn't slow to be physical. But besides his chest, he didn't move, didn't stop her and she expected he might and that he hadn't did not seem permission. She almost stopped. She still thinly glistening from their sex but his sweat now from another exertion. Little beads pooling in his chest's grooves, salt water in the channels like Florence. As if his body was trying to sweat out an acid. Her hand now directly above those marks on his belly and he reacting to her presence like her divining hand about to perform an exorcism, as if the maker of the markings lived inside him, whether originating there or after the act, had gone on to dwell, and her hand might just draw out that evil. Those ugly marks seeming animate, angry red circles like bore holes from mean worms, hot nails driven into his guts hiding smoking shanks, come to the surface where she'd collect them in her hand then cast them out the window: begone.

She lowered her hand and both of them seemed unsure about that. His belly moving with his fast breaths. She had never touched with such delicate deliberateness. She didn't put her fingers on a scar, just near one. How with an unfamiliar dog you never put your hand directly on its head. Just near those little angry circles. He breathed heavier. If she lightened her touch any more her fingers would be floating. He didn't sound so good and she figured she was making it worse so she took her hand away from his pockmarked belly and brought it to the side of his face and his face did not relax. Their heads lay together while one of them was being attacked.

She said quietly in the confidence of the bedroom, "Tell me what to do."

He didn't answer.

She didn't know what to say. She said: "I'm here." And could it even be possible to say anything truer or simpler, while of greater worth? "I'm here." Sounding like a claim concerning her own ontology, but said for the benefit of another. As if humblest words spoken truly were an answer to any doubt, any skeptic, she declaring her existence in his world, even in its darkness she couldn't see and with luck would never know.

She waited. She moved lower down. Her lips on his chest. Now trying to ease him without words. Kisses because lips touch lighter than fingers. She didn't ask she offered. A presence expectationless, open, receptive to all or anything or nothing. She just gave him that. She didn't say it would be okay. She didn't say she would always be there. She must have respected him enough to keep their intimacy free from the indignity of false promises. She just said, "I'm here."

She kissed above the scars. Lines get blurred and maybe in this moment more of a caregiver than a lover. But all true lovers are caregivers. His breaths if once scared now sounded angry, as if by taking in all the room's oxygen he might ready a larger defense. The sheet twisting in his hands. Her lips now the tiptoes of some fool thinking she could step around landmines. Her lips coming away slightly moistened. They weren't helping. She lay her cheek on his belly, one ear to the room, one to him. Trying to listen to what lies beneath, whatever side it might come from. For what needed to come out. But who's to say if what he needed was hers to give, if it was even his to let go. Who knows how these things work. His breaths just raised her head like a boat in a storm. She wasn't trying to command the waves.

Trying to let him know that if he had room for her, she was right now with him in his raft. Unsure if she got that across.

Then under her cheek she thought she felt one stomach muscle relaxing. Like the reverse of a baby kick. Like feeling something give up the fight. She both heard and felt his breath find depth.

So touch is your language.

If only it was hers.

Her body had spoken a language of compassion. To him it sounded like something else. His mistake could be forgiven, it was something he had never known. That was the night he told her about the scars. She listened and wiped her eyes and they lay in the dark. Days to come she knew he liked her a lot. She wished that was enough for her to love him back. She felt very bad.

Dealing with her rejection he became pressuring.

"Not tonight, sorry."

Became concerning.

"Please stop calling me."

Became distressing.

"Go home Trent. I'm sorry. But you need to move on."

The server asked Valerie if she was alright.

XIV

At twelve Trent was fostered by a childless, middle-aged couple. Shirley and Brent paid for an evaluation by a child psychiatrist. They wanted to understand how to better connect with him given his past, what words, actions, environments might trigger him. If what they had seen was normal child behaviour. They knew that the legal system allowed foster parents to adopt.

Shirley told the psychiatrist how last week she was sitting with him in the family room. She dumped the colourful pail of Lego onto the carpet then kneeled down beside him. Trent stared at the blocks. She like a blackjack dealer spread them out, the colourful pieces clinking on the grey shag carpet. She connected some, picked up a green rectangular block and put it in his hand and told him not to eat it or he'd ruin his appetite for cookies. He might have been too old for Lego and certainly for that piece of wisdom so it was mostly for the joke. She got up, touching his shoulder, and went to the kitchen.

"I watched him set down the block but he didn't touch any others." She had set down the electric beaters and started scooping chocolate-chip-studded dough from the yellow bowl, then dished it off with two spoons to the Pam-sprayed pan. "By the time I put the cookies in the oven he hadn't touched any blocks, he just sat there looking at them. I went over to put the Lego away and swap it for something else. I said we could kick the soccer ball around in the backyard while the cookies are cooling. I was gathering up the pieces and he grabbed my wrist." To the doctor's concern Shirley said not all that hard. "So I left the Lego out. The next day the same thing happened, he didn't play with it but he didn't want anything else, either. I showed him the Velcro dart board. The next day he built a small house that matched the picture on the Lego pail. Not matched, it *was* the house. The same colours, same size, same little Lego man standing outside." She turned to Brent. Then back to the psychiatrist. "What do you think of that?"

She had a pad and pen on her desk and hadn't written anything. "The average kid does peculiar things. Normal is not such a useful concept and in general I hesitate to read too much into any single event." She said for this child you should treat him like all children should be treated. "Things you're already doing. Be kind and patient. Set a good example. Make him feel safe and eventually he'll open up. Be open to learning his personality. Show him that you're two people he can trust—earn his trust. It might be slow to come given his past, but it'll come. They want that because we all want that, really. In the end, he's mostly going to be who he is. Studies show that the influence of parents is actually rather limited. Most parents with one child don't believe that. Most parents with two children believe that. Across all the parenting books there's a scandalous absence of how much genetics and random variation influence child behaviour." She waved a hand dismissively, as if cutting herself short. "Be supportive and nurturing of who he's finding himself to be in the world that does exist within his head, as well outside his home. But do keep track of anything you feel is noteworthy and we'll revisit." She set down the pen and scrolled the screen of her laptop. She said that for his age he scored very high in abstract reasoning and fluid intelligence, not the highest she'd ever seen but uncommonly high, especially for someone with his upbringing and history of school delinquency. "He scored above average in mechanical abilities." She scrolled. "He scored within one standard deviation of the other psychometrics. Except for verbal."

Brent said, "And should we be concerned about that? He hardly speaks."

On the drive there Shirley said, "I bet we come away with medication. And I don't want that for him. This boy's special. I know he is, in his own way." She looked at Brent. "I just know."

The doctor continued, "I'd say no, not yet. Absence of evidence is not evidence of absence. An abnormal trait does not an abnormal child make. Children develop at different rates so just give him some time. If we see his behaviour keeping him from finding his way, from finding his place in the world, or if we see him unhappy or unsafe or making others unsafe, we'll reassess. For now, let him open up on his own. Be curious without pressure. Sometimes, for certain this time," she was still scrolling Trent's evaluation, "still waters do run deep."

In the months that followed he didn't speak much more but he didn't need so many words to show his growing bond to Shirley. He set Brent's clothes on fire in the backyard. Brent came home from work and said hi to Shirley wearing her cute polka-dot gardening gloves with her polka-dot sun visor using the red-handled garden shears that he himself was not allowed to use, trimming her snap peas in the planter box beside the front door. She told him not to touch the lemon layer cake it's for dessert and he said you're not being fair at all. You couldn't see the smoke from the front yard. He sat down in a kitchen chair and it smelled like lemon. He drank a Snapple. He saw the smoke and slid the patio-door open and walked out to find a two-thousand-dollar pile of smoldering clothing in the round cinder-block fire pit beside the bird bath. His only two suits.

His three belts on top of the pile like snakes so charred they no longer writhed.

Shirley said oh my goodness and took off her gloves and went to go talk to him and Brent said no, that he and I also need a relationship. She was hesitant. He was firm.

Up the stairs he knocked on the Metallica poster as if he was thumping its bass drum. No answer, no sounds. He knocked again, this time not as a request as fair warning then opened the door. The boy sitting on the bed, his hands on his knees. He wasn't looking at him. Brent looked around the room. Clean, organized. He sat down beside him. The boy already big for his age, big hands. Brent took a second. The boy's eyes were on the floor. "Shirley feels the same way about pinstripe." Trent didn't smile and he didn't expect him to. "I'm not mad. Really. But you can't do that." He opened his hand and he didn't ask the boy for it and the boy reached in his pocket then placed the blue Bic lighter in his palm. That was the only lighter they had and he put it and the matches in a high cupboard above the fridge.

The next two months passed without incident. Two months later it's three a.m. Brent wakes hearing something and he's a pretty deep sleeper so he heard something. He looks to his dresser for the clock's indigo lighting then wonders if the power's out. He hears Shirley breathing beside him. He gives his eyes a moment and coalescing out of the dark like an image on a Polaroid is someone standing beside the bed. Brent's terrified pupils might never have been more saucered trying to extract the faintest illumination and see into the dark what he hoped isn't real. So when the flint wheel sparked it was shockingly bright. The boy's blank face flashing once from the lighter's sparks, and it will be that face Brent will remember long after the boy has been returned. Not the menace in it, the absence of emotion. Because even malevolence seems more recognizable than that cold vacancy.

His first reaction is to underreact, he just lies there in sheer terror but his hammering heart and body flushing with heat deny him the fantasy that this is a nightmare. His next reaction Shirley will later call an overreaction. He rises up in bed and swipes hard towards where the lighter just sparked and he contacts a hand and hears the lighter hit the dresser and Shirley turns on her lamp to Brent yelling at the boy what the hell's wrong with you. The unreactive boy.

She didn't know what happened but she went to him and had she known what happened she'd have gone to him. Brent was looking at him. The boy returning that stare, though the boy nearly looking through him. Shirley held Trent. Brent still in shock, restraining his rage. He looked at Shirley. He looked away. Saw the lighter on the floor wasn't blue.

The next day he came home early from work while the boy was at school and they talked but it wasn't much of a discussion. Brent felt bad. For everyone, but mostly for Shirley. She said don't say return, he's not a jacket that didn't fit. Brent said you can't put all the sharp things in a cupboard. "It's not his fault, but I trust him as much as a beaten Rottweiler. I'm sorry. We said from the start this was a trial not a commitment." She cried. She said he is not beyond saving. He said it's not your fault either. This all will strain them in years to come.

Trent would be taken into another foster home until he was convicted under the Youth Criminal Justice Act for theft over $5000. He stole a Ford Taurus. Repeatedly the officer questioned him but he wouldn't say where he wanted to go. At fourteen Trent was sent to a Youth Custody Centre in Burnaby, British Columbia. Eight months into his stay he left the facility. Trent's case-management officer didn't decline the requested leave because Trent didn't ask. Juvie is minimum security, control through staffing rather than architecture. It's not Alcatraz, and we broke out of that, we did.

Trent had never shot a gun before. A boy one year younger and half his size told him where he could find one. "In the shed. It's in a steel box on the top shelf." Trent asked how the boy knew that. "Because it's my old man." The boy said he'd tell the address but first Trent had to help him with another boy that had been picking on him. In the dorm that night nobody came to the first call for help and all the next calls were muffled by a pillow. In the morning that bruised kid was smart enough to not report it and blue body welts are quieter than black eyes. Two days later Trent left the custody centre with no more money than a couple or three city bus tickets worth. The boy had shown him on a city map in the small classroom where to go. Said the shed would be unlocked.

Trent midday walked to Richmond and snuck into the backyard. The shed had a padlock but its hasp unsecured. Enough window lighting through the silty panes that he didn't look for a switch. Two of the walls had rows of shelves and he stepped carefully around the clutter. Then true to the boy's words, a metal box on a top shelf just taller than his own height next to a dusty spool of twine and an old bag of peat moss. He pulled the box off the shelf and it was not so dusty. It was locked. It felt rather light but he didn't know how much a pistol weighed. The lid had a thin lip like a slim metallic overbite and he looked around and took up a garden spade and set its cutting edge to it but the spade was big and awkward and kept slipping. From a tool chest he found a large slotted screwdriver and a hammer, but then put the hammer back. With one foot on the box and using the screwdriver he pried up a corner of the lid but the lock wouldn't give way so he took up the spade and put the long wooden handle into the pried-up corner. He secured the box under what might have been an iron chassis missing its motor block and positioned a car battery as fulcrum then levered and the lock's latch bent soundlessly until the lid opened making a Coke-bottle pop.

He picked up the box. Opening the lid, its tight hinges croaked like a toad. A sound not so out of place in this musty shed. The box wasn't empty. It wasn't armed. He withdrew an old Playgirl magazine. A once glossy porno, winter-themed ski-hill edition. Mostly moustached men on the slopes with dicks soft, some hard. Some of them holding skis. Looked old, or rather dated, from the font, the fashion. He set the skin mag down and tilted the box like a drunk might tilt a bottle he knows is empty anyways. A single .22 cartridge rolled to the corner. He picked it up rather daintily between two fingers. Quite small, unassuming, like you'd never know by looking at it that the .22 cartridge has killed scores of people, even though you'd mostly elect it as a squirrel gun.

Trent in the early afternoon circled the block. At the fourth house he didn't see a security company sign or window stickers and no cars were parked out front. In the backyard he took off his jean jacket and held it up against the window of a back-door then tapped at it with a red garden brick. He covered his hand with the jacket and removed shards from the sash, like a glass-eating jeaned puppet, and slipped his hand through and unlocked the deadbolt. In the kitchen he withdrew from the knife block a large chef knife, but then slid it back and took a paring knife. A black backpack hanging off a chair he emptied of its sweater, which he will later regret. By the phone he found forty-five dollars and a small dish of loonies and toonies and quarters. He heard a soft cry. He turned. Where the living room met the kitchen called a kitten in a cage. He kneeled. It mewed. He watched it. It raised a paw against the metal mesh door. It cried again. He set a finger up against the mesh, its little rubbery paw pad touching his fingerpad.

He shouldered the backpack and opened the fridge and took an apple juice-box. From a jar on the counter he grabbed three cookies and put them in his pack and a fourth he held and as he walked towards the door the kitten walked directly in his way and he put the cookie between his teeth and kneeled and pet the cat.

The first motorcycle shop he called didn't recognize the name Trent had provided. He flipped a yellow page in the small phone booth then made another inquiry, looking for a custom fabricator of fairings and exhausts and gas tanks. Again he provided a last name which was his own. The guy said they rarely use him anymore. "Just for special orders and they have to be shipped in. He moved somewheres. But hold on a minute." Trent could hear papers shuffling. "Winnipeg." Trent left with a phone number and business name. Harrington Motor Sports. Winnipeg, Manitoba.

Late on a cold November day with a black pull-over hoodie under his jean jacket and a backpack over one shoulder and a paring knife tucked under his sleeve, Trent left Vancouver on an eastward bus. He deboarded at the Safeway drop-off where the Trans Canada Highway splits at Hope, B.C. He walked from there to the Petro Canada alongside the highway. The sun sets early in the late Canadian fall and when a passing car no longer spotlit his raised thumb he'd ball that thumb up and return a cold fist to his pocket. Two hours later a trucker fueling his semi said to Trent by law he wasn't supposed to. "Then there's the company policy against it. So that's strike two, bud." He was looking at Trent's jean jacket, a strong material but utter shit for insulation, the hoodie's drawstrings tied at the collar. "But the way the company's cutting back I expect the Christmas bonus to be a letter sayin' thank you for your twenty-eight years of service, when it's actually been thirty, and my name spelled wrong, and it's going to be my thumb in the air and

I'd appreciate myself in your shoes giving me a lift." The man was looking at Trent's tattered Reebok's with deflated pumps. "I don't expect the severance package to be any warmer than this friggin' weather. Cold, eh?" The diesel pump clunked off and he withdrew the dripping nozzle and screwed on the cap. "Heading east won't warm things up any, but if you're going anywhere between here and Halifax, you're welcome to climb up in. Just don't tell HR. I'm Les."

Trent shook his hand.

"Winterpeg, eh? Nice to meet you, Toby. Only rule: when I pee you pee." The hydraulic brakes hissed and Les shifted to first and they left Hope and rolled onto Highway Five, shortly passing through Othello, heading east towards revenge, Manitoba. Taped to the dash between the air vents were two girls in bathing suits. Les said, "Not twins but hard to tell? My girls." He pointed. "Seven, Jamie." He pointed. "Six, Jessica."

Eighteen wheels rolling north along the edge of the Western Cordillera, skirting the southeastern heel of the Coast Mountains, driving on down into British Columbia's interior plain. Trent slow to answer said he was heading to a family reunion, he seemed reluctant to divulge further details, or as if he himself was short on them.

Whether it was a half truth Les didn't feel like it was a whole one, and that was alright. If the boy was being untruthful that's forgivable in a world that raised people on lies. You don't hold a boy accountable for that. Les gestured behind him. "A load of farmed fish for Toronto. Then pick up a load in Toronto for Halifax and it could be anything. Car parts, dairy, maple syrup. Sometimes I don't even look 'cause they just load me up at the depot. Then pick up a load from the East and strangely that will also likely be fish. Scallop. Crab. Crab's a fish." He said that somewhere between a statement and a question but his passenger didn't help clear that up.

By Merritt, Les gave up on conversation. He talked at him until they hit Kamloops. It was quiet as they drove through Chase. Well before the ascent into the Rockies he just settled into the drive and that was alright. The CBC crackled then faded then fuzzed out in the gap's of civilization. He turned down the static to a volume just below the sounds of the highway they rode so he'd hear when the voices picked back up.

Night fell and driving through the night was its own thing. The quiet highway drone and the big headlights and the rocks and the trees passing by. Night is a country unto itself. Big high warm semi-trailer truck powering up the hills. Les looked over at him. His hood up, eyes closed, arms folded across his chest. Even quiet human presence drastically changes the cab and he was fine with adding to his cargo a boy who he would deliver to where he needed to go. He who lays mere bricks must always be envisioning cathedrals. He'd heard that once on a CBC program. This long-haul trucker had his own creed. He who shuttles loads...

Trent woke looking alarmed to what sounded like machine-gun fire as Les downshifted on their descent out of the Rockies. The sun returns on this cross-country cruise, daybreak over the Western Alberta Plains. Les said, "G'morning. Sorry about the Jake brake. Welcome to the prairies." Les watched him, figured it was the boy's first time seeing it. "If anyone steals your bag you just let them get a head start simply to make it more interesting. Flat as an old Coke in the sun. Okay, let's bring you up to speed. You slept through Mickie D's and it's probably more warm chocolate than hot and your Sausage McMuffin barely made it through Banff, Toby." He pointed to a Styrofoam cup, then lifted a brown bag with golden arches and set it closer. "I suspect you're wondering about the empty wrappers. Banff wasn't so kind to one of your hashbrowns. The other we lost back at Dead Man's Flats." He turned to the road then back. "I feel a little bad. You get through that grease muffin and there's black licorice in the console. You just help yourself, partner."

The rig cruised on level road and they fuelled at Medicine Hat then crossed into Saskatchewan. Big country with wide-ranging weather and though the highway through the Rockies was clear of snow, Moose Jaw here at midday had a dusting like fallen dandruff on the road's shoulder. "We'll make a pit stop at Rosie's. Maybe the best burger across ten provinces. I like a Big Mac but I would not put it on the short-list." He looked to the road then back. "If someone made the case for a Teen Burger being the best burger they would have my ear. I say across ten provinces because we're never contracted for the territories." He pointed left which would be north. "Not sure if the ten includes Labrador. I'm going to be honest, Toby, between us, I don't actually know what it is. Is it a province? Its own province, or like a jurisdiction? Special economic zone maybe? How come you never hear of it? When was the last time Labrador made the news? I'd ask their neighbour, the next one that I meet coming down from the rigs, but generally speaking you don't solicit a Newfie when looking to get somethin' clarified. La-bra-dor." He said it slowly as if the answer lay in its pronunciation. Shook his head. "So you want pickles on your burger or extra pickles?"

The perimeter highway allows through-traffic like transport trucks to circumvent Winnipeg's busy centre. In the busy city centre Les said, "Looks like the 'Peg has more snow than Sasquatchewan." Les asked him where he could drop him off and the boy said just downtown. Les confirming his guess, that he was running not returning, that probably nobody was waiting for him. He took him to the Greyhound Bus Centre, at least that would give him an option or two. He pulled into the bay as if this rig itself was scheduled for an 8:00 p.m. arrival and the concrete enclosure amplified the brake hiss. The dash display had the outside temperature at -8 Celsius. "I hope the city lives up to its license plate." He nodded to an old red Volvo. "Friendly Manitoba. I haven't spent any time here to say otherwise. I'll look for you buddy on my way back from Halifax. Bring you back a lobster if you promise not to talk my ear off next time." He offered his hand and Trent shook it and then looked down at the folded ten-dollar bill he now palmed. "I felt bad about the hashbrowns." Trent thanked him. Trent opened the door and Les said hold up and twisted in his seat. He rifled through a small duffle bag pulling out a red toque saying he had an extra. "If you order something you can stay in McDick's til late."

Trent opened the Yellow Pages. He took a city bus downtown and he did go to a McDonald's and ordered a cheeseburger and a small coke and a couple hours later when she asked him to please leave he ordered another cheeseburger. At midnight the restaurant closed and he started walking to stay warm. Streets thinly covered in snow. He warmed his hands on a big halogen lightbulb spotlighting the parliament and then shaped his hands and looked over his shoulder to see if they cast up a bat. He wandered north and generally the night puts the wind to sleep but Portage and Main here audibly breezy. He walked another few blocks north until firelight down a side street caught his eye. Something on fire down an alley. He had been walking the streets slow but now he walked slower. A few people standing around. In this year of 1997 he approached a burning barrel. As if each of his last hundred steps had walked him into a century prior. The City of Winnipeg in the winter drops them off outside homeless encampments as fire prevention and harm reduction. He walked up cold on colder feet. All three people turned. Two of them greeted him. A stack of wood pallets off to the side and a pile of flattened cardboard boxes. He nodded but his outheld hands were only for the barrel, a paring knife under the sleeve of his left forearm. Against one of the walls an old couch puking stuffing in two places. One person sitting at the end closer to him and at the farther end a young man curled up facing away, his back to the barrel. Beside the couch a faded floral-print armchair and while he looked at the caved and threadbare seat that seat got occupied. Trent looked at her gaunt face's eyes, like you hoped that story went untold. Or if she starts, beg her to lie.

Topics around the barrel varied but weather most prevalent. Observations, predictions. Cited sources ranging from almanac to bones. People joked. A skinny man, a young man, a woman. On the ground a couple stray cushions whose pattern didn't match the furniture. He kicked one towards the other and leaned one against the wall and sat down with his feet outstretched and there was some warmth. Vent holes had been drilled near the bottom and between his feet he watched the freckled fire. Political discussions both federal and local. Sports, one man arguing the merits of the Manitoba Moose and another saying hockey died for him when the Jets flew away.

Few other settings rival fireside for contemplation, but whatever were his emotions for the coming family reunion that he had organized whose sole other attendee would receive his invitation at the same time the location was determined and whereafter not much reminiscing, that very party would abruptly conclude, whatever were those emotions did not show on his face. Five years, it had been five years. And within his head whatever were those sentiments they did not distill into a few choice words. However contemplative fire is, if after five years he hadn't found what he wanted to say, one more restless night in a cold alley wasn't likely to inspire eloquence. Through to midnight the odd person came and went and the alley was cordial and the deepest hours of the night were quiet. He felt the cold ground through the cushion. He slept some and at sunrise a son rose.

He walked west forty-five minutes to the shop and the hours were posted and he had another hour before it would open.

From 7/11 he got a hot chocolate which he took to the glass bus shelter across the street from the shop. He scraped a hole in the frost then wiped at it with his jean sleeve. Sipped the hot chocolate from the white Styrofoam and scrunched his toes in his high-top Reeboks with broken air sacks. At 9:00 a man unlocked the front door. He couldn't see his face. It wasn't him. He could hear the door's small bell. The shop sold motorcycles in the summer and snowmobiles in the winter and in this November transition month few people seemed enthused about either. After a full day of surveillance he walked back towards the barrel while turning his head to every passing alley but found no closer fire. He bought a turkey sandwich and ate half.

This time there was space on the wasted couch. Not a corner seat but it was off the ground and closer to the barrel than those cushions still set up as he had left them, as if a past self still caved them. He sat down and crossed his arms with his hood over Les's toque and his hands under jeaned armpits and a stolen paring knife tucked up his sleeve like a penitentiary shank. He will try again tomorrow and if that proves fruitless to materialize dear ol' dad he'll have decisions to make.

The skinny man who last night rubbing his hands said that his knuckles inform him a high-pressure system is rolling in was right, because tonight these late-evening hours were already cooler than the recent morning's coldest. And the mercury still sinking as the night drew on to that most remorseless hour before dawn. Trent already had the drawstrings tied and brass buttons secured to their upper-most hole, so he turned up his jean collar which helped little. More people tonight came and went and already the stretch to midnight seemed longer than last night whole.

Dismiss astrology but know for certain the moon pulls on more things than ocean waters. Trent leans his head back on the couch. Inquiring lunar spotlight bathing the alley in a pale light, a cold light washing down on this scene where sits one lost boy.

Seated to his left a woman rocking was discussing with nobody laundry detergents. Tide and President's Choice and Gain with her hands extended and her fingers counting off their respective merits as it concerns colours versus whites and she would at times correct herself and at times she seemed to be losing the debate among herself or selves. Periodically her voice would rise, then settle. Gust then calm actually seemed more accurate. He had once been locked in a laundry room and wasn't let out until morning. And only then because his father came for a shirt. When the door opened he didn't say anything, neither of them. During that long night, scared and trapped, Trent didn't call out. Sometimes being remembered is worse than being forgotten. Sometimes it's better to be lost than found. Whoever spurned chance by saying the devil you know is better than the one you don't, simply had not met the right devil.

The times Trent was slapped for talking when he wasn't supposed to, or not answering when he should have, all mostly blurred into one except one time. He always cried when he got hit but that time he didn't cry. They both stood there in the presence of something new. A peculiar milestone on the road of abuse now marked by the novelty of his silence. He got hit and didn't cry. He hit him again, this time with his backhand. Not hard enough to level a man but it turned the head of one large boy. That second strike stuck out in his mind, and not for the force of it and not because that canine so new to the world would be so freshly chipped.

Another young man warming at the barrel was eating a meatball sub. Their eyes met and if between these two their age brought a bond it went unacknowledged. That young man looked away.

Trent could have lost the whole tooth so call it luck that women are the ones whose ring bears a stud. But his mother had left. That's how that story went in his mind. Left *him*—his father—not left them or himself. She had come into his room in the early morning after an ugly night. He pretended to sleep while she kissed his cheek. So his last moment with her had been a lie. A year later he was with child and family services. More than one dentist offered to fix the chip. Trent tongued it now. Still sharp. This physical cue to memory. This proof the past exists. He turned his head back straight from where tonight again the past had turned it.

The young man finished his sub and burped and tossed his empty one litre Orange Crush into the barrel. The lid was still on and shortly the bottle gave a small pop. The clean woodsmoke turned black and a draft coming down the alley found the barrel's low vent holes and stoked the fire while the plastic blackly burned and curled up like a fetus. The forked orange flames licked up above the barrel and one person there waited for toxic snakes to slither on up out of it. A seething from the wind as if it was carrying the serpents. A skinny man immediately downwind choked then coughed on the fumes and batted the air like he'd strike it down while incanting his magic or invoking his gods, white rabbits white rabbits white rabbits. He moved to safe ground upwind and drew on his cigarette.

The night drew on but awful slow. Hours to pass until dawn's safe harbour. When he did drift off it was one of those that immediately arrives the mind to dream. Eyes shut and dream. Dreams inspired by setting. Here, that's a problem. The vent holes ported to the draft funneling down the narrow alley made for a hungrier fire and a man attempting its satiation stomped a wooden pallet like a rib cage then fed the barrel snapped slats like broken bones. Overhead a looming moon so big one might question its disinterest, its innocence, and the skinny man looking up appeared to be doing just that. The lady to Trent's left finally seemed to have exhausted all angles of the detergent debate and dropped the topic, though had not stopped voicing her inner arguments. The woman would calm for a spell only to reanimate excitedly. Of course the constant internal dialogue did not make her unsound nor unique, only her voicing of it. So perhaps her mind not broke just her filter. Her reluctant audience becoming privy to various theories. Chemicals in the water, vapours in the air. "No Second Coming. No. He's already here." She looked to the moon and raised her voice, as if addressing it or speaking on its behalf. "I am the light that is over all things." She turned to the broken pallets. "Split a piece of wood I am there." She looked to a chunk of dislodged asphalt. "Lift up the stone and you will find me." She turned to Trent and asked if he was looking, if he was worthy of being found. She left the couch and scampered about, rather spry for such wither, asking the same to each in turn while also stopping to pose that question to herself or selves. Her body too frail to threaten, her words considerable in size. She approached the barrel and her sockets shadowed while her face glowed. "If you bring forth what is within you, what you bring forth will save you."

When she said that, Trent knew she now spoke to him. But all there believed the same.

She pitched higher. "I am the first and the last. I am the honored one and the scorned one. I am the whore and the holy one. I am the wife and the virgin. I am the barren one, and many are her sons. I am the silence that is incomprehensible." She paused, the wind abated, neighbouring streets trafficless. She continued quieter. "I am the judgment and the acquittal. I," she struck her frail breast, "I am sinless, and the root of sin derives from me. I am the hearing which is attainable to everyone and the speech which cannot be grasped." She paused. They waited.

"I am a mute who does not speak and great is my multitude of words."

At that a gust streamed the alley and the flames for a spell rose like a fountain with sparks for spray. She sat back down and lowered her chin to her breast. Her voice through the night didn't tire, only her convictions outpaced her articulation with her speech becoming pure babble. Hesitate to call that nonsense otherwise other domains are put at risk. Or is there no truth in music? The oscillation of her warped rantings took on an air of melody, hymn, song of anguish. Her sounds conveyed but worse they evoked. She'd jolt upright and spread her arms that you knew under her jacket were thin and veiny, spread them out as if she were trying to forewarn those who followed her, forestall what was coming. Her trembling hand just in front of Trent's chest. Her pauses so contrastingly stark seemed to convey as much as her shriekiest pitch.

The fire on this cold November night still hungry, as if it was trying to ward off something darker than nightfall. The skinny man who in his pacing had sucked much smoke, patterned her rising voice to barrel flares, and he now wondering if she wasn't its operative. He looked to her darkly rimmed eyes and she met his and he regretted that. The wind gusted and he shivered and the flames rose and she sang and the wood all burned up.

A man fed the barrel alley trash bound in white plastic bags. A foul smoke blew down the alley, on swirls, blew over the couch. The chemical fire contaminated Trent's lungs but it was her song polluting his dreams. Short dreams. He'd jerk awake. Every time he opened his eyes the flames no less serpentine.

One does not need logic, science, not even words for profoundest truth, and frankest proof was known in the hearts here of all who listened. And at that the skinny man pacing stuck his fingers in his ear holes. Not an uncommon sentiment, though usually more subtly performed. Trent didn't plug his ears. Perhaps his past, even in spite of its few years, had made him wise to the fact that if you silence your world you're deaf to its threats.

Around the corner another raving voice. Whether he was accusing an individual or a multitude was hard to decipher as the denunciations were addressed with *you* and *you* and *you*. Perhaps grievances cast at the world at large because the voice did siren so probably that raver was spinning.

In the dead of night, his hood up and his arms crossed, he woke with her crouched and rocking gently on the ground just before him. Her big eyes staring up at him. Her breathing laboured to a seething or a thin hiss from her ranting or her life or her health or all. They stared a minute, two, three. He uncrossed his arms and withdrew from his sleeve the paring knife, while from an inner pocket he withdrew the squished half sandwich. He set it on his knee and cut that half in two and gave her one and she with two hands ate it without looking away.

Into his sleeve he sheathed his blade, leaned his head back, eyes wide open. His face bathed in cold moonlight. Trent exhaled from deep down in his belly. He does that sometimes. His curling breath made smoky and luminous in this moonlight air. Like ghosts rising from his belly. Between alley drafts he watched them churn and waited for dawn.

You are marvelous, Trent. Trent, without you the heavens could not exist for a moment.

***

Trent pressed the button on the drink machine but the hot-chocolate spout only sputtered. Pressed it again. He slid his cup one spout over and pressed for his first coffee and smelled it and sipped it then poured in a hazelnut creamer and sipped it and poured in more then put on a lid and grabbed a day-old foot-long sub and paid and left. His spyhole had lighter frost than the rest of the glass and he set a thumbnail to it. Just after 9:00 a.m. he watched a tall man in a heavy parka with a long gait walk out from behind the building. Big shoulders, stooped walk. A street width away was just about the distance one might pick out facial features, but his collar up and his hat low and he wasn't looking Trent's way. And he didn't need to. Trent wiped at the glass then wiped it again then wiped it again. Five years but quickened breaths saying whatever he was feeling wasn't diluted by time. The man across the street sliding his key in the door coughed a familiar timbre that unlocked something in Trent's mind before it did the door. The little bell rang, the man entered the shop, his vapour hung around longer.

Trent with his hood up walked beside the shop and didn't see a car parked in that alley. He walked to the end and there were two parked cars on the street and room for others and he bent and touched each car's exhaust. They were cold. Had one been warm maybe he would have gone inside the shop now. Go make his peace now. Perhaps he preferred to make his peace in a private setting because he remained outside. By midday that chain-smoker still hadn't even come out for a puff. Trent looked for a backdoor but no. The afternoon drew on and twice in the bus shelter he did push-ups with cardboard under his knuckles to warm up. Twice he went to 7/11 for dime candy, sour keys, and heat. He read a man's watch. 4:30. Trent went to the alley where his father had arrived from. Don't go where the puck is, skate to where it's going to be. He recalled that from an interview on Hockey Night in Canada. So implicate the Great One in this patricide. He only went as far down the alley as would be the end of earshot to the shop-door's bell.

Winnipeg's fifty degrees northerly latitude doesn't hold much November sun and by 5:00 p.m., as if coordinating its workday with the shop, the sun had set and the eastern horizon was dim and the alley was getting dark. Streetlamps at either end simultaneously lit, a darkness hanging between their poles where Trent awaits his father. Trent's right shoulder leaning against red brick thinly frosted like the stubble of an older man's beard. If only it could offer some wisdom. He faced the same direction as would Dad. If he was coming. Hood up, toque on but ears exposed below the fabric. A car turned and before it straightened into the narrow lane he saw a Buick's emblem which then vanished behind the oncoming beams like twin trains sharing a tunnel. He squinted and when the car passed he heard behind him twenty, maybe thirty paces away, a man hacking as if lying on the snow, now redly speckled, might be half a lung. He heard steps. He heard the man hock and spit whatever his cough couldn't purge. Trent's right hand in his jean pocket choked-up high on a paring knife. The handle wet like his armpits like his back like his forehead itching under the red toque. Turn around and be made, even a sideways glance could give himself away. This boy too young to grow a disguising beard. Some snow crunches, others silent, this thin one squeaks and if Inuit really do have fifty words for snow surely such characteristics inspired their naming.

In the dark gap an unsuspecting father walks towards his past. Trent withdraws his left hand from his pocket and pretends to blow on it. He corners his eyes hard left, looking for a face Trent for five years hasn't seen other than most everywhere. But right then a woman entered the alley. Dad passed and a few seconds later she passed going the other way and Trent followed. They left the alley. Father and son turn right. Trent with his head angled downwards. Two blocks then down a sidewalk. Trent stayed a half-block behind. They went left down a street. Parked cars. A pedestrian. Trent watched him walk into Mirrors Pub Club where with his own size he might not get carded. Have his first beer on the same day as his first coffee on the same day as what was still to come. He stayed outside. In the cold and still air his short breaths lengthened. Waited five years what's another hour or two before properly getting something off his chest. Off his stomach. Something that had been eating at him. Two and a half hours later with his blue lips and body shivering and toes scrunched and one bloodless hand clawed around a vegetable knife, he knew he shouldn't get any colder and then his man came out and he entirely forgot about the cold.

But are we not all bleeding, Trent? Trent, are we all so different?

XV

Sometimes Valerie would go out for dinner alone. Like now. A friend once said don't you find that lonely? Valerie hadn't even conceptualized it as such. It's only lonely if you're telling yourself a lonely story. It's really nice, adventurous because who knows. It's definitely lonely if you believe it is, if you're living within the framework others built for you, then it's certainly whatever they tell you it is. She didn't say that. She said it was fun.

Valerie's reservation was for six and she arrived at six and was led up the stairs and seated at the bar seat furthest right, next to the kitchen. Had she not been she'd have asked for it. She draped her jacket over the back of the seat and hung her new handbag on the hook by her knees. The bartenders looked like Hollywood actors who were slinging drinks between auditions. One of them welcomed her and set down a menu. The dining room was busy while not at capacity and not all bar seats were occupied. Rap quietly played in the background. Behind the bar a tower of endless bottles like endless stories like they could all hold inside themselves a scroll, tell a history for every night they'd been tipped. Below the bottle-wall in the back-bar mirror beside her own image, a stalking wolf, low head and high shoulders. She turned and looked at the driftwood wolf, larger than life. She took the room in. A chandelier of wooden ribbons, something of a tumbleweed of adze curls so thin they became semi-translucent from a light like a centred ember. High on the far wall a circular exhibit of surfboards, their noses like rays of a bleached sun. How to describe it to Stacy. *Dear Stacy*, she started the text. High ceiling gives dimension, it changes the acoustics, the vibe, grandness blended with industrial blended with something else because the crew is wearing flannel. To her right, tantalizing plates didn't stay long under heat lamps. In the kitchen a crew scarcely speaking, fluidly moving. She figured that's something you only get with low staff-churn.

Dear Stacy. She tried to distill it. Aromas. Visuals. Sounds. I guess it's atmospheric? She saw an attention to detail showing up in small ways. That's how she knew what she was looking at. When someone cared that even the cornered speakers were hidden by matching paint. The glasses and plates didn't match and that was intentional. Every aspect thoughtful like chef now tweezing a green garnish to a mounded plate. She heard one server say to another, may I? A language of professionalism. *Dear Stacy.*

The best taco she'd ever eaten was years ago on a dirt road Mexican street corner. Before B2P. Just a folding table and chairs and propane burner, *Las Tres Hermanas* under a street light. Not even a restaurant sign, just three sisters cooking. One sister grilling strips of beef and frying onions in a cast-iron pan. One sister hand-shaping tortillas *clap clap clap* and you heard that before you arrived like a premonition of a satisfied diner. One sister plating charbroiled meat and onions onto a fresh tortilla leoparded with char. Lime wedge, hot sauce, nada más. That's it. Nothing more needed, none better.

It wasn't about a plate's price tag. It wasn't about affluence or status. People who think it is are paying for the wrong thing. The best coffee she had was years ago in Korea. Before B2P. A pop-up shop in a busy alley in the Bukchon Hanok Village. The guy with his straight-brimmed ball cap, headphones on. Only now did she wish she asked what he was listening to. Of course he could hear you order but he seemed half in his own world, at least. Organized, efficient, the way he set out on the little table the paper coffee cups equally spaced. The thermometer in the water. His variously sourced beans locally roasted labelled in their bags. "You pick." Whether or not he knew much more English. You could get coffee anywhere. People lined up. What is that? The price was average.

The other bartender, starting from the bar's other end, was refilling in a line the water glasses.

Something's good or it's not good. It's good or it's not good regardless of all that other stuff, accolades, awards, high prices. Talent irrespective of validation. Quality regardless of setting. Forty-dollar exceptional plates under a storied tower of bottles. Ten-peso perfect street tacos under flickering lamplight.

How to say it? *Dear Stacy,* still no more words in the message box. Those rare places of high achievement. What are they, what is it? What do you feel? Effortful pursuit for one's vision. *Close.* Mastery. *More.* Passion, discipline, creativity answering to no one while holding it to one's own highest standard. *Close.*

She couldn't quite put it into words. She sent Stacy a picture of that stalking wooden wolf. The bartender tipped the water carafe to Valerie's glass. Fabulous big gold hoop earrings, dark hair. Valerie said, "I love your earrings. They look so pretty I bet you could make a man jump through them."

She laughed. She poured. "I like yours."

Valerie touched a pearl.

"Have you had a chance to look at the drink menu?"

As if originating from the suggestive power of her own unconscious she ordered a Mexican martini. She looked at the dinner menu to see if there were any differences to what she had previewed online. Listed under *Share Plates*: *A six-pack for the kitchen.* She'd never seen that. She liked that.

A woman to her immediate left was paying her bill. "Start with that one," the lady pointing high on the menu. "In that dish the oyster itself becomes the pearl." That unsolicited endorsement was all Val needed. She ordered the shellfish appetizer and a six-pack for the kitchen.

The lady was putting on her coat. Beside her a man set down his book and pulled out his phone vibrating a text. "*will be late*". You mean even later. He wondered why the *w* wasn't capitalized. How does that happen? Like is she typing a lower-case *w*? He set his iPhone to the bar-top perplexed.

The lady with her coat said to Val, "Enjoy your dinner," and pushed her high-back chair towards the bar, turned for the steps that led from the second floor to the exit on the first. The six-pack must have been rung up because small claps of gratitude were coming from the kitchen and they sounded like a cross between fallen rain and Mexican tortillas which is a really nice sound. Well that was fun. She wondered if they knew she had ordered it, if her seat was listed on the chit. She preferred stealth tribute, she didn't look their way.

The man who had set down his phone heard the kitchen's brief burst of minor applause. He knew what it meant and he looked around trying to pick out the benefactor, see if he could infer it from their expression. He unwound his turn and looked right. He saw his barstool neighbour with her smile half-covered by her hand. This is funny, he thought. Small town Tofino, hey. Looks like we're on the same schedule: Hot Springs → Wolf. I respect that schedule. He turned back ahead. Damn fine schedule.

Alex hadn't seen her picture in any of the various interviews, online or print. He used to listen to Ted Talks but not in years and the one she had given was at the smaller Ted-X events.

He had no idea he held the door open for her at the Distillery because he had been on his phone. Seeing her again now he wasn't so surprised, repeated encounters happen regularly given town's concentrated layout, its central hubs and common routes of *grocery store to post office to beach walk*. Sometimes for a stint you just end up seeing the same random person every day. One more charm of living in a small town. He drank to the pleasures of small charms and small towns and picked up his book and would leave it at that.

Alex liked talking to new people and hearing where they were from and what they were doing. He enjoyed that aspect of his job, his fishing clients arriving from distant cities with unique lives. Some of his most significant and pivotal moments of his life had come from the most ordinary encounters, ones he almost had not initiated. A brief comment on the weather, an inquiry to what they were reading, and a snow grain snowballed. He thought that was kind of incredible. He was considering saying to the hot-springs-awkward-walker, I'm glad to see you're sitting, not walking, the world is just safer that way. But if Alina were to walk in while he was engaged in even the most innocent of conversations with a female sitting alone at the bar—never mind one that had literally stepped on her toes—that all just wasn't worth the hassle. He'd been down those tracks before. More than once. Those tracks led to a train wreck. He told himself, not pussy-whipped, just being practical. He looked to the stairs to see if his date had arrived. Just saving a headache as any reasonable man would. Then he wondered to himself if there was a difference. Jay one of the bartenders saw the furrowed brow and asked what he was working out up there. "Only the puzzle of ages, Jay."

It didn't seem like his neighbour here had seen him seeing her—though he did wonder if maybe somehow she was aware that he had looked her way for a second longer than cursory.

171

He had a theory on women that they had a couple extra senses than men, or enhanced senses, or that long ago they traded some rational acumen for alternate abilities. A private theory. So she very well may have known. He almost shrugged. He looked down to the menu. His hair was just long enough to tuck behind his ear but some strands now of their own accord became untucked and blocked sight of her. Probably for the best. He set the menu aside, widely parted his beverages, water and wine, to accommodate resting his arms on the bar. Pulled in his book. Just being practical, he told himself.

Pecorino cheese falling like snow, her strategic seat. Valerie didn't need to ask if the noodles were homemade. Chef set down the microplane then set the mushroom fettuccine under the heat lamp, followed by two plates of chicken, a ballotine as she saw each portion was tied with a string. By the time he had set two plates of white fish of which Valerie didn't need to revisit the menu as their thick cut could only be halibut, three servers had lined up with their hands held before them. She noticed that detail of their clasped hands. Some might think it was a posture of servitude. To her it looked like professionalism, a stance emblematic of the whole. She wondered if others saw that too. Or if maybe people didn't think about these things at all. She almost shrugged.

Three plates were carried past Val. The aroma of the pasta lingered longest. Valerie's heritage is French-Slavic but she believes her heart is Italian. She turned to Hoops. Smiled. Smile returned. Watched her drink being made. The background music mixed with the drink shaker sounded like Tupac had gone Latino, set down his MAC-10 and picked up a maraca. Changes indeed, thug-poet. The bartender's big gold hoop earrings swayed and to Val they looked like some form of perfection. Why was that? On the bar top the screen of her silenced phone lit with an incoming text. Dad: *Feeling good.* *Barbell emoji*

Maybe. Val knew that regardless of how the treatment went he would say that. She texted: *Yay! I'm so glad! Calling you later!* She picked the same barbell image then filled the message box with red hearts, as if there were any other. In no way did she feel ready to say goodbye to this man made of iron and heart.

She sipped. She realized that her father right now was the largest male influence in her life. My fault. I let my small circle become entirely female.

She had had a couple relationships that were significant. One relationship of three years had ended with infidelity. He had done the cheating but she had her own version, lies, that more common type of infidelity. And at first they weren't lies to him but lies to herself. Told herself that she really was into him in the same way she was when they first met. Why wouldn't she be now? What had changed? Fundamentally, nothing? She couldn't think of anything significant that had changed with them or their lives. Therefore, they could make it work, she had told herself. Love *loves* the word *therefore*. Just a seven-year itch that came at year three. That's all this is. Figure it out. Some people lie so well to their own self it's hard for even the person closest to them to actually know the truth.

Over time his language with her had lost its sweetness. Fewer thoughtful gestures, while she herself was making the effort. People giving a little less effort as the relationship aged must just be common, reducible to a predictable formula. For every passing year, one less care given.

At that time in her life she had been contorting and twisting who she was to the point she almost felt physically crooked, like maybe literally bent because she wondered if that's what was paining her neck. She'd wake in the morning feeling kinked. It affected her work. She was trying for them but that came out as feigning enthusiasm, hiding disinterest. Problem was the rest of her body couldn't pretend as easily as her words. Her body stiff, her skin unreceptive to his touch. As if preceding her self-admission, some deeper part already knew. Maybe one ought to add unconscious intelligence to the Love Languages, and doesn't its voice speak the loudest? He picked up on it.

She knew she had to straighten herself out or go insane. She called it for what it was: empty. She felt nothing for him. She was very sorry. Find more sensitive words but that would come at the expense of honesty. That had been her most successful relationship. Three years. God. Sometimes the residue of romantic failures wearied her efforts. Slid before Val was a skinny-stemmed, funnel-shaped glass with lemon-coloured liquid and three speared olives. Hello. She admired it a second. Then a few more seconds.

Your mother and I love you very much and we love each other.

We're going to be living apart.

Such experiences may cause a naturally inquisitive child to question how much of life is veneer. Maybe from such things grew the root of her contrarianism. Certain disillusionments do become formative. Perhaps a pattern. *I want you. I love you. Here's a disease for the rest of your life. Aw, that's very sweet, thank you, how did you know?* But she didn't think about *it* that often. All of that could undermine one's trust in words if not people. This sounds pitiable. It is not pitiable. It is freeing. Valerie would just decide for herself what is the world and who are its people. The thrill and carnival of discovering what simply *is*. That mindset came early. A young girly Euclid arriving at her own first principles. She had named her Monstera plant Euclid. She hadn't told anyone that not even Peter Mansbridge who sat next to its outstretched sunlit leaves.

When a magician says *watch this card* Valerie was curious what the other hand was up to. She tried to squint at the familiar. She didn't incline her head so much as tilt her mind.

It became pathological. On occasion she found some things generally considered heavy were light, some known to be cheap were priceless. She was still looking at the drink here but her vision became broad and the moment expansive. She, like Yeats, believed the world is full of magic things patiently waiting for our senses to grow stronger. The restaurant an impressionistic painting and not just the colours, all things smearing up together, kitchen aromas, colourful bottle-wall, voices blending with lyrics, notes of wine-glass chime and cutlery clink slotted between rap beats and you can let yourself diffuse into an amorphous moment without boundary to oneself, dissolve into the din, no shape, no size, a moment experienced while not appraised, not measured or weighed, not assessed as full or lacking.

Sometimes her uncommon perspectives manifested in large ways. The founding of B2P. But the small ways were to her also meaningful. During Covid there was a twenty-person line extending far out the door of an understaffed post office. A young mother with her young daughter walked up, saw a friend. "Oh man, we just got out of daycare and I have to get to work and still go to the grocery store. And now this line." She looked around trying to see the end of it. That young mother wasn't even complaining, simply stating another tall hurdle in the long track of a single mom. She and her daughter holding hands walked to the back of the line. Valerie stood second to the front. She saw two options. One: swap spots with the young woman. Two: she could ask the whole line if they would allow that young mother to take first spot. That option united the whole group in a selfless act. It spread the love around. It showed others something valuable hiding in plain sight and Christ how messianic that sounded in her head and not how she meant it at all. She asked the crowd to vote with a show of hands if the mother should take first spot. She hadn't told that story to anyone. That moment, in a sense, was symbolic of her life's work. In front of twenty people lay a diamond. None could see it. Glittering right there on the pavement. She saw it. It wasn't about being better than anyone—not at all. It was proof that often in this world there is value, goodness, beauty at hand. Regardless if others see it. Simply train your eyes. Valerie presently staring rather intensely at nothing specific, perhaps looking a bit peculiar because a fishing guide to her left had looked over, squinting, then looked over his shoulder, then looked away. The colours of this smeared moment divested to their sources and the yellow martini redefined itself in front of her and she finally grasped the glass and pleasingly sour it did help wash away the distaste of self-absorption. The thing is, the thing is: *mundanity is artificial*. That's what she felt. The world is utterly glowing. There is magic here. So why are you going to a silent retreat when what you're looking for is right here? Stray thought. Right here. Echo of a stray thought.

Every time she found a gem hiding in plain sight she wondered just how many that day she had missed. Perhaps there are always roses around you. Pay more attention and maybe you see wild flowers sprouting on city streets, scarlet begonias brushing bare ankles. She looked below the bar to her naked ankles and imagined inked flowers, rose vines growing up from her feet, petals and flowers and thorns. Val sipped the cool drink. She had arrived to the Wolf via Pacific Rim Navigators. Maybe just this one pretty drink or maybe one or two more. Val lightly flicked the thin glass and it chimed pleasingly. Her neighbour looked over like she had something to say. He looked to the stairs and seemed to twitch once and turned back to his book.

In more recent years she saw commonalities in her dates, men who gave little thought to small gestures that go a long way with women. Probably just her sample size. Men that couldn't ask a question which didn't reflect in some way back to their own self, not listening but waiting for their turn to speak. Their silence more often a polite patience for their turn to approve or rebut what she had said, rather than a genuine interest in what could be explored between them. Probably just her sample size. Or those men whose overly affected charm was a ploy to get her into bed. Then that charm and postcoital affection braked quicker than her Tesla.

She was becoming more fixed in her lifestyle, the routine that she liked. What in her organized and clean condo she wanted where and at what times she wanted to go to bed and wake and journal and meditate and run and read and when she wanted to dine, and those patterns, those rituals, time's flow was carving to greater depth with steeper walls. At times she wondered if what was diminishing inside her wasn't so much her ability to accommodate another, but her desire to. She used that word, accommodate. Lonely at times, but not a hollow lonely. A useful, instructive, grateful and inconstant lonely.

She didn't always trust men but she didn't always trust her own self—what she really wanted and what just sounded like something she was supposed to want from decades of swallowing the media's pictures and storylines selling her on packaged desires. The strong hands of culture slid the tube down her throat, she the *foie gras goose* being force-fed consumerist dreams and domesticated narratives, her poor unconscious fattened from cultural gavage. Telling her what a woman is and how one ought to behave. One time walking home at night through the park with her date she turned to him and pushed him back two paces to a tree and dropped to her knees and unzipped him and took him in her mouth. He got hard and she took him as far as it could go. Her eyes watered and she gagged and she pulled her head back and his cock slid out of her mouth and her cough broke the spit-string to his tip. Then she put him in as far as he could go. She wasn't even sure why. A gift to another if that's what got them off? An act of freely subjugating her own ego? A trust, a domination, a curiosity? A defiance to anyone, including any woman, who might tell her what a woman is?

She leaned for the martini. She wasn't entirely sold on the idea of monogamy like she wasn't entirely sold on motherhood. At times she wanted both. At times she wanted neither. Do I want to make sacrifices in my meaningful career to become the cook, the driver, the cleaner, load up the emotional and physical duress for not just nine months but all the years of it? Would my body no longer be my own? A body often tired? A body stretched and sagged? Within a culture that tends to appraise women by their appearance? Listen to me—temporary and trivial concerns in comparison to the grander project—right? Sacrifices for a family that might be less praising and encouraging of those efforts than expectant of those efforts? And that's fine, that's fine if it comes with all the love that a mother gets to know, and I suspect that not having a child may preclude me from a whole world of profoundest love and there is a chance that that is the single largest mistake I could make. I don't know. I do not know. Thirty-eight sounds like tick tock.

She took a sip. Her drink looked so pretty and her finger hovered over the Instagram icon because food-porn was fun. But this recent two week break from Instagram's exhibit of glossy perfection felt nice. She hovered her finger over a dating app, its icon's colour matching her drink. From some sense of classical romance as well her eyes feeling like sandpaper from incessant screen time, she hadn't tried dating apps. A woman from her team argued their case. "They drastically increase options, and you can still look to meet people in natural settings, this just ads one more option." She told her of one she liked. "You can be pretty specific, you can set your criteria. And on this one the girls message first." Valerie thought perhaps those eligible bachelors understanding the need to outcompete one another for the digital hand of a prized lady, would upload only their most gallant pics and write only the most charming quips. A dating app to restore her faith in men. She had downloaded the app a while back and made a profile but went no further. She tapped an index on the yellow icon. It started to update.

Over coffee one of her friends said to her she would meet someone. Well-meaning and all. But it implied she couldn't be happy on her own, and mostly she was. And it implied couples are happier, which she questioned. And really it invalidated the speaker. The fact is, a lot of people don't meet someone. She might not. Is life's beauty therefore limited? No. She had more respect for those who say, yeah, you might not, screw it, let's eat. Valerie said she was open to giving herself up to love without dependency. She was open to a relationship but didn't *need* one to be happy.

For her last birthday she dressed to an old Sublime song: she got her hair permed, she put a red dress on. They left the birthday-rosé-lunch for birthday-margarita-afternoon followed by birthday-cocktail-dinner. "One of the benefits of now being thirty-eight, Stacy, is that I don't have to do that shot. Twenty-eight, okay fine. Thirty-eight, not happening." She pushed the elaborate shooter away. One of her ladies said something and Val said, "Even if it is a girl-shot." Then in a few annoying seconds she caved under her friends' affectionate pressure. She even humoured them and put her hands behind her back and was about to bob her head when one of them said wait and tied her wrists with a scarf. She dug her tongue in the martini glass and tipped up the discovered jigger while trying to swallow a mouth of whipped cream. An off-side comment from Stacy had her choke and almost resurface that swallowed muff-diver. They went to a club saying screw it if we're the oldest. Jen checked her phone and then called home and then said she had to go home. "I don't want to go home," Jen said. They dropped her off by limo.

Stacy in the limo slowly pulled from her purse a boa like a pink Arabian snake, draped that feathery serpent around Valerie like an exotic queen. They danced and harassed the DJ with their outdated song requests. She adored these girls and swore to herself she'd not allow life's acidic busyness corrode their bond. Later in the night Nicole asked a man what Colosseum he just walked out of. That didn't really make sense because there's only one Colosseum. She asked him if he felt bad about all those dead beasts and men he just slayed. She told him he's the prettiest gladiator she's ever met. Holding on to his big arm she dragged him over towards their table saying there's someone I want you to meet, it's her birthday. "Valerie this is Thor." Trent said Trent. "A Roman gladiator." He said carpenter. Stacy looked at him and said tomorrow she's buying her husband a hammer. Later in the night his tight black shirt made the pink boa pop. Someone had put it around his neck. He said he wasn't a dancer. Valerie pulled him by the pink lasso out to the crowded dancefloor.

Before they left the bar Stacy wanted to tell her that his vibe was a little off, or something. Call it female intuition and how could that not exist after millions of years of physically smaller primates trying to avoid being raped. But Val the contrarian not always the most receptive to advice. And she sensed something in Trent she couldn't name and it made her curious. Before they left, Stacy said, "Babe, just be careful. You text me later."

Valerie in her red dress sitting on the kitchen counter. She had the boa back. He had peeled her top down and the pink feathery fabric hung down over her breasts. She lifted her wine but he didn't reach for his glass's slender stem because he was reaching for her slender stems. He pulled her closer over the counter and that hiked up her dress. He gave the boa one wrap around her neck, exposing one breast, and he put his arm around her waist and lifted her and turned and put her back up against

180

the wall. She with her arm around his neck and her other hand still holding her wine. He held her there against the wall and pulled her panties to the side of her bare pussy and lowered her down and her feet stayed off the floor. The boa with every thrust ratcheting tighter. Wine sloshing up the side of her glass. Valerie warm here at the bar like that wolf was breathing down her neck. She sipped. That next morning when he left, she righted a framed photo lying face down on a shelf. As if her dad, opting not to watch, had willed that frame to tip. Sorry about that, Dad. An old photo. He in a suit. His hand on her shoulder. She splayed the back stand. Better you didn't see that.

Valerie at the Wolf falling farther into a memory of a memory, Alice down her mind's own rabbit hole, back inside that little girl's head from the righted photo. Around that time her Dad had taken her camping at Porteau Cove. They were sitting by the campfire under Howe Sound's constelled sky. She roasting a marshmallow but really just burning it. Her dad, not a marshmallow enthusiast, was eating the charred ones, like six of them by now. She brought the stick to his face and he blew out the flaming glob and told her steady and she said trust and he pulled with his teeth that scorched goo off the stick, getting only a tiny gob on a cheek and then from the bag beside him skewered on a fresh little dessert pillow. She said thanks and he with three syllables said something fatly inarticulate. She said the next one would be perfect. He chewed a sticky cloud then swallowed and pointed at the sky. Nothing to see up there but spectacular stars. He swallowed. "There's you." Moved his pointing hand. "And you. And look, there's you and you." Poked her with the same finger he had pointed. He let her work out the analogy.

Valerie ascended from out of the head of that little girl living in a memory and back up to the bar. The app had updated. She read profiles. Men next to their dog or car. Occasionally shirtless. She swiped left and then she swiped left again. In fifteen minutes she had read *Partner in crime* three times. A couple of the dad jokes weren't too bad. Valerie looked from the two-dimensional men to the three—almost four—dimensional and tanned bartender with dark hair and big hoop earrings and the lips and the smile who held a microplane and a lemon. Nine glossed nails and one with tiny gold stars of varying small size studding a cuticle. She wanted to ask what makes that one special but preferred the mystery and watched shredded gold dusting the pillowy foam brimming a tumbler. The bartender looked at Val and Val said, "My name's Valerie." Said it about as soft as wolf step.

Hoops smiled. "Hillary. Ready for another?"

"I'm in your hands. Bartender's Choice."

"Oh that's fun. Let me see." Hillary turned to the huge bottle-wall. She asked while facing away, "What brings you to Tofino?"

"I'm here for a few days before going on a silent retreat. The Floating Gardens of Tranquil Cove. Have you heard of it?"

"I haven't. That sounds amazing though." She grabbed a blue bottle. From the garnish tray she picked out mint and basil leaves which she placed in her palm, slapping them with her other hand. "It releases the aromatics in herb-forward drinks. It reminds me of a doctor slapping a baby's back."

"I figured I should get out any cravings that might interrupt my practice. And I also wanted a drink and good food." Like that wolf took another step.

Hillary laughed and if she blushed it was hidden by her deep tan and light rouge. The curvy glass garnished with two lemon slices held an amber-coloured liquid.

"Quite pretty," said Val. Then she looked down at the drink. A bartender blushed.

One drink down and only a few minutes into this dating app Valerie was ready to delete this dating app. Her swipes of rejection, likely a touch animated by the alcohol's effect on this lightweight's body, had taken on a dismissive air of royalty directing peasants, had progressed into a gesture from some tired queen made disinterested from the routine of declaring *off with his head*. Swipe. She read the next profile.

If your love language is pizza we should talk. More loyal than your Shih Tzu. Decent cook. Grower of garden peas; tender of laying hens. Seeking that forever thing, that ride or die. Hit me back, just to chat, truly yours, your biggest fan, this is—

Her appetizer arrived. A little wordy but she liked the old Slim Shady reference. The semicolon on a dating app was a little weird. She looked above the bio. He almost looked familiar but the sight of one more man holding a dead salmon gave her concern that she might lose her appetite for this elegant oyster placed before her. Its display of culinary art arousing more feelings than all those dating profiles combined.

Val once wondered if food and sex and love and art and friendship were all linked by the same dopamine pathway. If one area is lacking, does another engorge? Alternate cravings to fill a deficit? A psychologist might suggest that she is eating her feelings. But she could go fuck herself. Not the shrink—Val. As in, in addition to a nice dinner out, she might just finish the night off with a little romance-for-one. Didn't feel bad about that prospect. Felt rather good about that prospect. If many men had their sexual desires caricatured by porn, her handheld electric friend did tend to spoil her.

At the centre of the small plate was a shucked oyster smoked in alder wood and bound in thin and long strings of potato, rather complementary to the chandelier's wooden ribbon curls, potato strings that twisted up into the air where the fryer had curled and fixed them. It looked artisanal. Or pagan or animalistic, resembling a nest sheltering an egg. It lay on a green-apple puree. In the depths of its savoury aroma she also picked up the acuteness of cilantro and citrus of lemon, at once softened and enriched by truffle oil. You don't mistake truffle oil. She was done with her phone and done with this app and done with this most recent digital man and she set her pointer finger to the screen and her final emphatic stroke of rejection extended a touch too far left and that finger hit the wine glass belonging to the gentleman two seats over. It didn't tip but it slid and sloshed and splashed. She looked to his white sleeve. She covered her mouth. The spots on his dress shirt. She looked to his face. *No way. No. Way.* She almost laughed. *There's no way.* Her hand over her mouth concealed only her smile not her laughter.

Valerie's last virtual rejection had been of the man sitting next to her. Albeit, this one looked a few years older than the pictures. She had rejected him in one world, then soiled his shirt in another. She truly wanted to ask, You catfishin' son of a gun, where's your salmon at? But instead, from behind a bashful hand she said, "Oh my God. I'm so sorry!"

Alex wondered if all this woman did was variations on toe-stepping and apologies. He watched her take up her lap's cloth napkin and proceed to mix messages: what kind of apology comes with this much smile. He set down his book and watched her. Her, not her hand that she was dabbing uselessly at his sleeve—some things you don't undo. Whether the sight of her smile is among them, red wine on a white cotton shirt certainly is.

The bullshit motto of the Local's Only Club, "Fucking tourist," was Alina's line, so he just tolerantly spectated her pointless dabbing. He looked from his speckled arm to his spotted shirt then back to the silly dabber.

She looked for his reaction. Their eyes met. One less love story went unwritten.

XVI

P iped lighting above the bar, cylindrical cages of electric-or-
ange filament like drops of glowing resin leaked from steel
tubes. Lighting softening as the host worked the dimmer. Alex
waited a second for her to recognize him from the hot-springs
boardwalk, which he thought was their first encounter. Jay slid
Alex a shot. Alex looked at him and thought that was funny
and strangely kind but he didn't want a shot and said that's
alright. He placed two napkins beside it, nodded at Alex's sleeve.
"Sparkling water, Alex." He refilled Alex's wine but corked that
detail in the bottle because the bill wouldn't tell that story.

A CEO sitting at the bar says to a fishing guide, "I'm really
sorry."

"That's alright," says the fishing guide. "Are polka-dot shirts
in style? Maybe my date won't mind."

"Oh yeah definitely." Valerie made an okay sign. "You look
great." She reached and touched his sleeve, her hand covering
the speckles. "I'm really sorry."

"Don't worry about it."

Following the lead of the lighting the music softened. Could
perhaps be described as emo rap, still G's on the mic, but even
gangsters get the blues. Alex looked behind him to the stairs to
see if Alina had arrived. He reached for his phone to ask her to
stop by his house and grab a shirt. He started typing and a text

arrived. *cant make it cant get my heels on ankles all swollen sorry not sorry*

The lack of punctuation bothered him almost as much as the cancellation. Just saying to hell with the period too then, hey? He asked Jay about texts lacking a capitalized first letter. "Jay you ever seen anything like that?" As if they were two detectives standing in some alley looking at a mutilated body. Alex was looking straight ahead at the bottle-wall, reflecting on being stood up. For about a minute. Less than a minute. He set his phone to silence and put it away.

Tesla said, "I'm going to pay for your dry-cleaning bill."

Tacoma didn't look over. "What's that?"

"What? What's what?"

"We don't have them in Tofino."

"Oh. I'll buy you a new shirt then."

"They don't sell dress shirts here. But. If it will help ease your conscience, I'll settle for one of those. Settle not settle." He said that last bit for Alina. He hoped she was somewhere somehow listening. Him making a private little requiem for their still-born romance. Run the Monte Carlo simulations ten million times, they could never be. He knew that from the get-go. He thought their cool bellies coming together at the hot springs was a bit sweet though. Guess that makes one of them. He snapped out of the reverie and pointed to his neighbour's half-finished appetizer and she about to take her second bite lowered the fancy mollusk and pushed the small plate towards him. Then she pulled it back. As if some things you don't joke about, the sharing of single exquisite shellfish being one of them.

"So you live here?"

"Yep."

"I'm jealous. Born and raised?"

"Nope. But it's where I spend most of my days."

She squinted and he squinted. Then before he told her how he had once lived in the geographical center of Canada and had moved out this way to fish on the ocean, he mentally slapped those parts inside his head so very numbed by routine in having told that story one thousand times. Then he told it again. One thousand and one.

"So you fish?" Odd question for one who'd already seen his salmon picture.

He lifted from off the cover of his closed book one nicked-up hand. "Fishing guide."

She looked at the book not the hand. "Fishing guides read?"

He half smiled. "After ruining my shirt you now insult my profession. Wow. You're really good at basic human interaction. You don't think fishing guides read?"

"It's not that. I didn't think fishing guides *could* read."

That brought the other half of his smile. Well, well. "Mostly we can't, no."

She looked at the book. *100 Love Sonnets* by Pablo Neruda. She looked at him.

"Don't tell anybody."

"So why did you bring a book if you're on a date?"

"Do you always ask this many questions to those whose clothing you've ruined and life you've greatly inconvenienced and profession you've insulted?"

She turned to her martini. Sipped it. Then slowly back to him, her eyes letting him know she wasn't going to dignify that question with a response and her stubborn gaze wasn't going away without an answer.

"Because women, God bless them, for all their very many talents, have yet to master the clock. Either that or it's intentional. Or subconscious, I guess." He looked past her and he appeared to be thinking hard. "Either way, I find that trait pretty dependable."

187

"I see. So are all fishing guides sexist, or just you?"

"I think as it concerns female punctuality, yes, I speak for all of the fishing guides. Also, the tradesmen." Alex went to take a drink and then stopped and said, "Also the accountants, the doctors." Jay on the other side of the bar was refilling the olives and Alex said raising his eyebrows, the bartenders? and then Alex said not in a question, "The bartenders."

"So how long have you and your lady been dating?" Like she didn't even hear him.

Alex thought there might be other questions nested in that question. Sometimes when he spoke with women he felt like he was in conversation with a Russian toy egg. He considered telling her how she on the narrow path was partly responsible for his new single life. Not entirely, of course, not even mostly, just partially, causal linkages, and all. "I think our love has just come to a tragic end. And after only three dates."

"You don't sound so heartbroken." She reached across the empty seat and touched his hand. "Will you be okay?" A question sweetly tenderized with melodramatic concern.

"Now that you mention it. I don't know. I feel very... vulnerable. Just... raw. I guess this technically puts me on the rebound. I shouldn't even be out in public in this state. Liable to make regretful decisions. I'm like a lost little doe out here." His eyes shifted conspicuously to the driftwood canine then back to her. "In the company of wolves."

She laughed. "Poor thing. Yeah, Bambi, you should be careful."

"So what were you doing on your phone there?" He gestured to it in her hand. "It looked like before you attacked me you were conducting a small orchestra."

Valerie took a sip of martini. "Just looking through some resumes." A euphemism isn't a lie, she declining to tell him how the algorithms of fate had for a third time crossed their paths. She knew it was the third time.

"And what do you do? And given how you just belittled the mental capacities of those in my honest trade this better be good. If you're anything less than a neurologist or philosopher or lawyer, and not one for the chemical companies, like if you're anything less than a public defendant for convicts slated for execution for their extreme environmental protests, I'm ordering my dinner as takeout."

"Defender."

"What?"

"And there's no death row in Canada."

"Then you haven't been listening to this night's playlist."

She liked that, the rap-label reference. She didn't show it. She said, "Guess."

"Guess. Guess your job." He cocked a brow. He leaned back from the bar and looked her up and down. Took a breath. "You're between jobs but thinking of getting your yoga teacher training. You're working on channeling your inner warrior and you're happiest in nature and have a dog which is the best thing ever and you're considering getting a second." He really smiled sweetly about the dog part in hopes of softening what some might take as caustic arrogance. Probably he didn't have a smile sweet enough though. "You love to travel more than anything," he touched her hand not unlike the way she had touched his, "except for your dog which you love more than anything. You meditate and jog and it seems to just come up in conversation how you meditate and jog. You're spiritual and an empath and believe your intuition is a gift. Your Instagram is mostly yoga poses and food pics—and your dog. After all these years your hormonal fluctuations still scare you. Mostly you're just trying to be your authentic self while living in the moment and speaking your truth. You came to Tofino to reconnect with nature,

189

and with *your* nature, to revitalize both your own wildness and inner peace." He leaned closer and did not smell sulphur and leaned back. "And given the fragrance of hot mineral water ionized by ancient stones, you were at Hot Springs Cove earlier today." He liked that last bit the best and was sure she hadn't noticed him earlier or why wouldn't she have said so.

Valerie didn't play poker but her face should consider taking it up. She nodded. "That's it. Wow. Nailed it. Impressive." Emotionless. "You've got me pegged. You're really good at understanding women and even better at telling them what they want to hear and you don't sound presumptuous or arrogant at all." She smiled very sweetly. "I have no idea why you're sitting alone at the bar."

"What did the pot say to the kettle?"

Words from smiling lips slowly poured like pure honey, "I actually don't have a dog but after listening to that I'm now thinking of getting one. Probably easier that way than for you to change your worldview. Our explorations of your worldview would likely ruin too many outfits."

He had no idea what that meant.

She didn't rush this pause, as if there was some pleasure here. "Flushing out all the birds from the pigeonholes you've put women into. In the name of fashion, let's leave it alone. But you didn't guess my profession, you just rambled off some lifestyle habits I'm guessing are common in your dates or the women you know, or maybe used to know?"

He leaned back.

"So that puts your listening skills on par with some men I know. Let's call them, most." Long hair tucked behind her ear she turned a pearl earring to him, spoke straight ahead. "But that's okay. Nothing wrong with being average Alex."

He could only see half her small smile given the whole was for Hillary who by her reaction had clearly overheard it all. And it sounded like his name ending that sentence was not verbally preceded by a comma. He realized she knew his name and he didn't know hers. He felt like some dynamic that started equal had somewhere somehow taken a tilt.

He was wrong. It was never equal. He had entered a rigged game set on an unlevel field. He had opened a door and before he entered, if he believed he might possess a bit of talent for the game, it should now be obvious there were certain arenas where a certain gender has the upper hand. Alex hadn't shifted on the bar seat and he didn't believe its stool legs had been sawed out under him, so he wondered why he was sitting less tall. About cut-in-half tall. He said he was too young to recall what it felt like that first time, but at least this day's circumcision made him laugh. He said in a soft laugh, "What's your name?"

She didn't even turn. Said like a boss, "Answer the question."

"Okay. Profession." He took another survey. How? he thought. Nicely dressed. What does that give me to work with? Approximately nothing. Double-breasted olive-green long-cut blazer. Low-cut white shirt tucked into black jeans. Bare ankles and white pumps. He came back up. Thin gold necklace. Long hair. He came up with nothing and said with confidence, "Let's see your hands." She turned and displayed her hands to him as if she were about to set them down on piano keys and he almost made a comment about her playing him like piano keys. He flipped them over. He so lightly raked his fingers over her palms, then pretended to study them—or rather, did study them, but pretended like he knew what he was doing. He squinted his eyes like he was puzzled by her lines, now troubled by them, now gravely concerned by them. He pointed and subtly shook his head and then with great burden whispered, "Ah no." A con man tried to buy a second with empty portent. He searched for something clever to say.

Nothing came.

He drew his finger down a randomly chosen line that he did not know was her heart line and she felt that tingle like a crawling spark or as if she held a comet with a long tail and he said, "But this here is truly interesting." He looked up at her then squinted. Back to the palm. He traced another line and the lack of firm contact seemed to increase the charge and she thought that was strange. He said, "But actually I would not feel right disclosing what I see. Morally, I mean. Ethically, is the problem. Not here, at least." He looked back up to her. "Having thought more on it, it might be better if you don't know. But just put that aside for now." Her lips came together kinda pursed and he had no idea how to interpret that. He lightly squeezed each of her palms, like one in a market might assess the ripeness of a peach. "These soft hands tell me you're not in construction. And with no callouses on the tips I now know you aren't a professional guitarist, and frankly, I'm a little disappointed about that because I love to be serenaded." He said that very seriously. "You aren't cut and nicked like me and at first I thought it would be adorable if we shared the same profession, maybe even dressed the same, get you some Carhartts. But now I'm doubtful." He turned her hands over. "No dirt under those pretty nails. So that rules out landscaper."

"I couldn't have just washed them?"

He took one of her hands and swept it between them to make her complicit in dismissing that silly question into the background noise of dish clatter and patron chatter and music that might now be described as jazz rap. From her upturned wrists to the bend of her elbows he softly drew a finger which at times slightly lifted, a Planck Length separating their contact, but that gap bridged by a spark they both felt and one of them wondered if when the apocalypse comes and the oil's all burned up and even the solar panels fail if this tingling voltage here might not just be strong enough to power the world. "I know for a fact tennis players have one outsized forearm. Same goes for professional arm wrestlers." He squeezed her bicep and did wonder if that was crossing an invisible line separating their personal space. He squeezed her other bicep because fuck it. "Cross both of those off the list."

She shook her head at this circus act. She glanced at the remaining bite of oyster.

He turned her wrists back over then put her hands together like he would now have her pray, covered hers with his, like he would lead them. "Given your cute nose's minimal freckles I think your time in the sun has been limited."

She wiggled it.

"That makes you not a professional dog walker." She made a comment that he should solve Scottish crimes and he said Watson don't ever interrupt me again or you can stuff your own haggis. "With your figure you just don't have the ass to do a plumber's crack justice."

"Charming." She unintentionally gave him what he needed.

"And your smile could light the dark. So now it's obvious. You are an electrician." He let her hands go, leaned back with the self-satisfaction of a sound deduction. Raised his glass.

Valerie was just cynical or realistic enough to wonder if he had repurposed some pickup line, but not so closed-off to silly efforts and tiny displays of very stupid gallantry. "Red seal." She held out her glass to him and a wine and a martini bumped hips. "To my first time having cheese with an oyster."

"Where are you from and what brought you to Tofino?" He demanded to know, now feeling like he'd earned it.

She said, "Valerie."

For a brief second he was confused. "Right. Valerie."

They both sipped.

He said, "Remember that time we were walking the beach and you said how years ago you used to find more sand dollars than now, and I said maybe it's the economy?"

"What?" She wondered if her de facto dinner companion wasn't perhaps neurologically diverse. "We've known each other for—oh. Is this how you introduce a joke?"

"Hi, my name's Alex."

Valerie shook her head and turned back to her drink.

"So what brought you to my fair town?"

Now she didn't even want to say why she was visiting because to a small degree it did kind of accord with his presumptuous stereotype. She looked for another answer and the only other honest one was her needing a little mental and physical distance from a bad breakup. All breakups are bad, she thought. A bit demurely, not quite bashfully, she told him where in three days she was heading. She kept her glass upright so this time it was only her light confessional laughter that spilled towards him over the bar.

Whatever it was, some charm through self-effacement or hint of humility, he felt something. It was touching. He didn't trust that at all. He thought he shouldn't say it but saying it was more fun and he said sweetly, even tenderly, "Or you could cancel on the silent retreat and just indulge in all Tofino has to offer."

He paused and she paused. What the hell, one of them thought, likely both. Dear Stacy, Tofino has one who kinda sounds like you. Her face unchanged. "Wow." Outside she did not laugh but inside maybe she did a tiny bit, so that comment's not-so-subtle insinuation must have been checked by something. Maybe his delivery. Maybe that they're both a drink in, or that she respected his gamble because she said, "You remind me of this ivy plant I used to know."

He thought a second. "Invasive?"

"A little creepy."

"Ah. Of course."

"Well that's a very sweet suggestion. But I think right now you should just silently retreat to your book. And maybe we should mount you in place of the wolf." She gestured towards it. "Hey predator?"

"So now you want to mount me?"

She shook her head. "You're projecting. That's not how I meant it."

"Put him on an ice rink and butter his feet, Freud couldn't slip any harder."

"Alex, sometimes a cigar is just a cigar."

"Yeah you wish."

She said on an unrelated topic have you heard of the mating tendencies of the mantis?

"Okay, weird, no Valerie I have not heard of the mating tendencies of the mantis. Tell me, is it most tender?"

"The female is known to remove the male's head before copulation."

Alex appeared tremendously confused. "But surely not before."

She just nodded and he looked alarmed. "No. But, how?"

"How does she do it, or how does he do it without a head?"

"Of course the second one."

"I don't know. Once you guys put your mind to something..."

"Well that's kind of a fucked-up thing to say in a fine-dining restaurant, Valerie. And Jesus that makes a Hallmark scene out of sea-otter coitus. Why does evolution like it so rough? Hey?" Alex at the bar imagining that green insect's lost little head spectating its own thrusting body. Probably its green alien jaw was still moving. He wondered if it was bemoaning death, or happy in copulation, even if that romance would be his last. Perhaps no truer picture of ecstasy and agony than a headless fucking mantis. Fucking headless mantis? he uncertain of the grammar. Undoubtedly the most disturbing nature scene ever to enter his head. "I think the male mantis needs a safety word." He turned back to her. "What should our safety word be, Valerie?"

"Oh I think your cheesy electrician pickup lines will keep you out of trouble."

Alex thought it was curious how her smile somehow sharpened the edge of her words. Like baking's strange chemistry where the addition of salt sweetens a cake. "Rather cynical. Original, I composed that line just for you. And your words now lie because your smile then didn't."

She touched his sleeve. "Aw, honey. That smile was pity, not arousal. Get it straight. I think my safety word will be cheque please."

Jay wasn't listening to a conversation that would likely rank high for this restaurant's queerest banter, hardly possible to classify as flirting, but now as if his listening unconscious had been alerted, he did look over. Alex said she's joking, Jay, that she will in fact be getting our cheque, he pointed to his stained sleeve, just not yet.

"Truthfully, Alex, I have exceptional orgasms without a man. So, you know, I'm good." Interesting smile. "I'm really good." Smile slightly broadened. She watched him. Watched him as if this all was entertaining, or like she was curious about his construction. She had met men made from different substances. She had read earliest man was made from clay. She hadn't met a clay man but she'd met several made from meat. Some high-end versions in Vancouver were made from very pretty porcelain. Sadly, she had cracked a couple of them and had to leave them to be repaired by their maker, their mother. Maybe she was curious about the construction of this one with the offside jokes and nicked-up hands.

"I see. Well, Valerie, that's about the loneliest thing I've ever heard. And that's where we differ." As if he set his barstool on a soapbox. "For me, sex is intimacy, tenderness and trust. It's like our hearts through our flesh are telling secrets." He slowed down and she bit her lip seductively and he wasn't sure if she was messing with him or genuinely moved or going to laugh or what the hell. It kinda tripped him up but he got the last part out. "The orgasm, Valerie, is just symbolic achievement of a shared vision."

"Do you see yourself as a great lover, Alex?"

"No more than the next man. So: yes."

"Not including the restaurant staff whose company you pay for, and the date who stood you up, do you have any friends?"

"No."

"Figured."

"Ruin my lipstick, not my mascara, Valerie."

She smiled at that one. "Excuse me." Valerie got up and took her phone and went to the bathroom and left Alex thinking about the puzzle of puzzles. When in a few minutes she returned she said, "If you keep making that face it's going to stay like that." Hillary inquired to her about an order.

Alex, as if they had just been talking about the enigma that is woman, interrupted their order. "I mean it just makes more sense that women are the puzzle." Said it like he had been thinking about it for a long time, maybe quite long, and might go on thinking about it. "We can't both be puzzles. We'd never get anywhere. Right?" He looked from one to the other.

Valerie and Hoops just stared at him. Valerie said kindly, "Alex, on the sane-delusional spectrum, you're not exactly straddling the zero hash, huh?"

He looked down between his legs, back up. "Maybe you can link some puzzle pieces for me. What's something you wish more men understood about women?"

Hillary punched in an order. Valerie played along because, meh, vacation. Where to begin? The female body? Too long a topic. Emotions? The mind? Longer. She considered saying that sometimes men scare her. That she was conscious of what hours she was at the gym or that sometimes a man walking too close to her car on a quiet street could put her on edge. Or that every single one of her friends had lived through some level of harassment. Every single one. She didn't say that. There was lots she could say. How sometimes when we share a concern we aren't looking for a solution we just want to be heard. Finally she said there's no answer. "It would vary depending on whom you asked. One woman can't speak for all women. There is no *woman*."

"Yeah yeah okay of course that's the correct twenty-first-century answer, but just play along. I'm asking you."

A moment in thought spent looking at him. "Love might look different than one's expectations."

"Like?" he asked.

"Like the blonde-haired blue-eyed big-tittied girl who's an angel with your parents and a devil in the bedroom and a talent in the kitchen." She squinted back at Alex squinting at her. "With a trophy salmon mounted above her desk where she's studying for her PhD in..." She took a second, "Marine biology..."

He gave no reaction.

"Whose researching quantum gravity..."

Alex cocked his head.

"Whose prepping her dissertation on classic literature..."

Alex thought to himself *the hell* and his face showed it.

"Who when you tell her about your story idea or your armchair philosophy, listens enthusiastically, nodding her pretty head—ponytail bobbing, of course—offers an insight, but doesn't deliver it as an insight, she says it in a way you yourself

198

think you thought it and now you take credit for it, and you will later explain that very insight back to her, where she will go on listening to you, with obvious pride and wonder at her incredible man. Thinking to herself, just how did she get so lucky. Daddy."

Alex blew a tiny wine bubble and nearly choked. He looked at this five-foot-two?-nut-job on a barstool. Then he swallowed both his wine and his impulse to pop her bubble, the one that she was living in wherein she housed her shallow conception of men. The same bubble now sized to about her self-righteous head that had her floating over the bar, as if an observation balloon to look down into the minds of men, where she could make her generalizations. Alex humoured her simplistic and shallow account of men. But his grace in letting her feel good about herself was now padding his bar seat and bringing him up to her height. She had floated up pretty high, and on that slow ascent he got a bit lonely. He got to thinking about that blonde, the big-tittied one, with the fish, who Mom and Dad were so fond of, the one who cooked the steaks, steaks? she said? who did those things you liked in the dark—all of them and made you think she liked to do them too. He had met her before. A couple times actually, but sadly it never worked out. Don't know why. Truthfully, that all sounded pretty good. Goddammit, he thought. Turns out she nailed him, nailed him to the bar seat because that all sounded pretty good. Alex smiling looked straight up past the electric orange filaments into the high ceiling.

Valerie didn't know what he was doing. "Inside joke?" she asked him.

"You tell me," he replied. "So, the literature bit. Where did that come from?"

She didn't say dating-app profile with a semicolon or that he was dining with Neruda. She said, "You're kinda wordsy for a fishing guide."

"Holy, pigeonhole."

"So, you're writing outdoor articles on the side."

"Okay maybe I am writing a bit on the side."

"Knew it."

"But mostly smut."

"Knew that too. What's your pen name?"

"Friendly Tickle."

"What's your pen name?"

"Mr. Curtains."

"Both of those aren't creepy at all. I wish you luck in your smutty endeavours."

Her touching back to livelihoods he realized he still hadn't discovered hers.

"I work online based out of Vancouver. A company focused on personal development and growth, social connection. We offer different workshops and activities and we're constantly adding more." An urge to check her emails even though she just did so very recently in the bathroom. "Things like yoga classes and breath workshops and meditation."

A small part of Alex was dismissive hearing these trending practices. But critiquing another's genuine efforts would be the very opposite of who he was trying to be. For all his flaws, that small voice got no microphone. "Cool. What's it called?"

"Base to Peak."

"I've heard of it. An app, right? I think I have friends using it."

"Yeah. We recently added nutrition and cooking classes, so this dinner here is basically just research."

Alex started listing off diets on one hand. "Keto, pesco, paleo, veggio, Atleo." The second last one he made up and the last one was the name of a floatplane company he randomly threw in.

She must have figured he was trying to be funny not belittle her trade. "Our nutritionists teach simple, whole-food eating. But none of it is very rule-based, none of it written in stone. Mostly just eat things you can pronounce. A big focus of the nutrition classes—but actually all the classes—is self honesty, ownership. People form meaningful bonds over shared pursuits and that accountability fosters well-being. We connect the student, class, instructor under one umbrella, one name."

"Base to Peak," Alex said.

In the split second before she continued she wondered if he was trying to regain some lost ground and redeem to her his listening skills. She wondered if her comment *Average Alex* had stung.

"What else is on the app?"

"There's cardio and strength training. We have affiliates in counseling and psychology. We use goal trackers and incentive-based intention setting and that's proprietary—we wrote and patented the software." She wrote the software. "Software that is now being used by other companies." She licensed it to them. "It's all really dynamic and fun."

"That's cool. And such passion. Every business would kill to have an employee like you."

She sipped. She hesitated. She said, "I started it. It's my company."

He tilted his head. "I guess you're living up to your name."

"My name?"

"Strength, boldness. *Valerie*."

"Okay and how did you know that?"

"Valeria. Latin, of course."

She waited.

"Alright maybe I googled it while you were in the can."

"Can. That's charming."

"Seriously though, I admire entrepreneurs. The risk and the creativity it takes. This vibrant and young town *is* entrepreneurship. So many of my friends are self-employed and it's hard to make things work here. The trade-off to live in one of the most beautiful places is that it takes some creativity to make ends meet. There are not so many traditional jobs and most revolve around tourism. Sounds like your livelihood is improving others. That's really cool." He said congratulations, not everyone gets to do what they love.

She didn't think she had said she loved it. "Thanks." Valerie's whiskey-sour arrived and she pulled with her teeth the cherry off the toothpick. She asked before biting it, "Do you enjoy being a fishing guide?"

"I do. Yeah."

Her silence.

"For a lot of reasons. The sunrises. The dawn colours. The water. The big blue water. I haven't really normalized its beauty and it's been fifteen years. The things on the water and in the water. Me on the water. The smell of the ocean. The blue ocean that sometimes is grey or green. A big salmon all dark and purple and silver and the shine of its body just under the surface. A bent rod, I just like how that looks and I don't know why and I don't really care why. As a rule, some things I do not question. Let beauty retain its mystery, you know? All my gear perfectly dialed and my hooks razor sharp. Fishing comes with all these aesthetics." He waited in case she wanted to *say fishing guides say aesthetics?* but she didn't. "Everything all quiet except the sound of a fish taking line off the reel, that metallic whiz. A man connected to a fish and the water. There's some things I just don't get used to even though you've seen it enough you should. But you don't. You know?"

She nodded.

"And my guests genuinely enthused. Grown men, sometimes old men being excited. Imagine a seventy-five-year-old man all excited and working his muscles and bringing home the fish. Just a fish on the line in nature. There's something there. A simple and good thing." He restrained an urge for continued redundancy, which for Alex was very, very hard. Either she got it or words were useless, as sometimes they are.

With sufficient passion, topic becomes unimportant. She didn't look uninterested. She said, "And the cons?"

"Let me wrap up the pros."

She thought that retort funny, borderline bossy, maybe minorly attractive.

"It's my boat my business my show. I don't need to have someone tell me when to get up and what needs doing or to do something better for me to do it and do it better. I need to show up if I want it to work. And not be numbed by routine even if the days are repetitive. I need my clients to be happy and to come back and to tell their friends to look me up. But that's easy because I genuinely just want them to enjoy their time. So there's this happy confluence of what's good for business being what I already want for my guests."

She noticed he said guests not customers. "That's really sweet. Your job sounds cool and you sound good at it."

He smiled. "How did you know I like compliments?"

She rolled her eyes. "Okay. Now: *and the cons?*"

"Cons. Alright. This isn't complaining it's just you asking. It can be hard on the back. Stack together enough southeasterly days and your knees feel it. Sometimes shoulder season isn't as busy as I want it to be and sometimes summer is busier than I want it to be. There aren't really any barriers to entry, as in, I can get another boat and train someone up, but if they save some money or get a loan, they might just start up their own business, get their own boat. So sometimes it feels like you're training your competition. And it's hard to find or hold staff without offering them accommodation when everyone in this town is short-term renting." He stopped as if abbreviating a longer rant. "But on the whole, there is other work I could do. There's no other work I'd rather do. I'm lucky."

The two mixologists shook and muddled and stirred, crafting stylish drinks flared with garnish. Four flamboyant cocktails were lined up before them as if Alex and Valerie sat front row to the catwalk. Valerie again excused herself for the bathroom. In the stall she scanned emails and then opened a text from Dad. *Send me pictures of the Bomber!* *plane emoji* He had linked an article. She skimmed it before the flush.

After Pearl Harbour, Tofino became Canada's front-line defence from the threat of invading Japanese. On Long Beach, barbed-wire fences stood to repel invasions. February 8th, 1945, at 23:00 a Canso plane was departing Royal Canadian Air Force Station Tofino on a routine anti-submarine patrol. After passing the end of the runway the port engine failed. The pilot attempted a 180-degree return to the airfield but tree tops clipped the fuselage. The pilot intentionally stalled the plane to bring it down as gently as possible and the plane impacted the side of a low hill. One passenger, himself a pilot with thirty top-secret missions flown in the European theatre, was covered in gasoline and thrown from the cabin and snagged in a tree branch where he dangled off the ground. The plane carried nearly 3000 pounds of fuel and 1000 pounds of depth charges intended to be dropped on submarines, but the cargo did not explode and all the passengers survived. In the early hours of the following day they heard a plane and the crew sent up a flare. The search-and-rescue plane returned a flare of its own and the downed crew sweated its arrival as they watched it fall towards their fuel-soaked, explosive-laden crash site. In the end the only explosion came when the RCAF made a controlled detonation of the depth charges which left a large crater still visible today.

Two empty seats to Alex's left, but the next two over were occupied. A man and a woman about the same age, close to Alex's own age. He recognized the dude. Alex heard him say, "Yeah I came out here six years ago to check it out. Then just never left. That's about the most common Tofino story there is. So you're from California?"

"Yes. I live in Cardiff-by-the-Sea."

"Rad. So that's us both then. I live in Tofino, by the sea."

"Oh, no, I mean it was named after a song—that's my city's full name. *Cardiff-by-the-Sea*."

"Oh." A pause. "Well that's about the most pretentious thing I've ever heard."

Alex almost face-palmed himself for a brother in arms saying something stupid on what looked like a date. It's hard out there, I know. He wasn't trying to listen in and now there was only silence anyways. He wanted to pat the guy on the back and say something encouraging but someone to his right said, "Okay local, I'm thinking of checking out the Bomber Trail tomorrow. Is it worth it? Any tips?"

Alex thought about the last time he trekked to that historical heap of twisted metal, passing the derelict and dank concrete building tucked away in the woods as if that was its keeping place when it wasn't featured in some troubled dreamer's apocalyptic horrorscape. He considered what to himself had always been a rather underwhelming hike. "Definitely. Yeah. It's just so fascinating. The old spray-painted crumbling fuselage all rusting-away there in the woods. All broken and shitty. But the thing is, you're going to need a tour guide. The town just enacted this new by-law. Alongside *All dogs must be leashed* and *No beach fires*."

Of course she knew he was extravagantly lying. "I see."

205

"The reason being we lost a whole convoy of Asian tourists last week. Two Germans last Thursday were eaten by bears trying to find the plane."

"The bears were trying to find the plane?"

"Anyways, like I was just telling the truth, bears said the Germans tasted sour. We lost fourteen Quebecois to cougars this year already. Cougars said they were poutine themselves in a forest where they didn't belong."

Valerie looked at Alex and with her thumb she slowly pushed away the dinner menu. She looked at Jay the bartender and said, "Safety word, please."

"Disregard that, Jay. She's trying to be cute."

"And do you happen to know any tour guides free on such short notice? Preferably one whose improv routine has very few puns. And of those few puns, even fewer that sound borderline racist."

"Oh Valerie. I see what you're doing here and I find it a little forward. But... maybe. I mean, maybe I could be convinced to lead this gruelling Bomber expedition. But it's going to cost you a glass of wine. And I'm going to need you to formally apologize, in writing—" he had only dipped one napkin in the sparkling water and saw a pen next to the straws and limes, "for denigrating my livelihood and those who work in my honest profession, the humble fishing guide."

She pinned the napkin to the bar top then scribbled lightly and slid it his way. Elegant cursive. *Fishing guides drink wine?*

He told her that there were some secrets to that trail that he didn't feel he ought to share with the greater public. It would be better if they got a private table for these privileged local insights. Alex had a table reserved for his date and inquired to Jay if it was still available and he checked and said very shortly, Alex.

Sometimes Fogust comes early and this town's affectionately-named, late-summer portmanteau enshrouded the Tofino evening. Restaurant guests sitting second-floor window-side watched Fourth Street in the fog. The sky above had mellowed and the music seemed inspired. Call it a kind of cloud rap. It was all very nice. He turned to her. "So. What are you looking for, Valerie?"

"Why do you think I'm looking for something?"

"A female sitting alone at the bar." He chose a better line. "I mean, mostly we're all of us looking for something. No?"

"And you're what I've been looking for? Will you save me, Alex? Will you complete me?"

He cocked his head and raised his eyebrows.

She said, "Why do I need you to love me when I can be broken on my own?"

He smiled at that. "A CEO-poet and a fishing guide are sitting at the bar..."

She figured that opener to his joke was also its punchline and she stayed on her tack. "Alex, do I need a man to tell me I'm beautiful?"

"So what are you looking for?"

"Someone to call me pretty and feed me Doritos." She batted her eyes.

"Doritos. Really?"

"Pick your battles, son. Doritos is not one you'd win. And what are you looking for, Alex?"

"You already did me. Big-tittied, blue-eyed, right?" Maybe that was the drinks or maybe he liked to keep her on her toes or test her limits or maybe he felt a very early hint of something that made him distrustful. Distrustful of himself.

She said, "You remind me of someone I almost met on a dating app."

"Inside joke?" He swiped an airy finger. "Hey, keep tellin' yourself there's always another swipe." To his left, the woman sitting with the man got up with her jacket and handbag and went down the stairs. Alex sipped his wine then set it on the coaster and turned it and was looking at his hand as he turned it. He said: "I'm looking for true love."

She looked at him. "But really?"

He shrugged. "Really."

"I'm not sure if as a mid-forties?" she inclined that word, "late forties-year-old man? you can say that. I mean, you can say that, but do you think it might sound a little ridiculous?"

"True love?"

"Yeah."

"*True* love."

"Yes."

"Fine. I'm looking for cheap initial thrills, followed by dysfunction, boredom, then sticking together out of habit, fear of loneliness, and financial commitments."

"Now isn't it easier being normal?"

"I'd love to be in a meaningful relationship. Like two, maybe even three days a week, I'd really like to be in a meaningful relationship. I could see that occasionally being sometimes fulfilling."

"You're on fire. You just don't quit, hey?"

"Oh Valerie. I wonder if the romantic bits are mostly dead inside me. And what remain are strictly for commercial purposes."

"Commercial purposes?"

"Well, those rare, tender breaks in the smut novels. Before the smut continues, you know?"

"You don't seriously write sex novels do you?"

"Wow. After having denigrated my primary profession you're going to besmirch my honest and scandalous prose workers of the slutty page?"

"So what mostly killed them?"

"What?"

"The romantic bits."

"Oh. Those." It actually wasn't the first time he had used that line, but that line hadn't gone any farther. He had to think about it. "It was a man actually."

She didn't know him well but she thought she knew him well enough to guess he wasn't bi-sexual. And already she knew him well enough to get the sense this was another baited line, so she just waited for the inevitable delivery, wondering how often he dropped the joke reel, and whether she herself even cared to know him on a subsurface level because at least this was entertaining, somewhat, and she was only here for three more days. In their weird little conversational journey this evening through cheap jokes and cynicism and cliché and sexual banter she felt like they were now furthest from any genuineness they may have momentarily touched on when sharing their profession. She waited for the punchline her own long reflection had likely killed of any comical impact.

"His name: Walt Disney."

She had been prepared to give the starving comic a charitable laugh, but she did give a small real one. Not at the joke so much but for the teller's silly delivery. Like he was kinda pleased with it but in an endearing rather than self-obsessed way. Like they could share the joke together. "Cute. So, is it like, you sleep for eight hours and you're sarcastic the rest?"

"Actually no. I have transient insomnia. It's mostly sarcasm."

"Well, Alex, your humour is of course fucked-up and you cross the line into several types of offside, and I think I can smell fish on your hands."

He raised a hand to his nose but his sense of smell was his weakest sense and his others weren't so Japanese-carbon-steel sharp themselves and he hoped she was just messing with him.

"But other than that, you almost seem like in the future you could have your shit together. Temporarily, of course. So I just have to ask. Why ever are you single? Why hasn't some local fisherwoman reeled you in?"

He put his palms to the sides of his neck, then leading with his thumbs kinda flapped them open a couple times like gills. "Such a lady that says the F-word and the S-word at the dinner table." He gestured to their bar. "Is that how women speak in Vancouver?"

"When in Rome—when talking to fishing guides. Now don't evade. Tell me: what's wrong with you besides all the obvious?"

He shrugged. "I've just been waiting for you."

"Touching." Valerie took a break from the B-tour comedy show and picked up the menu she had by now nearly memorized. The gap between them so stuffed with gags it was nearly an insulation barrier.

Alex made another joke but figured she must have missed it. He took up his menu. Bottom to top all he read on it was the question she had put back to him. *What are you looking for?* What am I looking for?

He didn't say: I don't want, could this work. I don't want, I think there's something here and I could see us being happy. I want fuck off I can't live without her. I want unreasonable expectations. I won't settle for less than that and if that's not in store for me, fine, so be it, I'd truly rather be lonely. I want are you even fucking real. I want sleepless nights trying to figure out how not to fuck it up because I'm not bad at fucking things up. He didn't say that.

As he spoke, a coincidental hush befell the music and the background murmur and the cutlery chime. He didn't speak any louder but the random drop in atmospheric volume was as if this evening's architect conspired to make him some lunatic yelling into the void. Her question: *What do you want?* His answer: "I want love, beauty, truth."

The man to his left now drinking alone paused the pint glass in front of his lips. The closest diners at the table behind them turned in their chairs. One bartender, one chef, one Valerie stared at him. His eyes shifted. Everyone waiting for something more, for an explanation of that absurd outburst.

But he only nodded, as if certain truths are self-evident. Then he took a drink, nothing more to say.

She assumed it was a joke and it may have been, but the lines of sarcasm and genuineness were now more tangled than the seaweed salad she was about to order. Valerie smiled amused at the silly one-liner from her most weird and chance dinner companion. Then she looked away. Alex had just about rendered his speech meaningless, this little boy at the bar had cried wolf one too many times.

From over Alex's shoulder a dish was presented before him. Its inadvertent timing as if a prize for his strange outburst. He hadn't yet ordered anything. He saw a savoury dish looking rather sweet. Elegant oyster. She eyeing the menu, not looking his way, with a bitten lower lip. Must have been when you got up for the bathroom, he thought.

Someone screeched a chair sounding like the rusted creak of the world returning to its spin, the background sounds and restaurant chatter returned. The music taking a break from hip hop, now onto some moody song, not so loud, base line and drumbeats and hi-hats but slow, subdued electric-guitar notes sounding explorative, lyrics telling some story about a creep and the skin of a crying angel. Something like that. He couldn't really focus on it. He looked to his neighbour who had squared her debt. Hey, Virtue.

He said, sounding less sarcastic, "I want to be worthy of love, beauty, truth."

Her eyes on the menu, whether she heard him or was listening to the song. But her bite released what could no longer be restrained and a heavy chord came from a distorted guitar.

XVII

The pain of severance is not in proportion to the duration two people have passed together, but by the depth of connection once had, now lost. Big deep unions don't need time's permission. Nobody even understands time. It's not an absolute cosmic clock evenly ticking, that we know. Your head in old age, that much further from the earth's core, will be one second younger than your wise toes. Certain things are safer from its advance while others are at greater risk from its stagnation. Two coworkers with neighbouring cubicles pass three decades together then hardly bat an eye when one retires. A mother with her heart forever broken over her purple newborn. All in the fullness of time? What's time got to do with it.

***

This evening Trent is parked on the street outside Mermaid Tales Bookshop. He tracked her phone and her arrival by car service in a black Yukon Denali. From where he is parked he can see, between a red car and a green Tacoma, the Wolf's glass door. When she had gone in he walked across the street to the pharmacy. Bought a toothbrush and toothpaste, soap in a travel case, a hand towel, a few other things. He recrossed the street for Shed Restaurant and ordered from the walk-up takeout window. While they prepared it he went inside.

He looked around the small bathroom. Black and white photos on the wall. A driftwood skeleton with big black holes for eyes. A portrait of a woman with long hair, her arm across her naked chest, a wildness about her beauty. A muscled young man in a tight undershirt, thumbs outside his jean pockets, head cocked. Trent looked at the young man for long enough it was like he expected that boy there in the photo to look away first. As if it takes more than muscles to make you hard. Trent lifted that picture off its small nail and dropped it in the trash. He removed the small soap bar from its case. Took out the small towel and folded it beside the sink just so. Took off his black t-shirt and went to hang it on the back of the door but it lacked a hook so he tucked it into the back of his jeans.

He looked at the mirror and the mirror looked pained. He looked away from his belly to his face. He hadn't forgotten about the beard he just wasn't used to it. He leaned to the basin and washed his face, then wet half the towel and washed his armpits. He hadn't told anyone the real reason. Only her. Grease stain from the stove when he was a kid, he said. Usually answering something like that. Car battery exploded. That was the other one. Some would go to touch the markings and he would stop that. Sometimes he didn't answer. He had had no plans to tell her.

Those belly scars in Shed's mirror looked like they could still smoke. But none of them had since the last day his belly was used as an ashtray. As a place to stub one out, stub several out. The first one was made thirty-four years ago and the last one thirty years ago. When he was a boy on cold winter days walking to school on Vancouver's East Hastings Street he would exhale and watch the mist. Exhale and watch the smoke. Sometimes on cold days he still does that.

He had no plans to tell her. Why tell anyone that? Why expose to another your deformities? Why reveal what can only repel? That night in the dark when she laid her head on his belly it just came out. If love is a drug it's a truth serum. It didn't feel good telling her. It didn't feel bad. And not something in between. Everyone says if it's not one or the other then it's in between. It's not always. A feeling indivisible to certain proportions good and bad, nor does it reside on a common spectrum and if there is a word for it he didn't know it. Somewhere between a shit and a birth and floating and sinking and drowning and catching your breath. Right in the very middle of that. All those rope-ends tied tightly together in one knot. That's the word.

A week after he told her, she left. He always expected that's how it would go. Then it happened. So he wasn't surprised.

Water dripped off his beard. He's a big guy. Takes up a lot of the mirror. Washing with his head now bowed, as if within its glass the face remained and he trying to evade its derision. He looked up. Saw what he saw. Dried himself with the towel's dry half and put his shirt on.

You are marvelous, Trent. Trent, if only you knew that the gods love ugly. And that we're all ugly. And if only there was a god.

Trent picks up his order and walks to his loaner car, a white Ford Edge. It's due back three hours ago a ferry-ride away. He gets in the car and doesn't start it. Across the street in front of him the hostess is sitting just inside the glass door. Above her the Wolf's upper-patio doors open. A server walks out. Then Valerie. Then not Trent. Watching through panes, patio glass and windshield, whether in scrutiny or rage, a pair of eyes do narrow.

XVIII

As if this restaurant's architect believed in the Many Worlds Hypothesis, The Wolf in the Fog has two bars, two patios, two stories. The waitress led them from the upper bar out to the upper patio and Alex asked Valerie if she thought an alternate though minutely different Alex and Valerie were on the lower floor. "Another story on the other story?" He said *that* Valerie had just made to *that* Alex a very promiscuous proposition. This Alex shook his head at this Valerie for that other Valerie's boldness. "Very scandalous of your alternate self."

This Valerie said, "There aren't many worlds enough for that other world," and he started saying something didactic about infinity but she cut him off saying, "Technically I was joking," and he said, "Oh. Good one."

Downtown Tofino in the warm orange evening. A trafficless four-way stop below them. The waitress presented the bottle of red wine and Valerie, approving the cork, tasted the sample. The server poured.

"There's your wine. Now start talking about the Bomber."

"Surprise surprise, a CEO all business. Gotta say, I'm glad that earlier you ordered yourself an oyster. I don't really think I could date a vegetarian."

"Aww." She tilted her head. "You think this is a date."

"Food is my lifestyle. Is basically my religion." He said how he caught all his meat, fishing and spearfishing and bow hunting, butchered it himself and had a big garden with chickens, smoked salmon and deer. How the ethics and sustainability of it mattered to him as much as the wild nutrition.

She listened to him go on with his convictions, at times charmed, other times wondering if suppose this was to turn into something, if he would one day, whether directly or passively, attempt to impose onto her his particular worldviews that underlay his subjective ethics. She had known a man who the only thing he held in higher regard than his arbitrary ethics was the sound of his own voice preaching them. Acting as if he had deduced or divined some objective morality that they now ought to live by, when really it was only his interpretation of right and wrong in the world, which he himself did not always live up to. Thus, hypocritical, flawed and arbitrary. When she had brought it up with him he did ease up some, but still affected a quiet judgementality. It wasn't exactly patriarchal, it just wasn't so fun to be around. It made it harder for them to play in the world. At least this one here is kinda funny, she thought.

"... and that makes it justifiable." He ended some sermon.

Two foodies discussed the appetizers like contract negotiators. Valerie said she'd take a hard pass on the foie gras.

They moved one lower and he said, "After watching My Octopus Teacher I just don't think I can do it. I have a hang-up when it comes to eating something smarter than me."

"Perhaps then you might consider becoming a vegetarian?"

He said ha ha and they ordered the seaweed salad. A man and a woman were leaving the patio and while passing their table she dropped her red scarf and Alex got up and picked it up and it wasn't dirty but he brushed it off and caught up to her and returned it.

The sinking sun shined on short buildings stunted by local bylaws. Down Fourth Street towards the harbour a crab boat was idling in to unload. One dock over, a fish-farm boat was unloading Atlantic salmon and restocking de-licing chemicals. Further down the harbour moored a coast guard ship that had one day searched Duffin Cove for the missing and one day to come would tow a flipped floatplane. On the patio of a waterfront restaurant with old brick boated in from a demolished Vancouver bank, brick that arrived from overseas to Vancouver as ship ballast, the owner with shoulder-length white hair falling from under a wide-brimmed black hat was telling the tourists how the foam on the surface of the water was the ejaculate of sperm whales. His shirt that referenced vagina, attire that might undermine him on some topics, oddly seemed to bestow him with a kind of credibility on the topic of sea sperm. Further down the harbour on a large pier one person said to her friend, "I wonder what that sign means, *Outfall*?" On that same pier an ambulance was parked and waiting, its attendants watching an incoming boat. Around the shore past Grice Point on a wooden observation deck off the Tonquin Trails, a couple shared a tall can of cider, and watched that sun now slightly more sunk.

The seaweed salad was presented centre table. Vibrant greens, puffed rice, red and white radish. Alex didn't break from his story. "She told me—*thank you*—that I didn't really love her."

Valerie was momentarily confused until she excised from the story that thank you directed to the server.

"She looked me in the eyes and spoke as if she knew better than me what was in my own heart." Alex and Valerie were trading some of their favourite failed romances. "I kissed her hand and told her, but Jackie, I *do* love you. She pulled away, in more ways than one. Then we napped in a group on the floor." Alex set two fingers of one hand side-by-side on the table. Then sighed. "Napped apart." He spread his two fingers.

Valerie's laugh travelled back in time to kindergarten and comforted young Alex suffering his first lost love. Physics allows for time travel, so though both young and present-day Alex were touched they were not so surprised. "Our relationship lasted less than a school week but she packed a curriculum of love into a few recesses. Taught me many things those bittersweet Winnipeg spring days." Alex should stop now with his audience of one mildly entertained and move on to something of meaning or just something else at all or just stop talking and let her talk. He did believe he could sculpt shoulders like a pommel-horse gymnast by picking all the low-hanging fruit from his everbearing tree of self-improvement. "I named my first vehicle after her. A dilapidated, mechanically suspect, loud and sweet piece of ass. A Jeep YJ with fuck-off big tires and half doors. I miss her. Them both. Both Jackies." He said their name wistfully.

"You're a clown." Valerie with her two index fingers made tiny claps, like tiny mouse claps for his small theatrical performance.

"Please tell me you also have a failed romance to share with the table." He gestured.

"I don't."

He regarded her suspiciously.

"I have many. Okay, I see your first crush and raise you a complex. I once got a valentine from my first beau. He had drawn me in crayon—so thoughtful. My head was big but my smile was huge. He captioned it: *Your smile is too big for your face. I don't like you anymore*. He stood in front of my desk and watched me read it. Then he explained it, just to make sure I understood, about my smile not fitting, pointing at my face then holding his arms out. More factually than cruelly. So it wasn't so much a love letter as it was a pictograph of my flawed physiology. Then he said something about my nose." She touched her nose.

Alex looked away from her nose. Then he put his hand over his heart.

"Yeah. Well I cried every night for a week and actually don't think I smiled for a month. I'm serious, a month, at least. And sometimes when I do smile, I still think about that. It's funny because it's so old and of course I don't care and it's just kids being cute and stupid and kids. But in one sense, it's just about the worst thing you could say to a kid. It's so subversive, the very root of happiness, a smile. Kids are funny at how perfect their cruelty can be."

"Yeah we figure that out early. Or more likely it came encoded with the software."

"My mom asked me what's up and I didn't answer. So she sat me down. I think after she got off the phone with his mom that boy didn't smile for even longer. I actually felt bad about that."

To Alex that last sentence said more than the others combined. "If we're going to just sit here and confess our list of broken, we had better ask Chef if he has eggs to make us sunrise omelettes."

"I think I dated him by a different name in a future year, a twenty-eight-year-old version. He put me on Rate my Face dot com." She laughed and Alex wasn't sure if he was supposed to also laugh so he drank. "Do you ever wonder how those early and silly traumas, that weren't so silly back then, affect you now? Or if every time you have a breakup, some part of you becomes thicker or calloused? Like when you breakdown muscle it grows back stronger and harder to break next time."

"Yeah like the UFC fighter who could tap you out by looking at you, meanwhile he's scared of fluffy kittens from some long-ago trauma."

"I sometimes wonder how many of those are messing with my own head. And it's not like they have to be obvious to still be twisting our outlook. As in we're probably all walking around with many of these complexes in varying degrees of significance. It would be fascinating if we could know our psychological history, see a seismogram of all the emotional quakes that shaped us, including those ones our motherly unconscious is keeping from us."

"Yeah. The story we know of ourselves is not an objective one. Isolated peaks of emotional impact rising up from vast deserts of forgotten though formative days. A shame that evolution didn't prioritize our capacity for introspection as much as our ability to run away from bears." Alex split the last of the salad dishing Valerie's first. A couple was led out to a table behind them. The evening cooling and Meares Island in the distance donning a tuft of cloud like a mountain's knit toque.

Alex said, "There was this old Simpsons episode. Homer is stuck all day with his arm inside a vending machine. The fireman eventually says to him, Uh Homer, are you just holding on to the can? Homer replies, Your point being? I wish I could say to my mind, just stop holding on to the can."

She set her hand over top of his. "Maybe you and I will be able to give each other a new complex."

"Aww, that would be really nice." They cheersed to their current complexes and those to come.

Valerie said, "If you go from watching a movie to playing a sport, there's about a one-hundred-fold increase in energy output. But if you go from watching a movie to taking a cognitively demanding math exam, your brain, as measured by FMRI and your body by caloric consumption, hardly shows an increase in activity."

"That surprises me. I thought the math exam would be sucking calories."

"I know. But conscious thought is just a small part of the mind's total processing. What *we are* is mostly subsurface. Like how you play an instrument better without thinking about the keys because some part of you is *thinking hard about the keys*. How ludicrous that some demanding tasks are performed better without thinking about them. I heard my mom—piano teacher—tell a student, the more you think the more you stink. The unconscious might be everything. Studying it was super popular in the early twentieth century, Freud and Jung. Then it fell into disrepute and was a good way to keep you from getting tenure. Now with new methods of inquiry, brain scans and falsifiable testing, it's popular again."

"Valerie do you think you should say *falsifiable testing* to a mere fishing guide you're trying to seduce?"

"Bribe with wine for local insights of the aforementioned Bomber Trail. Not seduce, Alex."

Behind Valerie, Alex watched an older couple cross the four-way. Their backs were hunched. He had a cane and they held hands. Old-style hats, a red beret and newsboy cap. Alex couldn't see their faces but he assumed by their movements their faces probably looked nervous. It was Monday evening but they were dressed for church. Alex was going to point them out and ask Valerie why they held hands. From love, or habit, or fear of a changing world? Or could their love be deepened by fear? Or were they just trying not to slip?

"I was on a second date with this man and I asked him if he wanted kids. His reply, I'm down for whatever."

"He sounds versatile at least." Alex slowed his eating pace so he wouldn't finish before her.

"One of the first serious relationships I had was in university. It took a little while for this to show up and I didn't get what was going on at first but then I noticed a trend. If I made a mistake he made me feel that it wasn't my actions that were flawed but my character. Like if I accidentally left the apartment unlocked *I* was defective, not my actions. *I* was pitiable for having an imperfect nature. Do you know what I mean?"

Alex while tugging at his collar said he definitely did not know what she meant.

"At first I didn't really get that this was an unhealthy dynamic because I just didn't have many others to compare it with. My parents." She shrugged. "And back then all the TV relationships were pretty ideal."

"Home Improvement. Rosanne. Full House. Fresh Prince. Cheers."

Valerie raised her glass and Alex shrugged but raised his glass too saying ah you missed a good one, Diane.

"After a few months with him I started seeing this other pattern. If I said I wish I wasn't such a procrastinator and could get my assignments done without cramming through the night, or that I thought I should exercise more or whatever, I noticed it was eventually coming back my way. When I figured out what was happening, I could almost hear him pushing that bullet into the gun."

Alex had the urge to correct her, it's not a bullet it's a cartridge and in most cases you don't really push it into the gun, more like load it into a magazine.

"It made me not want to talk about those things that I was insecure about, because it was like I was just giving him ammunition. I was young and just thought dynamics like that were normal."

Alex nodded. "Well, I'm glad you got out of that one. It must not have been easy and taken a long time. For a procrastinator." She actually laughed harder than she had that night because that joke was walking the thinnest of lines and Alex smiled knowing it. "He sounds like an asshole." Alex said that genuinely and lifted her cutlery off her plate and set her plate on his and laid their forks together spooning.

"Well, I know you're saying that to be nice. But sometimes saying that is part of the problem. I mean, what's his history?

How was he raised? No one exists on their own. There are no assholes in a vacuum."

"I gotta say *assholes in a vacuum* is the second most striking visual you've implanted in my skull, Valerie. Second only of course to the headless mantis thrusting his raging and final little insect boner." Alex flicked his pinky finger rigid. "Can't wait to see what my mind does to those two in the fantastic world of nightmares."

She smiling sipped her wine. "Should we order?"

The formerly warm orange sky was turning a cooler purple, magician's colour. As if this night with tricks to perform. At the far end of the patio came a metallic donk. Midway, another. He said to the approaching waitress that's okay her love warms enough and the waitress was actually not going to light their heat lamp and he said just joking I'm really freaking cold and then thanked her for lighting it. Under the hot dome's radiating heat he rubbed his hands then wondered if he looked like a pussy for being colder than she was and stopped and pretended he wasn't so cold and crossed his arms but then recalled that that is a posture of unwelcomeness and uncrossed them and picked up his wine with Reynaud-white fingers and kinda held the glass in a position that might subtly display the size of his bicep but then realized that was stupid because he was wearing a long-sleeved shirt, a stained one. "And what did you reply to that guy who asked about wanting kids?"

"Sometimes I don't. Sometimes I do. But I just turned thirty-eight. The ol' biological clock. I kinda need to get on that if it's going to happen."

Alex nodded. "You could always adopt."

"I could. But it's not something I'd want to undertake alone. And I dunno. I don't think it would feel the same. I know maybe you're not supposed to say that. Just for me, I'm not sure it would. For other people, I'm sure it's perfect."

"You don't have to attach the disclaimer. And you're CEO of Born to Peak."

"Base to Peak."

Fuck. Focus. "Base to Peak that's what I said. Can't you just buy one, or hire someone to kidnap one for you?"

"It's a good point you raise there. I actually did look into that, but it would probably mean I'd have to change our mission statement on the website and slogan on our t-shirts and mugs and all that. Just seems like a lot of work in the name of motherhood."

"I actually like the idea of making that decision with my lady. I could imagine a woman such that I could not imagine the greatest world existing without smaller versions of her. If we talked about it and believed that would give our lives the most meaning, I'd be in. Partly I just want to see my parents as grandparents. But I think I could be happy both ways. I mean, I'm happy now. Both could be fulfilling in their own way. If you get lucky at ground level and find your best friend, if you have meaningful pursuits and friends and all the rest, I just don't think anything else, even kids, is really missing from that equation.

"You know, thinking about it, your guy that said down for whatever. Maybe he just meant what I'm saying now, but said it differently. Maybe so many male-female relationships struggle not from incompatibility but from miscommunication."

"You realize that if you speak any louder about *male* and *female* in this era of gender fluidity you'll be denounced on social media before bedtime and cancelled when you wake up, right?"

"As long as you got my back, babe."

"Yeah I definitely don't."

"Two years ago someone said to me gender fluid. I said cleanup on aisle four. But now? Hey. I try to keep an open mind. To each their own."

"I feel like you could get a person cancelled by association."

He raised his glass. "May I never be so progressive as to disavow the grace of a woman's touch. Creed of the unwoke, motto of the old fashioned. Member: me."

Valerie shook her head and reached for her wine.

Alex said, "I have friends who say they don't want to bring children into this world. Meanwhile this is the best we've ever had it, on nearly every metric. Access to education, minority rights, gender equality, healthcare, longevity, and dozens of others. Half a century ago half the world lived in extreme poverty. Two hundred years ago, everyone did. Now it's less than ten percent. We'll eradicate it within our lifetime. That's simply utterly astounding and how often do you see that in the news? Never? That should be front page every single day. Getting that many people out of extreme poverty is legendary. People who say the world is going to hell have no conception of history. Not long ago there were no antibiotics or electricity. Dentistry was a shop of horrors. For a mastectomy you might shoot a jigger of whiskey in hopes of dimming the pain. Maybe the environment is in hot water but there's no obvious cap to the amount of people living green lifestyles that the Earth can sustain. Maybe it's not too late." He shrugged. "Well-raised kids are the antidote to our existential challenges. Saying you don't want kids because of the state of the world seems to me a bet against human ingenuity, which is really a bet that evil triumphs over good."

"I see why you write fiction."

"Smut—don't twist my script, Virtue." He looked down to the menu's mains. She had set hers aside. "A counterpoint to my optimistic lens. There's an old Greek saying, or was it Persian? A civilization approaches its downfall when its internet porno becomes predominantly incestual. *My Naughty Stepsister*, et al."

"Sounds like you've done your homework, Alex."

"A man who truly wants to understand his times must know his day's pornography—quote Hairyclitoris? Heraclitus? It's pretty funny that by solving captcha to access incestuous internet porn we're training the AI that might just destroy us all. I mean, if you wrote that plot nobody would think it plausible. And yet. Here we are. Stranger than fiction." He shook his baffled head.

The server collected their plates. Valerie asked for a lemon water and Alex holding up a peace sign said please make that two. "She's really thirsty."

Valerie said, "I just met him here. Please let me know if he's wanted back at the bar and I'll happily return him." Valerie ordered the pasta and Alex the burger and fries.

"Interesting choice."

"I respect a fine-dining restaurant that offers a burger and fries."

"Alright, back on relationships. Tell me about your marriage. Why didn't yours last?"

"Which one."

"That's funny."

"Is it?"

"Well, kinda. Right?"

"Glad my emotionally painful and rather expensive history of failed love makes you laugh, Valerie."

"Alright. Tell me about the last one."

"Nah."

"Then tell me about the first one?"

"I feel like I've been doing all the talking."

"Wow, wow, such timely self-awareness, Alex."

He liked that. "You go. Tell me about your last relationship."

Val thought about Trent. She looked down this sunset street underneath a smearing of pastel clouds and is every night in Tofino painted such colours? She looked over a row of parked cars. She looked at Alex and shook her head. "Me too, I'll pass."

"Okay great. We're really getting somewhere."

He sipped. She sipped.

A sea breeze rolling over the Pacific had found land at Wya Point, the rocky headlands sheared it and half blew on southwards and half north where it churned in Florencia Bay then built speed over the open stretch of Long Beach, tucked into Schooner Cove and rounded Portland Point, navigated the rocky crags of Radar Beach, it followed the deep curve of Cox Bay, the breeze stoking flames of an illegal beach fire now seen by a by-law officer and it rolled through Rosie Bay and into South Chesterman and the tide being low it passed behind Frank Island and onto North Chesterman Beach and stoked the flames of a legal beach fire which hissed from fat dripping off a smokie and it continued on over the sand towards beaches Mackenzie, Middle, and Tonquin and the girl on the bench watching the blood orange sky over this champagne coast passed that tall-can cider to the guy and the breeze hugged the curves of Duffin Cove where a gap in shore rock funneled it into town and it blew down Campbell Street to flutter the leaves of a rhododendron and like a pick-pocket it plucked pink petals off a cherry tree without swaying its branches then breezed on down the street but found little trash to stir until outside Big Daddy's Fish Fry it tumbled a discarded facemask half a sidewalk, like a drunk leaving a masquerade, then swirled it up, like a lone dancer making a few turns, as if behind that mask now came a smile, and the breeze nearly winded so far from the sea it set the mask down on the windshield of a white Ford Edge whose occupant turned on the wipers and it flowed through the four-way at fourth and Campbell Street where its final rolling puff breezed up to the Wolf patio and swept back a few strands of Valerie's long hair and Alex seeing her earring thought to himself it's the grit that makes the pearl.

"Alright. I'll go. Careful what you ask for." He sipped then set down his wine. "The first one we were eighteen. We were young and we were eighteen and we eloped and we both knew we had made a mistake. Basically that's about the whole story."

She sat with that. She nodded.

"The second ended two years ago. Six years together, four of marriage. And. I know this is not the answer I'm supposed to say."

Val noticed that for all the clumsy or verbose or provocative things he said he was not without self-awareness. Not self-conscious—he seemed rather confident in himself, borderline cocky, which did make her wonder if that was over-compensation for a deeper lack of belief—but he seemed aware of how what he said might be received. She so-far uncertain if that translated to emotional intelligence or manipulation.

"It's probably not what a woman would want to hear. But." He shifted in his seat. "I don't know. I'm not entirely sure what happened. I think many things." He paused. "Or maybe not the right things. I don't know. There was no cruelty, no infidelity. And honestly." He turned his wine glass on the table. "I was in love. I was very happy. I thought she was too. I didn't see it coming. I was very sad."

Alex's tone changed enough she questioned his verb tense. Valerie was a little caught off guard at this break from societal norms. Everyone knows in modern dating clothes come off before guards are let down. His words here inappropriate because sex precedes emotional disclosure and honesty has more shock value than a racy interjection.

"She said she was leaving. I asked why. She said she didn't know why. I asked her a month, six months, twelve months later. She said the same thing."

She thought his eyes were on his drink. But they were on his fingers around his drink. He was wishing he could blame those calloused fingers for lacking the sensitivity to feel those who had slipped through them. "I blame myself. Mostly. About a month before she left we slow-danced in the living room. At the end, she cried. Just a couple tears. She went to the bathroom. I thought they were tears of joy. I thought it was a romantic moment. I mean, for me, it was. I found out later they were not tears of joy."

He looked up to Valerie and was quietly smiling but it wasn't really a smile it was something else. "Can you imagine being so out of touch?" He was still smiling but it wasn't a smile. "Can you imagine having someone you care for the most leave you with little warning and you being blind to the signals? There would have been signals. Six happiest years then your lover, gone. Your best friend, all the inside jokes, not just the big loves but all the little loves, the couch cuddles, the road trips, the plane trips, the boat trips, the beach walks, all the dinners and breakfasts and fires, the hand holds, the confidences, the plans, the secrets. Who said your marriage proposal was the happiest day of her life. Who three years into the marriage said she thought you were becoming a better person, more kind and patient, who two weeks shy of your fourth wedding anniversary—left. Gone."

Don't trust the painted smile on a clown with downcast eyes.

She watched him. She didn't speak.

"I don't blame her. I wasn't perfect. I was not perfect. At times I was probably intolerable. I suspect that in my own unique way, I'm a very specialized type of intolerable."

231

If Alex lives to be old he will come to know that where once he thought there was virtue and a type of grace in honest self-admission of his faults, that in fact no redemption is to be found there.

She wondered if what he said was true, and if he himself actually believed it was true. It could be true. Or perhaps it was the type of self-denigrating claim one makes to endear himself to his audience while not entirely believing it true. She wasn't sure.

"But in the end, to me, that's hardly different than a father telling his son he no longer cares to be a father. A daughter telling her mother she will next Tuesday be disowning her. For better or worse. Sickness and health. Long as you both shall live. All that. Not all words are words, not to me. Vows aren't words. They're something else." He tipped his shallow wine empty, held the glass vertical a half second, as if hoping to slake some deeper thirst. "That's love. The truest love can break like a dropped pane of glass. Don't tell the kids it's all so brittle. Of course everyone will know inside their heart that theirs is different. They'll know for certain that ours was not the real thing. They'll think that but not say it. They'll know for certain theirs is different. Because they have a deep intuition about it. The cult of intuition. I knew what it was. I couldn't know anything more true. Heat is hot, truth. Water is wet, truth. Then, over. My fault, maybe, sure. But signs no larger than the periodic friction common to every couple don't always indicate the erosion's extent. One person might be breaking, or, is already broken. Is already lost. Is gone before they've packed their bags. No fighting, no major transgressions required. Why? Because people change and the magic dies. Just on its own. Sometimes it's someone's fault but sometimes it's out of your hands. Just the cellular death of magic. For all your efforts, sometimes romantic connection can have a natural lifespan that does not match up with its hosts. Never mind external pressures, never mind all the work stresses and financial insecurity and parenthood and all that. And if a couple avoids or survives all that, there's still the worst magic killers of all."

He gave her a shot at filling in the blank but she was just watching him. "Complacency, routine, resentment. The cancers of relationships, no? You tell yourself beforehand that will never be you. But that person who says that, that prior you, has no business saying that. Those two you's are in different worlds separated by a gulf empathy can't cross. You don't even speak the same language. Your future-self might one day be drowning in boredom, disconnection, and most ironically loneliness. Most relationships don't work out, so says the stats, even when the failing couple stays together. The clock is ticking for so many out there right now." Alex paused and they actually heard a ticking and Valerie looked at the heat lamp. He had a small smile that hinted irony. But it wasn't irony.

The server set down their waters and said their mains were coming shortly.

Her quiet eyes he momentarily glanced. "How bitter do I sound? Or just disillusioned? I don't even know. The lemon to itself is not bitter." He squeezed his lemon into his water. "I say I want love. I probably do. But I guess I don't trust it like I once did. Maybe now I'm just playing the romantic. Does that sound dramatic or self-obsessed?" He shrugged. "It might be true. For most of my life I made a mountain out of romantic love. I'm not trying to play the victim. But I think you never know even if you think you do and feel you do. Maybe I have a kind of doubt that I didn't have before." He paused. "Doubt feels like the right word." He paused again. "The lie of the fairytale is not that true love exists. It does. I've known it. The lie is happily ever after." He shook his head. "That does not exist."

Alex gave a rest to what he knew he shouldn't have started. The fool who spills those things he ought to hide away. The heat lamp ticked. Below, a car passed. He didn't think he'd said too much, he knew he had. Them in the shadow of a conversation of which the oncoming dusk in its wildest dreams could only aspire to such darkness. Here at the onset of twilight he felt his words had more than killed the vibe they'd banished the light. He tried to brighten the mood, such was his nature. He hadn't changed his smile but it was now a smile again and not that other thing. He said, "My complexes could make kittens out of your complexes."

Valerie said softly, "Don't bet on it."

She appreciated his honesty. Even the little sparrows she just now noticed trying to steal food scraps off the cement floor but picking up only crumbs of this conversation could tell this poor man was lost in time. The dim sky meant the lower patio where sat the other Valerie and Alex would only be darker. Maybe that Valerie had gotten up and left.

A server walked out to the patio, her face made angelic by a platter of wavering light. She set a candle down between Alex and Valerie. These two said at the same time thank you. He assumed in her candle-softened eyes he might notice some small change, some hint of her closing up and pulling away. Had he looked. But his eyes were on his hands. He said, "Show me someone single approaching middle age without a past. If your heart is free of scars you haven't risked it enough."

She sat with that. Across from someone owning a wound. For more than a moment. Then she said sweetly, "I thought you wrote smut not proverbs."

Alex looked up. Who would say such a thing after he had said such things? He was not sure what to make of this potential sociopath. This devil quietly smiling in beatific candlelight. Or, maybe after seeing a gash still inflamed long after its infliction, she hadn't turned away. Or an attempt to speak my language? An echo of the procrastinator joke?

She put a hand on top of his.

He said raspily, "Remember when you said no one truly is an asshole? I submit to the court, exhibit V." She rubbed his hand and the server stopped to tip their bottle, pouring a skinny stream of wine coloured savior-blood red. If optimism comes with one's chromosomes what a precious gene. Alex said, "At least I think I found my triggers."

"Nice one. Good for you." She still holding his hand patted it and let it go. "Do you feel comfortable sharing?"

"Yes. My house. The ocean. Cooking. A large portion of the English language. Music that contains instruments and often vocals. Mexico. That's about it. Oh. Duck dives, oddly, duck dives." He made the two-arm motion of diving a shortboard under a breaking wave. "Maybe in that motion the mind finds a psychological parallel. Submerge and resurface." He shrugged.

She rolled her eyes, assuming all that to be sarcasm or embellishment. It had to be or this poor man here was incredibly fucked.

The couple overlooking Tonquin waters passed the cider's final sips between them, witnesses to humankind's favourite star's nightly dip into the Pacific. The pair quiet as if listening for the glowing pool to hiss.

Alex's stupid jokes returned and to their punchline she added an extra laugh. Their conversation flowed from food to philosophy to movies to books, travel, work, then back to a prior topic, talking with the natural vibe that allowed even discordant ideas to slide in and out with the frictionless ease of those at play, just playin'. More things being said between words. Running barefoot on the wet grass of conversation, or perhaps a less silly metaphor, but one no less gay. Valerie had gone to the bathroom and checked her emails to make sure there were no fires to put out or ones that needed lighting. It had been years since she had a day with less work. She had mixed feelings about that. She texted her dad. *May have found a (most strange) tour guide for the Bomber hike—stand by. *plane emoji**

The orange streetlights now with more illumination than the sky. Besides the strange fishing guide watching her return to the patio, or perhaps him included, it was all rather indulgently nice. She sat and set her handbag down in the empty chair beside her.

"I ate your pasta. We're now on to dessert. Consider the mousse."

"Alex, some topics you shouldn't joke about."

"The waitress said our mains are coming very shortly."

"That's better." She looked down at quiet Campbell Street, below the sky's fading memory of pastels. "Do you ever feel guilty?" she asked.

"For eating your pasta?"

"You're living in a really nice town in a developed world with its democracy and quality schools and hospitals and general affluence and your town's forest-fire-retardant fog and rains to weather climate change and we're up here on the second floor of a fine-dining restaurant." She squeezed her citrus into her water.

Had Alex heard a different tone he might have squinted to shield his eyes from her lemon juice further soured by her own hypocrisy. "I'm not rolling in it. I have a truck but it's a few years old, my boat is for my job. I try to be a good person. I got lucky being born into a good family and in a country with a lot of opportunity for a lot of people. As long as I don't take that for granted and try to help others, I sleep fine at night—well, in theory, the transient insomnia thing. But same question to you. You're staying at a pretty nice hotel eating at a pretty nice restaurant. Is all that a little selfish given the state of the broader

236

world? The famines and the wars and the poverty and what have you. Do you think about it?"

"I do. Yeah."

"And? Does it wear on you?"

"Yeah. It does. But if I let myself think about it all day I'd be incapacitated by the sadness. So I try to bracket my concern. I don't think about it all the time and that's not callousness—compartmentalization for me is a survival strategy. When I do think about it I try to harness that dejection."

"Like?"

In an exploration of a real passion, she had raised the topic genuinely curious to hear his thoughts. "Similar to you."

"Well what kind of similar?"

And not to expound on hers. "I used to volunteer more, now mainly donations." She looked down the street. "That sunset was glorious."

He looked at her, whatever this was he was seeing. Some minor evasiveness, something. A peculiar reluctance. Those with tact would leave it at that. Alex said, "A little evasive, Valerie."

She hesitated. "A few years back I was listening to a Joe Rogan podcast."

"His first female listener. He'll be so excited."

"A friend sent it to me. The guest was telling a story, a thought experiment. You're walking to work beside a flooded ditch. You hear cries for help and see a child drowning. To save the girl means ruining your leather shoes and nice suit."

"I feel like this hits harder in Vancouver. Me I walk to work in rubber boots and Carhartts."

She gave him a look.

"But please continue."

"Of course you ruin your clothes to save her. What if you heard those cries coming from a block away. Would you run there? Two blocks away? A country away? Follow that argument to its logical conclusion. The idea really hit home with me, that the emotional impact of the cries doesn't have to diminish with the distance. If I listen I can hear them.

"Basically a philosopher broke my heart and opened my wallet—but out of compassion, not guilt. I looked into it. There's an initiative called effective altruism, the idea that some humanitarian efforts benefit humankind far more than others."

Alex had something to say but she showed more enthusiasm on this topic than all their others and he didn't want to interrupt.

"I found this all super fascinating. One hundred dollars in Canada doesn't go very far, but one hundred dollars in other places is the stuff of lotteries. Anti-malarial bed nets are really cheap and save lives, and there are pills that cost pennies but keep little kids from getting worms in their bellies. On a per-dollar basis that does a lot more than building a new wing for the art gallery or training a seeing-eye dog. So that brings the second part of this idea. Sometimes the best thing you can do is keep earning the high western salary and send part of it where it goes the furthest. I just find this to be such an interesting and underappreciated idea. I think if more people understood it it could really change things. Like, really change things." She was almost flushed.

He wondered if supposing she talked with similar passion about industrial air cleaning systems or colour variations of grey paint she'd hold his interest. Still with his stupid comments, but interested.

She looked around the sparse patio, the glass separating them from the busier dining room. "If one person in this restaurant did that, he or she may do more to help others than all the other people in that same restaurant combined. Maybe the whole street." She raised her water then paused it halfway. She mentally face-palmed herself. *Bahh.* Her eyes shifted. *Fuck yeck.*

She just got caught up in it and God she hated how that sounded because the *he* or *she* was obviously a *she*. Valerie had only been thinking in numbers and trying to illustrate it with an example close at hand. She looked at Alex who thankfully had no reaction, but still she wanted that comment back. She asked, "What do you think of the wine?"

"That's interesting." Alex nodded, no smile.

She thought he must have missed the self-congratulatory subtext, or that he was graciously letting her get away with it.

Alex took a sip. "Yeah, good wine." He held his glass up to a patio light, appraising it with one squinted eye. The waitress came by saying their dinner was just about ready. Alex said, "After our mains I was thinking of ordering the mousse. But now I'm not so sure. I'm pretty full on her self-righteousness."

Valerie laughed and smacked his shoulder. "He'll have the mousse."

"I didn't see it on the menu, but we were wondering if you have any hay we could order?" He stared at Valerie. "What? About half a bale?"

The server was confused and Valerie was confused and then Valerie said, "Oh. For my moral high-horse."

"For your moral high-horse."

Valerie said to the server walking away he's not mine he's one of yours. "That's not how I meant any of that and not how I wanted it to come out. So, y'know, screw you. Anyway, I looked into it. I set up monthly contributions to the best one I found."

"We're still on this are we?" Alex tremendously enjoyed finally having a chance to bust her balls back.

"Yes we are," she laughed.

He put the napkin on his lap to save time for when his burger came. "Well go on and say its name you're clearly on the payroll."

"GiveWell."

"Alright then. I'll check it out."

She didn't tell him that given her profile and public pledge to donate five percent of B2P's profit, one of the organization's executives reached out to her, inviting her to listen in on an initiatives presentation. After the meeting he asked her if she would consider becoming an advocate. Once a month for the next year she worked remotely with their team. She wrote an Op-ed for the Vancouver Sun and The Globe and Mail, delivered three talks at Ted-X Vancouver, Victoria, and Seattle. Valerie lowered her voice. "It's kinda like, no matter what else, anything I might screw up, in the end, people, God even, they have to judge me by those efforts. I don't need anyone's approval for how I've lived. I can tell myself I'm getting something very large, very right. Right? Is that a weird way to look at it? It's a good thing on its own, but it also corrects. It cleans. And nobody can take that away from me."

He knew for certain he was staring at the dry tip of an iceberg. But he couldn't tell if her enthusiasm for effective giving came fundamentally from a desire to help others or to square a guilt or what. Puzzle of puzzles, Virtue. He liked calling her Virtue, mostly in his head. Am I hearing passion or atonement? Just hard to imagine you with such a dark past, killer.

"Why are you smiling?" She squinted. "I actually don't love talking about it." The virtue signalling felt quite icky, as if she was presenting her preachy self as faultless. But she pushed through her own self-concern, practiced her delivery, then she got up on stage and did it—*killed it*, as much as one could kill a talk on altruism. "It just really matters to me, Alex."

"Stood up by my lady and picked up by a saint. I think to myself, what a wonderful world." He teased but he liked her so engaged. "I'm kidding. That's cool. But I think most people prefer local things. Online giving would be harder to pitch than cleaning a beach or teaching a kid to read."

"Close your eyes."

"Uhh. If they deliver our mains and I open them to find my pickle eaten, we're simply done here. Like we never met."

"Stop talking. Do it."

He acted like this was too strange but secretly he loved it. "Fine, weirdo."

"You're in rural sub-Saharan Africa so draw on a stereotype. There's a little boy in dirty clothes kneeling by a stream. He's barefoot. Do you see him?"

"Yes."

"He has a red bucket. Visualize it. See him dipping the red bucket in the stream. He's crouched there, right?"

"Yeah."

This was all part of her Ted Talk. "You can't see it but upstream is a city's pollution. Heavy rains flood the sewers. This is unclean water with parasites. But his mom told him to go get water and this is where they get it." Valerie was watching him and though slight his eyebrows did crinkle and she saw an empathic man. "Keep your eyes closed." She moved his wine glass. "Place your right hand on the table."

He did.

"Shape it like it holds your computer mouse. Good."

He liked the praise but he'd never admit to that.

"Navigate that pointer over the screen to toggle yes for a monthly donation. Click the mouse." She watched his index finger, they both heard it tap the table. "Take your hand off the mouse and type your master password. The software will populate your credit card."

He couldn't help but laugh at this spectacular weirdo with that smallest detail. He obediently typed, his fingers making sounds of their own private rain shower.

"Make another mouse click."

He did.

"Keep your eyes closed."

"I *am*."

"Now you're at the village. I've transported you there. Magic. The boy at the stream with his red bucket sees you. Tell him to come on. Offer him your hand. He takes it. You guys walk away from the stream to a pump jack. Its spout is shining. Why?"

"Because it's new, Valerie."

"You don't speak his language so just point where he should put his bucket. You can pump the jack for him if you want."

Alex was actually smiling.

"Tell me about the water, Alex."

"It's very clear, Valerie."

"But you didn't just donate one time. Did you, Alex?"

He almost laughed with her continual use of his name. "No, I didn't."

"Well that was really nice of you. I like that about you. You've been at this a while, it's been years now. Just small donations like drops in a bucket that don't have to be big if they're regular. The little boy leaves you. Next to that pump is a school. He walks in the door. You didn't build the school. You and I built the school together." She picked his hand up off the table and balled it into a fist and then bumped his fist with hers and though she only lightly touched his knuckles he felt that tender punch straight in his gut. To say he smiled there says nothing at all. Danger.

"Walk up to the window. You're very welcome here but let's not disturb them. They're at their desks. Look in the window and tell me what they're doing."

"Studying, writing."

"Books?"

"Yeah books."

"There he is, your buddy. His book on his table. What colour is the book?"

"Woah. Weird. It's red."

"Recess bell. The door opens to your right and they stream outside. All the faces streaming out the door. All of them laughing and playing. All healthy. How many?"

"So many."

"All the love. Somehow in this world, you had the luck, the utter privilege to help make that happen. And you did. Today you did. So how does that feel? How is it even possible, right? Tell me there's no magic here," she said. "Now open your eyes. Don't you feel lucky to have found that?"

His opened eyes. No longer seeing the school. Seeing something else.

***

In a minute there can be many days. Already they had taken a short journey together, from bar to patio. They knew inside and outside. They met with a sun in the sky and now they knew dusk. They travelled back in time and saw pivotal moments of each other's past. Shared emotional disclosures that might take some people days, years, or never do divulge. They crossed a conversational expanse as if its own type of broad geography. Their worlds altered. Their time aged.

"So a couple years back I was at the VAG," he said.

"The what?"

"The VAG."

"Repeating the exact same thing you already said once clearly, isn't more clarifying, Alex."

He laughed. "The Vancouver Art Gallery. I just like calling it that. Do people in your city call it that?"

"Fieldmouse leaves his coastal hole for the big city. What were you doing?"

"Mostly being scared and disoriented. I saw this exhibit. I haven't thought about it in years. This was not long after I first moved here. A woman sitting in a chair. People lined up for their turn to sit across from her. For two minutes you just sit and look at her and you're not allowed to talk. She wasn't anyone famous. Then the next person would sit down."

Valerie waited to hear about the exhibit.

"That's the exhibit. To me," he wafted a hand, "a little hokey. But I try not to be too dismissive of what's novel. Though mostly, I am. I watched some people sit down and some laughed. I saw a couple people cry. A lot smiled. A few showed no expression. I'm not sure what I think of it. But you and I are going to do that now."

Two servers walked out to the patio and placed their mains before them. A tall burger with lettuce and tomato and perfectly-asymmetrical, house-cut fries, tiny dish of ketchup. A plate of mushroom pasta greenly flecked with chopped parsley, like grass showing through a rare spring-pecorino snowfall.

Alex said, "Damn."

Valerie said, "Wow."

"Yeah you and I are going to do that now."

"But now?" She gestured to the food, her steaming plate.

"Funny timing. Oh man. But this makes it more intense. Yeah now, for one minute. I look in your eyes and you in mine and I don't care if this sounds cheesy and cliché—*I* am cheesy and cliché. Your fault for having dinner with the first fishing guide you met at the bar. Whatever comes, comes, and then—"

"For God's sake stop talking already and let's get this over with."

Their eyes had been locked long before they agreed to stare. Steam rising between their gaze. A candle unwavering. Tiny brown birds at their feet. Warmth from the radiating dome of the affectionate heat lamp. A sky with trace illumination studded with two earliest stars. Whatever on that lower balcony that other Alex and Valerie were up to. A man alone in a white Ford Edge. Wherever that couple on the Tonquin bench had gone. However many worlds.

They ate and Valerie forked some noodles onto Alex's plate and Alex said, "You know how I know you love me?"

"Don't read into it. It's a big portion and I'm pretty small."

"Large portions at a fine-dining restaurant aren't so common, huh? This Wolf just stepped ahead of the pack."

"Oh God. Who's on whose payroll?"

Alex took a fry and dipped his knife in the little dish of ketchup and he started to write but he screwed it up so he ate his mistake and then he took another fry and began again and it took some care but he managed to write V A L along the spud. He set it on her plate. Then delivered a couple more unaddressed.

She said quietly, "I know you like me like a fat kid loves cake."

"If I wrote you a love letter would you write back?"

She smiled.

Alex said, "I heard this song the other day. Bing Crosby or Dean Martin or someone with that kinda really affected, old-time crooner sound."

"We could easily find out who sang it." Valerie set down her fork and lifted her handbag from the empty chair to her lap and dug for her phone to type the coming lyrics and Alex said yeah but there's no phones at the dinner table.

Valerie with her hand buried in her handbag. Had he delivered a sermon *No Phones At The Dinner Table* her iPhone would have already been out, then it would have stayed out. Her hand on her phone in her bag like Mom had caught her with her hand in the cookie jar. She had clasped it but hadn't withdrawn it because she did share the value. She liked the idea of no phones while sharing a meal. So, either provide a counterpoint, or humbly withdraw her hand, a tacit admission that he was right and she was wrong. Unavoidably one would feel a touch diminished. That wasn't the dynamic he wanted but it's what he had unintentionally engineered here.

Her hand in her bag searching for a reasonable rebuttal. She put less stock in words than this smut writer here, but effectively those words stopped her with greater force than physical restraint. Touch knows only surface while words go deeper. For an independent woman who liked doing things people told her she shouldn't do and loved doing things people told her she couldn't do, this predicament was harder than it might be for others. Among a couple's *Firsts*—First Kiss, First Photo, First Dance—was the First Conflict. This tiny and most absurd one was theirs.

At the altar of your values will you sacrifice your ego?

She was looking at him and her eyes squinted mimicking her lips because this little dilemma was interesting. For all her independence, she did at times like being dominated—picked up, carried around, put down, throat held, arms pinned, hair pulled, all the rest. But this was not that. That was something else for another place. So that's not why her hand still in her bag had now unclasped her phone. And it wasn't just the shared value. At first she wasn't even sure what it was exactly. She just felt it. An intuition. She trusted it. Later on that night she would figure it out.

Later on he would ask himself if he had put whatever they were doing here at risk for something trivial. Between them something sweet was being baked, that was obvious, something he hadn't seen in a while and it didn't scare him, but it evoked caution. But he believed love doesn't exist without honesty. Aren't values a language of truth? He figured he hadn't really put anything worth anything at risk and hadn't been gambling at all.

With a kind of minimal smile he hadn't seen on her before, she withdrew her hand to her lap, accompanied by a silence he hadn't ever heard. If Inuit have fifty words for snow perhaps some astute language has fifty words for various silences. The space between them was pregnant or flammable or something. Some dynamic mixing up humility and deference and concession and agreement and reprimand and other things he couldn't discern. He had offended enough women and screwed up enough relationships to know that right then the wrong word, the wrong look, could abort or ignite this. This moment, fragile and uncertain, was balancing on one foot on the tip of a needle. He just thought she looked elegant, is all. That's all he was thinking. Very elegant. He didn't know what to say. You're elegant. He almost said that. He just smiled and looked away and she said what.

Alex almost forgot this whole strange moment was precipitated by a song. He finally continued on about the song and held towards her his plate of fries and Valerie laughed and pushed the plate of home-cut and salted, golden-brown fries away which was very, very hard and said, "No, I do that!" He hadn't even done it on purpose but she recognized his offer as some reward, a type of training, because she had done that to men.

He was oblivious to what just happened. His entire motivation behind offering her the fries was: *Fried potatoes with salt are very good. She will like these. I will share them.* Full stop.

After Valerie made it very clear she couldn't be trained and that she had left her phone in her bag for *her* moral vision of the world not *his*, then said, "Okay maybe for ours," she reached across the table and took a fry. Wagged it at him. "Get it straight, Alex." Then she snapped the fry in half and ate one.

"You are the strangest CEO I've ever met. Back to the song. I'm not saying I love that crooner sound from the man who we both agreed we aren't now Googling, but when I heard this, it just struck me. It's funny. Okay, here's the line." He spoke the line with no emotion: "Rainbows, I'm inclined to pursue. I've heard a million sentences. Maybe more. But that one, it's funny putting that word first. The dependent clause being a single word, then the sentence." Burger juice flowed over Alex's fingers making a gravy on the plate. He said you should probably not watch me this is going to get real messy-like. He didn't even attempt to deploy the napkin as that would be tissue paper at a tanker spill.

"Do you think you should say *dependent clause* when you think you're on a date and trying to be funny and or seductive?"

"Plagiarism! And one day I'm going to date a grammarian and you're going to eat your words when I text you how wet her panties got from me whispering to her dependent clause."

"Every time you say something weird like that it's going to cost you a fry. Please continue."

He pushed her the plate. He knew when he was beat. "Okay who can make the pause between *rainbows* and the rest of that sentence abnormally long without losing the effect of the sentence. Like so." Alex didn't clear his throat he just sang fairly quietly, "Rainbows." He looked around pensively, kinda shook his head like he was deep in thought, looked up higher, smiled off in the distance like he found what he was searching for and squinted like he was figuring out how to put what he'd found into words because in the domain of speech it didn't exist or at least was elusive, then he sang quietly, "I'm incliiiined to pursueee."

"Not bad." She brushed her fingers of fry salt and sat up. She set her cutlery down. She said, "Rainbows," while moving her head through a small arch as if she were traveling that colourful spectrum and ended looking down at its pot of gold. Subtly shaking her head there. She reached for her wine and held the glass reflectively before she would sip it and raised a single finger in a sign of *wait-a-moment* and didn't sip the wine, then kinda wagged that finger like she had finally figured something out, but right then the eureka of it all wasn't exclamatory it was savoury, perhaps because she'd worked at it for a long time, maybe a lot of her life with many failed attempts and had begun to think it wasn't even possible or didn't really exist and maybe she no longer sought it, so the revelation was not sharp it was warm, really warm and nice and easy, then finally, finally she sang too loud for the quiet patio and the calm evening in this dusky coastal town, which was also the perfect volume, "I'm incliiiined to pursueeeee."

On the other side of the window a table looked at her. Then from out in the wider world came what sounded like an echo, but it wasn't echo. It was resonance. Because one patio below in an alternate world, that other Valerie had sung the same line.

Alex said this wasn't a contest. But that somehow she'd still won. "Cancel the mousse. Let's get out of here and I'll take you to your prize." When the bill came she went for it but not quick enough. Alex tapped his card and put on his Patagonia.

"Hey Alex, there's not a puffy for every occasion." She teasingly pinched his jacket.

"Hey Valerie, stop listing your yoga teacher training as a graduate degree on your dating profile. And your comment concerning puffy jackets just offended half my town. Are you able to name someone whose toes you haven't stepped on today?"

She stepped the toe of her pump on his Blundstone. "I'm just Vancouver, Tofino."

Trent had watched her enter the restaurant alone. That's not how she left. Watched her and some guy outside Gaia Grocery walking up to a green Tacoma.

Alex opened her unlocked door saying when there's only one road outta town car jackings aren't a thing. He put Neruda in the console, took his keys from the drink holder.

249

Valerie said, "Speaking of values," and they hadn't been. She wasn't talking about his chivalrous gesture either. She held her hand up to her mouth and made two short exhales.

"Three glasses over three hours with food has little effect on me." She didn't look so impressed. "But I want you to be comfortable." He liked this look of hers better. He called for a Tofino taxi, a Whistle. Morgan said oh hey Alex, that she'd be a half hour and he told her okay no problem just come get us at Shelter.

XIX

T iki torches burning outside of a timber-house restaurant. They walked up the three steps to Shelter. "It's a good name. Fits well with the heavy winters here. *Seek Shelter*. I like that. Concise, alliterative, persuasive. I'm in." He slapped a pillar. "Timbre is one of my favourite words. Not the exclamation, the sound quality. *Timbre*. What do you think?"

"*Timbre*. It's pretty nice."

He opened the door for her. "Do you have a favourite word?"

She thought that was cute, like a boy asking a girl if she has a favourite colour, but in this case the forty-year-old smut writer inquiring of her favourite sound. She said chocolate was up there. Thrush. Babe.

"Yes?"

She laughed. "No. It's a favourite."

"Ah. Of course."

The music was beach house, chill techno, downtempo electronica. It smelled wood smoky and garlicky and delicious and felt warm and looked wooden. The big fireplace to her left, open kitchen ahead. Heavy wooden posts and beams with long cracks. Surf videos added to the vibe but distracted from conversation. Cozy, rustic, almost welcomingly homey, if a restaurant can be homey. She hadn't seen another restaurant with dining-room lighting as dark. Val thought it was the other places that were getting it wrong. The mood private, intimate. "Oh I like this." What does it mean when a spot you've never been to feel's like home?

Alex said hi to the hostess Lana. "Booth or bar, Alex?" At a padded booth their server filled their water glasses and Robin said Shelter had extended happy hour into the evening and she left the water bottle which was a clear wine bottle and two menus. Alex went for the bathroom saying to Valerie, "Please order me a Bailey's and coffee."

"The coffee doesn't keep you up?"

"I despise sleep and its nightly betrayal of reason, humanity, genius."

She suspected from his delivery it was a quote.

He stepped away and turned and pivoted. "Actually, okay yeah, decaf, por favor."

Valerie took out her phone. She opened a work email and looked through design submissions. She had hired a company to come up with a new logo for her brand. The backrest of her booth was a common divider. In the neighbouring booth sat a couple, the woman with her back to Val's.

"I don't want to leave either." Charisse set the menu down. "But we said we'd give it a year and see if things got better. That was three years ago." Kyle had one leg crossed over the other, as if the property-tax bill, folded in his back pocket, due in a month and payable to the town's district office, had him sitting lopsided. Tofino home prices meteorically rising, shifting demographics and loading debt. Tofino, this Canadian paradise many of its locals struggle to afford. Kyle looked at her and was going to say something. The waitress set down a Kelp Stout and a B.C. Tree Fruits Cider. He reached and slid and tipped and drank. Full-bodied, darkly rich, a touch of umami from the seaweed and a line of foam on his thin moustache like the pint itself left a tide's highwater mark. He cleaned that with his lower lip.

"Take the kids away from their friends? And you're not going to miss the surf?"

"Kids make new friends. It's what kids do. And they'll be closer to their grandparents."

"Yeah. But then we'll be closer to their grandparents." He sipped his stout, kept his head low to it like it was party to their conversation. "The surf?"

She shrugged. "We visit."

"Yeah. We visit. Ask our friends to hold a room for us during vacation season." He looked around the restaurant as if surveying its capacity. "Wish the spring rentals would pick up. The winter's."

Alex on his way back from the bathroom looked around for friendly faces and nodded to Darryl at the far end of the bar and saw Elizabeth in a corner booth. He looked to wave but she didn't look up from her books. He had a question for her. It could wait. He asked the bar to send her a Bourbon on his bill and he wrote on a napkin, *Did ever a dragon keep so fair a cave?* He asked that they not say who sent it. His smile was interrupted watching a lady lick whipped cream off an Irish Coffee. He sat and Valerie said, "Nabokov returns. Googled it while you were in the can."

"Can. Charming." Alex saw her mug's sugary foam was indented by CEO lips. Which looked like regular lips.

"I couldn't wait."

He slid his mug centre table and she met his for a dull clink.

She asked, "Do you rent or own."

He wondered if that question innocent curiosity, or evaluatory.

"I own. Got lucky with a nice spot. It's probably tripled in value since I bought it a few years back. No way could I afford it now. And I doubt that Tofino home prices ever come down, significantly."

"You think Tofino is insulated from a major bust?"

"I would think so. Back when it was a resource town it would have been more susceptible. Like in the eighties when fishing and logging slowed. But now its export is beauty in general. Stunning beaches in a country not known for its sand. Nowhere else in Canada comes close to rivalling the surf, not really. There are some breaks on the east coast, and some good ones down island, but this is Canada's premier surf destination for a reason. The consistency of swell five minutes from town is remarkable. Who knows which sports will last but it looks like surfing isn't rollerblading, you know? Short of a depression, war, epidemic, tsunami, earthquake—you know, all those very real things that could actually totally happen—it's hard for me to imagine the trend of home prices doing anything but rising." Alex with his nose touched the whipped cream then tried to lick it with his tongue but he couldn't reach and looked ridiculous and used a napkin. Valerie stirred her coffee making a creamy swirl then cleaned the warm spoon between her lips.

"Soaring home prices are wonderful for the newly retired looking to cash in their geographical gold pile. Hard for locals who can't be approved for such a large mortgage, or if they can be approved, just aren't so attracted to the idea of being house-poor vacation-rental owners while also working full-time jobs for the next thirty-five years. This town has its trade-offs." Alex caught himself mind-surfing a screen's perfectly peeling wave. That last one he leaned into a frontside hack and gouged the hell out of its smooth face, spray everywhere.

In the neighbouring booth Kyle's pint nearly gone. Charisse said to him, "And with the cost of daycare I may as well not work and just stay home with the kids. What's the point?"

"But you like your work. The break from home is nice, right?"

"Not enough to do it for what nets out to be minimum wage. You want the olives?"

"Split the burger?"

"We've what? Doubled our money on the house?"

"More than that. Even after taking off some for the reno's."

"We can buy the same size house in Port Alberni with a backyard and put down half on the mortgage."

"It smells there."

"Smells like a deal there."

Valerie caught bits and pieces of that and she wasn't trying to. She wanted to see what they looked like but didn't turn.

Alex watched the drink and napkin arrive to Elizabeth across the room who read it and didn't even look around, she just turned a page. Alex smiled, looked back to Valerie. "You said I remind you of someone you almost met on a dating app. I actually am on those dating apps."

"Oh really." Coyest inflection.

"I'm surprised at how often I see a woman who says she's looking for a guy who doesn't take himself too seriously. What does that even mean? How is anybody going to take you seriously if you don't take yourself seriously? I take my work seriously. And why wouldn't I? Same for my efforts of who I want to be and my health and how I want to treat others and all the rest. What I'm trying to be deserving of. Don't take yourself too seriously—what does that even mean?"

She curled a beckoning finger and he leaned in and she touched it to his forehead to turn his head and expose his ear and she leaned and whispered. "It means you're fucked, Alex."

Her lips grazing his lobe made him laugh as much as the comment. "And I don't know what half the abbreviations are. *ENFPQ. ENM+. FWBO.* Etc. Well, etc I know."

"You could ask the internet."

"Polyammorific. I could but I keep love simple. I'm mostly simple. I do monogamy. I don't share. My love is possessive. Is that a bad word? Then let me add this: my love is possessive. My lady is mine." He shrugged. "I don't share well, never have. I don't mean controlling—I respect her independence, but I get her body, her heart. That's all mine. Old school, unapologetically." He made a fist and held it sideways then another fist and pounded himself. He watched her while he said all that. It tended to polarize women and he had no plans to moderate it.

His phone vibrated and he caught Robin's eyes and made a scribbling motion on his palm. "So I was on this dating app—that's probably the worst story starting I've ever given. Okay before the story we need context. Ernest Hemingway is credited with writing the shortest short story. He said this would be posted in the classifieds: *For sale. Baby shoes. Never used.*"

"Ooo, that is crushing."

"Six-word tear-jerker, right? So I was on this dating app and this beautiful woman had on her bio—"

"What made her beautiful?"

"Keep interrupting. Her bio: *Hopeless romantic. With abandonment issues.* A picture of her. And her newborn baby girl." Alex leaned back. "Ahh guts me. And that's five words. Take the Shortest Short Story Award from Papa and give it to her. She beat Ernest by twenty percent."

Valerie sipped her coffee now half gone. She swallowed that and her correction: eighteen percent. "Yeah that's also crushing. So did you message her?"

That's funny. He figured they'd vibe on trying to come up with a shorter story than five words. He hadn't anticipated that query. "I did."

"And? What did she say?"

"She never got back to me. Prolly an issue with the app. Must have been a technical glitch."

"What did you message her?"

"I think I mentioned the Hemingway bit."

"You think."

He laughed. "I mentioned the Hemingway bit. I guess only one of us found it so interesting."

She nodded. "Prolly just needed a bigger fish."

His one arched eyebrow. He grabbed his jacket. "Let's go. I get to take you for dessert." The waitress had presented the machine and Valerie went to pay but Alex tapped it first. At the door she turned and looked at the couple. A dish of olives being delivered. One burger. Two plates. Candlelight.

They walked down the steps between torches as if ceremonially burning, a trial survived or one to come. His hand over her coat filled the small of her back. As if that hollow shaped for that very purpose.

XX

The Whistle taxi dropped them at the Outside Break parking lot and Alex asked Morgan to come back in half an hour please and Morgan thought that was strange but thought even stranger would be a cabbie offering unsolicited advice to two people whose bizarre banter made clear they were on a date taking place in their own world. She said see you guys soon. The Whistle pulled out of the big parking lot and a white sedan pulled in.

In the warm and dusky air they walked towards Chocolate Tofino. "Ah hell, of course." Alex now saw the windows dark. The dessert shop had been closed for an hour. "It only feels like summer today." He walked up the two steps and put his hands up to the glass and Valerie said you look about seven. He turned staring towards the dark trees as if through them he could see dessert options of Long Beach Lodge or the Wickaninnish Inn. He took out his phone to call Morgan back when one of the co-owners, a chocolatier, whose trade is basically happiness, came out from around the back. Alex smiled, looking like he had been caught about to rob the place for a chocolate tortuga. He knew the owners by name but he wasn't going to ask for a favour. But perhaps two middle-aged people standing outside a closed dessert shop did that for him because Carley said, "Does the guy who buys his vanilla-almond pints like clockwork need an after-hours hit?"

"I hate this town," he said. "Hi Carley."

"Hi Alex."

Carley turned on just one light in the shop and not the open sign. A sign above the back counter: *Hold my cone I have to pet this dog.* Alex nodded up to it and said look Valerie they knew you were coming.

"Every girl, Alex."

Alex asked Valerie very seriously if she trusted him.

"No," she answered. "But go ahead anyway."

He ordered two house-made waffle cones with coconut-chocolate gelato. "It's vegan and I don't order it because it's vegan." He put a twenty-bill down and wouldn't take change then handed Valerie her prize for the contest that wasn't a contest she hadn't entered that she'd won. Of course that's how he described it.

Late spring in northerly latitudes stretches out the dusk. They walked underneath the lingering afterglow from whatever the bashful sun and blushing sky had done together. Quiet parking lot of packed gravel and she stepped carefully in her pumps with low block heels. Their cones held before them in the budding night, like torchbearers from an occult sect of pleasure seekers. "So how does any couple make it last," she on a tangent from the cab's conversation.

Alex licked. "After my first failed marriage I thought, compromise. I want this and you want that, so we compromise. That makes some sense, right? Kraft Dinner pairing negotiations, baloney or hot dog. But I'm not so sure. That seems sort of transactional. Now I'm thinking it's about really trying to see it from the other's perspective and loving the person to the point you actually want them to get what they want and them wanting you to get what you want. So it's not really compromising at all. You're both truly wanting the thing you want, which includes gratifying the other person's desires. Their happiness becomes your own."

If she thought that was sentimental or idealistic or that his words had a greater chance of giving her a cavity than the dessert, she didn't say it. She looked pleased but most people do when holding gelato.

Live to Surf and Beaches Grocery and Wildside and Tacofino were all closed. They walked the parking lot and he told her stories of the town. As they neared a white sedan neither saw the occupant recline his chair into its greater darkness.

"Tofino originally started on an island. Clayoquot. You can actually see it from my hot tub."

She half-turned while fully turning her eyes and almost laughed. "Oh very subtle." She licked up a drip running down her waffle cone. "I like how you worked in a history lesson there. Hedge your bets, at once appeal to the intellect and the hedonist in me, hey?"

"Actually you're projecting again. That makes twice now. I think we need to spend more time unpacking your slutty unconscious. I propose we do that in the hot tub, seeing as how it's on your mind." He looked up. "I think we'll see moonlight tonight." He looked at her. "A soak and wine and history. I'll let you make the first wish on the first shooting star—no." He held up a peace sign. "First two stars. But this offer expires at the end of that cone. Don't answer right now. Take a minute."

"Other interested parties? All right, I'll think about it."

The opacity of her interest only made him want her more. "We might even be able to see phosphorescence at the foreshore." Though ecologically possible as he had seen such phenomena nearby, geographically improbable as he had never seen it at his foreshore. Call it wishful thinking.

"Here I thought you wrote smut but really you do cliffhangers."

Overhead, whooshing sweeps. The big bird too low to hide within the darkening sky. Wings large enough that the awkward creature seemed to struggle in flapping them, like this was all experimental. Wondrously gangly, trailing comically skinny legs. "You can tell by its rudimentary design that it was one of the first birds to have ever taken flight. Predates the pterodactyl." He licked his cone and made things up.

Valerie looked down from the ludicrous bird to this chocolate loon with gelato lips. Rare specimen, she thought. They both watched the bird fly.

He said, "As if the one who had originally thrown it up there had said, just before launch, *There's no way this will work, but, fuck it,* then threw an improbable and feathered dice into the air. *I'll be damned*, said God."

Valerie laughed.

"Watch out, it might fall." The bird flew out of the parking lot's low dome of light and into the anonymity of night. It called a most piteous sound, like a rusted crank, perhaps having a word with whom or what designed its flight mechanics. "It wouldn't be charitable to call that sound a song. It would just be wrong. Poor heron."

"You're a goof. Stop picking on the heron." She pushed his shoulder and her cone tilted and its single scoop fell. It didn't burst on the gravel it just plopped. Her licks had hardly shrunk it. They both looked at its sad hilarity. The little girl inside the grown woman felt a reactionary sadness. In a second or two, Valerie would laugh. She would laugh because it's only dessert. But for that second and almost two, she was a bit sad. An enduring little innocence that had somehow survived aging. Or maybe sustained it. Valerie stood looking at the scoop but the girl inside her, the one from the photo in her mind at the Wolf bar, kneeled beside the fallen chocolate. A woman standing, a girl kneeling. After those couple melancholic moments passed, the girl stood back up, but Valerie, again whole, did not return to her prior contentment. In their duration, Alex with one hand had peeled her fingers off her empty torch and replaced it with his still lit. Valerie smiled too big for her face. As if he had passed her something sweeter than chocolate. He held up the empty cone and she nested hers in his.

Valerie wondered why you never hear about positive complexes. Those experiences significantly happy enough to alter your psychological course for the better. Is that a concept and does it have a name? A positive complex? She figured she could find the answer with her phone. Her handbag over her shoulder, her arm she put through his. They shared one chocolate torch. As if some token flame of a larger fire.

While they waited for their Whistle, Alex again invited her over to his place. She had yet to answer. He felt like she was close. He thought the right words could dissolve her thin and uncertain resistance. But he was biased, he thought the right words were more powerful than Archimedes fabled lever. He told her again he would show her from the comfort of his moonlit hot tub the island where town started. He was considering saying a back massage with wine and a history lesson but that sounded creepy in his head and stressing the wine, however romantic, would sound like he had intentions to get her a little tipsy which of course he did which of course she knew and expected. His furrowing brow under a twilight sky, he searched for the right words to say.

She said, "I don't see the moon. History will be hiding." She passed him the cone.

In one hand he held a chocolate-topped doubled-walled waffle cone and in his other he held something sweeter and he pulled her in, her turning into his chest a little dramatically, abruptly, and the low light on the dusty trees from the grey gravel like all this not so far off a black-and-white movie. "Our first dance is in an empty parking lot."

She smiled but her eyes turned back up to the sky, the secretive sky, where she saw Venus, then Alex slow-turning them, where she saw Sirius, but the sky not revealing where it hid the promised moon.

He said, "Don't waffle," nodding sideways to the cone. Alex enlisting the seduction of a pun, now all hope for further romance was doomed. "I'm fabulously rich. Come on just let's go."

She smiled. In the warm twilight she kinda bit her lip. "Geez," she said. "I don't know."

Car lights turned on down the lot as if the sedan agreed but the girl uncertain. "I'll play your favourite song, darlin'."

"You don't know it." She finally lowered her sparkling eyes to him and she had all the sky he needed. The emerging vault of early stars having modelled its twinkle in light of her peeps. Her lashes two sweeping horizons over a Slavic blue this early night so deeply coloured.

"I'll play them all until we find it, darlin'. However many nights it takes. With luck we'll never find it." Alex's arm tightened around her back and pulled her in and she moved in a little closer. But only to lick the chocolate now level with the cone. If her smiling lips were saying something, he couldn't much make it out. So that would be his conciliatory prize. It wasn't such a bad prize, he thought. From the back of the lot a car started driving their way. And then the Whistle cab pulled in. Alex and Valerie embraced between opposing beams. "I planned this," he said. "One car is about to bring you flowers, the other has a violin. They're waiting for my cue. Just say you're coming over." He would have kissed her but the cars rather close and creeping forward over the gravel and they should probably move. But mostly he knew a kiss however sweet would keep her lips from saying yes.

She put a hand on his chest and he liked that.

She said, "Tonight I want to be back at my hotel, Alex."

He wondered if he could read into her wording. He said no problem then spoke into his collar. "Throw the violin in the sea and trample the roses." She rolled her eyes. He asked if the moon had come out yet. She says she has to go. He knew convincing words existed, of that he had no doubt. They just weren't coming. "You're here three more nights?" he asked.

"Yes."

"Let me cook for you tomorrow. Spearfished rockfish sautéed in a garden-garlic and wine herb sauce. Garden salad with homemade vinaigrette. Paired with mojitos from garden mint."

"Say garden again."

"I like to stress the garden." He had a policy of whether failure or triumph, he'd at least keep himself entertained. Garden.

They walked to the cab and he opened her door and she said pass me your phone and he unlocked the screen and did. Perhaps to his credit there's a certain grace in opening the door for that which you wish would stay. He walked to the front and said something to Morgan. She bumped his fist. Their car drove away and had he not stepped back the second one would have ran right over his foot but he barely noticed and didn't care at all and was just looking after the Whistle. Ask him what he thinks of her he'd probably say yet uncertain. But don't we so often desire what we can't have? Standing in the dark on the gravel. Still no moon and little more than a handful of lonely stars. He nearly wanted the poor heron to return. He raised the cone. Found the scoop gone too and a couple drops leaking out the bottom made a chocolate splatter on a Blundstone toe.

***

The cab's headlights lighting a dense roadside. Trunks and shadows and branches and shadows. Morgan said yeah born here and yeah she loves it, the summer but the quietness of the winter too, when the surge of visitors subsides like a slack tide. She slowed at the empty three-way to North Chesterman Beach parking lot. They turned right onto Lynn Road for the Wick and a trailing car pulled into the empty beach parking lot. The car slowed, then raised and lowered over a speed bump. Morgan spoke to the security attendant then continued to the entrance and Valerie took out her phone for its mobile wallet but Morgan said Alex had paid. "Oh he's sneaky."

Valerie in her room set her handbag on the dresser and slipped out of her pumps and opened the sliding glass door to her ground-level balcony. She climbed over the waist-high railing and walked barefoot on the hard-packed soil until her toes found soft sand moistened by dew, cooled by nightfall. The waves sounded loud as they always do at night, but they were just small. She walked waterside. The low-light pollution of an empty beach on the edge of a quiet town at the end of the road. The once sparsely-studded sky by every passing minute becoming a glittering dome.

The pursuit of B2P has come with costs. My this is nice. All of life comes with costs. I've missed small adventures so much. Everything has its trade-offs. She stopped and stared. Out. Up. Down the beach. A palely glowing tip peeking over tree silhouettes. She spied a slim lunar arc. To thine own self be true. So said Polonius. Harder than it sounds. Not so much making good on the pledge as truly knowing oneself. Murky minds make opaque humans. Long prior to Shakespeare came the Delphic maxim:

266

Know thyself. She turned slow under dizzying stars. But the self is a fragile construct. Nor are we static entities in a fixed world. When dynamism and flux are core, mustn't change be embraced?

She walked along sand firm and damp from the receding tide. Constantly told stories make discovery hard. Stories of self. Stories of deficiency. Not enough. Not loved enough, smart enough, strong enough. Stories of virtues and flaws. A strong woman. A kind woman. A boss woman. A pretty woman an ugly woman a nice woman. A childless woman instead of a mother. A single woman. A fit woman. A fat woman. A bitch woman a loud woman a whatever woman. Don't tell a woman what's a woman. Don't tell the world what is the world. She breathed in a brief cessation of stories, aspiring if only momentarily to cherish the world for what in the moment you experience it to be. A noncontingent moment, however flawed however cold, cruel, or beautiful.

A black gap underlay the pockmarked crescent moon. She looked from moon to stars to wherever began the wet horizon but sky seemed stitched to water like everything is connected, a tailor fashioning the sea's wet fabric in undulating silk starlight. Is the world so beautiful, or were our eyes shaped to see it? On the quiet beach, vacant and dark, she shed her clothes. The waves sounded large but they were not. She walked out and waded ankles in wet constellations. She walked in shallow water surging to her calves, as if the low sky itself was lapping, like waves of rolling night bathing her pale skin in starry light. She waded out until her hair floated limply on the cool black water's blurry stars, then submerged.

Such a vision seen by some could overthrow prior allegiances.

Valerie dried her hair and turned on the bedside lamp and airplaned her phone and put on a playlist, her fourth, *Chill The F Out*. She had an app that by timer slowly fades out music. She brushed her teeth. Panties and a t-shirt. T-shirt said, *It was all a dream*. The attribution wasn't mathematician-turned-children's-story-author Lewis Carroll, rather the acclaimed musician *Notorious B.I.G*. She unfolded a corner of the high-thread-count heavy sheets then slid in that fabric envelope like she herself was a letter addressed to a dream. Put two hands under her head and fanned-out her damp hair long and straight on the pillow. Turned out the lamp. Yo-Yo Ma playing *The Carnival of the Animals*, gradually drawing his bow lighter. Bow over string accompanied by waves arriving to shore. Harmony of melodies man-made and nature. Maybe that was her favourite song. Maybe she'd tell Alex that.

Funny man. The phone thing at dinner was a little strange. What was that? For a few minutes she was trying to parse out the elements of control and moralizing from a type of weird challenge or curious play. Or something else. A proposition? Invitation? A joint inquiry into life and values, as if the road to love is laid with the cobblestones of truth? Smut writer would probably like that line. Maybe she'd tell him it. Maybe she'd see him again.

She had gone home with other men while not having passed more time. She didn't not like him. He made her laugh. At times she thought she glimpsed a spark brighter than opposing beams—the dramatic turn, them between the cars, that was cute. She smiled now in the dark. He's cheesy and a little annoying and a little cute. Perhaps all in equal proportions. Vacation made sweet with sexual indulgence, so why not this time?

Traces of coconut-chocolate still lingered, not uncomplimentary to the toothpaste mint. The fading cello and the waves and the dark and the bed and she herself was enough. This wasn't about a man. Just her right now felt right. Nowhere to go, nowhere to be. This big glorious soft clean luxurious bed. Heavy clean sheets. Fragrance of the ocean at night, cleaner and cooler and fresher than the day. The dark room, her one arm across her chest, the waves sonically flooding her room. Not a boom. No scrabble of water pulling back over polished pebbles, not a crash like waves erupting on cliff faces, no deep bass of heavy shore-pound. She listened as if the ocean on its next surge might rise up the missing word.

Rarely is anything pure and various concerns creeping out of the dark because night is the playground for doubtful ghouls. Work. Her dad's health. Love, sex, loneliness, romance—those entangled things and in ways Trent and Alex seemed men not wholly distinct. She thought about that. Then she inhaled deeply, and exhaled them out over the bed and through the small gap in the open window where they were carried out to sea. Let the waves wash away her concerns.

The classical music faded out with the cellist for the night entrusting his rhythm to the sea. Or returning it, she thought. She was warm under the heavy sheets in the satin dark and then she was warmer and two fingers on her left hand were warmest. They circled slowly and dipped and drew inwards a little and came away silky wet, then circled more. Her eyes already closed in the dark. Listening to the water. Her chest rose and fell the sheets like wave crests and her breaths had started slow then caught the pace of the waves, matching their metre. Not a crash, not a sigh, not a heave. She exhaled and they surged. She inhaled and they receded. The fall of the exhale like the fall of a wave.

The pace of her breaths picked up and her two fingers were wet where they circled, less slow than before, almost quick, then quick.

Valerie stopped right before arriving. She opened her eyes into the dark. All the talk of the unconscious and complexes. This is funny, she thought. This is kinda funny. She realized in this very moment, in this most innocent and pleasing act, one that she had done countless times, she was literally massaging her past. The love language of touch soothing a secret that isn't a secret? As if communicating it's all okay? She had never considered that before. Is that what I'm doing? That's almost funny. Can't this just be a pleasant little self-love? Is there even a difference? Is nothing pure? Her two fingers moved slowly where they circled her budding clit, her pussy in the dark just like her puzzled mind. Not enough puzzlement to stop, but a mind most intrigued.

Her breaths slowed to once again pace the waves. Her hand in the dark only lightly touching. Relaxing under the heavy sheets in the clean room in the chocolate dark where the music had stopped but the cello waters still played. Her thoughts slowing. Thinking less, like her breaths slowly exhaling, slower than the peaceful waves quietly falling. Her last thought before whatever dreams might come, maybe falling is the word.

XXI

Alex could have gotten in the cab or called another but his direction was not hers and he wanted the walk. A far walk but he had walked it before. It was a nice night for it and he didn't have to work tomorrow. He didn't want to eat a double-walled waffle cone, so from the bike path he threw it in a salal bush for some lucky and soon to be manic raccoon and he wondered if she was even his type and he wondered what he could have said to have her arm still linked in his. A thrush was calling, as they do in spring evenings. Its melody sounding digitized, bejewelled, loopy and oddly concentric, like a pebble dropped in a rippling pool of song. Another answering on up ahead. A moon tip rising behind him like the emerging horn of a horizon-hid beast.

He wondered if he came off as egotistical or arrogant or garrulous. A car passed. He smiled thinking about how she got his moral high-horse joke, the hay. A long walk got short. Up the road, again those tiki torches looking welcomingly tribal. He felt their warmth far from their heat. The night wasn't so late and probably his friend Elizabeth was still in her booth. See if she could answer a history question. See if she could give him a nightmare before bed, she was good for that. For him, an amateur historian, she was better than Netflix. Mostly he wanted one last drink after a long and pleasant walk on this staycation night. Behind him a thrush called. Ahead one answered.

Lana was just inside the front doors. "You're back."

"I am."

"Bar?"

"Actually I'll join her." He nodded to a lady reading from a book angled against several others thickly spined. Shelter's dim lighting and her corner darker. Alex passed small round high-tops with oil candles. TV screens coloured surf blue. Elizabeth had her candle slid up against the bottom of an open book. Glasses, grey hair that the candle-shine silvered. Alex said smiling, "Did ever a dragon keep so fair a cave?"

She didn't raise her head she just looked at him over her glasses. "I knew it was you." She looked back to her book.

"Shakespeare," he said proudly.

She briefly peered at him.

"Seven books?"

"No." She flipped a page. "More. You can't see the ones I'm carrying on my shoulders." She gestured one hand idly to a shoulder.

She said stuff like that. He looked at her glass, knew what it was, but confirmed it anyways. "Bourbon?"

"Alright fine if you're offering." She looked around him and nodded to the server and lifted her drink off the table about as high as the highest book.

He knew she knew that's not what he meant. The women in my life, he said to himself.

She laid a pencil in the book and closed the book and set it atop the others. She looked at him with a weary smile or troubled grin. "I needed a break anyway." She pushed the stacks aside as if making space for conversation and that effort looked strained. She pivoted her reading glasses up her forehead and didn't rub her eyes so much as cover them. Black fingernails. "Yes, Bourbon, Alex. It's all one can do when reading history."

"Is Bourbon?"

"That or curl up shaking in a corner. After revisiting stories of Chief Sitakanim, I think I'll do both."

"I haven't heard of him."

"Count your blessings."

"I'll need to take my socks off to count all this day's graces."

"You do seem chipper."

"Who me? Nah."

"Good fishing?" She spoke absently, her eyes still covered by black fingernails.

He thought about that. "Yes." His smile.

"He keeps me up at night. I see him now."

"What's with the nails?"

"It's from the pages."

She said stuff like that. He liked her. "Why read it if it keeps you up?"

She uncovered her eyes and lowered her glasses. "I assume you want that question back."

He did. "I do."

"Don't turn away from what's ugly." She his elder mildly berating him.

"Okay, I'll rephrase. Why read dark stories so close to bedtime?"

"I need all the hours of the day if I'm to have any chance of understanding humankind." She touched the spine of the bottom book. "After Pérez," she touched the next higher spine, "after Cook, all was not well for the peoples of this coast." She drew her finger upwards over the remaining books while looking at Alex. "But neither was it before. Did you know that when Pérez made contact in 1774 he and the Indigenous off Nootka traded briefly over the side of his ship but the winds came up and his vessel was being blown towards the rocks? His anchor wouldn't hold and he had to cut the line." Her troubled grin. "As if the winds were trying to forestall what was coming."

"You'd make me curious if you didn't make me nervous." Alex was still standing, his hand on her table.

She set a hand on his. "You'd get nightmares, little boy." Her old voice wizened her tease. She pushed her glasses up her nose and Alex thought it's a queer gesture which appears at once grandmaternal and taunting. "History isn't for the tender souls. I wouldn't even tell you if you asked." Her hand still covering his, she now patted it.

Alex sat down. "Are all octogenarians so dangerous?"

She raised her tumbler, amber drink half-drunk but ice cubes scarcely melted. She looking at him over its rim. Her smile gone. She sipped. "You won't like what I have to say."

Alex unzipped his puffy. "Proceed, ancient."

"Young man. Some things once heard can't be unheard. You might not be ready for what I have to say."

He gestured an open hand to the space she'd made beside the books. "Proceed."

The server Patricia set down Elizabeth's Bourbon and before she asked him his order Alex said please make that two. "She's very thirsty." He his only witness to this shameless repurposing of jokes.

"The backstory to this is a story without end. So like all stories, we'll start this in the middle. Same place it ends."

He just shook his head.

She proceeded to tell him of the barbarous acts of Sitakanim, decapitating with a mussel shell eighteen prisoners on an island just off behind Shelter here, and then staking those heads to poles where they remained for years. She described how raids were often planned for the darkest hours of stormy nights, where warriors with painted faces, clad in wolf and bear hides, walked hand in hand up the dark beach to keep from getting separated, tip-toeing barefoot into the longhouses of sleeping enemies, raising stone skull-crusher clubs, whale-bone clubs, knives and spears looming over dreaming heads. She told him of the incessant wars of annihilation between the numerous Indigenous peoples of this coast, the endemic slavery and human trafficking before the arrival of the trade ships. She told him of Chief Wickaninnish, who desiring his own trade ship, convinced a mole in Captain Gray's crew to wet the primers of the Americans' guns so in the coming night they could sneak in and slaughter the crew and steal the ship. But Gray uncovered the plot and so that night his crew, listening to whooping cries coming from the forest, took up defensive arms, and fired cannons into the blackness. Then before sailing away he sent a crew to raze to the ground the seasonally uninhabited village of Opitsaht, that little village hardly a stone throw away from this restaurant. She told him of the historic partnership between the trade ships and the Indigenous to slaughter all the sea otters. She told him of Captain Brown, who, believing he had suffered a trade injustice by the Tla-o-qui-aht, captured some Indigenous fisherman out in a canoe, then bound them, whipped them, and threw them overboard to bob in the ocean while his men shot and killed them.

Alex stared aghast.

"Do you know what happened to Captain Brown?"

"Based on that look in your eyes, your claim of what history has done to your nails, I'm guessing, Elizabeth, you're not about to say happily ever after."

"Killed by Hawaiian Natives."

Alex shook his head.

"You know what happened to Captain Cook?"

"Don't say it."

"Killed by Hawaiian Natives. You know what happened to Captain George Vancouver?"

"Pattern recognition has served me well. On the poker table as well as other places. Killed by Hawaiian Natives."

"Alex, so cynical. I believe it was kidney failure."

"Ancient, they'll never dim this restaurant dark enough for your humour."

"I so lament the lack of early writing here because I want to know all the past. The oral tradition impoverishes all lovers of history. What I would give to read the diary of a Clayoquot woman in a cedar skirt picking salmon berries all day. What were her concerns, her joys, her fears, her desires? Was she happy? Did she feel her life had meaning? Do those very questions reveal my own cultural bias? Fine, be that as it may, I still want to know. Reading various accounts one begins to wonder just how valued she was by her people. But nobody wants to hear that story."

"Don't tempt me with a dark time." He smiled but she did not.

This time she hesitated. "There's an interesting diary out there. Maybe you've heard of it. A young British sailor is captured as a slave by a Mowachaht chief. Just north of here."

"I know of it. I might own it. Haven't read it."

She gave him a look.

"I will."

"1803. Jewitt records his twenty-eight-month captivity. He actually praises certain lifestyle attributes of his captors, and doesn't that seem to legitimize his testimony? Sometime into his enslavement the chief's elder brother makes an odd request. He comes to Jewitt, formerly an armourer and blacksmith, who the chief has tasked in weapons production. This man says he's having a problem with some of his property. Jewitt working away at his table, the man tells him to file his teeth, and he sits down and opens his mouth. Odd request, no? So Jewitt does as demanded, that's what slaves do." She stopped.

"That's it?"

"No. That's not it."

"Then, what?"

"Some say that among those ancestral cultures, coastal women were respected, and that within their community they were valued equally as men. What's funny to me is that it's always a man who says that. Here let me clear a spot for all the history books written by Indigenous coastal women." Elizabeth did not move. "Done."

Alex wondered if she was an enabler for his own sarcasm.

"So this man had recently purchased his wife—don't look at me like that, take issue with the records not the reader. I am not original."

"Oh you're one of a kind alright."

"He purchased his wife and she would not have sex with him. Jewitt, realizing his intention, attempted to dissuade him. The man said he carries no malice towards his wife. This was not a crime of passion because *A* he was not impassioned and *B* in his culture what he was about to do was not a crime. After he would perform the act he told Jewitt that a husband has a right to disfigure his wife in this way to prevent her ever marrying again. Just social custom." Elizabeth drank. "Well, let's move on. How's fishing been?"

He waited looking at her but she only returning his eyes, as if trying to read something in them. He asked, "You're not going to say?"

"Why would you want to hear this? What part of you wants to know? Maybe that's a question to ask? Hey? What curious darkness inside you, Alex?"

He waited.

"Leave now and only one of us is tainted."

He said quietly, "Go on."

"That night he went up to his wife and took her by the head and bit her nose off. Then he sent her back to her father." Elizabeth cleared her throat. She started, then stopped. "As touching as Deuteronomy, no?" Her voice cracked.

Alex offered his napkin, ringed in condensation as it was.

She waved it away. "It's fine." She touched her sleeve to a corner of an eye. "That's just where I leak Bourbon. Excuse me." She slid out of the booth.

Alex inhaled deeply then exhaled heavily. He looked at the table, at his own fingernails. Wondered how long it took. He looked around the restaurant, as if taking it in for a last time, as if he already knew what he will know soon, that he will never dine here again.

She returned from the bathroom with eyes no less red and slid back into their booth.

"Maybe a student of history ought to remind herself that it's always the blood and the guts that makes the books? For every atrocity go countless kindnesses unrecorded, no?"

She tilted her head. You couldn't tell what it meant.

"Or maybe in the name of a good night's sleep you give history a little rest?"

She looked at him, her face blank. Then around. Then back to him. Like she was restraining an admonishment of his ineptitude. "Point somewhere free of history, Alex, and I'll rest my eyes there."

Alex looked like he missed something.

"The vortex of history, you're in it. The present is history. Shelter is history. This," she raised her glass. "Bourbon is history."

She drank. "I want all the stories, even the dark ones, because they matter, if not most. I want to know what we are, humans, and there's no way to know that without the full and honest account. I want this absurd world's past in full colour and sensation. I want to hear the thunderous crack of Pangea breaking up then stick my toes in the saltwater flooding the gap. If an asteroid ended the dinosaurs, I want to feel the rumble under my feet, then smell the sulphurous, charred-reptilian air. I want all history, Alex." Her tumbler had leaked a bead of condensation onto the table and she poked it then drew a wet line over the back of his hand. "I want to touch the swamp-goo trailing the first daring fish to slink out of our old communal pond before the sun slowed, dried and baked her on her grand adventure."

He wiped the thin watery line on this character's black sleeve.

"I want to know the thoughts of our first obscene ancestor who precariously balanced for that fateful half-second on his two monkey feet. I want rock stories, fish stories, people stories. I want it all. I want to know what exactly you were crying about at your birth. What was on your mind, son?" Her thin smile.

"You do want it all. But that particular fact has slipped my mind. I guess sometimes vaginas make me emotional."

The music played on. A server passed. A table left. He sat and sipped. Ice cubes half-submerged floating in amber. "A question came up today," he said. "What does Esowista mean?"

"The name of our peninsula."

"No I know that."

"While on the topic of nightmares, huh?" She waved her hand at the candle and its flame bowed then righted. She set the tumbler down but didn't release it. "It's a transliteration of the original Nuu-chah-nulth language word, hisaawista. *Captured by clubbing the people who lived there to death.* The only account I've come across is from an ethnographer a century ago who recorded the oral histories of various chiefs and elders. In years just before contact, just before written history began here, several nations came together to attack a larger one. The motivations are said to be the chiefs' desires for greater holdings, and bad feelings of long standing between the two groups. Of course the Esowistaht people did not call themselves *the people who were clubbed to death*. So the word is a description of how their land was stolen. You don't like that word?"

"Is that the right word?"

She shrugged. "I would think the Esowistaht's opinion would be relevant to the discussion. But we can't ask them, can we? Exterminated people with an oral tradition aren't the chattiest bunch. Their's is a silent history. The last of the raiding parties would leave all the Esowistaht either enslaved or slain, children, women, elderly. After that conquest and a series of smaller wars of annihilation by those banded nations, who would later bear the name the Tla-o-qui-aht, the successful chief took a new name, Wickaninnish. One elder Kwishanishim said the Tla-o-qui-aht never raided twice. Fierce warriors greatly feared. What I would give to hear the Esowistaht's side of the story."

He just watched her. "Not sure if such stories will make you any friends."

"Does a girl with a good book of conquest and subjugation ever really feel lonely, Alex?"

He almost smiled to the sound of her scratchy voice calling herself a girl. "You're like a hundred."

"I'm more concerned with making sense of the world than friends within it. I have Bourbon."

Elizabeth lived two blocks away from Alex. For a time he had seen her around but they had not met. People had told him about her. One evening he was driving home and saw a lady in a black robe talking to her roof. Bourbon, Bourbon, she called. He slowed to watch crazy. He kept driving. He came back in about seven minutes with an extension ladder and shortly afterwards descended with scratches on his arms and an ungrateful tomcat held squirming against his chest. Black cat, of course. It leapt away at about rung six. She invited him in for a drink. They talked—she talked of history and he left with nightmares, Elizabethan horrors he called them. They were friends ever since.

"Anyone who spends time reading the old histories here will find that this coast's past before the settlers was marked by conquest, genocide, and slavery. One wonders how the ocean retained its colour. Then along came the trade ships and with them further injustice, among them resource exploitation, residential schools and the reservation system." She sipped her drink and watched him.

Four tables remained in Shelter. Now three. He rattled his cubes. "Well. I should get started on my cougary and nightmarish walk home."

"I'm ranting."

Alex didn't say no. He half shrugged. "Ancient, I happen to find you interesting."

"The day I picked up my first history book I got my first grey hair. I opened the book, and so went all the rest."

"Elegant silver."

Her smile.

The oil was low and the candleflame small. She said she had better go too, but only he was standing. Alex on his way out stopped at the bar. He turned and saw her looking at her books but not opening them. He paid her bill.

XXII

Midmorning, Valerie with her laptop at the Inn's restaurant. Big centrally-located copper and glass fireplace. Circular layout with an elevated and expansive view of North Chesterman Beach and the broad Pacific. She sat window-side and worked while drinking an oat-milk matcha latte in a white porcelain mug thinly flared.

"The freshly squeezed juice-of-the-day is basil-raspberry-apple-mint."

"You had me at basil." She ordered the Pointe Breakfast, swapping the meat for a small side salad. Between emails her scanning eyes over vast blue water. She asked the server if she's seen any whales during this year's migration.

Two poached eggs in a shallow saucer. She scooped one and set it on a piece of sourdough toast and ground pepper with the small and slender push-button grinder. Her slicing knife spilling orange yoke over the bread and onto the plate. Second day with no messages from Trent and that made her happy, happy for both of them. She hoped he was in a better place. Later in the morning a text message from an unrecognized number.

Morning Ms. Roy. Would you happen to be free for a tour of the town? Then perhaps a cheeky afternoon garden mojito from the garden with a tour of the garden?

The strange fishing guide returns. She named his number in her contact list. She texted: *Do you muddle or shake?*

Alex had actually never made a mojito but the greens in his garden from the combination of salmon blood and chicken droppings and compost and rainwater and sunlight seemed to be doping the plant's growth. He was concerned that if the mint would continue at its current rate he would by fall be living in a peppermint forest. Not that that sounded so bad. Similar to a gingerbread house, a thought for a children's story. Alex that morning watched a mixology video. It was very simple. He watched it a few more times so he could fake an old talent. Like the redneck he in part truly was he made a muddle stick from a dowel in the garage, rounding its one end.

As it concerns mojitos, the only shaking is my head for those that don't muddle.

He had a few versions of that quickly populating his brain. An unmuddled mojito is a shaky proposition, etc., but he just texted that first one.

The sun was out and the flowers in his yard seemed to appreciate that. Pulling up to First and Neill Street he tried to gauge the weather by the sky. At First and Campbell's four-way, a pedestrian was crossing the streets diagonally, preventing all cars from crossing. Alex tapping his steering wheel reminded himself that often it's he who is the kook. Patience. Construction in town delayed him a few minutes and he wondered if that's why Valerie was already out front under the archway. Dijon sweater over a collared shirt and black jeans. He would have taken long odds she'd have him waiting at least a couple minutes. In Tofino there are no dry cleaners, dress-shirt stores, or windshield repair services. Through his truck's cracked glass, like an ill-fated premonition, he saw her.

She came smiling to his side and he lowered the window.

"I'll just be a minute."

His mind said of course but his mouth said no problem. He held out to her the yellow spring daffodils.

"Funny looking roses."

"It starts early, hey?"

"I'll be right back." She passed him a duffle bag through the window and he set it on the passenger seat and held the flowers. Last night Val plugged the charging cord securely into her iPhone but in doing so it came partly unsecured from the wall. She hadn't noticed its low battery on her morning run. Right before Alex rolled up she texted her dad and saw the red battery icon. Less work, more Tofino. Make good on a promise. No problem. She returned without her phone. She felt a little naked. It felt good to feel a little naked.

Alex was distracted checking the weather on his phone and didn't open her door and mentally kicked himself for that. "Morning Ms. Roy." He passed her the flowers.

"Thank you. Beautiful."

"You're welcome, sunshine."

"What kind of air freshener is that?" She dipped looking behind the rear-view mirror where nothing hung. "Tropical. Or watermelon?"

"Close." Alex opened the console and took out a small cardboard package the size of a hockey puck. "Blue surf wax." She sniffed it and he pulled away from the entrance with her asking him his favourite smells.

"Fingers invisibly stained with scents of fresh-picked tomatoes. You go."

"Spring rain."

"Fallen brown tree needles baking in the sun of a warm forest floor. That takes me back."

"Blooming flowers." She smelled the bouquet. "So if you dreamt you slept with your friend's husband do you apologize the next day? I'm asking for a friend."

"Are you that bad of a lay?"

She sheepishly looked at him.

"Yeah you should. As long as I'm there to watch. I really think you should, yes." He slowed for a speed bump. "You know what I've wondered. Suppose you have a dream about someone you know and they wronged you in it. Or the opposite, they were really nice. Do you think you hold a trace amount of emotional residue for them in your awake life?"

"I think probably, yeah. But maybe you've always had some kind of subsurface emotion—whether resentment or affection—you just didn't know it, but it was always there colouring things. Only now it surfaced for you to recognize it in a dream."

"Interesting take. Kind of like the ol' classic *egg or chicken* dilemma."

"It's chicken or the... You're messing with me. Too early." She looked back ahead. They both waved to the security attendant at the outer booth. Alex slowed for the three-way-stop then turned left for town. Valerie said, "The other night I had a dream of dinner with friends I hadn't seen in a while. I wondered if maybe the dream isn't so much exploring or pointing as it is delivering. Endorphins, dopamine, biochemicals that underlie social connection, maybe they're being released in a dream and the body has a type of self-sustaining mechanism. Like it's growing then feeding itself what it's hungry for. Some psychologists say that as it concerns our well-being we have the ability to manufacture the very commodity that we seek. I was in the audience when Dan Gilbert, Harvard psychologist and happiness researcher, gave a talk on it. Positive psychology, how to make happy people, happier. B2P is going to be offering workshops on it in the summer. Seems like spiritual savants can attest to that, their deep equanimity even while just sitting alone in a cave from the relationship they've developed with their mind. Pretty fascinating, I think."

"Not to mention tantric-sex explorers."

"It's true though."

"It's definitely either the most self-empowering or loneliest thing I've ever heard."

"So did you sleep any better last night?"

"Spring is a funny time at my little estate." His place was fairly large as far as Tofino properties go, but for certain not large enough to be called an estate. Sometimes he said manor, more often sanctuary. "I basically live in a bird reserve, or a sanatorium for mad robins. This time of year the first one starts at about five a.m. We're all up at about five a.m."

"Why don't you wear earplugs?"

He shrugged. "'Cause then I wouldn't hear the robins."

She shook her head.

He pointed out some Tofino sites. It was fun playing her personal tour guide. At the start of town they passed the white barn-like building of Tofino Resort and Marina where down the drive was the beautiful harbour patio that Alex would sometimes drink a mid-afternoon stout and watch the boats offload their catch. They passed Surf Sister where a barefoot girl with her windswept hair stands holding her board forever watching a wave, who Alex for some twelve years now had a crush on. One day he'd find her. He right now in his head said something really sweet to her. Long Beach Surf Shop on their right. Tofino Coffee on their left. Then Alex said, "Holy shit."

"Woah."

He stopped in the middle of the road stopping cars behind him but nobody honked. To his left a smoking rubble. Like they'd arrived to some isolated warzone. "How didn't I notice that? I drove past this picking you up." A smoldering lot. Charred timber posts. Wisps of smoke like rising ghosts from fallen Tiki torches. Most of the stone fireplace still standing but blackened. The big kitchen exhaust fan hanging on a dilapidated wall, the only one still half-standing. Last night's fire trucks and police cruisers and dozens of bystanders that had crowded in front of Shelter Restaurant's raging structure fire no longer here. Smoking and sooty aftermath of a local dining legacy. He looked at her then back to what no longer was and someone honked and he pulled over. He checked his phone, Facebook, the Westerly, texted a couple buddies. "I can't believe that."

"What does the news say? Was anybody hurt?"

They drove down Campbell Street and Alex was quiet. They turned left at Fourth Street for the quiet roads to Tonquin and he wasn't talking much.

A hundred sneakers hanging from power lines. They passed the skate park. The caged basketball court. Tennis courts confused by pickleball lines. The liquor store and the hospital. He turned left on First Street and drove past Centennial Park. The concrete ping-pong table with its stainless-steel net, which when he first saw it believed was constructed to survive the apocalypse so future archaeologists would know Tofitians' love of play. But right now he was only thinking about the fire. In the middle of the small park on the grass a mother with her little girl dunking a dipper, blowing soap bubbles into the afternoon's slack air. Thinnest rainbows in their fragile surface.

Near the end of the road they right turned down his steep driveway and Valerie bet that these bordering yellow daffodils had six freshly cut stems. With her empty hand she punched him in the shoulder. He perked up, such was his nature. Arching the driveway a red rhododendron. They drove under its floral yoke. Spilling between the house's wraparound deck and the yard's big cedar trees, glimpses of blue water. Two rock doves grazing the parking lot's weedy gravel flapped up on whistling wings then turned in the air, flying above them, flying away not fluidly but in pulses, dips and surges. To one side of the lot were four old iron anchors painted bright white, each standing about three feet high, spaced a car-width apart. He nosed his Tacoma up to one as if a ship making fast.

"Okay how does a fishing guide get this place?"

"Mostly luck. For a time my fish guiding was interrupted by some other endeavours."

"Well that's cryptic."

"Isn't it?"

She waited.

"I won it in a card game. Sorta." He cut the engine. He said he used to play a lot of poker, and that it kinda worked out. He didn't expand on the *a lot* part. The long hours behind three computer monitors, sometimes passing on trips with friends to stay and grind the digital felt and for his efforts at times losing many thousands of dollars, sometimes with losing weeks even losing months, hitting his daily stop-loss of ten thousand dollars where he would get up from behind the screens and go sit quietly and be quiet and doubt himself, then get up and work out and clean something and do it again the next day. He just said that he went on a *heater*, a good run that lasted a long time. "So when you and I play some evening make sure to dress in layers."

She took a second on that one and he opened his door.

"I wrote out some letters of inquiry for this area of town, and for those owners who weren't home I tucked the note in their door jamb. These guys weren't home. It wasn't for sale. Turns out it was an older couple who were ready to move on. The lady called me the next morning." He got out and she got out leaving her bag. "They were already considering selling and I made an offer and got a good deal. A month later I was moved into my dream home. Probably that rarely works. Just lucky. This was right before a big price boom in Tofino properties. I kept on playing poker. Put the winnings into a few investments. Looking back, that was reckless. Lost on most of them. Got lucky on a couple. They paid off then paid off the mortgage. Bought the Outcast. Put the rest into low-cost broad-market index funds."

"Your boat's name is the Outcast? Should I be concerned?"

"Yes you should. Though actually it came named." Two truck doors shut. "Have you seen the movie The Gambler? There's this great speech in it by John Goodman. IMDB rates that movie a six. That's a joke. That movie is a solid eight-point-five, at least. I've never trusted movie ratings again. Anyways, what to do when you go on a deep run in the black? I did exactly what Goodman's character says, basically word for word, but I did it *before* I saw that movie. That's just too funny to me. Like the common wisdom of degenerate gamblers."

"And now you fish?"

"*And now I fish!*" He said that like a bizarre proclamation. "Folded my cards. Cashed in my chips. Now: *Catch fish. Write smut. Seek love*. With a bit of *fuck-you-money* in the bank. Or what some might more delicately call a financial cushion. That movie is underrated in so many ways. We should watch it one night. I'll make you popcorn as long as you don't put anything weird on it. If you put nooch or sugar or something, then we'll have to resort to *his* and *her* bowls. I'm traditional in my dating and my popcorn: monogamy, butter and salt."

The fishing guide seemed to be talking at her more than with her and she moved away from her side of the truck and turned and looked around. The still cedar boughs suggested the afternoon windless. Sight of blue water. Scent of magnolia.

"Let's go this way. I'll show you something." He beckoned an arm. "I should have mentioned this earlier, but I live with three blondes. Do your lips get all pouty when you're jealous?"

They left the small parking lot for a treed fringe of his property and he ducked under a branch with big glossy banana

290

leaves and she following looked up at the magnolia tree. It had bloomed a single big white flower.

"Oh wow. I think it's even prettier than a lotus." She leaned in.

He turned. "Oh her. I agree. She's my favourite here. More than once I've suspected her of being her own quiet god. Oddly she doesn't just bloom in spring. One here, one there. As if she knew her own potency and if she flowered all at once she'd just spellbind the world."

Valerie touched a big white silky petal. So pretty, but probably not prettier than the one from that song she heard driving here. It's very hard to be prettier than something from a song. From below the branches she looked up at a high bud whose tight leaves restrained bloom.

In a forested corner was a small shed with a ten-foot mesh-wire run, a galvanized water-feeder hanging from the roof, oddly, a large mirror. Alex pointed at it and told her they are surprisingly vain. Some scattered oyster shells like a caged man had a happy hour. "For the added calcium." He didn't tell her about the rats in the shed, how he was snapping necks and stacking bodies like it was a military coup—war-time crimes, girls, I'm your soldier—he just presented to Valerie, the Golden Girls. "Las mujeres rubias."

"Why Spanish?"

"Because in my mind they're Mexican."

"You speak Spanish?"

"Just enough to get my heart broken."

She rolled her eyes at his constant playing of the tragic romantic and he asked her what in the heavens of her dismissiveness she saw up there. She answered: "What are their names?" Plump golden birds with proud chests waddling under roosting bars in the packed mud run. Pecking among the dirt and pebbles for a doomed wood bug.

In truth he hadn't named them, he could barely tell them apart and believed them to be amoral and feathered contemporary versions of small dinosaurs and felt quite certain that had he been their size and found himself in their cage, that even though he had given them a fair life of ample wandering room and the reliability of organic feed and fresh water and protection from predators, that their maltreatment of him would be the thing of nightmares. He could see it in five of their eyes—one had been pecked out. The names he just now pulled out of the air.

Alex pointed to the one with the bigger chest and ass. "That's Nicki, formally, Ms. Minaj." He pointed beside that hen to her smaller friend. "That one is Lil' Kim." He pointed to the third at the far end of the coop. "She has the best cluck of the three. Haven't heard her use it in years. Her on the small mound there." Alex turned to Valerie. "I wish her heart still was in rhyming. I'll give you three guesses."

Valerie needed one.

"Guess we have that in common. Such a voice. *Even after all my logic and my theory, I add a motherfucker so you ign'ant neighbours hear me.* At once polished and coarse—Ms. Hill, be still my heart."

"Neighbours?"

"I'd rather not say the N-word, but sometimes a guy can't help but sing along, you know?"

"Alex, I question who should free-range and who should be in the cage."

He led her through his sanctuary, while the head of a bi-national, multi-million-dollar company looked quite innocent carrying a dainty bouquet. A narrow path between trees where nailed to trunks were small cedar planks bearing scrawled quotes. He pointed to one. *Cultivate empty space as a way of life for the creative process.* One above a garden gnome holding a book and smoking a pipe. *The cosmos bear the imprint of*

292

our minds. Another set on a stump. *Caution the undisciplined pursuit of more.* Nearing the greenhouse he with a hand up cautioned her about the mint. "I'd never find you again. You'd starve in there. Or like, get nutrient deficiency, I guess. Obviously you'd try and eat your way out."

"Keep going," she said, perhaps wondering how deep the well of his weak mint jokes.

"In all of human history you would be the one that died with the freshest breath. Then your spearmint ghost would refreshingly haunt my garden forever." While walking he turned to her for her reaction and she said, "Boo."

"I'm going to interpret that as the sound of the mint-ghost, not your reaction to the joke."

"It's your world, Alex."

"Please, this way." He opened the greenhouse's sliding glass door then waited for her to enter first. The small greenhouse was warm and humid and organic smelling. It measured about the length of the span of a yellow hammock with a comfortable sag. On the tables and sills were pots with darkly rich soil, small green shoots and some larger. "Baby tomato plants," he pointed. "Spinach and lettuce and those two are peppers." Alex dipped a carafe into a rainwater pail where the fermenting seaweed he hauled up from the foreshore was releasing nitrogen. "Plant crack." He watered. "I call this my second office."

"So, this is where the magic smut writing happens? Smells fittingly pungent."

"Okay but it's not just this." He pointed to the *Collected Works of Shakespeare* beside the hammock and said but not just that. He took from his back pocket a small red notepad bound spirally whose curls held a short pencil and laid that on the tome. He got in the hammock and took from his pant's front pocket a folded pocket knife and thumbed it open and said my granddad always carried one and then with the smallest little curled shavings he sharpened the short pencil with the book and the notepad beside him and the plants around him in the warm greenhouse with the yellow hammock and the lush and organic fragrance until he'd shaved that pencil's conical lead to needle point. "That," he said. "All of this. I really like it." From the hammock he extended a hand to her, uncertain if she'd take it, hoping she heard enthusiasm not egotism, with this, with everything, gratitude and wonder, not self-absorption.

The walls of the greenhouse tenderly creaked under the hammock's doubled weight. Them wrapped in a yellow cocoon, she half-nested into him, her head lying over his arm. She couldn't see his small smile but she could feel his heart. He touched his toes to a shelf to rock the hammock over the gravel floor. He said I thought the beautiful thing is supposed to leave the chrysalis not enter it.

She flicked him in the chest. "Is this where you come up with these lines for your Tinder dates?"

"Yes. Do you have any plants?"

She told him of her creeping ivy named Alex and the fat and jealous jade named Jade. She told him about the monstera plant called Euclid the Monster. "A good monster, like Frankenstein."

He asked her why she named her plant after an early geometrician.

"Because people will tell you what is this and what is that. What is art and what is woman and what is life and what is bird or anything." That she wanted to know more of the world through the world. "Less intermediaries. Find out what rain is through rain. Listen to it, feel it, smell it. I stay open to the possibility that rain, even if just on some nights, or even some drops, might not be exactly what we take it to be." She talked about breaking patterns and establishing her own first principles. "Basically, just playing in my world."

From their fabric banana Valerie detected the aroma of basil and pointed to a row of green stunted shoots and he confirmed. She asked, "Have you heard of the Proust Effect?"

"I know of the writer, but no. What is it?"

"It's when a scent involuntarily triggers a vivid memory."

"Okay yeah I've definitely thought about it, I just didn't know it had a name."

"But sometimes I can visualize a memory so acutely, I can feel the texture and see the smallest details and occasionally, I can even smell it."

"Without it being present? Without the stimuli? So like the inverse of the Proust Effect?"

"Exactly."

"Huh. Give me an example."

"Okay when I was a little girl we had a cocker-spaniel puppy." Valerie laid the flowers on his chest and Alex looked down at this symbol of death. "Not even as big as my two hands." She held up her cupped hands and he actually did see a puppy within them, whether or not they were looking at the same one, floppy brown ears, tan and white little warm body. "Just a cute fur-ball of love."

"Knew it. You do want a dog."

"Every girl, Alex. I played with him before and after school as much as I could out on the grass. Sometimes when I think about that I can smell that new puppy smell." She brought her cupped hands to her nose.

"Can you now?"

She shook her head. "Maybe there's too much here, the greenhouse." He said let me try and she shared the cupped puppy but he only got trace scents of her candied skin. "I've Googled it but I'm uncertain if it's a recognized phenomenon. It's probably in the psychology literature somewhere but my keyword searches always trigger Proust Effect or synesthesia. Maybe olfactorisation or a type of hyperfantasia." She shrugged.

"I'm calling it the Valerie Effect."

"So what will your memory of me smell like?" she asked.

"You?"

"Yeah."

"Us?"

"Okay."

"This?"

"Sure."

He didn't turn his head he shifted his eyes around the small and sunny and warm shack. The garage was his, the tools and boating equipment, the hunting gear, but he once lived with a woman who called the greenhouse the *she shed*. Traces of her presence here and everywhere more substantive than a ghost and if he thought about that now it would likely sadden him but he did not think about that he looked at the plant green and soil black and wood brown. He smelled the baking lush organic warmth, which was a good smell. My God I hope you don't take this from me. Other things have been taken. I've lost whole geographies I've lost waters. Will you take this, Valerie? Do you take this Valerie. You open up to someone and you've let them in. Caution, there's thieves at the gate. Not all demons have to be invited in and did one just come in through the sliding glass door? He turned his head to her. She was looking up at the opaque ceiling.

He put his nose to her neck, not unlike a puppy might, and sniffed from the base of her neck to behind her lobe and she squirmed from the tickle and what a gesture that makes a grown woman giggle. He joined her gaze at the wavy, diaphanous roof. He said faintly, "Valerie, my virtue or my plague?"

She turned to him and exhaled into his ear sweet words like expelling cherry smoke, "Fuck around and find out."

He laughed as much from her lips grazing his lobe as the comment. He asked if all CEOs are so adorable. He said mine was Shakespeare and she tapped the big book beside them and said she figured.

"So what will your memory of me smell like?" she asked again.

He turned his head once more to her, this time a bit higher, her hair. "Like candy and danger."

"Why danger?"

"You can be coy but you can't play dumb."

Her small smile.

Alex pointed to the garden box outside the open door and they watched a robin in the soil. He was wondering if it would eat his carrot seeds, if that's why he struggled to grow carrots, while potatoes he had to beat back with a stick, and the ambitious mint has already been mentioned. The bird sniped at nothing then sniped again under an overwintered kale plant and pulled up a wriggling worm dropping small bits of damp soil. He was pleased that the world in places conformed to his stereotypes—female punctuality, dietary habits of select birds. It's just easier that way. The hammock swept low, its fabric underbelly nearly grazing the gravel.

On a few shelves were various containers and pails. Valerie asked, "What's on your bucket list?"

"Is it *in* or *on*? 'Cause the *bucket*, you know? Fuckin' prepositions kill me." The low swoops of the hammock dipped low as any bucket. Maybe you're my bucket list. He didn't say that. "I want to engage well with my world. I want to be a good friend and good person and give effort. I want to stop reading all the books so I can know a choice few on a deeper level and work out hard and cook food I've hunted or grown and eat it with my favourite people and try to be worthy of the love I seek. I guess

I want to be worthy of the love I seek. Just engage well with my world. That's the entirety of my bucket list."

"Okay great and all but that's not a real answer, Alex. Here's what a normal answer looks like: *the pyramids*. You want to see the pyramids."

"I want to see the pyramids," Alex said.

"Good." She reached up and blindly patted things like the air and his shoulder and side of his face until she found his head to praise.

He liked that but he'd never admit to it. "Go see what all those back-broken slaves incentivized with a whip and a bowl of wheat managed to stack together."

She stopped patting his head and flicked it. "Do not soil in my bucket list. And slaves didn't build the pyramids."

He doubted that was true but didn't argue. "I actually don't vacation much anymore, besides the odd short Mexico trip. I find travelling alone a bit lonely. And why go anywhere when I'm living where I would otherwise vacation to? Tofino. It's like, no one living in Hawaii has ever gone on vacation. Ever. Not one. This is Canadian Hawaii, but with fewer sharks and better beer. Pretty much everything I want is here. The surf. The boat. The garden. The beaches. The patios. The food. The people. Spear fish, write smut—what more does a guy need? What else would I do? The pleasure sought on vacation is often much closer than foreign shores. There's your proverb. People talk about getting away and I just can't relate. I want more Tofino not less. I want to distill this place and concentrate it and shoot Tofino up into my veins."

"Oh Jesus." She tried to leave the cotton swing but the ranting monkey she shared it with wrapped them up in glorious yellow saying we're not done. On one of the highpoints of the hammock's low arc she reached towards a vine of New Zealand spinach sneaking out of its box and she pinched off a leaf and brought the leaf without looking at him to his mouth, green gagging his ranting. He ate the spinach but held her bound. "Where was I? I was saying something very important and not pointless at all. Oh yeah, if I were to travel, I tend to pick my vacation spots based on cuisine. How's Egyptian food? Papyrus rolls smothered with nectar of the gods or something? I never hear about Egyptian food. That concerns me, Valerie. Dates? Is it a lot of dates? That scene from the original Indiana Jones about thirty years ago where the monkey eats the dates. Where was that? Egypt?"

"I think that was Turkey. And the monkey dies."

"Right. Turkey. I'd go there."

Valerie just sighed. The hammock rocked like a middle-aged cradle. He said, "Bucket list, okay you go."

"Who me? I thought this was the Alex show."

He flicked her.

"I think I'd like to learn to play the piano. My mom plays. She plays beautifully. She used to play for me when I was in my crib."

"Bach."

"Furball?"

"Composer."

"Ah. No, Brahms, she tells me. Of course I can't actually remember that. But I can feel it. I actually can. It's not a defined image but it's there. It feels real, like there's something there like a memory before language, an impression or shape. I don't know. I'm going to make time to learn to play. I think in some ways her playing for me literally shaped me. Those classical lullabies rocking me to sleep shaping a neuroplastic mind."

They idly swung.

"Sometimes I wonder how close our versions of the world are," she said.

"Yours and mine?"

"Or just people in general. Like there are big discrepancies in how individuals experience the world. For some, hearing music is nearly as impacting as being struck over the head by the guitar. Music to me just sounds like truth. Its notes more precise than letters, its melodies more true than words. Truth that transcends the intellect and it's easy to understand but also inexplicable. It's almost a violation, how it just doesn't ask permission. Sometimes when I hear the ocean I think you could not have life without music. That would simply be a contradiction in terms."

He listening. Them swaying. "You think music means so much to you from your mom?"

"I'm not sure." Her eyes on the occluded roof. "Maybe. But maybe it's bigger than that. Than Mom."

A hummingbird flew inside the greenhouse. Elegant emerald torso. Beak like a swordfish. It hovered buzzing in place surrealistically like only a hummingbird can do. It looked forwards but flew backwards. Its beauty as if the designer of birds used most of her allotted time to work on this exemplar and then on day six was about to get to work on the mammals and turned and saw in the corner of her studio the ill-formed clay of the poor heron, all gangly and ridiculous. Oh fuck, right, the creator said, slapping her forehead causing tremors to rumble out in all the worlds. The hummer's rapid eighty-wingbeats-per-second flight, sonically enhanced by the small enclosure, sounded like a biplane. Alex and Valerie stared wide-eyed. It hovered as if pinned in place. It flew a small circle around the greenhouse and ended back where it started. Then it flew away.

They turned their heads to look at each other but in the cozy hammock their foreheads touched. "Well that was incredible," she said very close.

He considered licking her nose. Or their first kiss. But this forehead touch was nice too, like a meeting of the minds. "Yeah wow. Outstanding." They spoke closely. "And this whole room is windows and it didn't fly into one. It just flew out the only opening. How very clever." He kept talking, as he does. "For absolute certain if that was a robin it would be laying concussed on the ground right now and we'd be trying to nurse it back to health."

She turned her head upwards leaving him with his regrets. "Rufous?" she asked.

"I think Anna. They migrate north. When you get your dog you should name it Rufous."

"Ruf. Ruf."

"Yeah."

"That green vest of his was so sharp."

"So sharp! Just beautiful. Ah the magic greenhouse."

He toed the shelf to swing the hammock through a few last low arcs. "Can I show you the house?"

"Yeah but first, tell me about beauty, Romeo."

"Beauty?"

"Yes."

"I mean. That hummer. What else to say. Or, the ocean." He nodded back in its general direction. "Those words." He pointed a finger without lifting it towards that thick seventeenth-century book, often obscure but sometimes quite beautiful. "Sometimes I feel I just live in beauty. I am very lucky."

"Talk to me of women's beauty."

"Oh. That." He'd never been formally invited to enter a minefield. "Not sure about that."

"Not sure you have an opinion, or not sure you want to voice it?"

"Yes."

She turned to him. "Come on, don't be scared, this isn't a trap."

"Except that it certainly is. I don't see what the point would be. It's all subjective, right? And what does my view matter when I don't represent all men."

"Oh well this is interesting." She called him on his trepidation she hadn't seen before. "Shy or fearful Alex? Or is your hesitation from thinking I can't hear it."

He looked at her.

"Talk." She pinched his side.

"Ow. Isn't there some legal clause establishing my right to not self-incriminate? Does Canada have that? We should."

"Go."

He took a breath. "Female beauty. Well. For me, it's not everything. But."

"That's what I thought. Keep going."

"It's much more than I want it to be. It has too much power. Maybe most men see things differently. I don't know. I don't ask most men. Pretty sure men like pretty women. Alright. A beautiful woman could almost bring me to my knees. The word intoxicating is the right word. It's unfair and it's not right. Truthfully I'm a bit tired of evaluating women by their face and bodies—I don't expect to stop, but I am a little tired of it. I mean, I know in doing so that I'm really evaluating my own shortcomings. It's probably a deep-rooted character flaw. I have no illusions—or, I have a lot of illusions, but not with this. So you show me where in my mind that superficial switch is and I'll eagerly flick it off." He flicked her. He was absently looking at the spot where the hummer vacated. He half turned to her. "Me saying this is at my expense, right? This is me signing on the shallow line?"

She didn't answer.

"But it's stupid. You love someone for many other reasons that matter so much more, and you'll keep loving them deeply when looks fade. We get wrinkly and love deeply. I know that.

So I welcome a coming blindness to current false idols. And I'm getting older and greying and all the rest so why not just grow up? I tell myself that. What part? Unconscious? Conscious?"

Whether or not her curiosity on the topic arose from the stunning hummer, or a lingering memory of his hot-springs companion, she didn't say. If she did harbour a prejudice, however slight, or subconscious, because the harshest critic of another woman's appearance is often another woman, her's was silent.

"Now you be honest. That makes me just a little ugly, right? Immature? Pitiable? Something."

She took a second. "I think you're allowed to like what you like."

"If I made it sound like it's everything, it's not. I need that intelligence, kindness, play, all the rest. Whether or not I'm deserving of that, I need that to feel anything. But I've met a few women with those attributes and it wasn't enough." He shrugged. "My poverty." He looked at her. "Probably honesty is overrated."

They lay in deep yellow in the absence of a hummingbird.

***

He stopped them in front of the greenhouse and said, as if they were standing in front of a crab tank, "Pick yours." He passed her garden shears. She added leafy mint stems to her small yellow bouquet. They walked up the steps to the front door but he said come check this out. The wrap-around deck with an elevated view. The sky and the water both blue. They stopped where the railing cornered. The backyard below, the water beyond. Clumps of mashed-potato clouds shadowed the water's surface. Alex was leaning into the railing with his head turned to the blue, full of mystery, potential. Then he looked away from her eyes to the water. "I think this is your colour."

A kayaker off in the distance. Towards Vargas Island, the Cape Anne, a red and white coastguard boat. Small turbulent eddies, larger calm pools. The backyard was salal bushes, cedar and hemlock trees, bedrock outcroppings, a couple winding brick paths. The hot tub surrounded by a huge pink-flowering rhododendron. "On warm days a garter snake sun bathes. The rock doves coo in the yard. The eagles hunt the cove waters from that tree," he pointed. He said the paths disappearing behind shrubs and trees lead to secret alcoves and private nooks. "That one to the firepit and from there there's a short trail down to the foreshore." There was a lower deck fronting the cliff. A sauna just back of that which looked like a huge whiskey cask. "That's the truth barrel."

"Oh cool, then we're going in that. And I love that bench." She pointed with the bouquet to a pretty, red iron bench.

He nodded outwards to the cove where the Outcast tethered her orange mooring buoy. "I just like seeing her out there, facing into the wind. Outcast, you sea rebel, holding down your isolate buoy like the renegade you are."

"Are you talking to your boat?"

"This is Duffin Passage. If we watch long enough we'll likely see porpoise or otter. For a few years now I see this one sea otter regularly. He's probably here every day. He dives down and finds a clam then floats on his back and eats it. And always there's one seagull with him. The two of them, sea otter and seagull. It's never two seagulls. I find that funny. I always think I should write a children's story about them. Those two pals just living the easy life eating clams together. Getting into all kinds of shenanigans and hijinks."

"The smut writer with the children's story. Sounds like an offshoot of the hooker with the heart of gold. I'd read it. Why don't you write it?"

"Just working on other things."

"The love story starring a fishing guide."

He pushed her away from their shared corner of the railing. "Have we spent that much time together already?"

She turned back to the ocean. "It's all beautiful. You're very lucky. Do you ever see whales?"

***

With its uninsulated cedar walls the house was more like a cabin. Several bookshelves. In the middle of the living room a commanding stone fireplace. Big picture windows overlooking the water. He pointed up to a vase in the kitchen for the thirsty daffodils and she had to have heard him but kept browsing, and he reflected how women at times seemed to share attributes of cats. Framed photos on a shelf. Friends and family. He watched her pick one up and smile and though he had that photo displayed there for years he only just now wondered if having a picture of yourself holding a fish is self-centred. It was a really nice fish.

The kitchen was 1966 original with green laminate counters and plywood cupboards. When he first bought the house he figured he would redo the kitchen. He redid a lot of the house. But the layout was functionally ideal and though unsightly, nothing needed fixing. As years passed he grew very fond of it. If being charitable one could perhaps call it, as Alex just did, "Charmingly vintage. Maybe. No?"

Valerie didn't need to move closer to see that where the wooden cupboards opened they were permanently darkened from decades of finger grease. That the counters were stained and the sink was dark around its lip. She thought the kitchen was ugly, bordering unsanitary. But she didn't pull on his thread of charitable interpretation because it would only too easily unravel the onesie of his illusion and leave him standing there naked in his old and grimy kitchen. She circled the stone fireplace. She walked over to the large bookshelf. "So many." She dragged her finger along a row of spines, as if making a glissando over piano keys, and each author might sound a word. She pivoted fat Tolstoy out on his heels as if he was about to fall over backwards and opened to one of the many dog-eared pages. A passage starred in pencil. *Pierre's insanity consisted in the fact that he did not wait, as before, for personal reasons, which he called people's merits, in order to love them, but love overflowed his heart, and loving people without reason, he discovered the unquestionable reasons for which it was worth loving them.* "Why do words mean so much to you?"

He opened the fridge but looked at her. "The right words are beautiful. For what they say. But sometimes for what they convey without exactly saying it. They're the thing that occurs between the boundaries of individuals. The catalyst, the bridge, the thread, the spark, baby." He had a red kitchen towel over his shoulder and set limes on the counter and displayed with a small amount of pride some ghetto muddle stick.

She closed and squeezed fat Tolstoy back into his slot. She flipped through a Dostoevsky, *The Idiot*. "Someone saying happy birthday means less than someone baking you a cake and giving you a massage. That second person proved it, the first just said it."

"I'm not sure I agree. Actually, I don't. I think it's easier for most people to buy a bit of gold than say something truly heartfelt. Those genuine words are hard to fake and the right ones can mean more than just clicking buy on Amazon. Words.

I guess my connection to them comes from my faith in the world they try to describe."

"Truly sounds like you write the most elevated smut." She closed and reslotted the mad Russian. "Love, beauty, truth." She said that like a delayed echo from his absurd statement at the Wolf.

He smiled. "Yeah. I guess I have just enough faith in all that." He put cracked-peppercorn kettle chips in a bowl and said guilty pleasure.

Valerie sat a stool at the kitchen's big island cutting board. A bouquet of thirsty flowers in her hand. She separated out the mint stems and plucked leaves which she laid like lily pads alongside his elaborate mojito operation. She saw him look at her. In exploration of love's languages she almost let her thoughtful silence stand for her counterpoint. "But words are only ever symbolic, or so often, just empty. They aren't actions. They're the stuff of broken promises."

That statement was more loaded than his twelve-gauge two pre-dawn minutes prior to September first, season opener. He thought about using the muddle stick to pry open whatever she was harbouring. Not her first allusion to distrust. He sliced limes into wedges, then shook his head and stepped to the freezer. "I thought I had baggage." He gently teased. He got out the ice. "I'm making yours a double. Triple. I better just pass you the bottle." He pushed the rum her way then started muddling the limes and sugar and rum.

She smiled. She went to his side of the island and reached up above the sink for a vase and added water, then happy daffodils drank heavily. She set them on the long wide slab of a varnished cedar dining table. On the counter by the fruit stand Valerie saw a full peanut-butter jar upside down. She righted it.

Alex flipped it back upside down. "I find stirring a new jar of crunchy peanut-butter kinda annoying and messy."

"Your life is hard."

"I had this revelation—epiphany, really. Oil sits at the top. One day I said to myself, what would happen if I store the jar upside down? Valerie you may have created a multi-million-dollar international company that flipped the script on dysfunctionally isolating technology—*but behold*." He displayed the upside-down peanut butter.

"Does it work?"

"Ah this is actually the first experiment. We have to finish eating the other jar first. Stick around to find out the results. Bring bread, crackers. I could shave off like forty oppressive seconds every month. Total that up over the course of my life, and I've saved, what? An hour? Two?" He marched one step in place while opening a sparkling water. "And humankind advances. They say genius is looking at the same peanut-butter jar everyone else has seen, but imagining what none others do. Quote Sophocles. Or was it Testicles."

"Visionary, Alex. Modest and visionary. With all that self-love I guess any interested lady better hope you're polygamous." Dozens of spices on a shelf above the stove. Pictures on the side of the fridge. Among what she assumed were family and friends, and younger Alex in the snow with a large furry dead mountain goat, were pictures of a girl successively advancing in age. "Who's that?"

He didn't turn. "My daughter."

"I see. I'm definitely buying that. Mostly because of the hijab."

"Zainab. I sponsored her to attend school in Afghanistan."

She looked from the picture to him. She was squinting. Then back to the photo. "Sponsored. Why'd you stop?"

"For six years she said she wanted to be a judge. Now she's in scholastic limbo because the Taliban have taken back control of the country and have proclaimed that girls reaching the developed and wise age of twelve no longer need education that the Koran cannot provide."

"Well that's very sad."

"Valerie. Please do not be so denigrating of another culture and its interpretation of its holy book as it concerns women's rights. Or the lack thereof. Who are you to fault the word of God and his equitable and coherent theory of human rights." He finished engineering the drinks and dried his hands of lime juice on the red towel draped over his shoulder and joined her by the fridge. They were looking at the beautiful and smiling and hopeful girl with big brown eyes in the green hijab. He shrugged. She was tremendously beautiful. "Yeah. It's sad."

He handed her a fizzy, rather elegant looking mason jar, the limes and the curled mint suspended between ice. "It's a special kind of asshole that keeps a girl from going to school. My friend Elizabeth says rationality is our greatest attribute." They were still looking at pretty Zainab with enough intent you'd think the photo might just animate and pan out and show wherever in the world she was right now because Alex wrote her last and hadn't gotten one from her in ages. Right now she not knowing someone out there was thinking about her.

"What do you think?"

She hadn't raised her drink. She hadn't looked away from the photo. "What. The greatest attribute of humans?"

"Yeah."

Staring at the girl she considered rationality. And intelligence and the ability to create and awareness of one's own mortality. Finally she said, "No. I don't think so."

"Then what?"

"Compassion."

He held up his jar and said to compassion and she said to Zainab and he said yeah definitely and they cheersed. "I think a good story would be, after all these years of her and I exchanging letters, she and I lose touch. Then down the road I'm in Afghanistan."

"So, realism. Just some casual Afghani tourism, hey?"

"Yeah exactly. A casual trip, like maybe I want to treat my heroin addiction to the Disneyland of poppy fields, or I'm an up-and-comer in the world of international arm sales who everyone is saying such good things about. Anyways, I get into some trouble. And. Anddd..."

"And Zainab did end up becoming that judge and she presides over your trial!"

"Hurray!"

Valerie's face in turning from the fridge to the fishing guide lost its elation. "Except her loyalty to *truth and justice* trumps her gratitude for the man who sponsored her, who made that very education and her position as judge possible."

"Oh no. What a plot twist. I so love a good plot." Alex turned from Valerie to Zainab, who controlled his freedom, who held in those pretty brown eyes his fate.

"In the end," Valerie's voice lowered gravely, "honourable Zainab sentences you to life in prison. But don't worry." She reached and brushed a few strands of his hair to behind his ear. "That dirty-blonde hair in Afghani prisons means you'll be treated real nice. Well loved, special guy." She stopped brushing his hair and stroked his cheek. "I can see it."

He closed his eyes and willed himself to think of the headless thrusting mantis to protect himself from whatever image her playful smile now suggested she herself was witnessing in those Afghani prisons. His eyes closed, she clinked her mason jar to his.

"Ah shit, Zainab. What the hell. Well, I'd respect her for it at least." He said he'd tell her more of his story ideas, the hijinks and capers of the sea otter and gull, as well his half-baked hammock philosophies—an even less rigorous version than arm-chair—if she joined him in the hot tub, and she said if he promised he wouldn't she would.

"The bathroom is just down the hall." Valerie went out the front door and grabbed her bag from the truck. Alex got his bathing suit from the clothesline and changed on the back deck. Coming inside he said loudly, "When I travel to new places I think it's both polite and respectful to adhere to local customs. Do you or do you not agree, Valerie?"

"I'm changing," she half-yelled from the bathroom. "I can't hear you. That makes me quite happy."

He came down the hallway and spoke louder. "Some traditions are worth respecting and it's respectful to follow the values of others when in their locales, and being tolerant of other worldviews makes the world a better place so when I visit another culture I do things that might at first seem strange Valerie because I believe that's respectful. And so I'd ask you to respect Tonquin's local customs. Bikini tops in the hot tub are offensive to me and my people. It's like wearing a church in hat."

She gave a single laugh on the other side of the door thinking he screwed that line up because maybe he was actually a little nervous, as some boys get excited around boobies.

"A hat in church," he corrected.

"Sure no problem tits out got it."

She came out of the bathroom in a one-piece blue bathing suit.

"Disrespectful." His shaking head. "Classy and disrespectful."

She pushed on his chest walking him backwards. "Take me to the hot tub or lose me forever."

"This way, Goose."

***

The hot tub sat on a small deck bordered by a railing. You stepped up between two large garden planters, each growing a four-foot-high pine tree. A big pink rhododendron spanning the back railing. One side of the hot tub faced the ocean. He flipped open half the lid and it smacked the other half and he slid it back on its rollers. "Nobody can speak for Tofino. That said, I will. Tofino is a few things. It's a Japanese cherry tree town and a dog town and a yoga and fishing and food and taco and surf town. And it's a rhodo town. That island right there has over a hundred varieties." He pointed.

Valerie stepped up to the lip then down into the water and said ahh in the hot and effervescent water and submerged to her shoulders. The water fizzed like her drink she sipped fizzed. Her head low to the water, from her perspective the ocean lay just beyond the tub lip, like she found herself in a warm and pleasantly turbulent saltwater back eddy. Alex followed up then down and said ahh yes this is good and they cheersed again because you can't really cheers too much when you're on vacation or staycation or just whenever really.

"I once operated a B&B." That story was approximately true because one of his former wives did most of the work while they split the income. When he framed it like that, it did make him pose himself some serious questions. On the topic of ex-wives he tended to excise them from stories to save all the 'my ex-wife,' 'my first wife,' which he figured didn't help further his romantic cause on dates. "I almost named it, *End of the Rhodo B&B*."

Valerie plugged her nose, whether from the odour of that pun or her plans of submerging to escape them. He turned on the bubbles. He pointed out to an island's sand spit, the one

312

Elizabeth had referenced, and he tried hard not to think about staked heads. "Finally we arrive at your hot-tub history lesson. Clayoquot Island, also known as Stubbs. It was a fur trading outpost. Town started there because there weren't any roads. It had houses, a pub, a hotel, a jail. The mail arrived by steamer. People held a festival called Clayoquot Days that started in the late-nineteenth century and ran for decades and it brought everyone living in this area together, all backgrounds and ethnicities. Wheelbarrow and canoe races, tug-of-war, greasy-pole climb, everything. You had singing Scots, chanting Natives in full war-paint, Norwegian Viking tunes, Gaelic songs, baseball, piano playing, a tennis court on the grass fenced-in to keep the local bull from eating it. Eventually Susan Bloom of Bloomingdales department stores bought it, and for decades the island's caretakers were gardeners and soap makers. I use the soap. It's quite nice soap. The local doctor said in his diary that venereal diseases were so common he scheduled a day a week to paddle around and treat the infected. He called it Dirty Friday." Alex smiled at that anecdote and looked from the island to Valerie and Valerie excused herself for the bathroom.

Alex wondered if she had to pee or if history was not her first love. Her wet tracks on the stone path. How long would it take this midafternoon's drying sun to disappear them, or after her departure, for time to vanish the footprints she'd walked across his mind.

Valerie descending the steps was eating a chip.

"You were gone for a bit. Everything okay?"

"Chauffeur, bartender, C- maybe even B-list comedian, historian, soap spokesman. How does a girl get so lucky?"

"Well."

She resubmerged and he passed her her mojito. A robin called. She looked towards the lower deck that fronted the cliff, the big cedar. On one of its low swooping branches, two robins looking back at her. She breathed measured breaths. She blew at the bubbles, then laid her head back. Pink flowers bordering puffy clouds. Waves lapping the rocks below. "So how do you live in a fairytale?"

He looked over. "By staying loyal to my delusions."

She fanned her arm through the surface of the water raising a small wave that from her corner travelled his way. "It does sound like you've got a couple of those." Whatever that meant, whether she was referring to his story of the sea otter sharing his clams with the gull, or to his childish belief in true love, or that good will triumph over evil, or whatever else, as surely there were more.

From his side of the hot tub he moved towards the middle and once established there he pretended to front crawl. He wasn't moving. He turned around and pretended back crawling, this wet fool, the hot tub not so big as to really accommodate this. She did smile. He switched to some stationary version of the breast stroke and he said that was his favourite stroke and while still paddling with one hand he slowly reached his other hand over the water towards her bathing suit, her half-sunning chest rudely covered by blue fabric at the waterline. She watched those fingers approaching and when that slowly-moving hand got close she inhaled which swelled her chest and then as his hand got very close her own came up from below the water like a sea monster and drowned his hand. He took his hand back and pulled his arms through the water like he was wading through a swamp to propel himself closer to her and finally arriving said I swam the whole length of this Pacific hot tub and you have no idea what I had to go through to get here to save you, the steam that nearly blinded me, the chlorine dispenser I had to slay. He put his arm around her. They watched the sea.

***

"I'm all pruned." She looked at her raisin fingers.

He looked at his. "I'm also poached. I like going from the tub to the cold shower to the sauna to the ocean, back to the sauna."

"Hot—cold—hot—cold. Just like your love life, eh?"

"Nice. I like knowing you guys in Vancouver aren't too city for *eh*." Alex got out and walked barefoot down the rooty path and turned on the barrel sauna whose glass door fronted the cliff. He came back and pointed to the outdoor shower. "Rinse? The water isn't heated. It's pretty intense. Truthfully, it's kinda horrible. I think I have low pain tolerance for cold water. Women have more body fat than men so you might be okay." Nice, idiot. You called her fat. He turned to her. "Obviously you're not fat. Just factually women have a bit more fat than men. Right?"

"Is that a fact."

"Maybe? Evolution's insulation for the wee ones? The water is cold, but don't worry, pain can purify."

"Then turn it on and keep it on."

He liked that and wasn't sure why. Why is humility endearing? What is that? He wondered if we're attracted to those who might fill our deficiencies, balance our excesses. Hard to imagine an evolutionary adaptation more advantageous.

The outdoor shower shared the sprawling breadth of the big pink rhodo. To its other side was a lilac bush flowered purple. A chain-switch hung from the large and shiny rain-shower head she stood underneath. A wooden post in front of her hid the water hose behind it and she now saw he had actually scrolled words into a small cedar plank mounted at eye level. She pointed at the sign while looking at him. *Pain can purify. Pull for truth.*

315

He was pleased that she only now saw it. He told her to pull the chain to the shower of truth.

"I thought it was the sauna barrel of truth?"

"Everything's truth here. Get it straight, Virtue."

"Please now stop talking so I can enjoy this."

"Only a sadomasochist would enjoy what you're about to experience."

"Are you secretly in love with yourself, Alex?"

"I've never been good with secrets." He smiled hoping she was only teasing. He playfully defending what he hoped could be considered a healthy amount of self-satisfaction. He knew he didn't deserve any of this because his life was all luck and he knew that could change overnight, sometimes for the better but eventually and inevitably and permanently for the worse. An uncertain and risky path led him to this place, to his life. Pure enthusiasm. "Isn't that what all your self-help books profess? Love thyself."

She had stopped listening to him well before she pulled the chain that silenced his words, for a minute, silenced the world.

He watched water beads fall glitteringly, her eyes closed in her private rainfall. He could pick out individual drops falling in some slow division of time. He heard bird song, but if it was a robin its notes were being stretched. In the space between the next bead to wet her head he wondered what this memory would one day be. This right here seems like something that wouldn't be swallowed along with most of one's life into the abyss of forgotten time, all the big dark gaps of memory. Here I am at the inception of a memory. Will it be happy or sad? What will be its scent? Flowers and chlorine? Will you take this? What about the greenhouse? Did you already take the greenhouse? Maybe that's the real Valerie Effect. What will you leave behind? Her hair down her chest, one hand on her shoulder, the other on the chain. And one day you'll be an old man living in the crossed-circuitry of the sensible world with your random and partial accumulation of former days, smelling memories and seeing ghosts, hearing voices and tasting the bitter past. Beads dripping off her elbow. Some bird's stretched song. Her parted lips wet with running water. Water wicking down her hair down her chest down her blue stomach, her eyes low and her shoulders rolled in.

She let the chain go but the rusted valve delayed. Her bowed head, her hair shrouding her face, as if whatever she was experiencing had become more private. Her closed eyes. Moisture enhances smell. For the large size of this rhododendron its fragrance minimal, the water with a clean smell, and the blooming spring lilac was mythic with scent. Her cold body tingling acutely. The lilac perfume so strong she felt awash in flowers. The soft rain of a thousand wet petals falling over her. One for each beautiful thing in the world, who could count them all. She smelling purple and feeling flowers under tingling rain.

"Valerie," he whispered again. "We just entered Stage Two water restrictions. It's now mandatory to not shower alone. Local customs, you understand."

Her head unraised, he watched her lips shape to a small wet smile where words like rain beads like molten quartz dripped from her jewelled lips. "Then don't get us in trouble."

He stepped into her synesthetic world. He held her waist. The rain shower quit to odd drips, a robin flew over, another chased, they both looked up at the birds and he looked down first and when again their eyes met, Alex kissed Valerie. A kiss as an arrival and not as a stop along the way, a kiss you'd not trade for any other riches for none in that moment compare, a kiss fateful, that for all its softness you felt sparks or upon their contact came a silent ignition. Every star above them pulsed once but the sky was too light to show it and anyways their eyes were closed. Where his hand sweeps her hair behind her ear, where his arm pulls her wet body against his. A kiss whereafter lips slowly separate, two small smiles grow between them. A small kiss to silence ten thousand words.

XXIII

C old Winnipeg winter night of reckoning. As if the mercury sank to match the coldness of the boy's heart. A father comes out of the pub and a son follows. Trent gauges his walk. The man doesn't teeter, doesn't burp or sway. Just coughs. He walks much as he had before, a mild stoop. That is best. Sobriety allows for full emotional presence.

Vacant quiet street. He's walking on ahead and hasn't turned around once. Trent still hasn't seen his face other than everywhere. Trent's pluming breaths are soundless like his sneakered steps over sidewalk snow are soundless. His sweating grip on the knife and if it would shake it would not be from the cold. Trailing close enough behind he hears him cough. He halves the distance without betraying his pursuit and that wasn't hard.

A jangling sound sharpened by the cold. A streetlamp's orange light, the big man with his house keys. His father turned off the sidewalk and walked through the open gate of a waist-high chain-link fence. Walked up the short and narrow path to a small house and fumbled a second with the keys then opened and closed the front door and he didn't look behind him. Trent didn't stop at the house, didn't even turn his head. But he slowed and held his breath and listened for a deadbolt. He kept walking to stay warm and allow him some time to settle. He went to an Esso and bought a Mr. Big and a Red Bull and stood by the magazines and didn't read them. He walked back towards the house, disappearing then reappearing in the gaps between the streetlamps. As if the cold streets themselves pulsed with revenge.

No television hue in the living room window. Trent had pocketed his toque and wore his hood up. A streetlamp behind him had him following his own shadow through the open gate. Up to the front door. A handle with a thumb latch. He set his thumb on the cold brass curve. He pressed down slowly. The latch gave way but the door did not and in the cold air the small metallic click sounded like he'd fractured a steel girder. Then stillness. To his left the window wasn't open but the colluding streetlamp suggesting a narrow gap might accept a knife blade. He slipped his short blade and levered carefully, his other hand pushing up on the top rail until he had a gap large enough to fit his fingertips. The window stiff but it did slide making a tiny squeak like a wounded rodent. He stopped moving and stopped breathing and his open mouth as if he hoped to swallow that sound. His hands hadn't let go of the sill. If the man were to wake, the most likely outcome would be that sill slamming down on eight fingers.

The winter evening refound its silence. You could hear a half-block away a chugging car slow down for an intersection, then drive on. He squinted into the dark square hole he had made into the living room.

The winter cold made the sounds of the pump-action shotgun so clear and detailed it was as if not just the gun's metallic guts but the sound itself had been machined and lathed. Rearward sliding bolt, internal hammer cocking, cartridge pulled to the elevator, bolt sliding forward and the cartridge lifted to the chamber and the gate closing, all so very articulate.

The darkness of the room and the streetlight off behind Trent's head obscured his face where it sat at the end of the shotgun's sight rail. Had the windowsill been breached by an arm, a leg, the shooter's ears would have been temporarily deafened, while the ears of the home invader might have been the only part of his head still present in the open window. In that moment before obliteration, the muzzle blast would have illuminated a face. A father in a flash of light seeing his son. What thoughts in that elastic time would have outpaced the bird-shot flying down the bore? But so far that sill unbreached and the young face therein darkened by the halo from a background streetlamp. Had the man seen something other than a common criminal, perhaps he might have chosen other words than those he just dryly spoke. "Wrong window."

A far guttural and grating voice than the one from Trent's memories but enough dark timbre to shape in his mind the face he couldn't see. That face just outside of arm's reach, just on the other side of darkness. Trent didn't turn away and he didn't leave, though he'd now been asked to do so in two languages, whether a third was coming. He could make out the bore's rim, thinly lit, like a skinny moon you squint to see if the tips of its crescent touch in the gap. Everything behind it the dark kept for itself: the smooth metal of the stainless-steel barrel, the defender-series pistol grip on a synthetic stock, a cigarette-stained finger curled around a trigger capable of unlocking Trent's mind and setting flight to his bad memories caged in his skull like penned black birds, release them flapping into the winter air behind him, a hundred bats of bad memories streaming out of their cave.

Trent had five years to find the right words for this moment. Never found them because he found too many words. Too many to figure out where to start, how to put them in any kind of intelligible order. Try to gather them all closely to sort through them, but even though the past had stopped, their volume increased until it was like he was wading in a pit of marbles rising up to his chest and he couldn't touch the walls and then they covered him over and he choked on all the words he couldn't speak. He'd try to start again. He did that over and over for five years and tonight in the dark gap of the shotgun's crescent moon he tried to figure out what to say to his abusive father. These first tears soon to freeze on his cheeks unlikely to help articulation. All the words rising up overwhelmingly. Trent just grabbed one. Grabbed a second. Saw they were the same word. He hadn't been able to link them up because they were all the same word: why?

He was about to say that word when the man holding the gun spoke first. Three words like burps, esophageal speech from a man lacking a larynx. "Wrong. Fucking. Window." And that third warning emptied the halo. The open window returning to empty street light.

It wasn't that night Trent was served with a restraining order. That first one would come two years later. It wasn't that night he was charged with assault or a weapon's offence. None of that was in response to actions taken against his father because he never saw him again. Never saw that face in the flesh again. He died less than a year after that night. Trent didn't know of the funeral. He didn't lay his anger down into that grave, if such an action is even possible. As if his father's final gesture was a dead hand reaching up to close the coffin lid on resolution.

XXIV

T he swell surged on the rocks below the wooden deck fronting the cliff. The sauna was a couple dozen feet farther back. Three large metal bands wrapped around the curved, tongue-and-grooved cedar barrel. It looked like a huge whiskey cask some giant had drained of its hooch then dropped in a gunnera grove.

"What are these?" On three sides of the sauna were eight-foot-high plants appearing to be some type of prehistoric rhubarb, thick and spiky stalks supporting broad leaves six feet across.

Alex told her how he cuts the gunnera down in the fall to protect their roots from frost and a month into spring they regain their full height. "Baffling growth. If this whole place is my sanctuary then right here is its temple. My goodness I love this thing as much as the day I bought it." His hand on the sauna's door handle. "Okay here we go." He hadn't yet opened the door and he told her to be quick to not lose the heat and they ducked through the hobbit-sized doorway, each taking an opposing bench mounted to the curved walls.

Baking cedar air. Alex lay back against the back wall, his knees bent upwards, looking towards the water. Valerie mimicked his pose. Mounted low to the back wall the 220-volt electric stove between them, its small quarry of rough-cut granite stone where below glowed cherry-red elements. Tiny ticking like the Wolf's heat lamp. Valerie rung her hair onto the sauna rocks and they hissed and steamed. Alex unscrewed a tiny vial and tapped three drops of essential oil onto the hot rocks. "A potion from those soap makers." The barrel now infused with eucalyptus. "So Valerie, this misty barrel is a place of quietude, reflection. I'm really going to have to ask that from here on in you not talk."

"You're the one always talking."

He closed his eyes and his sarcasm got faint. He exhaled, "Please now," his words trailing off, "just be quiet now." Barely a whisper. He turned his head from where he lay and looked over at her across the gap. Her face flush with the transition of cold to hot. Her wet hair. She rolled her face his way.

He said, "Truth Barrel. So tell me. What's love?"

"Have we discussed Doritos yet?"

"You're pretty. We have."

"I think we've covered it."

A seagull called. A wave rushed.

"A tsunami is coming. It's going to float away our little barrel like a cork on the sea and we might not make it. My last request, I need to know, tell me what love is."

"Play. Intimacy. Integrity. Effort. Care. Listening." She paused. "Listening more. Honesty and chocolate."

He lay with that.

"Now you."

He thought. Then he thought another minute.

"Remember that Christmas when I knew you really wanted that cigar box for your paperclip collection?"

Given that their history could be measured in hours and did not include holidays, she had no idea what he was talking about. "Yes. Of course."

"But nobody would hire me and my only possession I could sell was my duck. My beloved rubber one. Recall?"

Now she actually did recall and there was no doubt in her mind that he was an idiot. "You really loved that duck."

"Christmas morning comes and you're so happy to see the cigar box. *I* was so happy to see *you* so happy with your cigar box." He gestured to her when saying *you,* to himself for the *I.* He turned his head towards her bench. "It truly was a nice piece of square cardboard. Do you still have it?"

"How could you even ask that."

He nodded, looking back to the wood ceiling. "I tell you to go get your paperclips so we can see how they look in it. What did you say to me?"

"Not now."

"Not now. That's right. You said open your present first. Okay, so I do. What do I see?"

"A soap dish."

"Yeah. Yeah. But not *a* soap dish. *The* soap dish. The one I really wanted."

"For your duck."

"For my duck, yeah."

Valerie was not actually tearing up at that most cheesy and excellent story from her Sesame Street television youth. Or maybe in quiet subdued weeping hilarity she was. The sauna sweat does mask things.

"That's real love, baby. That's ride or die, that's we bury the bodies together." He rolled his sweating head her way. "You feel me?"

She was laughing quietly. "You are a Muppet, truly." She wiped the corners of her wet eyes. She realized something. How is laughter not one of the five love languages? Send that book back to its editor.

They breathed and the tide surged. They breathed and the tide surged. They breathed and the tide surged.

When the rhythmic water rushing the rocks receded, a silence swamped the gaps. Baking cedar barrel of truth. On the last surge a dread washed up through the planks of the sauna floor. She felt it. She had had the conversation with a few men. Not the one about love. She had the conversation so she was used to it. It wasn't ever easy but she was practiced. Maybe now is a good time to bring it up. Normally she disclosed it in the bedroom. But this seems good. The quiet and intimacy of the barrel almost like a confessional. I don't need to confess what isn't a sin. Like a confessional, side to side, not facing one another. The low light. What would that make him? I have nothing to confess. Not unholy if we are the spectacular unwhole. I don't owe anyone anything. I don't owe explanations. Do it now, then it's done, makes it all less personal this way. I'm not looking for his approval. Who's then? Just put the words in the gap between the benches. See what comes of them. A wave surged. Receded. Maybe now in this silence. Another wave crashed. Or now.

She usually started it with, *There's something I want to tell you*. But nothing good ever came after those words. That sentence ought to be culled from speech or classified as explicit. One time she didn't preface, she just said, I have an STI. But it sounded too abrupt. Never before had she such hesitancy. Open up ugly. Just open up to ugly. You are not ugly. The sauna hides anxiety, everyone sweats here. No judgement in the truth barrel. Didn't he say that? She leafed through pages looking for words on how to broach it this time, this time starting to feel like it might matter more than other times. *I am... One time when I was young... Alex, everyone has imperfections...* She settled on a classic. She started to say, "So, I have—"

Alex had been deep in thought and he didn't intentionally speak over her, it was just how his engrossed mind sometimes operated. Her words didn't register until he'd layered them over with his: "What scares you?" Oddly, words not so far from

326

her preoccupation and there exist more tenuous theories than unconscious communication. Maybe a subsurface part of him sensed something in the barrel's silence. If the rests between notes are just as vital to the song, silence is a part of music and maybe in the gaps he heard something. Perhaps her sweat laced with biochemicals of anxiety related a pheromonic insight, talents of an animal that for eons relied on more primal knowings than words.

She didn't answer.

He asked again.

She didn't turn her head. She retreated from her confession that wasn't a confession. "You go, I'll think."

"Alright but we're coming back to you. I want to know.

"I think when I was younger I thought I could resolve more. That there are answers and you just have to give effort. But now I realize there's less clarity. Not more. Maybe for everything, or all the big things. Even the foundation of what appears concrete, math and science, is far less robust than most people realize. And given that's the case, it's hard to name anything safe from doubt. You start to understand how shaky this all is. How much you don't know and never will. You get older and realize you don't move towards certainty you move away from it. That those biggest Why's, those biggest How's, they don't get answered. The world is fundamentally mysterious, I believe that now. And that being the case, we are then to our own selves mysterious. Who we are. What we are. Now I know I'll die in the very centre of my confusion, and quite likely, surrounded by my regrets."

The water, a wave at a time, continually carving channels into the rocks below, one wet cutting stroke after the other, since ever there was rocks and water.

"But I guess that's not what scares me. More a frustration than a fear." He looked at her. "You're thinking."

She with no shortage of fears. All the ways for B2P to collapse and letting her clients down. She thought the state of the environment should be concern number one but it wasn't. Getting older. She saw it in her skin, between her eyebrows wrinkled from concentrating for hours on her screen. On some nights a new grey hair came with more preoccupation than the ocean's deoxygenation. She didn't tell people that. Fears. Things finalised, decisions I never made being made on their own. The window for motherhood slowly closing as if the poor stork has been losing a feather a day. Living alone and getting older and growing old alone. I can be happy alone. She ran a hand through her wet hair the sauna made hot to the touch.

"Here's one," he said. "There's a rumour about me going around. More than one person has mentioned it to me so it seems everyone knows it. But I hesitate to circulate unsubstantiated claims. Allegedly—this is how it goes—I'm going to die. As in, *me* not existing. That doesn't quite slot into my worldview. I'm not sure what to think of that. I think there's a real chance I'll take the world with me when I go. We'll see." He looked over at her looking up at the slats. "Peace that passeth understanding—I could do without." He looked up. "I'm scared of the coming realization when I know it's all over and everyone is going on and I'm left behind and it starts to sink in how I didn't love enough. Too many days distracted with petty concerns. That I should have savoured more, the water, the trees, the people, the everything—given more, done more. Loved more. Done more for others. Finally see that light in the tunnel but it's only from the oncoming train and there's no way off the tracks and it's carrying my cargo of regret and that feeling is the one you die with." He exhaled.

He gave her space to speak but she still so quiet.

"I woke up early the other day. Even before the obscene robins. Sometimes something wakes me. Not exactly anxiety, but it's not all that clear to me what its name is. It has no image. It is existential but it's not exactly fear." The relentless water scoring the rocks below. "Sometimes at night I'm capable of doubting everything, everything. I just." A breath, a wave. "Fine. I'll take the weight if I get the levity too. When I'm lying in bed at night in the dark and I can't sleep I say, thank you. To nobody and not to a god. Thank you. To existence. To the ideal of gratitude itself. Thank you for the capacity to endure what little pain I've known. Thank you for this beautiful breath, may I be so lucky to find myself awake in the morning and drawing one more. Thank you for doubt. If it all ends then even the darkness will end. That's sad. Tremendously, heart-breakingly sad. Knowing sadness will ultimately end, is, to me, sadder than that sadness. Seems most women I ask say that they are okay with death." He looked at her. "My God, I am not. Non-existence is a real problem for me. Screw the Stoics and the Buddhists, there we differ. My general state of contentment may not be entirely dispositional, it's a recognition of scarcity. It's knowing this finite tree has finite fruit. I love life. How else to say it? Goddamn it I love it. How fortunate that we don't have to understand something to love something. I've got a fundamental froth for this all. I could die tomorrow and this would all have been a most excellent ride. But I don't want to because goddamn it I love it. For a long time I did not exist. You know? And now I do. I'm here." He was lying down with bent knees and he raised and replaced a foot, this sweating sauna lunatic stepping his own version of a lunar claim. "I'm just so happy to be here. Thank you for having me."

An odd address, as if he spoke to the many gods of his world, those residing in honest words and those who colour the ocean blue and those who keep the coals warm and those who live in magnolia blooms and those who linger on your fingers after picking a tomato, those that leave the glade just before you arrive to find pine needles baking on the warm forest floor. And other gods too, he had them. He reached out blindly across the gap. Found her arm. Found her. Didn't turn his head just held a part of her. "Still with me, Goose?"

She still quiet. He let her be that. Then she laid her hand on his.

"I apologize," he said. "The truth barrel." He reached up with his other hand and pressed on a slat. "Don't know if it can handle all that. First time I've tried filling it to the brim. Might crack the cask."

She so awfully quiet that he is now concerned. "Woman. Speakest to me. How you doin' over there?" He squeezed her arm he still held.

"My dad dying."

If she meant that in the sense that one day she will lose him, it sounded to Alex like he was heading that way now. The heat expanded a stave and the wood popped. He asked about it and they talked. She hadn't talked about it with other men. She told him about the chemotherapy, how the cancer had spread out of his liver. Her voice didn't waver and the sweat from the sauna hid her tears like it had her weeping laughter like it had her brief moment of self-imposed shame. She was not one to sob and Alex didn't know she was crying. It wasn't the first time he had been blind to a woman's tears.

***

Over the course of the day several cars had passed by the Chesterman Beach parking lot including earlier a certain green Tofino Tacoma with one Vancouver Valerie seated in the passenger front, a window that would have directly faced Trent's rental car. But her phone stationary he had no reason to scrutinize vehicles and Tofino has nearly as many Toyota trucks as puffy jackets, and it has a lot of those. She was still at the Inn because her phone was and he'd never known her to leave it. Some patterns you can bet on, nor is it surprising if someone doesn't leave a luxury inn.

Why are you even here? What are you doing? What will you do?

What monuments raised, what waters swum, what mountains climbed, count the feats inspired by a one-sided connection. Men seeking what cannot be or trying to reunite what never will be again. Maybe if he can't have her no one can. Maybe certain burns sear a sharper pain than even bellies scarred from snuffed cigarettes.

He walked up the beach just as he had twice earlier today just as he had last night. Walked a path by a carver's shack. Wandered a wood-chip trail passing huge Sitka spruce armoured in bark plates for this harsh coast. Trent looked for a side door to the main lobby of the Wickaninnish Inn but no. He walked up to the main entrance. Big yellow-cedar doors, each with an engraved eagle, talons meeting at the centred handles. Talons now parting, the doorman from the inside opening one. Trent entered the lobby and though this was his first visit you'd never know that by watching him. He didn't look around to situate himself. He didn't marvel at the vast view. The restaurant was beyond the welcome desk and he wasn't walking that way, he had his phone out and it looked like he was using it. He turned his body halfway back towards the door like he might have to leave because of that text message he had just read that didn't exist. His head low and his eyes raised. A hallway to his left and one to his right but he couldn't just aimlessly wander looking for her.

He didn't look at the front desk. His phone now to his ear and one of them said good afternoon to him and he raised an index finger. Down one of the hallways was a bathroom sign.

The front desk's phone rang and the attendant answered. The man on the phone said he was sending flowers as a little surprise to his wife Valerie Roy staying at the Inn and what was her room number please?

Hard to say how often that would work. But it's made more likely in a town where endemic staffing shortages curtail hours and close businesses, where seasonally-staffed entry-level jobs have a high turnover.

The attendant, herself a romantic, said oh that is very sweet. She said just have them delivered to the front desk and we will certainly take them the rest of the way.

He said for a personalized touch he'd like to put the room number on the card itself.

The attendant thought that was a little peculiar, but she was not unfamiliar with odd requests from the occasional high-maintenance guest and didn't think it violated company policy and when in doubt default to the maxim: the customer is always right. "Valerie Roy? One second please. Room 450."

Trent exited the bathroom and walked the closest hallway. The room numbers stopped at 200. He turned around and walked back and waited at the end of the hallway and it wasn't long until new arrivals were checking in and then he crossed. His pace was deliberate without rush, his face mildly preoccupied and he passed the doorman again who by company policy or personal preference kept a courteous silence. Again talons of twinned eagles parting. Outside at the end of the grand walkway he turned right. Picked the closest building and saw that the room numbers were conveniently displayed outside the door. 350-500. He looked at the door and didn't pull it. There wasn't anyone around and in casually turning he didn't see any staff so he knelt by the door and untied his shoelace. Retied half the bow and waited like that for someone to leave the building. So still he nearly could have passed for one of the statues populating the grounds. The shiny heron metallically feathered hunting in a pool of dry rocks. The iron-winged owl forever swooping silently. After a few minutes someone inside was coming out. The only issue would have been if it was her, but the beard and sunglasses and hat, seemed he'd roll that dice. Hard to say what he would do. Whether if even he knew.

When the person was a few paces away he tied his shoelace and stood and extended his half-palmed credit card to the key-card-locked door and then he turned as if to look behind for someone, and as the woman exited he caught the door saying thank you and walked in and didn't look behind him. Room 450 was ground level and he walked a pace past it then leaned against the wall. He crossed his big arms and gave it some time. He didn't hear anything. He texted her an empty message and he did hear a faint ping. Behind him a cleaning cart was being pushed up the hallway. He didn't turn. When the cart with its spray bottles and clean towels passed by, she asked if she could help him. He looked up pensively from his phone, then declined, saying that she'll be out shortly. He looked back to his screen. The cart passed and turned a corner.

While he listened he looked at the hotel's website, confirmed what seemed obvious on Google Maps and Images. He left the hallway and went outside and walked around to her ocean-facing suite. He didn't have to climb the railing to see in and there was nobody in there and he already figured that was probably the case. He heard a piano ringtone. On the farther nightstand her charging phone was lit up with an incoming call. Running shoes by the door. Laptop by the desk. The bed was made. These story fragments not telling him so much. He walked the grounds. The spa. The book room.

What about last night? What about that green Tacoma outside the Wolf? What about that?

The sun half-submerged in western waters. He cruised the streets and nearly every other vehicle was a Toyota. Saw a few green trucks but one had a cap and one was too old and one a different shade and one a Tundra. Spring evening was setting and a coastal temperate rainforest is far from prairie cold but a cold feeling lowered with the dusk, a cold reminiscent of a long ago Winnipeg winter night. He tongued a chipped canine. He cruised slow, down then up the residential roads. Hellesen Road and Black Bear Lane and Vinyl Village. He drove all the town's roads but that's not saying much nor did it take so long. Looking for a truck like a stray piece of green Lego. Maybe enough observation? Maybe about ready to put that block in its place?

Trent, one may leap to heaven from the very slums. Trent, only rise and mould thyself to kinship with thy god.

XXV

After the sauna Alex rinsed in the outdoor shower and Valerie used the hot shower upstairs. While she was in the bathroom he started prepping dinner. Valerie opened the bathroom door to the sound of a wine bottle uncorking. When she came into the kitchen he handed her a glass of red wine and she said, "Oh vacation. Thank you. Love the apron."

He was wearing a beige cooking apron embossed with a picture of a blacktail buck, subtitled, *Lucky Dollar Meats. Est. 1967*. "My grandpa's butcher shop. My dad and I each have one and wear them when we butcher a deer in the fall."

She felt the urge to check in with her dad and irresponsible for leaving her phone.

Alex peeled then cubed beets. Dead-serious looking at her he said stop making a fool out of me. Then from his phone to the Bluetoothed speakers he hit play.

"Oh you didn't just put this on."

"How many guys have done that to you? If it's more than just me, I give you permission, just this once, only one time, to lie to my face. Right now. Here we go. Am I the charming first to play you Amy Winehouse singing Valerie?"

"Yes, you are Alex."

He set the oven to 350. His fingers tinged red like a murder scene but his only crime will be if he burns her dinner. He put the beets in a bowl and tossed them while adding olive oil and salt then dished them to a pan and got the rockfish fillets out of the fridge. Butter and salt and pepper, garlic.

"I like adding a bit of oregano to the seared fish."

She looked for the herb and didn't see it and said let me help and started opening drawers. "Where do you keep it?"

"The oregano? In the garden. Where do you keep it, Vancouver?"

In addition to the herb mission Alex charged Valerie with the duty of harvesting kale. "Yell if you get stuck in the mint. I'll fire up the chainsaw and come save you." He started making a vinaigrette in a small mason jar then shook it into emulsification. Onto the baking beets he drizzled balsamic vinegar and honey and scattered chopped walnuts.

She returned through the backdoor and exaggerated a sniffing motion and said oh my and he came over and took the greens and she wasn't even looking at him she was raised up on her tiptoes like a spy-hopping whale lured by sautéing garlic and he put in her hands the kitchen shears and said her second mission is parsley and chives. "Godspeed."

"Yes, chef."

"Oh I could get used to that. Finally we found our roles."

Departing through the backdoor she raised him an eyebrow.

He laid the seasoned fillets in the hot iron's melted butter. After a few minutes he set that skillet under the broiler and when the dishes were done he finished them with flakes of Maldon salt. In the big stone fireplace he lit the tinder and blew on the flames and laid two logs and closed the heavy iron-framed squeaking glass door. Outside the big living room window, in the gap between Wickaninnish Island and Vargas Island, the spilled sun was being absorbed by the blotting dusk.

Alex and Valerie sat at a small table, a candle between them. Her eyes on the water coated in bright and rippling slag. A rose-golden light coloured the room. What she was considering disclosing in the sauna was not on her mind now because the lighting was not right. So it was not on her mind at all. She turned to their dinner. Herb-encrusted browned rockfish topped with chopped chives. Glazed beets with crumbled feta. Simple green salad.

"I mentioned how I spearfished this?"

"Twice, I believe."

"With a spear. While I held my breath. Under the water."

"Wetsuit or loin cloth?"

"I leave that to your imagination."

"This looks incredible. Thank you."

"Well your vegetable harvesting is second to none. Good team." He smiled. "This is nice." The burgundy horizon, their glasses meeting between them like they held two cups of poured sun. "Can I put on a song?"

She didn't call him out on that first cousin to hypocrisy, bringing a phone out at the dinner table, she just said, "Please do."

He put on a slow song and he said he's actually not going to talk for once because his voice among hers is pure criminal. The emerging dusk amplifying the glowing arc, red-hot with the day's final burn. They listened. Valerie rather delicately chopsticked a beet to her mouth, held it cooling between her lips. The singer sang about love and the sea while the violin entered all haunting and slowly drawn and though its plaintive melody seemed committed to sorrow its burden could not deny its beauty. Valerie exhaled oh wow. They let the song play out.

In the quiet aftermath he said, "Maybe beauty can save the world."

"Pass the pepper, Fyodor."

He laughed. He passed it. "For someone who alluded earlier to a distrust of words you've read a couple books."

She didn't look over at *The Idiot*, the one on the bookshelf, she just smiled.

He looked at her over his raised wine glass, then tipped and drank and looked at her through it. As if distorting an enigma might help clarify it. He shook his head and she said what and he went for the bottle in the kitchen and pouring hers first he was trying not to drip. She watching him close enough he felt on stage giving a little performance. The stream skinnied-out and as he lifted the bottle that he didn't turn, a single drip fell to the table and that misstep only a drop but his self-scorn sized to a puddle.

She leaned for her wine and strands of her hair fell from her shoulder.

He cleared his throat. "I think the biggest question might just be a meaningless question: what's the meaning of life. It sounds like a fair question, but it's probably closer to asking what's the square root of water. It doesn't have an answer because it's not a valid question. This all might just be a fortuitous cosmic experiment in a laboratory that nobody built."

"Alright so what do we have then?"

"That's the better question. Not meaning *of* life, meaning *in* life. And I put it back to you. What's something that when you're doing it, you just know it's right? You don't need to ask if it's worthy of your time or justify it to anyone. It's just good. It's self-evident. Do you have that?"

Over what had become one full day she had heard his original tone of shock-value and sarcasm gradually sweeten. Heard it at Chocolate Tofino parking lot. In the truck. In the hot tub. Like a mug of tea that hadn't been stirred so well, and now each sip brought a bit more honey. It was cute. He served her a couple more beets. The sky outside becoming a confessional dark. Why even think about it. We're just two people getting to know each other over a nice dinner after a nice day. Tell him now and get it out of the way now. Tell another man what you received from another man. Go on and kill the moment. If you can't handle me at my worst you don't get me at my best. This is like a little privileged intimacy. She detested it. Would you see Stacy as less if it was her? Tell yourself what matters, tell your unconscious to get over it. Because that's how it works. You speak and it listens. Your life by design. Just not this. Not this. Or not anything. Her hand reached for the glass.

Alex said don't worry about it and he went for a kitchen towel and smiled getting it. He liked that she spilled the wine. It just made her real. This human here was actually a bit daunting. Women did not make him nervous. She made him a little nervous, whether or not he'd admit that. He wiped the red towel over the wooden table, scarcely more than a splash, wiping up his drop too. She looked a bit agitated and he said don't worry it's nothing and she wished that was true.

He figured she was working on his question and he saw no need to rush the machinery of her mind. The night was young and together they could solve the riddle of life as evening drew on. She had turned to the twilight water. Alex skipped a track, landing on a melody moody, atmospheric, broody. The music and the dusk waters and the candle and the fire and the woman cast the moment in a spell, a Gestaltic moment greater than the individual elements comprising it on this early noetic night. Those things that can't be put into words. Those things too amorphous and dynamic and large and awesome and true and fearful and beautiful for the primitive structure of language. Sometimes greater erudition leaves a thing unnamed. May your virtue be too exalted for the familiarity of names. Don't bind it up in letters like an orca in a pool. Don't try to constrain something as deep as the ocean as wide as the sky as profound as her blue and ponderous eyes that she just turned back to him. Looking into her eyes his stomach dropped. A moment fully appraised. Infinities move among us. Eternities go here. This here is dangerous. Alex moved his hand over the armrest towards the chairback. That was unconscious, as if reaching for a ledge.

***

Valerie brought the candle with them to the kitchen. Instead of turning the lights on they just did the dishes together by low light and warm suds. Perhaps something budding, something young, something as fragile as a soap bubble.

Looking out a kitchen window Valerie drying her hands saw light on the water in Duffin Cove. The playlist was between songs and they could hear the faint bass and low rumble of a boat returning for harbour. The narrow beam of its bow light over water.

"Usually loaded with crab when they're going that slow." He was drying the carbon-steel Japanese chef knife he had gotten on a trip to Japan and quite adored and showed favouritism above all the other knives. "Did you get enough to eat?" He was gauging the speed of the boat and was preparing to swim after it with the chef knife in his teeth and the dish towel wrapped around his face to hijack a crab if she said she was still hungry. That's no problem.

"Yes, thank you."

Alex put the tip of the knife in the block. "You're sure?"

"I'm sure."

He slid the blade home. That crab boat got lucky and Alex was thinking maybe he would too. He wished he could offer garden-fresh strawberries and vanilla ice cream but that season was still months away. "I can only offer you dark chocolate for dessert." He took a bar from the stack in the cupboard.

"I don't understand what you mean by only. Can we walk down to the deck first?"

Early dew wetting the rooty path. The crab boat rounded the point leaving only its trailing bass as the night's final rumour of commerce. Then that was spent leaving the priceless wash of the sea. Dark enough that Alex couldn't even see the swooping cedar bough he knew was just beyond the railing.

"Just out here in these waters in 1899 a cargo schooner caught fire. The Hera. A November night. The crew evacuated out by Lennard Island but the ship drifted on through here." He pointed at waters too dark for his gesture to indicate anything more than their collective imagination. "Among its cargo were cases of beer and instruments. It went down just out here. Burning masts and blazing grand pianos sinking in the night."

Like a passing ghost ship, the wake of the disappeared crab boat now swamped the rocks. Valerie gazed upwards. The sea was dark and the trees were dark but the stars were not. Twinkling pockets of them. Between clouds she couldn't see she looked into the heavens that had no end. Valerie said she's a little cool.

It's only a matter of time. Alex before that thought was fully composed lingered appreciating its beginning. "It's only a matter of time until we see a shooting star. The Lyrids." He cleared his throat, as if it was the wine that made it dry. Valerie traced the W of Cassiopeia. Alex looked for Ursa Major, the big bear. He looked for Sagittarius the archer. They both saw a satellite disappear between clouds and watched for it to reemerge but in the next starry pocket came a streaking meteor. "Make your wish," he said. He was quiet just in case he might hear hers, but unless she had requested the wash of the sea, she kept it to herself. A man who in occasional and private moments was more saccharin than NutraSweet used his wish to wish hers came true and when she asked him of his wish he said, "I think you know the privacy rule of wishes." She wasn't facing him and he wondered if she was smiling. She poked his side and he figured she was.

She said, "The temperature dropped so much since we sauna'd."

From a distance that was hard to judge but sounded close came a sharp blowing noise. Like the ocean was venting through a hole in its liquid skin. "*Pfff. Pfff.*" Two holes.

"What is that?"

"Super weird. I'm not sure." A sound as if the scoffing sea was incredulous at Alex trying to think of something clever to say instead of doing something obvious. Two quick puffs. "*Pfff. Pfff.*" They were squinting at the water and it came again, short and fast jets of air. He asked her half-seriously if she wished for a whale and she said no, "I wished for two." They squinted uselessly and when it came again he said, "I think it's porpoise." Two harbour porpoises hunting like samurais in the night. A wave sonically flushed up the bank to the deck where in the shoreless night Valerie made one full turn like the porpoise swam all around them.

He moved behind her. He put his arms around her in her sweater where she stood cool against the railing. She was quiet. She didn't sigh but her body kind of did. Whatever was on her mind that went unshared in this secretive and wishful dark. Above them another shooting star but she didn't see it and he wanted for nothing in this night's good fortune and so he let that star streak on, unwished, for a less requited dreamer. He pulled her in very close. Held her there, his arms around her. Her deeper breath. Her back against him and she felt his heart like he would push it through his chest and into hers. You can have this. He took his hand away from where it wrapped her up and regretted that and when it had done what it set out to do he returned his arm securely across her chest. Securely for whom. He lifted away her hair covering her neck and his grazing fingertips ran her a chill that stopped high up her back, warmed, covered by his chest. His eyes now adjusted enough he could make out her pale skin. Beauty at times may be delicate but that which could fall you to your knees is never weak. Danger. Her bare neck that seemed to him so delicate, that she allowing its exposure was her trusting him, his privilege of her bare skin too naked for even the modest cover of night.

He kissed that sloped and alabaster skin. Just once.

Her chills.

He kissed her neck again. Then joined her gaze looking out into the depths of what cannot be seen and there is always uncertainty in such depths, and though it too is capable of inspiring chills these of hers came from some other source. She leaned her head back and his wordless breaths breathed over her ear. She turned within the enclosure of his arms, turned towards him. Her back against the railing. She put her hands on his chest as if to stay his heart. Her back braced by the railing, more of his weight leaning against her, and she wanted that. Hint of lume to the whites of their painted eyes in this night of stars and eyes and wishes. He brought his lips closer. Hers barely parted, so intimate yet not so open that a secret might slip between them. Two pairs of blushing lips met, locking for a moment, as if secrets don't need to be told, or if told were safe in locked lips. They kissed and a star melted. They kissed and a star melted, another. Drops of star slag landing on their heads as if the heavens are crying. Rejoice. Alex couldn't care less about the melting sky because life is nothing without love.

"It's raining," Valerie said.

"No." He kissed her. "It's just star drip. Phenomenon of the Pacific Northwest. Very common." He brought his cold nose to her cold nose, more intimate than even wet bellies. "More rare than bioluminescence." He went to kiss her and she said, "Okay then. Maybe we just stay out here."

A tone Alex hadn't heard from her. "But I want to see you." He took her hand.

Robins asleep in the trees. Damp grass bordering the ascending path. He held her hand. In the kitchen she took the candle, carried its light down the narrow wooden hallway. Behind them the music of some lost romantic still playing. Candlelight on wooden walls. He held her hand in this bachelor's sparse bedroom made tastefully minimalist by decorative candlelight. The bed was made and the room was clean and warm. She set the candle on the dresser below a hanging ivy plant and it cast curls and spades onto the walls. He put his arms around her and they kissed and he moved them towards the end of the bed. Supporting her back he laid them down.

Valerie embracing his weight, her eyes on the ivy shadows. Curls and spades. In the sauna she knew she would tell him and now she knew she would not. It actually doesn't matter from a health perspective and it's just so common, if people only knew how common, she told herself and told herself to lift it out of her mind like her sweater now up and over her head.

He laid that away.

She was justified in keeping it to herself because they would use protection and she hadn't had an outbreak in five months and female-to-male transmission is actually quite rare. Her blouse opening one button at a time. He took his shirt off so they could be equals. She pushed it out of her mind. She reached up and touched his chest, his stomach defined in candlelight.

He lowered down and kissed the top of her neck. He wanted places of her none had praised and he sought them out. She tilted her head back and he kissed under her chin, along the ridgeline of her jaw, around to a small depression behind an earlobe. Her collarbone. The top of her shoulder. Their bellies touching, skin on skin like some communion, some prayer there, like some truths can only be embodied. He leaned down, their chests only separated by her rude bra. He reached behind her and she arched her back. She rolled her shoulders in and her lace cups loosened. He slid one dainty strap down from her shoulder. The other one. He while looking in her eyes lifted her bra away without breaking from her eyes. In this permissioned moment. Then he let his eyes lower to her breasts. Naked is honest and honest is holy and them half-naked not fully blessed. His hands warm he cupped them to the bottom of her breasts, their soft undersides, as if receiving them. He laid his chest down onto hers. Rapture of flesh, riot of sensation. Skin on skin was religious, so worship in the bedroom he heard someone say. Her breaths a bit short and movements a bit rigid he could tell she wasn't totally at ease, but nerves at first naked are common and he tried to affect his own calmness about them. There was nowhere else in the world, nowhere else in time he wanted to be.

And all that together made transmission very unlikely and just giving it all this much thought she knew in her head she was acting justly and that made her a good person—and that turns imperfection into its opposite and so it's okay—her past bursting its tomb, concern for the disclosure couldn't be bracketed off like news of a third-world famine—it's okay, it's okay, his chest against her breasts where her heart beat saying it's okay it's okay and this will be my first panic attack in a bedroom so here we go and it's not even a big deal anyway because her mom said so, her eyes on the looming ivy shadows and a breeze must have come in through the window because the candle wavered and the plant, like a crib's mobile, cast dancing spades on the walls like you can count all your flaws.

He kissed her quickened chest. This confident woman become vulnerable like some innocent queen. He put his arms around her back. One budding nipple licked, teasingly held by his teeth, warmed by his mouth. He searched on, wanting what of hers went uncherished. He kissed the bend of her elbow, kissed the side of her ribs. His lips down her belly. Her belly rose and fell and when it dipped he didn't move his head he just waited for her breaths to rise it back up to his lips. He lifted her leg and held her calf level like a bar of gold. Pulled one sock off while kissing her ankle. Then her other. His fingers on the button of her jeans. Sliding her zipper down. Their jeans on the ground and pant legs tangled up together. Her knees bent, his hands on her knee caps to part her thighs and there was resistance there and he with testing pressure like one turning a screw feels for tension before stripping threads and finding that he would stop but then she does allow their parting. He lies down in her valley. His forearms beside her head. She feels him through her panties. She puts her hands around his back. He trails fingers over her chest, over her waist, over her panties. Fingers sliding below the band. He's looking at her in the candlelight. Then Alex says to Valerie, ever so gently, "Why are you crying, babe?"

***

Alex pulled the duvet up to their shoulders. They lay with their heads facing one another sharing a pillow.

She said she had something she wanted to say. She looked sad. She asked if she could whisper it.

He said of course and turned his head towards the ceiling.

She thought of all the ways she had divulged it in the past. This woman who did not owe anyone anything and did not need anyone's approval to feel worthy and sexy and whole and

346

she moved closer over the pillow, narrowing the gap. She chose her words very carefully. She whispered most delicately, "I'm tainted."

She didn't believe that because she was not supposed to believe that and her mother and girlfriends and people that love her would tell her not to believe that. Not that word or any like it. But maybe she did believe it a tiny bit. And if in part that's how she saw it, maybe there was more strength in admitting that to herself. Truth is hard. Who should tell her what to feel? She said a word she had once heard from a boyfriend. He called her that. Its specificity seemed to imbue it with credibility. So she kept it, held onto it. Hadn't said it before. Tonight she wanted to see what would happen if she put a word, one a man had called her, back in the ear of another man. Kinda like returning it.

Alex didn't need it explained. Over the years he had had a lot of sexual-health conversations with women and STIs are not uncommon. He hadn't heard it framed that way though. He thought it was one of the sadder sounds he'd heard. A sound like in the night you had stepped on a violin. Something of great beauty, capable of beauty, making a broken sound. Not as sad as all the wars and plagues and all that, just epically, individually sad. Sad for this sweet woman smarter than him, certainly kinder, not funnier but quite funny. A woman who he was sure people warmed to like cold hands to a heat lamp. Who wielded wit like a broad sword that kinda cut him off at the knees. Yeah maybe she was funnier than him. This stone-cold drop-dead most-rare undeniable catch of a woman saying something like that. It sounded untrue.

Whatever emotional intelligence he'd earned from many failed relationships, those lost loves and fallen robins of which at times he was one, Alex was just smart enough to know she didn't need a man to repair or validate or approve her dignity or self-worth and that she'd probably just tell him to keep his mouth shut, and maybe she didn't even mean those two words because she kinda operated on a level above him and if he now offered her any of the patronizing and sweet things playing in his head, their effect might only work against him. He wasn't sure. Women were a black box at the best of times and this one here on this night was octahedral. He kept his mouth shut. Safer that way. He set his eyes on the curls and vines cast on the cedar ceiling.

The man of too many words had not spoken so she lay with his rejection. She pulled the duvet up higher. To confirm it, she reached a finger and softly poked his cheek. Like how a cub after the thunder of gunshot pokes her motionless mother.

Hidden clouds fall private showers. Two porpoises hunt in the night. A flame wavers. A cheek indents. A dumb bear comes back to life.

Alex rolls his head. Looks at her in the sanctity of candlelight. She's not far away at all but he brings his hand up and with a curling finger, motions her in even closer. She scooches, close, comically close, their noses touch. Nobody is smiling. He has to be strong to not laugh because at times she kills him and he is concerned if they spend much time together he might die many little deaths and then one big one when she leaves. He puts a finger on her chin and turns her head to expose her ear and Alex disregards his own intuitional advice. So fault him for it.

"I think you're the definitional opposite of that word," said the moon snail.

They talked openly under the security of a down duvet pulled up to their shoulders. He said her sharing made him feel privileged. He said her honesty hadn't killed the moment it had deepened it. He said we're all imperfect and thanked her for her disclosure.

This time she kissed him. She slid her panties off and moved on top of him while he reached for the night table and opened the drawer. For Alex the sex appeal of a condom was like arriving to a world-class spa and seeing the inviting steam and warm pools and the floor of small polished stones waiting to be felt pleasantly underfoot and anticipating all the sensual warmth and then the spa attendant handing you a raincoat and rubber boots. He passed himself a raincoat.

She felt him press at her. She felt him press and not much. She tried to help him. He did something with his hand and tried again and she didn't feel him and she wondered if, despite his words, it was from her disclosure. If he thought she was unsexy, unclean.

"Sorry. Sometimes condoms feel like George St. Pierre is giving my cock a rear-naked choke."

She didn't laugh. She didn't like condoms either.

He told her an analogy about a spa and a raincoat but he said "Helly Hansen." He thought that specific mention of that rubber suit really conveyed it. He had one by the backdoor. "Stand in a typhoon that fucker'd keep me dry."

He kept trying while using his hand and she just wondered if it was her. Didn't wonder, she knew. Performative truth, his words empty when his body says otherwise. Right now the only thing penetrating her was her insecurity of her sex appeal on this uncomfortable night. The spades of the hanging ivy danced again. Intimacy felt as far away as Tofino and Vancouver. She could hear the rain on the roof. She wondered if it was raining in Vancouver. He smiled with the awkwardness of the condom's imposed inadequacy. She turned her head to the wall furthest from the candle. Maybe climb that vine shadow out of here. She turned inside herself, but it had begun to rain inside there too.

She was about to climb off and she put her hands on his chest but he put an arm around her back and sat up and lifted her and swept her to lie on her back. His weight on her. "It's not happening. Sorry." He told her stupidly what she already knew. His chest was raised above her and he sighed because this sucked and his chest deflated and settled down onto her. They lay in disgracefully well-ordered bedsheets, in a queen-sized bed crowded with bad sex. She wiggled and he lifted his lower-body weight and she closed her legs. She put a hand to his shoulder and lightly pushed for him to roll away and waited for him to take the hint. He didn't. Or, he got it, but he didn't comply. Alex just lay on her, his weight fully over the length of her body. He put his arms so deep under her back that each hand held opposing sides of her waist. She in the vice of his stubbornness.

He said, "You're beautiful."

She heard trite words his soft dick made false. She turned her head to the laddered vines.

He knew she was going to tell him again to get off. With his hands he bunched the sheets up on either side of her, tight against her shoulders. "It's not the first time a condom murdered the moment." He shook his head at her. "Don't feel special."

She didn't smile and his humour, so often overdone, was now just annoying. He lowered down and playfully bit an earlobe because he is a stubborn pest. She batted him away but that just pushed him to her other side where he bit her other lobe. She gave only the tiniest smile at this stupidest clown. She said get off. He whispered fuck that. His mouth right beside her ear he breathed in and out rapidly, which for her would have been pretty loud, sounding like an animal sniffing or a playful small one getting all excited, and the air tickled and she tried not to laugh. He said, "Though my cock is presently soft I promise you my heart is rock hard." She burst out laughing not knowing what the hell that meant and how could she when neither exactly did its source. Her head tilted back and he set his teeth fully over her exposed neck, her laughing throat playfully mawed.

She felt her stomach drop. She followed it. Didn't reach for a vine because the ones she saw were all shadow and she was leaving a shadow behind. And she liked the feeling of falling. Wasn't sure she'd felt it before.

Take me to church or lose me forever.

Alex held her bent knees and kissed her knee caps, then physically made his request and she accepted their demands. Her legs parting and again her valley. He kissed downwards, alternating lower along each inner thigh. His hands on the outside of her thighs, sliding down at the same pace as his lowering head. His head kissing lower until he couldn't go lower, until he found who he wanted to speak with, and his hands searched over the sides of her thighs, sides of her hips, up to her waist, over her belly and to her chest, each hand full with a breast, and his mouth between her legs speaking to her and her hands in his hair encouraging his language while he lapped up her beauty and ate her sin. Her thighs at one point did press against his ears made deaf to a world he cared not to hear. He stayed there in the sweet darkness of her vulnerability because what's love without it. He stayed there until he had said all he needed to say without saying a word. Once, he said her name. Once, he looked up, chin glistening in candlelight. "I searched," he said. "There is no flaw in you." Her hands in his hair. Who knows if there was candle or music or spades or night or light or time or anything. Her whole body blushed, her face flushed pink like spring bloom and he between her petals.

Outside in that other garden, the magnolia's restrained bud burst blooming into the night.

She woke in the night. She lay listening. Sounds of soft rain. Whatever is the rain, whatever it may be. She heard sounds of the sea. Rhythmic and soothing. She heard him sleeping, his breaths. She rolled and faced his sleeping face. Very quietly, hardly audible, she hummed. Just a couple bars. She turned back around and went back to sleep.

XXVI

I n the grainy light he had his arm draped over her duvet-covered shoulder. Her waist tucked into his. Outside the window, first notes of dawn song. The slow light lifting the room's satin dark revealing an exhibit. He studied the slope of her neck. Paintings are worthless. Her latest breath deepened.

"You weren't kidding about the birds," she said dreamily.

A barred owl sang its distinctive call. *Who cooks for you, who cooks for you-all.* A thrush, a sparrow. The dominant song was the robins' hormone-fueled musical round, spring season's horniest melody, a cacophonous overture of wild lust, jealousy, love and heartbreak. "Pretty beautiful," Valerie said. He kissed her bare shoulder. His arm tightened around her. "Morning to you too," she said wiggling.

What had tripped-up Alex last night seemed no problem now. They followed the cue of the birds, and afterwards, when the horizon relaxed its clutch of the sun, Alex of Valerie still had not. Lying there they agreed to look into options. Valerie said, "Maybe we can look into transmission rates without wearing a Helly Hansen."

He said he would like that.

"And I didn't suffer through that fucking IUD for nothing."

He assumed that military jargon was another inside joke. He was funnier than her.

Their heads sharing a pillow. "Wednesday," he said, "but it feels like Sunday. You can still have church as an atheist. Slow coffees by the morning sun. Beach walks, books, gardening, good food, hard workouts, surfs. What does your worship look like?"

"That's hardly a morning question. Here's a morning question, Alex: cream or sugar?"

"Almond milk or oat milk, Vancouver?"

"Oh wow. Very good. It's never too early to talk dirty to me."

Valerie went for the shower and Alex considered inviting himself but morning-one might be jumping the gun and he liked the remorseless outdoor shower anyways. He dried all frigid and had his socks and gitch on and she Arabian-like came back into the bedroom, a towel around her torso and one around her head. In passing she did some little dance, mostly hips, fists on her towelled waist, entirely seductive. She sat the end of the bed next to him and pulled on a sock. Alex pointed. "Those are the most pretentious socks I've ever seen." Each with a corresponding L or R at the corner of their toes.

She pointed at the ones he was wearing. "Hypocrite."

He pulled his jeans on. Lifted a black shirt off a closet hook and sniffed it.

Valerie didn't say anything.

He sniffed it again, as if his research required a bit more data.

"Hey Alex, here's a good rule of thumb. If you have to sniff it twice, don't."

He took her advice and tossed the shirt at her head and pulled a clean black shirt off a hanger. He wasn't sure if she had said what her plans were for today and in trying to recall, his eyes cornered replaying their yesterday's scenes. "It's weird how memory is visual. Like, for example, tell me what Leo Tolstoy wrote."

"Fifty Shades of Gray."

"Correct. I think most people when they recall things don't just pluck it as inert data out of their mental ether." He sat down on the bed. "I'm seeing that book's black and blue cover. Okay, humour me. What sound does a Canada Goose make?"

"Typically they can be heard squawking in the early morning about Russian authors and half-baked psychological theories."

"I guess that does in some sense satisfy my request to humour me. But how about just answering the question, smart ass."

She flatly looked at him and said dryly, "Honk. Honk."

Alex laughed. "Now who's the silly goose?"

She shook her head pulling on the other sock.

"But okay your eyes went to the right for a split second when you tried to recall their sound. For some reason we access memories by moving our eyes to ocular corners."

She repeated ocular corners. "I bet never in my life do I hear that again. So where will your eyes go when you remember me? Up for the angel you lost. Down for your broken heart?"

He pulled his shirt on and she touched his chest. "Oh I'll probably just roll them like you do."

She brought her face so close that their eyes crossed.

He said, "Yeah this one. I'll cross my eyes when I think of—"
She interrupted him with a kiss.

"Here are your breakfast options. One: toast with smashed avocado."

"Why are you always so aggressive?"

"Two: any style of eggs from the golden girls. Or my go-to standard breaky..."

He started telling her about oats, something about organic, blah blah hand-milled, blah blah small batch, blah cacao nibs or was it hemp hearts, whatever whatever flax seed and makes it every day and just doesn't get tired of it and what a small win simple pleasure that is, hand-picked wild virgin blueberries etc. etc. special special.

"Wow. That all sounds elite and wonderful, but also, what are your thoughts on a donut? It's important I respect my indulgences while on vacation."

"Ah. Now it's clear. To Valerie Roy I am just a vacation indulgence." He stood up. "And yet, I think I'm okay with that."

"Yeah, exactly." She pinched his jeaned bum. "Nice ass though."

"How about a French donut? We can even paddleboard to it. To Savary Island. Do you know how to paddleboard?"

"I do, yeah. B2P lists classes of aqua-yoga on SUPs. I went to one. So how far away is this island?"

"Oh. No. I mean Savary Island Pie Company. It's a café. It's just around the point."

"For pies?"

"Oddly no. They have other things than pies. But I didn't go there for a long time after they opened because I thought it was just pies."

"And you don't like pies."

He shrugged. "I actually do like pies. Especially with ice cream. I guess I just didn't get a pie urge for a while. Y'know?"

"No I definitely don't know. I think we need to wait for the blood to return to your brain. But okay sure, breakfast pies it is. Though I think by definition, paddleboarding to a pâtisserie makes us hipsters. Are we sure we're okay with that?"

***

Alex outfitted Valerie in one of his jackets. He looked like he was really enjoying holding it out for her, the puffy. "Wow, you look good. If you keep your mouth shut you might pass for a local. Actually, you might sound more local than me." He had to think about that. "Anyways, tell me how much you love wearing that puffy."

She pinched the amorphous stomach and pulled at it with obvious distaste.

The morning was cool. Duffin Cove was calm. From the foreshore of Alex's property he had built a wooden walkway lashed to big boulders. You could walk right down into the water. They took their shoes off and Alex stowed them in a backpack. He set her paddleboard on the water then held it in place for her, some twenty-first-century version of a gentleman steadying a lady's horse. While she mounted he didn't miss the opportunity to describe it to her as such. They paddled over the shore's tall kelp. Orange and yellow sea stars on the rocks just below the surface, nudibranchs and tiny shad. A school of needle fish threaded the electric green and waving eelgrass. Alex's motorboat patiently moored to her buoy. They looked for the storied duo of sea otter and seagull.

"They're probably out getting into all kinds of hijinks," Valerie said. "Oh, you didn't tell me, what are their names?"

"Valerie and Alex," he said.

"You're okay with being the seagull?"

A small boat passed and Alex waved. They pointed their inflatable crafts directly at the oncoming waves. Valerie paddling said, "Favourite sexual positions. Go."

"Missionary."

"Me on top," she said.

Alex paddled. "Missionary."

"Uhh. Me on all fours and you from behind pulling my hair."

"Well. I think that covers them."

Valerie laughed. "Postcoital sex-drive lower than the tide, huh?"

The tide wasn't so low but he let her have that one. A short paddle took them around Grice Point. "I was once with this girl."

"Girl or woman?"

Alex was never sure if he should call a female a girl or a woman, woman just sounded so formal and older and some women call other women girls, so he wasn't sure what to do and went back and forth. "I was once with this woman. Not once, we spent time together but we weren't a couple. Friends with benefits cheapens it. It was better than that. No label required. And one night we were together and she had already, you know, she had arrived. Like you last night." He raised his eyebrows twice.

"Okay. Smut writer who can't say orgasm. Continue."

"Generally not before breakfast."

Valerie a stroke ahead had stopped paddling and their crafts now cruised together.

"She said she'd say anything I wanted. We were having sex and she told me to tell her what I wanted her to say. She'd be anything. Say anything. Nothing was off limits, I couldn't offend her. What do I want to hear? she asked me."

A couple ideas ran through Valerie's mind. "Alright and what did you request?"

"When I asked her she looked at me almost laughing like she knew that was too much, like she was smiling because for certain that crossed the line and if she had asked that question to other men, none of them came back with that, like there were fetishes and then there was this. Lines you don't cross. And I remember her little uncertain laugh like danger. Things you know you aren't supposed to say."

Valerie was looking straight across from him now. She wasn't even paddling.

"I asked her to whisper in my ear that she loved me."

The bay broadened to a wide channel but they stayed close to shore. Alex loved being by the harbour in the morning. The sea smells, the docks and boats and seagulls, the sounds of water. They paddled under a tall pier supporting a vacant blue building. "Formerly the Ice House Restaurant." His voice enhanced by the heavy wooden platform above them. He tapped a paddle on a barnacled pile. They ducked under a beam and paddled in to the small sand beach. Feet on the cool sand in ankle deep water. They lifted their boards by the central handle and moved them up just past the tide line, dropped their lifejackets. Maybe the sugar weighted the scent because low on the foreshore here they could already smell the bakery.

They had planned on croissants but they hadn't anticipated this baker's world. Alex said hi to the staff. Carrot cake and brownie. Scones blueberry, raspberry, and cheddar-chive. Morning Glory muffins acting as some middle ground between responsibility and indulgence. The cashier said she liked to think of it as a safe space where people can order pie for breakfast. "We don't judge here."

Valerie saw that she wasn't just referring to raspberry-rhubarb or lemon buttermilk with berries. There were Guinness meat-pies, chicken pot pies. Valerie without looking away from the glass display reached sideways for Alex's hand. She turned her eyes to his and he wasn't sure if they were asking for guidance, strength, or blessing. In an attempt to satisfy all three he said, "Follow your heart."

After some deliberation they agreed on sharing a butter croissant and a cheddar-chive scone, an oatmeal chocolate-chip cookie for later. He got a cappuccino and she an oat-milk matcha latte and he had his card out to pay and Valerie took it and threw it on the ground and paid and they took their score to the bakery's little waterfront patio and sat at a small table. Piano from the café's speakers drifting through the open windows, a melody paced to the unhurried morning air. Valerie thought it might be *The Goldberg Variations*, one of her mother's favourites. Mostly simple, sometimes embellished and elaborate, at times achingly beautiful. On their patio table, clouds floated between their porcelain mugs and a seagull flew across the glass.

Alex watched two happy dogs leashed to the railing chewing grass like tethered goats. One time he was here by himself in the morning with the sounds and smells of the harbour, drinking a black coffee, eating scrambled eggs on house-made sourdough toast, one of the best breakfasts there is, and a little sparrow kept coming close and he shooed it a couple times and again it came back and he whapped it with benign intention but it hit the railing and flew away all funny. He didn't tell her that.

Alex heard thunder and he looked to their right. A pickup truck rumbling over First Street's big dock, its creosoted black and heavy timbers. To their right the Tofino Air floatplane base.

Valerie pointed to a silver and green, weird-looking rowing-machine, permanently mounted on the grass in front of them. "What's that?"

"Good question. I've never understood it." Next to the contraption was a girl, young woman maybe. Baggy sweatpants, an oversized hoodie and a toque. "I think women's fashion took a wrong turn."

Valerie looked around to see if anyone else had heard that. "Alex. When she dressed herself this morning she may not have had you in mind."

"That's not exactly how I meant it."

"It's definitely how it sounded."

"Okay fine. But I won't apologize for assessing a woman's beauty. I'm a man. It's what we do. Some of us. This one. Unapologetically. All male animals if not just all animals do since forever, right? It can't be wrong. Society's overreaching if it thinks it can come clip my balls. Calling it objectifying is too fancy. It's just what we do. There's no biological driver more foundational than sex. Sex starts with attraction, assessing beauty."

She listened to a man whose nose tinged red from years of fishing in the sun, whose weather-cracked hands were not young hands, whose crooked teeth were impurely white from his love of coffee that he had mentioned twice today. She listened amused to him in the pleasant morning air as he opined on superficial beauty.

"Should I apologise for being attracted to a certain shape? A certain shape is a sign of a woman who takes care of herself. Health, fitness. Again, evolution, no? A toned body as a woman who might save my ass from a cheetah."

"Cougar."

"Exactly. Impart good genetics into the kids. To me a woman who works out is sexy and not just because of the shape. It shows discipline and effort. That's not bullshit, I mean that. I'm attracted to effort. It's a valuable signal. I give my world huge effort."

"Alright. I'll let all the women know you'd prefer them to walk around in yoga pants and tank tops twenty-four-seven so you can evaluate their character and discipline. You should expect this to work out well and with no backlash whatsoever. So all that's left is for you to tell me all your social-media passwords and I'll get this going for you. Make sure to read the comments."

He turned to her. "Will this help book sales?"

She thought about it. "Yes. Because to burn a book you first have to buy it."

He turned to the harbour, rolling that over in his head like that wave rolling through barnacled piles. The wave collapsing on the beach like his concluded thought. He nodded his agreement. He didn't look at her, he just held out his fist sideways for a pound and she stuck her napkin in its little clenched hole. He just kept it there and raised it and wiped the corners of his mouth. He raised his coffee mug in the cool morning's sea-scented air and smelled the harbour and the rich scent of cappuccino and said my God it's the best. "This is all the best," he said. "I love mornings."

A raven landed on a big black iron anchor.

"Baaachh," Alex said profoundly.

"Mmm," she agreed listening. "Furball."

"Yes. I like him."

"Yeah."

"And he's fun to say."

"Bacchh. Yeah. He's beautiful."

His mug before his lips. He blew softly. "You're beautiful." He sipped his coffee. She poked his side.

They descended the bank to their paddleboards. The tidal currents were ebbing and Valerie and Alex hardly had to paddle home. Rather than standing, they sat on their boards and agreed that saving the cookie for later was ridiculous. They passed it back and forth between them a bite at a time. Scattered clouds over a western horizon, the day yet to decide whether to disperse them over sea or blow them inshore. They were back in the bay and he couldn't believe he hadn't mentioned the orcas he saw three days ago. He followed up her enthusiasm, "Maybe we could go for a boat cruise. You want to get a feeling for Tofino, the water is the biggest part of the story. It's the plot, the arc, the climax." He winked on climax. The fates of tide here momentarily separating them just farther than outstretched hands. Alex put the cookie on his paddle like a serving platter.

"I think I got a little feel for Tofino this morning." She returned his wink. She reached for the cookie.

"Um. A little feel?" He set his paddle to her SUP's stern and pushed to turn her around, but its deep fin stably tracked the water.

"I mean a big fulfilling all a girl could ever hope for ever in her wildest dreams big feeling for Tofino this morning."

"Better. Yeah the water is everything. It's what supported thousands of years of people living here. It's what brought trade and education. And miseducation. And hospitals and plagues. Brought people together and pulled people apart."

"The ocean did all that?"

"I'll have to check the schedule of my staycation, but I could maybe squeeze you in for a tour." He squinted to falsely emphasize a maybe which was no maybe.

"Oh yeah? What will it take?" She waiting to hear his pick of sexual favours.

He looked over at her. Kneeling on the SUP, her legs folded under her, her bare feet. Her suspended paddle dripping water drops. Wearing his puffy. With the hair and the smile. "A picnic," he said.

XXVII

A lex waited in his truck outside the Inn while Valerie changed and grabbed her phone. She and her phone reunited after their longest separation in a decade. In her room she scrolled in triage through texts and emails. A missed call from Mom. An empty text from Trent and that was weird. A text from Dad last night saying he's feeling pretty tired. First time she'd heard that language. If Superman says he feels a touch unwell that translates most grave. His text said don't call I'm just going to try to sleep. She called. It rang and rang.

Alex checked a couple websites and merged their conflicting weather forecast into: moderate winds with a chance of anything. He looked out at the sky. Flying in from the distance came a flapping heron. Its eternally gawking neck like a hillbilly forever stuck in a guffaw. He shook his head at it. He wondered if it was the same one from two nights ago at Chocolate Tofino parking lot. He watched it glidingly descend and outstretch webbed feet and land entirely gracefully on the highest drooping branch of a hemlock. It didn't flutter to find its balance like even the eagle or the crow will. Remarkable. Alex just knew for certain his vision of the world was askew at best, altogether distorted at worst. He wondered if with the privilege of time he would one day as an old man live to see all his convictions overturned and finally arrive to know nothing at all. He returned to fortune reading the textured palm of the greying skies.

They pulled away from the Inn with his hand on her knee. Passing North Chesterman parking lot why would he notice the white car that fell in behind them, that turned left with them towards town, that turned when they turned up Industrial Way. At Picnic Charcuterie they picked up Castelvetrano olives and Genoa salami and Carr's water crackers and island-farmed old-cheddar cheese. Valerie said she had heard of the donuts at Rhino Coffee House and requested a pit stop.

Arriving to town centre Alex was saying it would be good to get out on the water now because the wind might come up. He pulled over and a Ford Edge pulled over and she walked into Rhino. Alex in the truck scanned busy sidewalks, looking for any familiar faces. Outside Rhino, people with their coffee sitting block benches. Small brown birds scavenging for crumbs. Rhino's door was open and he could see Valerie at the end of the line. She turned to him. Someone passed by her with a glazed donut with rainbow sprinkles and while looking at Alex she pointed small and clandestinely at the donut while mouthing wow or woah and then shaped her hand into a circle and extended the index finger of her other hand and violated her donut hand, twice.

He shook his head at her, this lewd cartoon. He looked around. In the rearview mirror he saw a familiar face. He got out.

Trent got out.

Alex and Trent walking towards one another and then Alex said to Jeremy, "Morning."

"Morning. What are you up to?"

"Morning date."

"Oh reeeally. Alina?"

"Nope."

"That was fast. So is it a morning date that started in the morning or a morning date that started last night?"

"You know I don't kiss and tell. What are you up to?"

"Actually I do know that you kiss and tell. Grabbing coffees and meeting Ava and the boy at the park. See you tonight?"

A fractional moment of hesitation. Building the dancefloor. Right. Alex was standing on the edge of the sidewalk, running that schedule in his mind, when a hard shoulder of an oncoming pedestrian impacted his own shoulder. Something must have caught the guy's attention because he turned his body at the last moment causing the impact to have greater force and Alex got turned outwards. Smarted. He looked at the guy in passing. Big guy who kept walking without rush. From the side profile he saw a beard. Dark blue hoodie with his hands in the front kangaroo pocket. Dark sweatpants, hat, sunglasses. The guy didn't stop or look back, he just nodded sideways and raised a hand in what seemed a silent apology. Then turned left into a store.

Narrow sidewalks in a tourist town, it happens and Alex let it go. It would take a freight train to derail the morning he was having. He looked back to Jeremy who was still looking after that guy.

Jeremy said, "Town gets busier earlier every year, hey. See you tonight?"

"Yeah for sure. See you tonight." Two bumped fists.

Valerie stepped out of Rhino with a small brown bag. She looked right, Alex was to her left. Three small birds at her feet. He watched her pinch them a crumb. A few crumbs. He waited to see if they would alight her shoulder or fly up with a ribbon in their mouths to tie a bow in her hair. She walked up to the truck and finding it empty looked down the sidewalk, Alex emerging out of the crowd. He walked to her side and peeked in the small bag. Two donuts. "Nice. Thanks."

"For what?" She pinched off a crumb for him. He ate it and opened her door and she said I got you an old-fashioned and he didn't get that pun until he was opening his own door. Two people got into a truck. One man walked out of a store. The store was called Storm.

Over a quiet coastal town the Pacific-Northwest sky has made its mind up. Heavy clouds are rolling in.

XXVIII

They drove down Arnet's dead-end road and turned down Alex's driveway. "Beside the mint is a lemon balm plant." He took his small pocket knife from his jean's front pocket and thumbed open its black carbon blade and passed it to her by its white handle. "You want to cut us some and I'll make a thermos of tea for the boat?"

In the mudroom he put a couple jackets in a backpack and grabbed some things from the kitchen and carried them outside where Valerie met him with the leafy stems.

"Why do you have so many coolers?" Lined up beside the house were four coolers of various sizes.

Alex pointed to the small red one. "Why did this one tell that one it couldn't hang out with him?" He pointed to its larger neighbour.

"Why?"

"Because I'm just a little cooler." Alex said he stole that from a friend.

"Hey Alex when I go boating, I consider it a place of quietude and reflection. I'm really going to have to ask that from here on in you not talk." They paddleboarded out to Alex's boat. He got in first and turned to Valerie standing on her SUP who had her hand on the gunwale saying, "Permission to board, captain."

369

"Too easy." Alex extended a hand. She stepped over the gunwale and into his world. Valerie put her bag in the cuddy cabin and Alex looked up at the sky asking it to hold, then trimmed the motors down and fired up the girls and they sounded throaty and enthused. His house in the background, he didn't look at it so he didn't notice the man in the living room window. He went to the bow and bent for the buoy to unclip the two stainless-steel carabiners from the hull but between the buoy and the boat, bull kelp was all wrapped up with the two tether lines. He reached for his blade and then said please pass me my pocket knife, honey. Perhaps that teasing address not without a sliver of hope or a testing of waters.

She said oh shit and he knew what that meant. He tried to break the kelp but three were braided together, as kelp tends to do, and so he tried to lift them up over the buoy but they were tangled and heavy with the mooring line. He pulled them as high as he could and lowered his head close to the water and bit three times and spat three smile-sized lengths of hollow kelp stems. "We're good." He lashed their paddleboards to the buoy.

In front of them a large whale-watching boat heading out to open ocean was plowing through the water trailing a white rooster tail. This one looked similar to that doomed one from 2015 but he didn't mention that sad story. Alex waved and Valerie waved and a few of the passengers on the large open bow heading towards sinister skies waved back. The winds weren't up yet and that's what mattered. "Choose our own adventure. Do you want to go for a tour through the sound? Or straight out to open waters?" Alex with his arms out sideways pointing the opposing options. Valerie put two hands on Alex's left arm causing him to lower it and they right turned towards protected waters. They drove over the ghost of the Hera with its drowned pianos and later they would drive over the ghost of the Tonquin, and other waters with their sleeping ghosts.

They passed a red sea buoy. He slowed approaching Beck and Stone Islands and then turned and idled closer to Arnet Island. A sea lion floating on its back eating a crab. It dove down and resurfaced with another and used its mouth to rip off the crab's claws and eat the large claw meat then bite through the carapace. Its whiskers smeared and dripping with green guts. Alex put the boat in neutral and went to the bow and picked up the round crab trap saying I just have to put the pot on for dinner. He heaved the crab pot out splashing beside them. The mesh of the trap dissolving into watery hashmarks, peeling loops off the coil of line tied to a small cylindrical buoy. They idled over shallow water. Anchored off their north side was a green floathouse. Solar panels on its roof, rainwater catch system, outdoor shower, a small tin boat lashed to its dock. Alex nodded to it. "Could you do it? Would you want to?"

Garden boxes with kale and mustard greens. She imagined a dog on that old mat. A downward dog on that other mat. "I adore the water. I know I always want to live close to it. I think so, yeah, for some of the year, at least." Looking at this quiet floating home she thought about tomorrow's silent retreat. She cultivated an allergy to unreliability and cancellations so she wasn't going to do that. She looked at its deck. Two chairs in the sun. "But some things seem all idyllic until you're actually in it."

"Yeah. Whether all that isolation becomes meaningful depth, or just lonely. I'd drop off care packages for you. Golden diva eggs and Rhino donuts and floating-house booty calls. At an initial frequency of twice a day. Eventually tapering off to about once every five to seven days."

"Very thoughtful of you." Three floating diving-ducks so tiny they looked like toys.

"I wonder how much art was created from lonely people. Whether coupled or single. That urge for human connection probably underlies a lot. People trying for greater connection with their world. What do you think?"

Valerie watching to see if an eagle head would poke out of the large nest in a tree top on Beck island. "If I had to guess, I don't think beautiful creations are mostly from the deficient, no. Some, lots, but most? I doubt it. Art comes from praise, play, exploration. Sometimes I think a little loneliness is underrated. And how many relationships are only hobbling? And mediocrity might be worse. I don't think to be alone is to be incomplete and to be with someone is to be whole." She looked from the floathouse to him. "That story made more sense in older times, hunter-gatherer and agrarian societies."

Alex in rocky waters trimmed up the motors. "I think it's more fun to be with someone. Someone to share my jokes with. Someone to help weed the garden, trim the mint. But I hear what you're saying. Being on your own can be motivating. And yeah, I'm probably a better friend, a more thoughtful person, work-out harder, dress sharper when I'm single."

She assumed the dress sharper bit was referring to his only dress shirt she had stained and not his current rubber boots and old puffy with a faded hat. "Yeah you look good."

He shook his head.

"And you feel you can't do those things while being in a relationship?"

Alex was mostly trying not to run them aground on these reefy waters. His eyes on the sonar. "More like..." He trailed off and further trimmed up the motors.

She seemed amused by his fluster.

"It's a different type of hunger when you're dining for one." That sounded stupid and he wasn't sure if it even made any sense, this poor multitasker. "A little loneliness is harnessable." He felt like that condensed it well enough and anyways he was mostly trying to agree with her while not dinging a prop and likely she'd leave it there.

"Okay but why not just do all those things while you're in a relationship?"

"You're just not letting me out of this, huh. I guess that's the struggle against complacency. Sometimes a relationship dulls my urge to improve and grow." He smiled. "Alright that sounds terrible when I voice it." He reached behind himself without looking and squeezed his seat. "Leather talk-therapy couch? Nope. Vinyl boat seat."

"So the relationship stunts your growth? The *relationship* does that?"

"Yeah not me the relationship." He was smiling without looking at her. "I'm guessing B2P doesn't outsource its bullshit testing, huh?"

"We keep that in-house." Purple seaweed stripped with blue iridescence wavered in the shallow waters. "I guess I'm just pretty happy, mostly. So *if* a relationship it has to enhance that shared life."

"That's what I'm saying. She has to elevate me." He knew she was looking at him. "For fuckssake I'm trying not to run us aground here," he laughed. "You know what I meant."

They cleared the shallow section and Alex trimmed the motors back down and idled them towards Meares Island. "Look." A small herd of feral cows were grazing eel grass on the exposed foreshore. "What the hell, right? They were brought in with the missionaries. But the residents never really took to cattle raising. I guess after four thousand years of living comfortably without cows they were like, nah bro, we're good. Incredibly the cows seem to take to coastal life." A wild bull with short curled horns and impassive eyes looked up at them, dripping-wet eelgrass drooping from its lateral chew. "Do you think he's thinking what we're thinking?"

"Yeah, definitely. He looks like he's thinking that."

"They've survived a hundred years. How in the hell. I mean, just, what. They live wild and nobody feeds them and have to face wolves and cougars and bears and hard winters and y'know, no hay or prairie grass. It just baffles me. Don't bet against life. The common Jersey cow, one resilient motherfucker." He turned. "This place, huh. Cows on the beach. Goats on the roof. CEOs in your bed. Welcome to Vancouver Island, coast of your wildest dreams. Come dip a toe."

Behind the cows were houses pink and white and green and red, a small colourful waterfront community. "Opitsaht. Something like a hundred and fifty people live there now. Prior to George Vancouver the population was in the thousands." They looked at the houses facing the houses of Tofino, where in between, a few absurd cows, utter-deep in salt water, grazed eelgrass.

They idled past Stubbs Island and the sand spit they saw from his hot tub. Mussel shells on the beach. Staked heads eternally sun-baking in his mind, black birds landing on those morbid scarecrows, claws in their tangled hair as they bend to take the eyes, skin tightening to blackened leather, gaping jaws silently screaming at the sea, at the sun, at their enemies, if not the world entire. He didn't offload that story onto her. He only said after a quiet moment, "The waters of this coast should run red. Red for the otters. Red for the whales. Red for the salmon blood. Red for the people blood."

Valerie actually looked down into the waters. As if expecting to see some scarlet ribbon, an errant clot or bloodline slipping through the currents. Cruise over a shallow sand bar where a shad swims through the eye sockets of a lost skull. They idled on. He said that though this coast's history is at times harsh he found it all fascinating. "You start learning some of this area's past and you can't turn it off. There's a lot I want to read. People I want to talk to."

They idled towards Tonquin Beach at the end of the Esowista Peninsula. A young girl in a white dress walking barefoot scattering handfuls of red petals from a woven basket. As if to seed the sand in roses. A gathering. A cellist. The curved wooden body between her thighs. A groom in a blue suit standing under a driftwood arbour. A father walking his daughter in a red dress barefoot in the sand and her train raked rose petals, as if the garment had been tailored by a florist, or a tailor fashioned it from a flower.

"Would you get married, captain? I mean again again?" She was sitting beside him and poked him twice under his ribs. He embellished a wince.

"Don't prod the captain. Ever tried. Ever failed. Try again. Fail again. Fail better. I assume Beckett was talking about matrimony." He looked at her. Her face was studious. "I do like that traditional idea. The promise to make something that lasts. It's still sweet to me. So far I've been reasonably successful at defending it from my own bitterness."

He didn't accelerate until they had idled far enough away that the sounds of the throaty twins wouldn't pollute Pachelbel.

The horizon's low clouds now darker than the sea but a boat named Outcast feared them not. Alex zipped up her puffy. "I'll show you something cool." He throttled up and their accelerating boat pitched then levelled into Templar Channel. The washboard water from strong currents running up against an opposing tide. The heavy weight of the fibreglass boat cut smoothly through the small chop and then the water flattened out like a pulled bed sheet, a contrast so oddly distinct it was as if two separate bodies of water had been abutted together. They made twenty-five knots over slate-blue water under a roiling fateful sky, all ashy and leaden.

XXIX

"What do you feel?" he asked her. The sea surged on McKay Reef. Alex slowed beside black jagged rock. "This coast is called The Graveyard of the Pacific and no doubt this very reef here changed some life plans." Remorseless stone sharpened by the ceaseless stropping of hard water. "More sunken ships per kilometre of coastline here than anywhere else in the world. Over two thousand shipwrecks. Ships smashed to bits all over this indifferent coast and salvage attempts rarely successful." Ahead of them a limitless sea, not even a cargo ship in sight, so broad, vast and blue.

"It's like a cliff without a cliff." She was looking out towards the thin horizon. "It's just so immense, and like you can feel a sense of both beauty and power. It's sublime."

Their boat on the fringe of open ocean he put the motors in neutral. The ebbing tide drifting their boat southwards. Just up ahead on their left, Surprise Reef, the sister to McKay. A seagull cruised then angled for the choppy water, lowering orange legs. Water crashing on the jutting rocks. Today the sea's swell small but her might undiminished. The surging water erupting on the dark rocks, then the ocean sucking back. Rhythm like respiration. The water drawing back, the water surging. Valerie wondering if that's what makes music so elemental, rhythm like breath, like waves. The sea sucking back like the whole Pacific was receding, the whole ocean in concert, the water by the reef lowering five feet exposing more of the hard outcrop, a sulphuric yellow band, water draining off the reef through fissures and cracks, rivulets running from clefts scoring deep channels. Millennia work here. The next wave rushed and flooded, roared and swamped. A force seismic, sea spray nearly volcanic. The action of the water seemed intentional, if not animate itself. A tradesman at once detailed and brutish. Polisher of pebbles. Carver of clefts. Smasher of ships. Wet malevolence, raw wrecking power indiscriminate, implacable. Alex saw this every day and he never got used to it. The awesome instills more than caution it elicits humility, fear. They listened to water with such roar one wonders if the very belly of the world isn't angry. Them spectating only a surfaced glimpse of her power, where below were stacked fathoms of blue muscle. The roar and the boom and the spray, vertical spume and frothy water.

They coasted with the current. Alex steering had his other hand on his knee and Valerie placed a cracker with salami and cheese on the back of it. He raised his hand like a platter and ate it. Surprise Reef transitioned to a watery gap, to the rocky fringe of Lennard Island. Six black oystercatchers stood on a low rock, each of their beaks pocketed in a wing pit. One pulled out its bright orange beak and looked at the passing boat then started peeping. Then five others turned and peeped. Nature cartoonishly ordered. Valerie laughed at them, calling them hilarious.

They drifted towards Lennard. She was already looking at it when Alex peeped, "What I wanted to show you." A lighthouse tall and slender, its observation deck capped red.

Valerie was wondering if it shined only at night, and about three seconds later that question got answered.

"One of the last manned lighthouses on the coast. A husband and wife run it. Probably anachronistic, seems to me it could all be automated. Nevertheless, romantic."

"So picturesque, very cool. Thanks for taking me." She cheese-and-crackered him. "That floathouse by the harbour, maybe I could do. This would be really intense. Man, the storms they'd see. I imagine they've gone through the entire gamut of roleplaying, huh. No, you were naughty schoolteacher last week."

He laughed and they coasted southwards steadily as a baggage carousel. On a flat section of exposed reef, Alex watched water broadly drain like melting reality. He might not be the big-deep-forever romantic but he knew he was the big-deep-forever romantic. He knew he still was. Always would be. Through lost loves' fallen hearts and broken stars. All the while he had kept open to it, kept looking for it. Trying to be worthy of it. On past dates wondering if it could work, if they could make it work. He had said that to himself more than once. The little contrasts, the small mismatches, the humour and language close, but a bit off. Right now he wasn't evaluating, he was looking into the sea's late-afternoon midnight-blue. Just staring blankly at those luminous bars of vertical light that moved and faded-out within it. Realizing what had happened. What would have been obvious to someone looking from outside in. He wondering if it was sudden or gradual. Fallen like a trap door or fallen like sliding down a plane tilted from countless small attractions. A smile, a gift, an idea, a laugh, a touch, a disclosure, a humility, a vulnerability, a song, a revelation of passion of intellect of laughter of wit of kindness of play. Beauty not attributable to a single feature, rather: alloy, mixed and irreducible. He was attracted to pretty things, he couldn't help it. He looked over at this pretty thing looking at the lighthouse with a residual smile from her own joke. Maybe no definable tipping point when he'd fallen— There it is. So you name it. Calling it what it is. Naming what a part of you already knew. At each moment our eyes see a thousand things

379

but our awareness so narrow. How long did some part of you know? As early as the Hot Springs? At the Wolf? Or only a moment prior to now. But there it is. A felt conviction. So there it is, hey? Too many dates to count and then this over three days—*three days, Romeo*. He swallowed. She laughed but he didn't catch it, another role-playing joke about a stranded captain and an innocent sea wench but he missed it because he was distracted by something. He looked briefly at her smiling to herself like she ordered a six-pack for the kitchen. He was distracted by a feeling, an old feeling, been a while feeling, by a feeling you weren't so sure you were still capable of feeling, wondering if your body forgot the biochemical recipe, or if with every year you desensitized to the potion, or you blew your chances and you only get so many and you had it before but never again and every year you swap a dream for a regret, the big clock's advance cracking a fissure with every tick until a part of you once foundational becomes brittle, or shrivelled, weak numb defective dead can't hear the signal like a cat out in the cold that's forgotten its name, like an atrophied muscle with fibres beyond rebuild, but now he didn't wonder because this feeling felt so real it scared him. This woman's trailing laughter and the sea breeze blowing and the boat lightly rocking and the oystercatchers peeping and the waves rhythmically surging and he knew he could say something stupid right now or say nothing or be uninteresting and maybe you're mine to lose. You know now what she is and now you know what you can lose. The female mantis takes the head, he knew a species that takes the heart. You never know for certain who you've invited in. Danger. It just boiled up now and got sharp and acute and true and starkly real and he felt it deeper than a belly laugh and you understand that nothing can be promised nor vowed, not truly, so maybe it's better without the pledges, and maybe this doesn't work out, life in a series of moments so take what you

380

get, and maybe it even ends today, maybe it ends now, right now, and all we got was three fine days but right now my God it's nice and maybe we don't make it but that doesn't matter because in the end nobody makes it. We don't need to wait for time to tell, our story can be concluded now: it does not work out, that he was sure of. No spoiler there because in the end, it always doesn't work out. Count on that. So stretch this moment out, make time so slow tomorrow is nothing but a passing concern, stretch it like taffy before it's all gone. It will be all gone. I promise. I guess some promises can be trusted. His body was pitted and light and heavy and warm and twisted and hopeful and fearful and thrilled and then off the starboard the water erupted gigantically as a seventy-thousand-pound creature blasted through the surface then quarter-spiralled with sea water twisting away from it and the whale arched its huge back towards the surface—nearly its whole behemoth body out of the water—and it was parallel with the water, and that flash second was slow enough that Alex saw water dripping off its long serrated flipper, and its long thin mouth in a curious smile was not nearly as surreal as just how inanely quiet that fractional moment was before what was coming.

Then the humpback landed spectacularly flat and the squished water exploded sideways, spray jetting out dozens of feet. The whale submerged and the sea closed back up making a huge wet clap raising a twenty-foot-high wet mushroom cloud. Just: *BOOM*. Two jaws dropped. Spray peppered their puffies as they watched a marine fountain recede. Valerie's eyes were huge and she turned to Alex looking the same. "Holy shit." She didn't even exclaim that. It didn't need exclamation.

"Woah." The surface roiled and fizzed like the ocean was carbonated and the Outcast rocked.

"A humpback!" she exclaimed. She was sniffing. "Oh my God I can smell its breath! That stinks!"

"Holy crap that was close. It absolutely did that on purpose." The waters still fizzing. "I could see its barnacles."

"Tubercles! They're hair follicles!" Valerie went towards the bow and leaned over the starboard gunwale. "I wonder if there's two. When humpbacks are courting they dance."

"Like you in your towel! You just saw your spirit animal. What a fluke."

She was going to say I know! but realized he was making a pun. "Sometimes when they mate they breach. Nasa sent their song into space on a golden record aboard Voyager. Fifty-four human greetings along with the humpback song, the most complex call in the animal kingdom. I wonder if it's hunting krill maybe." Her whale facts from a childhood fascination now surfacing like those watery ovals. The whale spouted some sixty feet off their stern, its gnarly back rough like exposed reef. They turned their heads in unison.

"Wow."

"Wow."

"I'm going to jump in."

"Sweet," Alex said. "Don't come back without a couple crabs for dinner."

Valerie unzipped Alex's puffy.

"Keep your eyes open for echinoderms. I'm so hungry I could eat the balls off an urchin."

Valerie put his jacket on the seat.

"Woah wait what. No you're not. Zip that back up. Hey, nut bar, it's about eight degrees in there. Three minutes you'll be cramping, six you'll be drowned."

She went into the cabin and came out with Alex's wetsuit.

"Woah woah woah. It won't even fit."

"It'll help."

"Look just look at the current." He pointed. "Look at our drift. You'll be swept out to sea."

"I'll be moving at the same pace as the boat. You'll be beside me."

Technically that was true. Alex looked around. She had his wetsuit in her two hands.

"But I won't do it if you say no."

Hell, don't say that. Alex looking at her.

"People dive with whales all over the world. I was looking at a trip to Tonga for just that reason. It's safe. Safe for the whales, safe for the divers. They come up to boats all the time, like it did now." She gestured towards its last surfacing. "They're playful and inquisitive. It's an animal and we're animals. It's a type of paternalistic specism to say the whale doesn't want this."

In another setting he might have laughed at paternalistic specism, this freak.

"Its brain is three times bigger than ours, it knows what it's doing. Imagine how much ocean advocacy and opposition to illegal whaling would come from diving with whales. It's a good thing. So, captain, may I have your permission to go on an interspecies ambassador mission?" She brought her heels together and rather mannerly held the wetsuit before her.

"You should give a Ted Talk on bad ideas."

She didn't look impressed. "Why though?"

Fuck. Why. Why. Why. "'Cause you'll die." He said that almost seriously.

She tilted her head because that was stupid.

"Eating a ton of krill a day is a lot of Valeries."

"Stop. They're gentle giants."

"Tell that to Jonah. I dunno. Just feels risky. Just doesn't feel right."

The whale spurted, now a little farther away. She looked and he looked. "I don't think it is risky. Not taking risks is risky. They're curious and gentle and things like this make the world special, I think."

"Okay look at it this way." He took a breath. He figured if he primed himself with that opener his brain would solve for the rest. He was waiting for his brain and then Alex and Valerie were both waiting. "Even supposing you're right, there are do's and don'ts in small towns and some are worth respecting even if maybe I get what you're saying. This feels like one worth respecting." A look of her's he hadn't yet seen. Not reproach, not even disappointment. He wasn't sure, it might have been pity.

"Well. I disagree. But okay, I understand. I won't do it if you don't want me to, Alex."

She put the wetsuit down on a seat and she didn't look sad and she wasn't hamming it up and she wasn't guilting him and all that made it much worse. Why do you kill me? Hey? What is it? Maybe you just do this all better than me. No. For certain you do this all better than me. What is this here? He hardly understood it. He looked around, not like he was looking to see if anyone was watching, more like searching for something he could point to to help illustrate this bad feeling. Turned and saw the big lighthouse behind them. Where its light warned of dangers, captains about to crash and all that. He turned back around to see her watching him and maybe she saw in his eyes that he hadn't entirely closed the conversation because she said sweetly, "Take your hand out of your purse."

He wondered if in time he could get used to always showing up to a gunfight with a knife. She returning his line from the Wolf he had never quite said. He lightly shook his head and that motion enough to free his restrained smile. Okay. I talk a good one. He didn't want her to go but he really wanted her to go. What's sweeter than getting your most desired thing? Giving it. To be the giver. The privilege of giving at your expense and not wanting anything in return. He felt like he'd be giving up something here. Something that mattered. Far more than a rubber duck and a paperclip collection. That kinda felt right. A man in the Outcast floating at a strange and watery crossroads of opposing values. At the altar of your whatever will you sacrifice your whatever? How did that go? Fuck it. He wanted her to have this.

Poker player without a poker face, she saw he was wrestling with it and said, "Alex, I don't have to go." She meant that.

And that sealed it. And so together we bury the bodies. "Okay. Yes."

"Really?"

"Yes. Be more than careful," sternly. "And don't touch it," sterner.

She said very quickly already starting to change, "Alright I won't touch it!"

He went down into the cuddy and came out with his three-foot dive fins, his mask and goggles. "None of this will fit you and you'll just be a baggy mermaid and most likely it will make things worse and I expect that you'll drown and sink. Sink then drown, rather. So at your funeral when I take the podium—pulpit? podium—I'm going to look your mother in the eyes and tell her that you held a fillet knife to my balls." He put the gear on the empty seat beside him and actually took the fillet knife from the console and put the knife's blunt spine between his legs over his jeans and said just touch the handle and then it's not a lie. "I need to be able to look your mother in the eyes in good conscience when I say balls."

She was changing but leaned over and put her hand on his chest to steady herself.

"And I just want to come out and say it to you now in case this is the last I see of you before your rosy cheeks lose all their life and colour: I don't even like you because I don't, is why, and also you be really really really careful. Babe."

She was zipping up the wetsuit. "Aw. I will."

"Say promise!"

"Promise!"

"Alright." He picked the fins up and she came over and he offered them outwards but she didn't take them she just kept coming until the fins were awkwardly squished between their chests with her neoprene body looking like a funny seal that swam from Vancouver waters to put her arms around the neck of a cedar monkey and her arms around his neck and her smile and her eyes and it was over before that but now it was really over. All over.

"You're sure?" she asked.

"I am, yeah." He said that a little raspily.

The last spout had the whale swimming westward away from Lennard, taking it towards deeper water, calmer with the distance from the island's turbulence. Alex engaged the twins. At four knots he tracked the whale. Twice it came up spouting. She found his dive socks in the flippers. Everything fit comically, if not uselessly or most likely dangerously baggy on her. But reef-camo ling-skin never looked so good. He went below and got his rubber weight belt and slid off two pounds of lead because he didn't want to sink his treasure, just make her a little less buoyant to give her an actual shot at seeing the whale. Of course strapping her with lead seemed ominous. But what he most expected here was for her to jump in the water, immediately be cold and swamped and see nothing, then quickly want to come out and to hell with the whale. He wrapped the belt around her waist and oddly felt like a hockey dad lacing up his son's skates and set the buckle's prong to a new hole he had to stretch to poke. "Hey skinny love, I'm going to fatten you up after this."

"Thanks cap'n." She spat into the goggles and he said hot.

"I'm going to drive up ahead of it and you tip back. Alright?" He widened his course so they wouldn't run up on it or spook it and he throttled to about six knots to outpace the whale they

386

couldn't see. He did feel like Ahab, and isn't everything sinful sweetened by the badassery of it? He took them to what he guessed was about a hundred yards ahead of its last surface. After a few minutes of cruising, the whale blew at their five o'clock. It hadn't veered.

"Oh my God I can't believe this is going to happen." Her voice had gotten nasally and her upper lip duckish.

"You look good," he told her. "You should be fine. But I get your Tesla."

"Bring it in," she said like a CEO at a shareholder meeting and he thought she meant bring the boat into position and he nodded obeying and started to steer to line them up but she grabbed his puffy below his chin like a schoolyard bully and leaned him towards her and set duckish lips on his then pushed him back and put her snorkel in and said something that he couldn't understand but was entirely willing to agree with.

He said, "Say what you want about the crazy girls, they tend to keep you on your toes."

She just stared at him, then tapped a three-foot flipper onto the tip of his Blundstone.

He added, "I hope there's room for me in Vancouver after you get me excommunicated from my beloved town."

She said something inarticulate through the snorkel but her goggled eyes were squinting.

Alex was thinking that for several reasons this won't work. Primarily, the whale can turn off or dive deep or just not pass that closely and Pacific Northwest waters are about as clear as the typical male's understanding of the typical female. Something as obvious as seventy thousand pounds and fifty-feet-long could just about smack you in the face with a fin and go unnoticed. "I'm going to slow and turn and you tip back over the starboard so you're not near the motors."

She waddled to the other side.

"Hold your goggles to your face when you go."

She nodded then gave him an okay sign.

He returned it. "Good luck," he said.

The Outcast turned and Valerie tipped back. Turns out five-feet-fuck-all displaces little water. He looked around. The big white lighthouse behind them. Alex saw its light revolve, no longer a beacon for ships, now a jail-yard spotlight. Good. He felt excited for her and he'd suffer the backlash, town or law. He didn't watch the accusatory light come back around because he was tender to a mermaid.

She hit the surface, the freezing water on her exposed hands and cheeks but its cold sharpest flushing in at her neck and flooding down her back. She took a big deep belly breath and held it and dove. She spat the snorkel out underwater like she recalled from her PADI. If you shallow-water blackout your jaw clamps shut, an evolutionary reaction to keep the water out. Doesn't work so well if you've ported your lungs with a snorkel like a funnel to the sea.

Alex watched Valerie's back round and he checked the time on his phone. He watched his long carbon-fibre flippers go vertical then kick downwards, flexible fins waving goodbye. Both the girl and his heart sinking. He couldn't see her after about six feet.

She didn't need to descend very deep to search out a surfacing whale and at what felt like a dozen feet she levelled out and began scanning for a sea giant. She could hear the low rumble of the motor and then that quit. The wetsuit worked really well at becoming baggy in the armpits and small of her back and holding very cold water very close to her. Water hung around her waist from the weight belt like she had a belly or a baby. But the goggles didn't leak and that mattered most. She was cold and searching and two bubbles came from her mouth because she just smiled underwater thinking that this was the Trojan wetsuit of free dives, latex-in-a-spa type of deal, or however he phrased it. She saved that joke for him and her smile receded because someone was singing.

She tried to source the sound but the sound was coming from everywhere. She turned in place, suspended in a medium of blue song. She scanned the empty water that faded-out to a dusty and opaque blue. Then she stopped her frantic scan that would only shorten her breath-hold and just listened. It sounded at once bovine and canine and Chewbaccan. That description in her head did not sound so pretty but truly the melody was. She wondered if there weren't two of them, knowing that they danced and sang in courtship. Every other sound was inflected and she wondered if species other than humans question with inflection? Wet melody haunting, mysterious, beautiful. Her diaphragm contracted, like a weird internal hiccup. Its brain so big, whatever that does to its song. Very few species have big brains, an evolutionary expense, a resource hog of an organ. The human brain makes up only two percent of body mass yet burns twenty percent of one's calories. A dinosaur twice as big as a whale only has a brain sized to a tennis ball. What was this creature doing with such cognitive power? she wondered. Acoustics aquatic, melody piping through a wet medium. Her diaphragm contracted again. Then again, deeper spasm, intervals shortening. She didn't want to come up. Eyes squinting through dive glass. Then she looked up to that luminous and wavering ceiling and kicked and kicked.

She broke the surface looking out to sea and gasped and held it a half second in a recovery breath. She turned in place to find the boat. She saw his eyes, their equal mix of concern and curiosity. She gave an okay sign and he mirrored it. She remembered that for however long you hold your breath you should double your surface time. She didn't. She took a big breath down into her belly and rounded her back and left surface waters the stormy sky was darkening and a tender atheist in a boat said a little prayer to any god who might be listening.

Alex hadn't consciously held his breath, he noticed he was holding it and then he kept on holding it. He had hoped that after that first dive she had had enough. Though now getting to know her he wasn't surprised she hadn't. The whale hadn't spouted. He restarted his stopwatch and he watched and waited. The law says a boat must be four hundred metres from a whale. Alex gauged the distance now and figured he was about four metres, give or take. He touched each of his wrists. Assessed how well they would each handle a spike. But really it had nothing to do with being caught. It was about squaring it with himself. He told himself he could justify it by subjugating his values to his heart. If lover before law abider then no breach of character here. He said that in his head and listened to its ring and it didn't sound too bad but he figured it was mostly bullshit. This was probably closer to selfishness. He replayed her arguments. He distracted his concern for her by diving into his own cognitive dissonance. Only three days ago he felt a little pride in respecting the required distance from the orcas. It felt good to treat the animal with respect, be part of a community with values. But maybe it's different when they surface beside you like an invitation? Or maybe she just really wanted this and it did not seem evil and nobody was getting hurt and maybe I just really wanted to give it to her. That sounded more truthful. Alex topside checked the time. Moral compromise in thirty-five seconds. Call it a record.

How to describe it to Alex? Sunken tonal howls of a crying water puppy. For a man who might worship words she came up with that to try to speak his language. Who are you singing to? Your baby? Your mother? Your lover? She couldn't see the whale and she didn't need to. This was enough. The music was enough and it was incredible and she turned within song and she didn't need to see the whale because she felt the whale and that was something very special and then out of the aqua murk like a spaceship floating through this galactic blue, came the whale. Directly at her. Gigantically silent. Unnaturally large. She had forgotten to spit out the snorkel but it came out now. The whale veered slightly. The creature long enough that at first she couldn't see its massive finning tail obscured by murky water. Splotches of white on the side of its big head and white on its jaw under its thin and curious smile. It cruised by, no rush at all. As if its weight would slow the world to its own pace. Its wide and thin serrated flipper coming towards her. She searched for its camouflaged and small eye but couldn't find it. The whale propelling itself sleekly, grace irrespective of size, this colossal ballerina. Her diaphragm contracted. Her outward arms stabilizing her suspense in this liquid dream. The flipper gliding through the water like it wanted to be touched. The gap closing between her small hand and its gigantic fin like the wing of a 747. She pulled back just enough to allow a tiny gap she'd swear was filled with charge.

Valerie's dad lost consciousness.

The whale coasted past her, its force enough to perceptively buffet her. Ocean sea-blimp cruising in a wet hazy sky, its big tail arching upwards showing its white underside. The trailing edge of its tail all scratched. She was slowly turning watching its big grey bulk dissolve, dissolve and disappear and fade into blue.

Alex's diaphragm contracted again and this fool topside holding his breath might just black out before the swimmer does. iPhone showed fifty-eight seconds. About as long as he stayed down on his own free-dives. This is a bad feeling. Internal hiccup. What a shit decision. This was stupid. No. Not this. Me. I am stupid. His chest contracted. Situation like this, the cold and the murk and the current and the excitement, a minute would be a hell of a long time for her, for most anyone. At least all this slow time gave me enough time to figure out that I'm an idiot is what this comes down to. Godgoddammit. Internal hiccup. Fuck it. He unzipped his jacket fast and knocked off his hat and boots and shirt and drew a huge lung-filling breath and topless in jeans stepped a bare foot up to the gunwale and picked his spot to dive and right there is where she surfaced.

This time she broke the water looking right at him. She took an enormous breath. He couldn't see it in her blue duckish lips too numb to smile, but he could see it in her zealous eyes. Like someone strong with new belief. He was really happy for her.

He extended the short ladder off the transom and she kicked over and he didn't want to speak first. Let her float in that realm where words only anchor. She took a fin off and passed it up and then the other and he set the fins down beside him and extended his hand and she took it and a CEO in ling-skin ascended the ladder in the floppiest of dive socks. She stood on the deck and water flooded out the ankle cuffs while her watery paunch deflated. He could not resist poking it. She took off her dive mask, the rubber leaving a ring around her gleaming face like it was highlighting her joy. Her cheeks rosy from the water but her skin perhaps surfacing a deeper glow. He was really happy for her.

She undid the weight belt and more water flushed her cuffs and he wrapped a towel around her shoulders and another he draped over her head and this hooded monk gave him a cold wet kiss. From inside the towel's cotton cave she said like a new-age worshipper from the sect of Gratitude, "Thank you very much."

He said my pleasure.

She said, "I'm freeeeeeeezing." Then laughing blue lips asked him, "Why is your shirt off?"

He looked up at dark skies. He privately thanked all the gods of his world, each one. "Sun tan," he outrageously lied. He poured her tea in the thermos' cap-cup. "Well, tell me."

He sat in his chair and she put her back against him with the towels around her and his arms around her while she held the small steaming cup. They both looked over the water while she tried to put it into words. That took some time. Behind them the lighthouse watched. Tower of judgment or keeper of secrets? Oscillating light searching for threats over the moody sea under ominous skies. She brought the small mug chalice-like to her lips and then up beside her head like an offering. He sipped. They didn't talk. Call it something other than comfortable with silence when your world isn't lacking a message. They drifted and watched the water for a spout. The big graceful creature gone back to its depths to sing under heavy layers its haunting song. Valerie could still hear it. She'd always hear it.

The roiling sky a royal grey but potentially a mad king. The first sign of the incoming southeasterly streaked the surface like spine hairs bristling on a dog you don't trust. She changed and dried and he said some women would pay good money for how your lips look right now. "Engorged and duckish."

She said I'm so cold and hurried into his oversized puffy she seemed downright happy to put on. They started their cruise back, her arm around his waist. He liked that tremendously.

Alex felt similarly to when a fishing client would reel a beautiful salmon to the boat after doing everything else right and all the gear was tight and the drag was set and the lines were not tangled and the hook was perfect in its snout and he could see the beautiful fish in the water all perfect and played out and tired and everything came down to him doing what he had done a thousand times and he swung with the gaff and missed and bumped it off and screwed it up. That feeling. Not wholly, just partially. Like he'd let down his end of some agreement. Or disrespected something.

What's town? There's no town. Town is people. Some would vilify me and some would think it's cool and some wouldn't give two shits. One privileged person jumped in the ocean with a big mammal. And? And then? No that's it, that's the story. Oh. Sorry, I was distracted by all the wars and famines and trying to get my bills paid and my kids' lunches made. The whale is fine, the diver is fine. The world is no worse. It's squared. But talking big values and then not following through is the definition of shitty character. He just wanted to make sure he hadn't let himself down. He was his own reckoner. He'd always been that. That's what was going on here, to thine own self be true.

Nearing the harbour she said, "You've been a little quiet captain."

He didn't want to spoil her experience by voicing his own minor and lingering conflictions. Maybe this secret will be a little sweeter for its sin. He looked into her investigating eyes. Then above her and off to the Tofino shore and leaned in and kissed her forehead and said and meant it, "I'm good. We're good."

She gave him a detective's squint. Her arm was wrapped around his waist and her fingers pinched his side. They cruised on. They stopped and checked the crab trap but found only juveniles. They cruised into home cove and slowed and puttered towards the orange buoy in the bay with their tethered paddleboards and he moored the Outcast and raised the twins, cooling water draining out their lower end. Paddleboarding in Alex mentioned his commitment to help a friend for a couple hours.

In the kitchen unloading the cooler they heard knocking at the front door. "House calls are actually extremely rare here. Half the time it's missionaries. I usually invite them in and offer them tea and try to refute their God." He opened the door and said oh right.

"You forgot."

"Nope. Okay yup."

Michelle held a bottle of champagne and a glittering tiara. Pulling in were two cars full of half-drunk ladies with food and more bottles. Somewhere squished in there was a no-doubt tipsy bride-to-be.

"But this actually works just fine. I was heading to Jeremy's now anyways to go help build. So the place is all yours. How's our special lady doing?"

"Better now than she will be soon." Devilish smile. "Thank you again so much. It's really great to have it here."

"It's nothing. It's my pleasure. I like sharing this place. Just come inside if it starts raining or whatever you want."

"Okay that's very sweet, we might. I came by an hour ago and knocked and thought I heard you so I just opened the door and said hi. Then I went down to the deck and put up a few decorations."

"Ah. I was out boating. Just got back."

"Weird. Something banged. You didn't get a dog without telling me did you?"

He shrugged.

"Well have a good dancefloor build. I hope the rain holds off for you guys."

"Yeah for you guys too."

Michelle half turned for the front steps as Valerie sidled into the doorway. Michelle said, "Ohhh." A long, curious, little nosy, little happy kind of oh. "*You* were just out boating were *you*... And who is *this*?"

"This is an American fishing client named Steve."

Michelle tilted her head like you're an idiot.

"Okay he sometimes goes by Valerie." Alex was slowly closing the door on many half-drunk inquiries from eight opening car doors while saying, "But we better stay out of your guys' way." He smiled and before the door shut Michelle said, "Bye Steve."

"That was for your own protection. If we sneak out the backdoor we might avoid the inquest." Alex grabbed a few things from the house and put them in a canvas grocery bag. Walking past the shelves next to the big window overlooking the bay he didn't notice a picture of himself had been laid down. That a couple things had gone missing. They left through the backdoor. The line of laughing ladies was on the other side of the house walking for the backyard and Alex thought the two of them might actually be able to sneak away. His hand on her waist walking to the Tacoma, he diverted towards the greenhouse to grab his pocket knife. Couldn't find it and he asked her and she said by the lemon balm but it wasn't anywhere obvious. "Doesn't matter I'll get it later." They opened the truck doors and Michelle leading the bachelorette troupe turned stopping them all. She said in the tone of an elementary schoolgirl, "Bye Alex and Valerie!"

In wardrobes to defy the weather or charm it into benevolence, floral dresses and hands on summer hats, a dozen pretty heads turned. Valerie waved. Alex with one hand waved and with his other hand held up high and specifically directed at Michelle he raised an affectionate middle finger. She blew him a kiss.

They drove up the steep driveway and turned left onto Arnet Road that shortly joined Tonquin Road. Tonquin Park on their left. Basketball court empty. Ping-pong table vacant. No girl blowing fragile soap bubbles. Two vehicles left Tonquin, two drove through town then turned down Lynn Road. Only one continued on to the security booth.

He knew it was too early to say it. Was it too early to feel it? That's not how this works. Things tick by their own time. Certain gravity can squish a century into a finger snap and he felt something sizable here. He pulled up to the Inn's drive-through drop-off and put the truck in park and his hand left a bit of moisture on the wheel. Don't schedule it. Don't tell it what time we're expecting you. Some guests don't wait for an invitation. Would saying it now be crazy if feeling it now was true? She leaves tomorrow. Tomorrow. The only swing he knows is for the fences. He didn't want any other kind than crazy love. Love with abandon. It's the only one I know. What if unreciprocated? Or what if you wait until tonight? He'd played a lot of poker and knew it rarely hurt to hold your cards close.

She said, "Finally we get a much needed break."

He cleared his throat. "Yeah it's been getting a little much. I'm really looking forward to some time apart. Finally."

"People would have started to talk. Looks like your friends already are. Your hand on my waist towards the truck. Alex, they'll say you're in love."

He didn't know what to say to that. "Don't be thinking about me swinging a hammer all masculine-like."

"I've already forgotten about you. Alexis, was it?"

"Yeah ditto. Tell your dog I said hi."

"The thing is, a girl needs to eat. You want to cook a late dinner together?"

"Yes I do. I'll try, but we might have to make it dessert."

"Okay that works. Who knows, I might let you caramelize my brûlée."

"Hey Virtue, I'm the smut writer here. Stay in your lane. I'll text you when we're done with the build."

"Okay. I'm going to run out to the Bomber Trail quickly and get some pictures for my Dad."

His eyes on the truck's digital clock. Cautionary thoughts flooding his head like sea water into an oversized wetsuit. "Well that's cutting it close." At least with the new boardwalk trail it's not so bad. "If you leave now you'll be alright." In the console he kept a small pepper spray and he got it out and displayed it and stuck it in her bag and then reached to the backseat for his canvas bag and the headlamp he had brought in case carpentry ran late. Then with no risk at all of being patronizing he strapped her head at 4:30 in the afternoon with a headlamp. The headlamp was pretty large. She looked like a miner. "Whatever gold, diamonds you find out there, we split. Say deal. Be careful, have fun."

She didn't know what that meant. She was funnier than him. She said, "You like me."

"I do not."

"Kiss me."

He obeyed.

One fat raindrop splattered on glass.

XXX

T rent at North Chesterman Beach parking lot exited his car and started walking towards the beach. He heard a car arriving to the three-way. Again the green Tacoma. Nobody in the passenger front, so a woman was returned to her phone. He walked back towards his car.

A dark sky washes over Tofino. Not raining but first spits. Not storming but stray gusts. A white car rides the tail of a green truck. Maybe another time Alex would have noticed, maybe another time he'd have seen in his mirror that same face from the sidewalk.

Alex pulled into Jeremy's driveway. Several stacks of lumber, 2x4's and plywood 4x8's. Not just a couple hour's worth. He took a pic and texted it to Valerie, captioned it, *Uh oh...*

Valerie read a text from Stacy demanding an update—food pics, beach pics, boy pics, something—because it's raining in Vancouver and trapped inside with three kids this mother is losing her mind. She checked the boat pick-up time for her silent retreat tomorrow. She called the front desk and while it rang she ran her hand over the fabric of a red dress that she would wear for their dessert that they will not have tonight and when the front desk picked up she asked if they had rain gear she could borrow. She hung up. Her phone goose-honked. Sender: Strange Fishing Guide. She read his text. She typed, *About to venture off to the Bomber without my fishing guide*. She emojied a face with a single tear and an umbrella. Then she highlighted it all and deleted it. Sent two emojis: *strong arm* and *hammer*. She texted her dad: *Bomber pics incoming. Standby.*

Alex walking up the driveway thinking that it's light until late so she should be fine. He held his hand out flat catching the odd spit and looked up at the sky. Jeremy was kneeling on a wooden frame in a white undershirt, jeans, hat and a toolbelt. Alex nodded. "Sun's out guns out, hey?" He took off his long-sleeved.

"Looks like you came well-armed."

"You think you can offer your labourers less of an hourly wage if you pay them compliments?"

"Is that a new under-shirt? It's really nice." Jeremy stood and looked up. "I hope it holds."

"You know you're in Tofino when it's already raining and someone says I hope it holds." Alex surveyed the lumber, the humidity amplifying scents of pine. "So, I take it we're building a new community centre? Or like a series of town amphitheatres?"

"Don't worry we've got a pizza each coming. We'll see Justine on her delivery scooter here promptly. I like to keep my workers well fuelled on pepperoni and cheese. If we were building indoors it'd be vegetarian to comply with labour codes on proper ventilation."

"I'm just wondering what we're gonna do with all the leftover wood when we finish building a life-size replica of the Trojan Horse. Guess we could knock you together a half-dozen rental units."

"Hey. I didn't design it. Just following orders." He passed Alex his set of carpentry tools: a hammer and a Tofino lager.

"Well that kind of yes ma'am attitude bodes well for a happy marriage. Would have been kind of you to share such wisdom a couple divorces ago." Alex cracked his beer and held out the end of his hammer handle and Jeremy tapped his own. "I just saw the beautiful bride-to-be at my place. Bride to be a little hung-over tomorrow." Alex buckled the toolbelt and filled a pouch with nails and said they should make these with beer holders so a guy could actually get some construction done.

"When we get done the floor we can whack together a standing frame. Tomorrow we're going to put some bed sheets over it as a photo booth." On the gravel parking lot they toenailed 2x4's into frames about the size of two doors. The long side of the current one became the inside edge of the next, overlaying the ground with rectangular honeycombs. When they finished a frame they laid a 4x8 plywood sheet over it. After they had a small section of the dancefloor built they tested it by standing and bouncing. Jeremy said, "Oh yes that's gonna have a nice little spring to it."

"Dancefloor's gonna be a jumpin'." Two grown men bouncing on an empty red-neck dancefloor, someone go ahead and write that country song. "I'm looking forward to this. Who's the DJ?"

"You're presently dancin' with him." Jeremy had ear protection around his neck that he wasn't wearing, but he now slid a muff up. "DJ Hammer. White cousin of MC Hammer." He extended the hammer out sideways as if he would scratch a record with it. "Been working on this playlist for half my life. Expect banger after banger."

"Fuckin' A." They were still bouncing and it wasn't the liquor because this was first sips of beer one. Alex was thinking of a certain whale-diving sup-riding CEO that he wanted to slow dance with tomorrow.

"Slegg heard that the lumber was for a wedding. Reduced their normal delivery fee of one hundred fifty dollars. New price after taxes came out to free."

"See that's the problem with this town."

"Jordan's going to buy all this lumber to frame a home build next week. So I'm not even out any money on it."

Alex shook his head. "I might just move."

They knelt back down to build the rest of it and they weren't planning for the eighty attendees to take turns dancing. They started gambling. Fewest strikes to drive the nailhead flush with the plywood won a beer payable in the future. If you missed and struck the wood you owed a beer. Between the whacking Alex was telling about his day. As if he would fully square it with himself by confessing it to his buddy while squaring a dancefloor.

Jeremy stopped hammering. "You guys jumped in with a humpback? Just now? Out at Lennard?"

"I didn't. I tendered while she swam. But I gave her the go-ahead, yeah."

"Well." He stood a nail. "That's pretty damn cool." He drifted the nail home in two heavy strikes. "That's two."

"That's a beer."

Jeremy got up and walked to frame-one and stuck his hand in the plastic bag and withdrew a spiked fistful of nails and refilled his pouch and came back and knelt down. Alex drove his nail home with three strikes. Jeremy lined up a nail and asked what Valerie was doing now, he said bring her tomorrow. Alex told where she was and where she'd be tomorrow: the Bomber and gone. He didn't change his tone when he said it.

Jeremy had pinched a nail vertical ready to be struck but he didn't drift it he just looked over at Alex.

Alex swung and missed sinking a crescent moon in the plywood. "Fak me that's a beer." Some accent.

Jeremy with the pinched nail. "So she's off to the Bomber alone. This girl like one who you say you might not have met maybe in a while or maybe in ever. In a town with approximately fourteen single women. And you've struck-out with about fifteen of them. This girl's off by herself on a swampy-ass cougar hike and then off to a place that isn't here tomorrow? Hammering no doubt making me deaf and I should stop treating these like neck decorations." He put his ear muffs up, said louder, "Probably I just heard you wrong."

Alex laughed standing a nail, raising a hammer. "Yeah no, that's the story, bud." He went to swing and Jeremy reached up and grabbed his hammer and if only that photobooth was already built.

The social life of a forty-year-old man is not that of a twenty-year-old man and small transient tourist towns get smaller when old friends move away or lifestyles diverge. Sometimes people move away without moving away. Who hits middle age and couldn't chronicle their life by friendships lost? Is that such an uncommon story? Sometimes lost just down the street. Common for married men to have few or no true friends, or bonds so thin you can see through them. Social events of kids' birthday parties and school concerts don't count. Men you go away with from your house, catch something or ride something or kill something then cook and eat and drink something then burn some wood. Jeremy was a good guy and people liked him. Doesn't mean he set out a third hammer.

Two hands on a raised hammer that though hadn't been swung one of them already felt struck by its guilt.

Jeremy said, "Sorry, son. This is a union job. The pace you're working you're making everyone else look bad. You're fired. Pack your shit up."

Alex said no no it's all good, she and I had a great day and Vancouver's a stone throw away and we might do dessert later, and he hadn't let go of the hammer and said really I'm just here for the pizza where the hell's that scooter at and Jeremy was bigger and he just yanked the hammer away.

"C'mon. You'll be here all night."

"I'll get it done. Or I'll be putting my tipsy beloved to work when she gets back. The dancefloor that drunk love built. If we build it on a slant it's just going to keep people moving. Feature not a bug."

Alex looked at him. "Ah I don't like this."

Jeremy slid the hammer over the dancefloor and it slid easily over smooth wood wet from rain spits and it thudded against the bag of nails clinking with some kind of finality on the matter. "Tell me what you'd tell me to do if roles were reversed." While Alex was thinking about that Jeremy said, "Checkmate, son."

The guilt and the spring love and this bromance mixed with the rain must have been rusting the parts of Alex that churned out weak jokes for it took him a second: "I'd probably quote Herodotits to you: He who contemplates the fairer sex during construction will find himself with ten blue fingers and two blue balls. Thou shalt get back to building my flippin' dancefloor, stud."

"Truthfully I just didn't want to share the pizzas with you. Text me how it goes."

"Alright. Alright. Put me down on the clean-up and dismantle crew. And maybe you should hold the nails for the bride. If the missus misses and hits her ring finger and you can't slide that gold band on tomorrow, I'm going to feel like a real jack-ass." Jeremy was sinking nails two strikes a piece and the rain spits now largening to drops were only water coolant for this well-oiled machine. Alex hadn't stood. His first beer half-full beside him. "And save me a dance tomorrow."

"Count on us kicking our heels up to Thank God I'm a Country Boy. Good luck. Now you're just ruining my concentration." He drifted a nail home with one heavy strike as if no matter the sky's rage no storm could ever live up to man's thunder.

"That's a beer. Hell that's a case. Alright." He was still kneeling, kneeling on wood, under rain. In a posture one could mistake for reverence, if not worship. As if something most holy to this man went about here.

Two small nods and a couple pounded fists.

Alex buttoned his long sleeve and walked the driveway listening to hammer strikes. He figured pretty soon he would be walking funny if he kept going from moral bind to moral bind. What a day. A day not over. So go find Virtue. He started the truck and the wipers swiped. He increased their rate. He looked back at Jeremy. But he told himself sometimes you have to allow a friend the privilege of giving a gift even if receiving it is hard. The rain falling on his friend's back and a hammer rising. It looked like defiance but it was stronger than even that. Alex didn't need the photobooth to take this one with him.

Cell service is poor at the Bomber and he was a little surprised when she picked up.

"Hello strange fishing guide."

He thought he could hear it in her voice. Hear something in her voice.

"Hey ocean love."

"Am I so blue?"

He thought he could hear it in her voice. He knew you should hold your cards close. But sometimes in rare moments you say fuck it all-in and lay those cards down and put it to chance.

Tofino said, "I'll be your ebb if you be my flow."

Rain peppering a windshield and silence over a phone.

Tofino said, "You're the red wine stain on my white cotton heart, babe."

A silence. Then Vancouver said, "Yeah. Yeah. Said the pot to the kettle."

Thrushes and robins and porpoise and whales and perhaps even rain and cranes and most certainly spring.

"Where are you? I'm coming."

"I just parked at the Radar Hill lot."

He said change of plans, that her tour guide was en route. Said he'd see her very soon. But cell service at the Bomber is not very good and right then her reception died.

***

Humidity engorges the weather. Brisk wipers shed fat drops. But even the wettest storms never soak deeper than skin and the soul's beach of new love only knows sun.

Still in park he texted so his message would find her at first possible delivery. *Tour guide en route. In the interim do not get eaten by wildlife.* There was no real rush now because he could hike them back in the dark and everyone knows dusk only adds to romance.

Swirling leaves and swaying trees, he pulled away and Trent pulled away. The first speed limit was fifty and he wasn't doing much over that. Then same for sixty, then seventy. White car tailing too close for good weather, tailing dangerously close for bad weather. He squinted in the rearview. Saw a beard. His eyes returning back to the road then again to the rearview. Asshole in the rearview. Not certain but pretty sure it's buddy from outside Rhino? Funny, he thought, small-town patterns. Normally he'd just slow down to let the car pass but there aren't many passing lanes on the Pacific Rim Highway and he himself had places to be. Fine fine, keep up, dip-shit. Eyes back to the road.

Valerie had already walked a little ways down the path. Through spotty cell service his text arrived and she read it and was still smiling when she put her phone in her jean's back pocket and Sampha's piano ringtone started playing. For a moment the wind swirled the melody. Had the musician composed it for the news it carried he might have written a more somber tune. "Hi Mom." She slowed. She stopped walking.

Valerie jogged back to her car and got in and turned to the highway for the Inn and put weight on the pedal of a silently rocketing sedan that on a quarter-mile track leaves Vipers and Mustangs in its exhaustless dust. She wasn't sure if she could get a ferry that night or if a floatplane could get her across island this evening or first thing in the morning or if she should start driving now.

The sky seemed willing to die for its convictions, sending kamikaze rain down onto the glass. Three cars increased their wiper speed. Valerie was returning north with her tires gripping the pavement through a turn, her finger wiping a tear like her wipers with the rain. She barely drifted over the centre line.

Alex had just looked to his rearview at a driver practically pulling into his truck's box. Rounding the turn he barely drifted over centre.

Valerie looking at Alex, Alex looking at Trent. Then Alex evasively swerving and right before impact: lovers' eyes lock. In a frame of frozen time he saw her in the truck's cracked windshield.

Their vehicles like passing meteors grazing contact. Two mirrors explode into shards. The Tesla skids to the right and slows and head-on hits a tree and the airbag deploys. The impact registers in the car's crash-detection system and initiates a call to emergency services.

The Tacoma's swerve is more pronounced and its tires smoke bluely before it careens to the shoulder. Loose gravel, deep pothole, high centre-of-gravity truck. The narrow shoulder merges to a shallow ditch and the truck tips then rolls. Materials violating engineered intentions make unnatural sounds. Snaps, bangs, groans. Alex hears drums, kettle and bass. A brass section, but that's his chest hitting the truck's horn and he was trying to place a more subtle percussion note of his collar-bone snapping.

Chunks of fender and headlight are thrown into the air. Pitiless G-forces bounce a brain off a skull evoking the senses, colours and sounds and smells, hyperphantasia in a car crash. The truck rolling on its side he feels his jaw clench so tight his teeth grind enamel which he thinks is shattered sea shells powdering his tongue and he hears it's the grit that makes the pearl. His concussed mind, vivid and inharmonious. As the truck rolls upside down he with a bird's-eye-view sees a salmon swimming in a wheat field, its iridescent body purple and silver and dark green parting golden stalks. *Oh God, how beautiful*. He distinctly smells cedar and violet and sweetness and candy and danger and senses some childhood fear that presents itself as a shape that he can't identify or describe but knows well as he used to lay in bed nightly with it as a boy.

The truck rolls up the shallow ditch and its passenger door smashes against a heavy log-pile left from clearing a bike path. The truck, oddly righted level, contrasts its mangled body. Piece its story together from a trail of broken things. The hood jacked open like already someone had come to have a look. A small engine fire. Rain sizzling on the engine block like water drops on sauna rocks and he's sure he's back in the truth barrel. So what do you want to know? Nothing to hide here, you've long been naked. If one could test for truth by fear then in brief half-moments of clarity he's sure he's going to die.

Alex is confused why he can hardly move his arms and legs. He's tugging lamely at the seatbelt. Shirt partially pulled up. He's staring towards his feet. Wonders why he set out that day with only one boot. Tries to replay dressing that day but mostly he can't, just sees a towelled seductive queen dancing, all hips. If he could better move his head he might see his boot in the backseat. He sees his jeans down low are dark and wet and wonders where he's bleeding, but it's not blood it's an oil stain about to catch fire. He can't see the engine fire only the black smoke and his foot without the boot is warm and he feels it warming. Alex tries to lift his head but it's so heavy. He rolls his eyes upwards and sees the webbed windshield before him. He pats his pants for his blade but can't find it. Nothing much to do but wait for this web's big spider.

Valerie opens her car door and takes some steps before falling to a knee. She puts her hands on the pavement to help settle the road back into its place. Her hands beside her foot like a sprinter having a nightmare because she can't run. She tries to right her dizzied self but wobbles to her side. She can't see the truck because two cars in the middle of the highway are blocking her view. Both cars white. Both driver doors simultaneously opening. Two big men get out with their hoods up like anti-prophets, like synchronized cult soldiers. Matching beards on these hooded twins with twinned movements too precise for choreograph. Then her fuzzy double-world begins to merge. Begins focusing into a singular scene: one car, one door, one man, one Trent.

Recognizing him doesn't help clear things up it only brings distrust of her spinning mind. The nonsensical world of dreams seems more coherent than all this. Why is he here? But the pavement on her hands feels cool and wet and she smells wet pavement and by all that she believes this is no dream.

Trent didn't look at her long and now he turns and walks around the front of his car. She can't see his one hand disappear into his hoodie's pocket and then reappear. She tries to follow but falls. Below her, small roses bloom on the wet pavement. As if today the heavens are bleeding. Or that little flower girl from Tonquin Beach had seeded this asphalt. A couple drops of nose blood fall on the road, a short-lived bloom, then diluted they go runny in the rain.

The air Alex breathes is hot and his world hazy and he isn't in pain and in fleeting moments he has enough lucidity to figure that is a problem. The black smoke at his feet has turned to flames. No explosion so the fire burns oil. Coming up his leg. Like a fighter pilot in a shot-up plane he sends his sticky fingers out in search of the eject button. He finds it, he presses it. Great luck. Then again. Doesn't realize it's the wrong seatbelt, but spatial awareness is the least of his problems and had he found the correct one he'd find the mechanism crushed. Those scents of sweet violet rain now turn pungent. Hot engine smells and oil and burnt hair and black smoke. Small flames by his ankles like a den of snakes exploring for the first time the outside world. Nothing much he could do but watch them. He presses eject uselessly. Corn snakes or some orange coral serpents living in a Pacific Northwest reef slithering up his legs. To his thighs, their hot heads on his belly. He feels his belly burning. His wheezing inhales drawing black smoke. Who knew lungs could squeak. His head all bungled up and his brain swelling. Alex senses its presence. He hears its crawling claw tufts tapping the roof. Sees its web in the cracked windshield. He's sure it's the spider's presence now shadowing the side window. He wonders if it's that same wretched one from Hot Springs Cove. He hears from the side window: tap tap. He read that orb weavers, those creatures crawled out of a nightmare, catch in their web grown hummingbirds. *Me Rufous. Don't you know I'm too beautiful to die in a web.* Louder tapping at the window, death never so formal. Fuck you, he once thought he'd say and he'd say it in tears if he had to, but that is all nonsense because he is purely terrified and anyway his wheezing lungs could only contribute a gurgle. He tries turning his head to follow his eyes and with that he has a bit more luck than raising it. It lolls loosely to his left shoulder. He corners his eyes looking to see the spider darkening the window.

The window starbursts then shatters to the sound of a struck cymbal. Alex's lungs make soft squeaks. He doesn't see a spider. He sees the hooded reaper. Their eyes meet.

A moment there, a man with a burning belly, trapped and scared.

Alex watches as the arm reaches in. He feels his hair being gripped and his head tilted back causing his mouth to gape and there is red blood that tastes like candy and danger trickling from his lower lip to his chin dent and a couple drops fall to his neck hollow. He recognizes his own knife, watches it slide across his upper chest once, then down by his waist, and he thinks if it's his knife he must be saving himself. Alex is actually smiling. He's smiling. Because he can hear it now too, faintly but increasing. The whale song.

Valerie sees Trent returning. As he comes around the front of his car their eyes meet. He stops and puts his hood down. Trent breaks their gaze. She watches the white car pull away until her eyes register the beaten truck across the ditch. She sees Alex lying on the side of the road. Valerie running to him only falls once. She kneels beside her man. "Alex. Alex. Hey *Alex*! Alex! Look at me. Hey. Look at me." She shakes him lightly but doesn't like how his neck moves. Her sounds merging into the evening's melody. His squeaking breaths, rain sizzling on an engine block, and a siren in the rain.

Epilogue

L ong Beach is the first beach you see when you arrive to Tofino. The last one on the way out. Endless sea and long sand. Clumps of seaweed and scattered driftwood, driftwood latticing the headlands, seagulls and ravens. Where a cooler sea breeze arrives to warmer sand rises roiling mist. Big water. Under its surface is vitality and bloom. Deep depths fade sunray reach, yet life thrives.

Sometimes, like now, a pale-blue sky holds a few high skiffs of clouds. Sometimes nobody around. Or just one. This one who takes a deep breath. The pale sky and reflective water. Water that can turn from grey to green to the blue of your dreams.

A warm wind. Warm sand. Sounds of waves on the beach—crash, fall, lap, thump, rush, surge—sometimes words will always be chasing. Like some will always be chasing.

Toes scrunched. Toes stretched. Warm toes digging into the sand. The warm sand.

Dedication

Dedicated to the women who throughout my life have tried to help educate me. Those who have long given up and those I hope will keep trying.

Also by Tom Stewart

Under Big-Hearted Skies

Immortal North

Immortal North Two

For free books every month, bonus material, and early access to new work, join Tom Stewart's newsletter—*where the literary life meets the wild coast*: https://tomswords.substack.com/

substack

About the Author

If you enjoyed this book to the extent you want others to find it, please tell someone about it, and rate and review it. That keeps me writing and I'd appreciate it. Thanks. — Tom

***

Tom Stewart is a novelist living on the coast of Tofino, Canada. He is the winner of the 2023 WIBA Fiction Award and a finalist for the 2022 Somerset Literary Fiction Award. Tom grew up near Winnipeg, Canada, where he studied literature and philosophy at the University of Manitoba. He worked in northern Canada as a fishing and hunting guide and as a bush-plane pilot before becoming a full-time poker player.

The author would like to thank his Patreon supporters: Roberta R, David G, Hermit, Kelli B, Keren J, Ruth Z, Sylvia VG.

Manufactured by Amazon.ca
Bolton, ON

46669807R00247